FOOTPRINTS OF THE DEVIL

Championship surfer Dave Tregenza returns to his native Cornwall for a surprise visit, only to find his sister-in-law and aunt in turmoil because Jonathan, his brother, has disappeared without a trace. Then, several days later, Jonny's dead body is discovered on a remote beach within a few miles of the huge satellite earth station at Goonhilly Downs. The police suspect a link between Jonny and the site, so DCI Channon, who has had previous experience in suspected sabotage, is called in from the adjacent police authority. His investigation proceeds without success until a second murder occurs...

FOOTPRINTS OF THE DEVIL

by

Olive Etchells

Magna Large Print Books
Long Preston, North Yorkshire,
BD23 4ND, England.

British Library Cataloguing in Publication Data.

Etchells, Olive
   Footprints of the devil.

A catalogue record of this book is
available from the British Library

ISBN   978-0-7505-2667-8

First published in Great Britain in 2006 by Constable,
an imprint of Constable & Robinson Ltd.

Copyright © Olive Etchells 2006

Cover illustration © visitbritain.com

The right of Olive Etchells to be identified as the author of this work
has been asserted by her in accordance with the Copyright, Designs
and Patents Act, 1988

Published in Large Print 2007 by arrangement with
Constable & Robinson Ltd.

Magna Large Print is an imprint of Library Magna Books Ltd.

Printed and bound in Great Britain by
T.J. (International) Ltd., Cornwall, PL28 8RW

For my sons, Andrew, Jonathan and Daniel

For their invaluable help and advice,
I would like to thank:

Once again, David Price,
Police Superintendent (retired)
Sheila McConnochie SRN, SCM
Ian Whitaker of Porthleven,
an enthusiastic man
David Etchells (the 'Ancient Mariner'),
my nephew and my friend

Chapter One

Windswept and deserted, Kynance Cove lay beneath a cloud-strewn April sky. Dave Tregenza paced the cold sand and told himself that after two whole days it still seemed strange to be back in Cornwall. Even to himself he couldn't use the words 'back home', because didn't people say, 'Home is where the heart is'?

He didn't know where *his* heart was – he didn't even know if he had one. Oh, he had a reliable pumping machine inside his chest, part of the physique his coach raved about when he had his check-ups; but a heart that felt things, that loved, that – that yearned? He didn't go in for that sort of stuff, not any more. What was the point of it, analysing and agonizing and tying himself in knots?

He had a better way of dealing with life now; he kept it on two levels, mental and physical. His mind decided what he must do and then his body took over and did it – end of story. No emotion, no tension, no trauma; and those times he couldn't get his mind in gear he simply followed his – his what? His instinct? Yeah, that was it – his instinct.

Was it instinct that had brought him back? It certainly hadn't been a considered decision, nor for that matter had it been some sort of tugging at the heartstrings, or whatever the romantics might call it. One minute he'd been with the crowd in

Hawaii: eating, drinking, laughing, waiting for a real big surf. The next he'd been on the phone to the airline and making weird, false excuses to his friends.

What was even more weird was that once he was back in Cornwall the sense of urgency had evaporated. He found he couldn't – he simply couldn't just roll up at the house with a cheerful 'Hi there, I'm back!' – not after seven years. Instead he'd skulked around a bit, seen what he'd needed to see; seen *her* – from a distance, through glasses – hanging out washing in the garden of a house called Lookout Cottage above Porthmenna harbour. He could remember the old guy who used to live there – a retired coastguard who was always on the jetty with his cronies.

So ... since he got back he'd seen a few things, done a few things: hired a car, booked into a hotel in Helston where nobody was likely to remember him, then zoomed around all his old haunts. He'd saved the best until last. Kynance had always been his favourite, not for the surf, nor even the caves, but for the atmosphere of the place, its sheer, unarguable beauty. It might be deserted now, at nine o'clock in the morning with half a gale blowing, but people would come before long, rain or shine, they always did. It had been on this very rock, the huge one next to him, that he'd decided to leave home; here, with the flower-decked grasses above him and this silver-gold sand between his toes.

Had he been right, that was the question. He put from his mind the people he'd left behind and asked himself how Cornwall itself compared to lands across the seas: to Thailand, Australia, Hawaii. There could be no argument that the biggest surf in Cornwall was no match for the great glass-green rollers of the Pacific, but what about everything else?

What about the age-old landscape he'd roamed as a boy, with its isolated farms and granite cottages, its roads edged with dazzling gorse? What about the ruined engine houses of its tin mines, the little coves that had once harboured smugglers, the sea that could change in an instant from grey to blue to turquoise and indigo? What about the smell of it, the unique salt smell of English seas breaking on English rocks outside an English harbour? How did all that compare?

Deep in the heart he wasn't sure he possessed, Dave Tregenza knew the answer to that one.

Frances heard the car and rushed to open the front door, but one look at the face of the young woman outside brought her to a standstill. 'No news, then,' she said. 'When I heard you arrive I thought–' She stopped herself. Why say it? She headed for the kitchen. 'I'll make us a coffee. Are the girls at nursery?'

'Yes. I could see no point in disrupting them even more. They're unsettled enough without Jonny, and I'm sure they sense that I'm in a state.'

The two women faced each other across the kitchen table: Frances in her customary trousers and shirt, her dark hair needing a cut and swinging with each turn of her head. Opposite her, Delphi Tregenza pulled out a chair but continued to stand, as if she'd forgotten how to bend her knees. Well on in pregnancy, she was long-legged enough to have retained a certain grace, but right now she was gripping the back of the chair as if for support. 'I've just been to see the police again,' she said, 'but it was the same old story – it's too soon for them to get involved.'

Frances busied herself with the coffee and wondered whether to admit that she was trying to organize a search of the whole area. 'Trying' was the word, because the Lizard Peninsula was tricky territory and she didn't know where to start. No, she couldn't say anything – it would look as if she expected something awful to have happened to Jonny, when as far as they knew he'd simply gone off somewhere on his own. After all, his brother had done it for good seven years ago, though at least he'd announced his departure and hadn't left twin daughters, nor a wife who was ready to produce child number three.

She placed a mug of coffee on the table. 'Decaff,' she said gently, 'and filtered water.' Delphi's ideas on protecting her unborn child had become an obsession in the last few days. There would be a psychological reason behind it but Frances didn't want to go down that road. 'Do sit down,' she urged. 'I'm sorry about the police but they did make it clear about not taking action yet. Listen, though – you know we talked about loss of memory? Well, I've looked it up and it's a distinct possibility. Apparently it doesn't only happen in stories.'

'I know, I've looked it up as well. But if it's a memory thing, how did he go, and where from? He didn't take the car, he hasn't got his licence with him so he couldn't have hired one, and if he used the train he would have had to get to either Penzance or Falmouth. There's been no sighting of him, no record of using his credit card to buy a ticket.'

Frances eyed her with concern. Delphi was Cornish born and bred, yet the obvious hadn't occurred to her. He could have gone somewhere by sea. He was familiar with tides and currents, he knew how to handle a boat, and to travel any distance he could have hired a vessel and if necessary somebody to sail it for him. He could have paid in cash if he'd been keeping money aside for that purpose.

The younger woman was chewing at her lips. 'You haven't got hold of Dave, then?'

Why admit to all the international phone calls? 'I have no address, nothing except the number of his mobile and that's been switched off for days. The last proper address I had for him was in Western Australia, a place called Yallingup Beach – pretty remote, I think. When I last spoke to him there he said he was moving on.'

The younger woman opened her mouth to speak but Frances flapped a hand at her. 'Yes, I did ring and leave a message there in case he makes contact with them.'

'If you'd managed to get hold of him, would you have asked him to come home?'

'He was close to Jonny when they were young, very close, so I was hoping I wouldn't need to ask. But even if he did come, what could he do?'

'He could be *here*,' said Delphi. 'Even if he's still in a strop with me, surely he must feel he

13

owes you something? He – he might have some ideas.'

'We don't want ideas,' said Frances abruptly, 'we want action. I must admit he was always one for action.'

It was somewhat delayed action that took Dave Tregenza back to his childhood home. Out past the summer lets and the tasteful little new-builds and along the single-track road that led away from Porthmenna. How often had he and Jonny careered along here on their bikes, with the waves crashing below them on one side and the flowers tossing in the hedge on the other?

He didn't know what he would say when he arrived, or what he would do. All he knew was that the weird sense of urgency was back and he was regretting the two wasted days. He stopped the car where the road became a gravel track and for a moment looked down at the scene that had once been the setting for his entire life. On one side of the track was farm pasture, on the other the grasses of the clifftop above the sea, which was now at high tide, its white-capped waves roaring below the house. The house ... it was just the same: stone-built and solid, its shutters still painted blue and strong enough to withstand the winter gales. All at once something inside him twisted and cried silently, Home! This is my home!

That's enough, he warned himself grimly; no getting tied up in knots. He left the car and with deliberate slowness bent his head to the wind and made for the house. Much later he was to wonder why he hadn't knocked at the front door that faced the track. After an absence of seven years it would have been only polite, but from long-established force of habit he walked round the side of the house and opened the kitchen door. The wind blew it from his grasp so that it crashed against the iron doorstop on the floor.

The two women stared at him: Frances with a mug of coffee halfway to her mouth, Delphi clutching a tissue, her jaw slack at the sight of him.

They both got to their feet and Frances said just the one word: 'David.' Years of pain and resentment were swept aside by a surge of joy so intense she could have rushed across the room and covered him in kisses. Instead, she forced herself to remain still. This was the boy – no, he was a man now – who had pushed her away more times than she cared to remember. Her nephew, her ward, one of the two sacred charges left in her care by their parents.

Sacred charge or not, this one had caused her nothing but worry, hard work and quite often anguish. Right now he looked fantastic: lean, deeply tanned, his hair bleached by the sun; and he was taller, broader than the gangling lad of seven years ago. 'You got my message, then?' she asked. She could hardly believe he'd got here so quickly.

But Dave was looking at Delphi, a cynical twist to his lips. Pregnant with number three, he told himself sourly. He'd missed that when he saw her behind the washing line. He hadn't known that pregnancy could make a woman look so old.

There were shadows under her eyes, lines from her nose to her mouth. He'd left home, left England because of her; she'd been lovely then, enchanting, like a wild rose, but now she looked ancient. He gave a mental shrug and told himself it was a relief to find nothing left of the passion he'd felt for her, the obsession with her every gesture, her every word. He'd been a mere kid at the time, of course...

They were waiting for him to speak. He'd say something in a minute, as soon as he got his head round being in this room again, with both of them at once. That was more than he'd bargained for. Then Delphi spoke. 'Thanks for coming,' she said, nodding her head wearily. 'We need you.'

At that, the question Frances had asked registered with him. Uneasily he looked from one to the other. This wasn't exactly the return of the prodigal, was it? He hadn't expected the fatted calf treatment but surely something was a bit odd? He pushed at the door behind him, closing it against the battering of the wind, and at once the room became quiet. 'What message?' he asked.

'I've been trying to reach you for more than forty-eight hours,' Frances told him. 'I left a message with a man called Morgan in Yallingup Beach just in case you happened to contact him, and I've been trying your mobile for ages. It's Jonny, David. He's gone missing.'

'Missing?' Gentle, reliable Jonny, the brother he'd grown up with? This was unreal. Unreal, maybe, said a cold little voice in his head, but this is what has brought you back. His heart gave a

16

single heavy thud, then settled. 'Missing?' he repeated, trying to sound merely puzzled. 'What's going on?'

'Come and sit down,' said Frances. 'I'll get you a drink in a minute, but first tell us how you got here so fast and then we'll tell you all we know about Jonny.'

Dave sat down and said carefully, 'I didn't get any message, Frances. I just decided to come. I suppose you could say I followed an impulse. I was in Hawaii and I felt...' Lord, it sounded so *spooky*. 'Uh – that is – I had a sudden urge to come back. So I came.'

Delphi was fixing him with her amazing dark blue eyes – at least those hadn't changed. 'When?' she asked intently. 'When did you get this sudden urge?'

Careful, he warned himself. In a minute you'll be telling them you've messed about for two whole days before coming here. But Delphi's face was very near, she was staring at him with the eyes that had once haunted his dreams and were now circled with dark shadows. This was no time for half-truths or evasions. 'It was Monday,' he said reluctantly.

She let out a moan. 'That's when he disappeared! Something's happened to him – you sensed it – the girls are always doing it with each other and they're only three. You knew something was wrong. That's why you came back.'

'Hush, love,' said Frances, reaching for her hand. 'David and Jonny aren't identical twins, they're just brothers.'

'Brothers who were very close – you said as

17

much only five minutes ago.'

'Yes, I did, didn't I? Look, tell David exactly what happened.'

Delphi moistened her lips. 'Jonny went out on Monday evening. He'd read the girls their story like he usually does and when they were asleep we had supper. Then he changed his shirt and said he was going to the Dancers' to look at a job and give them a quote.'

'The dancers?' Dave repeated. 'What dancers?'

'They're man and wife. It's their name. They've bought the big house at Trevant on the downs and they're doing it up. Jonny's done some work for them on the timbers and there was a bigger job in the offing. He thought he'd get it. You know it's his special thing, old stuff, especially on properties that are listed?'

'Yes, yes. So what happened?'

'He didn't come back.'

There was an emptiness in the words that chilled him. The back of his neck felt cold as ice. 'He didn't telephone?'

'No.'

'What did the Dancers say?'

'That he'd left their place at about nine. They saw he was on foot and offered him a lift home but he said he'd go back the way he'd come – by the short cut across the fields. There's no reason to think they're lying. Why should they?'

Frances had been listening intently and now she broke in. 'All that area's been searched, first of all quickly, by the two of us, and then by half the men in Porthmenna.' She flashed him a warning glance. 'Just in case Jonny had been taken ill, or

18

broken an ankle, or something.'

Dave nodded and went back to his questions. 'Has he done anything like this before?'

'No, of course he hasn't. If he's out on a job he'll ring me if he's going to be late, but on Monday he didn't take his mobile.'

'What about the police?'

'They've taken all the details and put him on the missing persons register, but they won't actually investigate unless there's suspicion of foul play. There's no such suspicion.'

'How long will they leave it before they take action?'

The shadowed eyes closed wearily. 'They haven't said. Look, I'll have to go and pick up the girls in a minute. Then I must be at home for the phone.'

'I have a pupil coming in the lunch hour,' said Frances, 'but I'll be round about two so you can try to have a sleep while I keep an eye on the girls and give them their tea. I'll stay the night as well, if you want me to.'

'Oh, please! You know my dad stayed last night? Well, he's not staying again. We had words at breakfast time – it was a stand-up row, actually. He let slip that he thinks Jonny's got another woman.'

They both stared at her and she stared back, one hand pushing at her hair and the other cupped against the mound of the child inside her.

'Utter rubbish!' said Frances stoutly. 'Come on, love, I'll see you out.' At the door she said over her shoulder, 'Your room's ready, David, if you're staying.'

Dave watched their departing backs. He was

staying, all right. What else was he to do? What else did he *want* to do? Nothing, he told himself, except find his brother.

The Harbour Stores in Porthmenna was crowded with customers sharing in the morning exchange of news, with proprietor Lizzie Bannon in charge. She knew more than anybody about local affairs, because most things that happened were revealed in the shop sooner or later.

Sometimes she was teased about running a gossip shop but she would have none of it. 'If customers want to exchange a bit of news while they buy my goods, I have no objection,' she would say, and she meant it. Trade from self-catering holidaymakers could boost her takings four- or five-fold, especially in the school holidays, but what she called her bread and butter earnings, her year-round income, came from the locals. She needed them like they needed her.

The doorbell pinged and an elderly woman squeezed in. 'What news on young Jonny?' she asked above the chatter.

They all waited for Lizzie to answer. 'Nothing yet,' she said, putting a couple of still-warm pasties in a paper bag. 'Nobody can understand it.'

'If a child was missing, every policeman in Cornwall would be out,' said a tall woman choosing tomatoes, 'but they won't get off their backsides for the breadwinner of a young family.'

There was a chorus of agreement, then a little woman in a cross-over pinny spoke up. 'I know folk don't like it said, but I can't help wondering if he's gone off deliberate. Planned it, sort of.'

20

An angry murmur built up, but it was Lizzie who answered, one hand keying in at the till, the other lifting a tin of baked beans on high to silence them. 'It's no use all of you getting annoyed,' she said firmly, 'because it's not the first time that's been said. The fact is we don't know – nobody knows. What I do know is he's a good young fella, and I for one can't see him leaving his little girls, nor his wife when she's only a couple of weeks off giving birth. Now is there anything else, Minnie?'

One by one they paid for their goods and went home, leaving Lizzie tidying the counter and looking forward to closing for an hour at one o'clock. The bell pinged again and a slim woman in cord trousers and a tweed jacket came in.

'Mrs Dancer,' said Lizzie politely. 'Can I get you anything or will you look round at your leisure?' She hadn't got the measure of this one yet, she thought. Like everybody else she'd heard plenty, but it cost nothing to be civil.

Nancy Dancer selected odds and ends from the shelves, finishing with clotted cream and locally baked bread. She liked the village shop – it gave her pleasure to pick up her everyday needs there rather than going into Mullion or the super-market in Helston, and though Lizzie Bannon was a bit of a battleaxe she was a mine of inform-ation. She put her basket of purchases on the counter and asked, 'Have you heard any news of Jonathan Tregenza?'

'No, nothing at all, Mrs Dancer.' Lizzie couldn't help sounding cool. Jonny going missing was a Porthmenna matter, whereas this woman and her husband had barely warmed the seats at Trevant.

Nancy noted the coolness. 'My husband and I are concerned because we were probably the last to see him,' she pointed out.

The shopkeeper's keen dark eyes peered into the younger woman's glasses. 'We're all of us worried to death,' she admitted, 'but we're hoping he'll turn up safe and sound. You see, most of us have known him all his life, and his mother and father before him, God rest their souls. One thing I will say – there's a bit of feeling round and about that the police should step in.'

Nancy Dancer nodded calmly. 'My husband says they'll take over very soon.'

Lizzie leaned across the counter. 'Does he now? What makes him say that?'

'Our geographical position, Mrs Bannon.'

'You mean our position here in Porthmenna or yours over at Trevant?'

'Both. We're nearer than all of you here, of course, but this very harbour can only be, what? Four or five miles away as the crow flies?'

Lizzie was no fool. It had been mentioned before, here in the shop, but what on earth could that place have to do with young Jonny? 'You're talking of Goonhilly?' she asked blankly.

'Yes, I am. The world's biggest satellite earth station is within a few miles of where a man has disappeared, so far without trace. There's a nationwide alert in force to safeguard special sites against terrorism and sabotage, you know.'

Lizzie was nonplussed. They'd all been proud of the station on Goonhilly Downs when it was first built back in the sixties. It had been the talk of the

22

Lizard, of all England, come to that, but they'd got used to it, it was just – there. They called it 'The Place' or 'The Dishes', and watched as holidaymakers went on family visits there. 'Terrorists?' she said uneasily. 'They're foreign folk, surely?'

Nancy Dancer's eyes were hazel, but at that moment they looked like two gold orbs behind her big glasses. 'Innocent people could become involved with them,' she said quietly. 'I think my husband is right, you know.'

'Maybe he is,' agreed Lizzie thoughtfully. 'Maybe he is.'

Dave looked round the familiar bedroom and saw that nothing had changed except that his desk was tidy and maybe the walls had had a lick of paint. As for the view, it was as spectacular as ever: limitless ocean and to the side of the house the exquisite little cove they used to call 'our beach', at present swept by rough seas even though the tide had turned.

If Frances had painted the walls, she'd put up all his posters again, almost as if she'd expected him to come back. Had he ever intended to? Not at the time he left, that was for sure. He'd been too full of pain and fury that Delphi was going to marry his brother. Lord – he'd been besotted with her. The joke was he'd thought *she* was besotted with *him*. How wrong could you be?

A year later it had eased his pride a little to send them a cheque as a wedding present, for all the world as if he were well established abroad and earning good money. They little knew he was washing up in a greasy-spoon beach café and thought himself lucky when he won the odd fifty dollars in a surfing contest. Still, prize money had funded the cheque. They might be surprised to know what his income had been in the past year...

He'd always known what was going on here in Porthmenna, of course, Frances had seen to that. If she knew his current address she sent long, newsy letters and every month or so she would try to reach him by phone. Give the woman credit, she'd kept in touch, and what was more she'd done it without a word of criticism about him leaving. No doubt she'd said all she had to say about that the night he told her. Oh boy, that had been the exchange of home truths to end all exchanges, for ever and ever amen.

By the time the twins arrived he'd been able to accept with scarcely a twinge that Jonny and Delphi were a married couple with children, that he was 'Uncle Dave'. Frances had never sent him photographs of his brother and Delphi, but she'd kept him well supplied with snapshots of his nieces. At first they'd looked pretty gruesome – a pair of blobs with screwed-up faces, then after a while they started to look like actual babies, and all at once, amazingly, they'd turned into two little girls. They were called Sophie and Dorcas and he'd be seeing them soon. They could talk, he knew that, but could they hold a conversation? Would it be gibberish?

Thinking of conversations, the biggie, the one with Frances, was yet to come. No sooner had Delphi gone home than his aunt had taken a couple of phone calls, then she'd whipped him up an omelette and salad for lunch. Two minutes later a kid arrived for a German lesson and stayed closeted with her in the sitting room for an hour, and as soon as that was over she had to go and hold the fort for Delphi.

'I'll be making an evening meal over there,' she told him, stuffing a basket of food in the car. 'We'll eat about seven when the girls are in bed, so you can come across any time before then if you want to eat with us. You know which is their house, don't you?' With the wind buffeting her she got into the car and said, 'If Delphi goes to bed early, perhaps we can talk.'

Talk? Oh, they'd talk right enough if it was anything to do with Frances. How often in the past had she pinned him down for a discussion when it was the last thing on earth he wanted? Right now, though, it wasn't going to be talk, but action. As a start, he was going to walk to Trevant, taking the path his brother had taken four days ago. That would be better than staring at the sea, remembering.

Chapter Two

DS Bowles was not a happy sergeant. Routine paperwork bored him, he wasn't as good as he'd like to be on the station's new software, and he'd just been told yet again that he needed to work on his 'people skills'. He knew that was because he hadn't given the kid-glove treatment to a weepy old bird whose cottage had been burgled. She hadn't even known what was missing, so thieves could hardly have made off with the solid gold dinner service or the Rembrandt. He'd thought her a bit thick – either that or senile – but she'd been with-it enough to put in a complaint against him and DC Jolly.

Well, everybody knew that Jolly didn't live up to his name, and Bowles had been a bit on edge at the time. Earlier that day out on the street he'd spotted his ex-wife drooling over a spherical bundle of joy in a pushchair. He'd known for ages that she was expecting, but it had been a real kick in the you-know-whats to see her all rosy and chubby and coming the smiley little mummy.

The thing was he could bump into her any time, so why on earth did he stay in this dead-alive neck of the woods? There was no crime worthy of the name apart from the odd GBH, a trickle of possession and dealing, and the usual breaking and entering. OK, last week there'd been a double drowning in the Fal which could

26

have been interesting – two young women – but it had turned out to be a genuine accident. Tragic, the papers had called it, instead of the more accurate sheer carelessness.

The fact of the matter was that if he did apply for a transfer, the top authorities weren't going to fight each other to take on a DS from a rural force, even a tough customer like himself. What had the DCI said a few weeks back about his methods? 'You need to soften up a bit, Bowles, you're too abrasive. A metal rasp might go down well with the Met but down here we're happier with fine sandpaper. You're a good detective. Stay with us, remember what I say and you'll do all right.'

That had been Channon, old clever-clogs himself. He'd worked closely with him three times in all; oh yes, it had been Bowles the lackey, Bowles the gofer. The funny thing was, when he'd been with Channon he'd *had* to soften up, and all three times they'd cracked the case. Talk about 'Softly, softly catchee monkey' – if somebody put words to music it could be Channon's theme song.

But back to the salt mines... Reluctantly he reached for the stack of regional print-outs sent down from the DCI's office. As usual they were mucho-yawno, but he wasn't such a fool as to think routine didn't matter. Minutes later he was rereading reports, back-tracking on memos, taking a large-scale map from the rack. Well, well, well! Parliament and Buck House might be in London and not Cornwall, untold millions might live in big cities compared to mere thousands in the towns and villages down here, but that didn't

27

mean there was nowhere in Cornwall listed in the manual on Prevention of Terrorism.

Suspicious incidents, individuals, behaviour; suspicious this, that and the other ... so what was laid down about it? Hey hey! *All must be investigated.* And who was the Big White Chief in charge of such investigations for half Cornwall? Who had found those two busy little bomb-makers hiding down here in benefit-land? Who had tracked that Semtex gang to Bodmin? None other than DCI Channon, that was who! Old clever-clogs had masterminded the only two cases of national importance in the area in the last nine or ten months. A success on the national scene was just what Bowles needed on his record. Then the Met would be after *him* and not some high-flying twit on the fast-track for promotion.

Trying to transform a wolfish grin into an earnest frown, Bowles left his desk and headed for the stairs.

Well, he'd spotted it... Detective Chief Inspector Channon leaned back in his chair and listened, thinking that the sergeant could be quite eloquent when he had a point to make. 'I've checked the map,' he was saying now, 'and the man disappeared within four miles of Goonhilly and not much more from Culdrose.'

'Culdrose comes under the Royal Navy,' said Channon. 'They can look after themselves, they cost enough and they have the manpower.'

'Well, what about Goonhilly? I know there might be no connection, but on his way home the missing man could have seen something or heard something out there in the middle of nowhere, then whoever was up to no good could have realized the implications and made sure he wouldn't talk. Can I go to the Lizard and suss it out?'

'The local beat-bobby has put down his thoughts on the matter, Bowles. Did you see his report?'

Bowles shrugged dismissively. 'It's only his opinion,' he said, then it sank in and resentment tightened his mouth. 'You already knew about it?'

'I'm paid to know things,' Channon told him gently. 'As a matter of routine we're sent details of every missing adult reported to the Devon and Cornwall force – you must be aware of that. You must also be aware that most of the cases just sit in the files until something happens – they come home or turn up elsewhere or they've been involved in an accident. Very rarely they're dead, sometimes by their own hand. In the case of this Tregenza fella we'll have to look into it, both because of his circumstances and the proximity to Goonhilly. Having said that, a couple of years ago a chap dropped dead in the car park there and at first it looked like foul play. We spent time on it and so did Goonhilly Security, but it was perfectly innocent.'

'So can I go?' persisted Bowles, eyes glinting.

'Yes,' agreed Channon, 'under certain guidelines. The missing man has two young children and a wife who's due to give birth very soon. Naturally she's distraught, but by all accounts well supported by family and friends.' Channon's straight dark gaze met that of Bowles. 'You treat

29

her gently. You don't upset her more than she is already and you give her no false hopes – we both know there's the chance of a bad outcome. Also you do not raise with anybody whatsoever the question of sabotage or terrorism, or suggest any link to such things. Is all that clear?'

Irritation was rising in Bowles. He'd thought this was *his* brainchild, yet Channon had already organized the whole shebang. 'Very clear, boss,' he said tightly. 'Anything else?'

'Yes. Keep away from Goonhilly – I'll talk to them while you're over there. I want only general enquiries at this stage – local enquiries. See if anything strikes you on the home front – family, friends, Porthmenna itself.' Bowles didn't fancy doing the PC Plod round a grotty fishing village, but he managed not to roll his eyes. Then Channon said, 'No going solo on this, mind. If there's anything suspicious along the lines you've suggested, we'll deal with it through the usual channels. You'll take somebody with you, of course.'

'Of course. The obligatory watchdog.'

'That's right,' agreed Channon. 'I've made Yates available. He comes with the deal. Take it or leave it.'

Oh, marvellous! DC Yates, the 'good interviewer', the 'good with people' man, the little white hen that never laid away. 'I'll take it,' Bowles muttered ungraciously. 'Can I interview anybody else I think might be connected?'

'Yes. I've already spoken to Helston, as it's their territory. Written report, signed by you both. I'll give you till eight thirty tomorrow morning for it.'

Without a word the sergeant turned on his heel, leaving Channon staring after him. A prickly devil without an ounce of tact, he told himself, but he could be thorough when he wanted to be.

Eyes narrowed, head turning from side to side, Dave Tregenza trod the path from Porthmenna to Trevant. Thoughts were tumbling around in his head, questions jostling each other, but he didn't want to deal with them. In particular he didn't want to think about that sudden urge to come back from Hawaii, because what lay behind it was bad; that much he sensed, just as Delphi had sensed it a couple of hours earlier.

Concentrate, he told himself; think about where you're walking, about the places you and Jonny knew as children – the secret places. Maybe he went to one of them and was taken ill? Maybe he saw something he shouldn't have seen, perhaps a light where there was no house – it would have been nearly dark when he left Trevant. Had he seen a crime being committed, or stumbled on somebody moving stolen goods?

Not far away was a quarry – actually an old serpentine dig where local men used to excavate the spectacular green stone of the Lizard; he and Jonny used to play there until it became flooded and was fenced off. Had the village search party examined the place? Had anybody been to the engine house of the old copper mine in that gully across the fields? He would go himself after he'd been to Trevant.

He was walking up a narrow valley now, cut by

a stream that tumbled along on its way to the sea. Once on top of the Lizard the land would become flatter; a bright golden plateau of fields criss-crossed by narrow roads. The ravines, the cliffs, the gullies and the caves were all on the seashore. Keenly he eyed the coarse grass, wishing that Jonny could have left one of the signs they'd used years ago when they played at tracking each other.

At last the wind had dropped. It was now very quiet, so quiet he could hear the rhythmic thud of the waves far behind him; he fancied he could even hear the beat of his own heart. All at once the questions were back, rattling at the door of his mind. He knew he could ignore them no longer.

This business of the sudden urge to come back. It was no use pretending he didn't know what it was all about. He might as well admit that there'd been other such urges, long ago. The time he'd leapt from his desk in the middle of geography to run to the gym where Jonny's class were having PE. There he'd found his brother unconscious on the floor behind the vaulting horse, the teacher bending over him in bewilderment. Jonny had overshot the mat, landed badly and knocked himself out. Dave hadn't known how to explain why he'd come running from another room, but he heard the teacher muttering to the head about ESP, and when Jonny was safe at home and in bed, he'd asked his mother what it meant...

Then, much later, when their parents were gone for ever, there'd been that time in the cave on 'their' beach. Knowing about tides and currents from an early age, well-trained in all kinds

32

of sea-lore, he and Jonny had made a den out of dry sand and driftwood in the depths of the cave, aware that there was more than an hour to go before the tide came in. All at once he'd shrieked at Jonny and dragged him from the cave, only for them both to be knocked flat at the entrance by a sea surge heading a freak tide that had astounded all the Lizard. That had been a close call – they'd had to swim for it through a swirling mass of foam, and Frances had gone berserk when they trailed home in their wet clothes and she realized what could have happened.

Other incidents came to him: nothing shattering, nothing earth-shaking, just odd little bits of – what? Foreknowledge – that's what it was, and in every case his brother had been at risk. He himself used to pretend it hadn't happened because he couldn't understand it; it was weird, a bit creepy. He was the reckless one, a bit wild and always in trouble; creepy things were soft – a bit girly, not in line with the image he had of himself. Now he was beginning to see that he – the younger one – had been meant to keep his brother safe. Not easy, not even possible when they were grown up and on different sides of the world.

Enmeshed in memories, Dave came out from the fields to a single-track road, its low stone walls topped by the bountiful gold of the gorse. Ahead of him lay Trevant, he could see the old granite building and a cluster of cottages. He turned full circle and saw that the house was at the head of the narrow valley he'd just climbed. He could see Porthmenna's harbour wall and the two great rocks that locals called the Eye Teeth.

What a position, what a view! Quickly he turned back to face Trevant. It was time for a word with Mr and Mrs Dancer.

Peace had descended on Lookout Cottage. Frances cleared toys from the floor and relished the silence. Delphi was in bed, tossing and twitching in a restless doze, and the twins were having their afternoon nap on the sofa, their faces only inches apart, as if each needed to feel the other's breath.

Frances looked at them with the disbelief that had swamped her mind since late on Monday night. It really was beyond belief that their daddy had left them from choice. He adored them – they adored him. He adored their mother – she adored... Surprised at herself, Frances halted her chain of thought and made a correction. Delphi loved Jonny dearly. What *was* all this? she thought. She was worried sick and completely exhausted. They were all in crisis, so it wasn't the time to deceive herself about anything. Delphi loved Jonny, she relied on him, but she didn't adore him.

Picking up a toy ironing board Frances stood quite still, staring at it. From this moment on, she vowed, until Jonny came back or was traced, she would have truth in her mind – truth as she saw it. She might not be able to speak the truth to other people, but to herself she would make no pretence – about anything. That way she would have an inner core of honesty, no matter how disturbing, that was open only to her. If she didn't have that she felt she might crack under the strain.

She found a tiny iron and put it on the ironing

board along with a teddy's T-shirt and a doll's dress. Dorcas was the one who liked to iron, she knew; Sophie preferred pretend cooking. At that moment the doorbell rang. The girls slept on, so she closed the living-room door behind her and answered it.

Two men faced her, flashing ID cards. The taller of the two, thin and sandy-haired, was clearly in charge. 'Detective Sergeant Bowles,' he announced briskly. 'This is Detective Constable Yates. We'd like a word with Mrs Tregenza.'

'Oh, thank God,' said Frances in relief, 'come right in. I'm Frances Lyne. It's my nephew Jonathan who's gone missing. His wife is asleep upstairs and so are his little girls, in there.' She knew she was gabbling, and made herself slow down. 'Have you brought news, sergeant?'

'No,' said Bowles, 'we're merely making routine enquiries about Mr Tregenza, on the orders of my superior officer.'

Hope glimmered in Frances's mind like a shaft of weak sunlight through cloud. Police ... that meant manpower, searches, experts on the lie of the land; police would know about the passage of vessels, have links with the coast-guards. The relief of having them here was intense, and if she didn't warm to the sergeant, at least the younger one seemed a kind, earnest type. 'Would you mind waiting in the kitchen, so we won't waken the children?' She left the two men and hurried upstairs to get Delphi.

Bowles looked around with interest. All the olde-worlde stuff seemed pretty good for a seaside cottage. There was none of the pseudo fishermen's tat of so many places he'd seen. The auntie wasn't so bad either, for her age, though he preferred them with a bit more upholstery. At his side Yates waited uneasily, knowing he'd be torn by pity when he saw Mrs Tregenza. He could hardly bear to think what his own wife would have been like if he'd gone missing when she was carrying young Jamie.

Delphi appeared almost at once, fully dressed but heavy-eyed and with her hair tumbling around her shoulders. Remembering Channon's warning, Bowles bared his teeth in what he hoped was a reassuring smile, and made introductions. 'You've already given the local police a recent photograph of your husband, I believe,' he said, 'but we're here now to get more information on him, and then we want details of all the family. Perhaps your husband's aunt, here, can give us those if you need to rest.'

The three of them sat at the big table, while Frances hovered nearby until she was needed. 'Full name of you and your husband, first of all,' said Bowles, and when Delphi gave hers Yates looked up from his notebook and asked blankly, 'Is that short for Delphinium?'

Even Delphi almost smiled. 'No, it's the name of a Greek town. My mother was born there.'

Then, for what seemed like the hundredth time, Frances listened as she related how her husband had gone to Trevant House and never returned home. This time, though, she had to give every detail of his physical appearance, his clothes, the likely contents of his pockets, and the names of his doctor and dentist. The sergeant seemed ob-

36

sessed by Jonny's line of work and qualifications, and having satisfied himself about that, asked what Delphi knew about the Dancers. Were they locals? Were they British? Was Mr Dancer retired? What had made them buy Trevant House in preference to anywhere else?

At last they were finished and with a nice show of concern Bowles suggested that Delphi should go back to bed. 'We'll be in touch when there's anything to report,' he assured her, 'and if at any stage my superiors think it necessary, you'll be allocated a special support officer, maybe even DC Yates, here.' The pale eyes flicked to the younger man and gleamed with barely concealed mockery.

Delphi saw it, but merely gave an exhausted nod and went to the door of the sitting room. 'I'll keep my children from seeing you,' she said. 'They're a bit unsettled.'

Yates also had seen the mockery and was stifling resentment. Bowles might be good – he was sharp as a needle and tough as they come – but he had a malicious streak. Not only that, he'd been known to bend the rules in order to get a quick result. Everybody at the station knew that he marched to a different drummer than the rest of them, but the lower ranks put up with him because they had no option. As for a support officer for Mrs Tregenza, that was pushing it a bit when as yet there was no evidence of foul play, nor even suspicious circumstances. And even if the DCI *did* allocate somebody, surely he would choose a woman?

The sergeant was beckoning Frances to join

them. 'Now Miss Lyne, if you'll just give us full names of family members and later, when it's convenient, make out a list of all Mr Tregenza's friends and acquaintances?'

'We have many friends, sergeant; in fact, everyone in Porthmenna is a friend. I'll write them all down for you. As for family members, there aren't very many. There's me, Frances Lyne. I became legal guardian to Jonathan and his brother David sixteen years ago when their parents died in an accident – I'm their mother's sister. I came back to look after them in the family home and I live there alone, now. It's a house called Seaspray, out on a little no-through-road called Sands End at the far side of the village.'

'And the brother?'

'He's been abroad for the last seven years, but he arrived back from Hawaii at midday today.'

'Where is he now?'

'Out searching for signs of his brother.'

'When did he arrive in the UK, Miss Lyne?'

'I'm not sure. Last night, maybe. I think he'll be round here later on, so if you want to see him I'll tell him to make himself available. To go back to the family, there's only one grandparent still alive – Mrs Alice Tregenza. She has Alzheimer's and lives in residential care. Oh, and then there's Delphi's father. His name is Pennant, Terence Pennant, he's an artist. He lives just this side of Poldhu Cove. I know the house, but I'd have to look up the exact address.'

'Thanks, but we can get it if we need it. Tell me, does Mr Tregenza own a boat?'

'No. He can sail, of course, and he knows the

sea around here – it's a dangerous coast, as I'm sure you're aware. Howard Sandry is the man to talk to about what goes in and out of the harbour. His son runs pleasure trips and takes people out fishing. I don't think there are any long-distance boats for hire to the public – it's not safe unless you know the waters.'

'Miss Lyne, what do *you* think has happened to your nephew?'

'I don't know, sergeant. What I do know is he would never desert his wife and children.'

Bowles nodded with apparent respect and agreement, while thinking he'd heard that one more times than he'd had hot dinners. 'Thanks a lot,' he said soberly. 'Let's hope for good news very soon.'

Even as he spoke his mobile rang. It was Channon. 'Bowles, where are you?'

'At the Tregenza house. We're just leaving.'

'Good. Say nothing, get back to the car and ring me on my mobile.'

With a bland smile of apology at the interruption, Bowles made his farewell and at once left the house. Behind him, Yates wondered what all the rush was about.

Dave found Trevant House very different from the place he remembered. There was scaffolding against a side wall, windows sparkled in freshly painted frames, new lawns were laid amid sleek swathes of gravel, trees and shrubs had been cut back or replaced. He decided that the Dancers must have real money, which probably meant they weren't Cornish. The moneyed types usually moved in from elsewhere.

A woman who might have been in her late forties answered the door; neat and small-waisted, she was wearing cord trousers and a cream shirt. Light flashed on her glasses, but Dave caught the widening of round hazel eyes at the sight of him. He swallowed a sigh. Over the years he had found that women liked the way he looked, maybe because he was big and blond with a permanent tan. It was just the way he happened to be, and if it made women warm to him who was he to object – just so long as he didn't get too involved. He liked women, but did he like involvement? No, thanks.

'Can I help you?' the woman was asking. Her eyes and her small red mouth said 'in any way you like'; her actual words were merely polite.

'I've called to see Mr and Mrs Dancer,' he began.

She held out her hand. 'I'm Nancy Dancer. My husband's around somewhere.'

'Dave Tregenza. I'm trying to help trace my brother Jonathan.' Small and damp, her hand was still gripping his, so very gently he relinquished it. 'I do realize you must have answered loads of questions about him, Mrs Dancer, but I feel I must call here before I go anywhere else.'

She wrinkled her nose, shook her head and said, 'It's quite a puzzle, isn't it?' Dave eyed her curiously; the words, the tone, were more descriptive of a crossword or a jigsaw than the disappearance of a husband and father. 'Come in here,' she went on, leading him into a room just off the hall. 'We call this the snug, but in time it

40

will be our office. We're in the process of transforming the house into a hotel, you see.'

'That sounds great. I hope it goes well. Now, about my brother–'

'He didn't look like you,' she said thoughtfully. 'He was darker and not nearly so big.'

Dave stared at her. 'You're using the past tense, Mrs Dancer.'

She blinked defensively. 'I'm sorry, I didn't mean to. The difference between you struck me, that's all. I suspect I'm making small talk because I simply don't know what to say to you. You must be worried sick and so must your sister-in-law. Sit down for a minute and I'll fetch my husband.' She laid her hand on his, squeezed it, moistened her lips and hurried from the room.

Dave paced up and down. She was a bit weird, wasn't she, sending out a come-on when she must have seen that all he wanted was to ask about Jonny. He hoped the husband would be easier to deal with.

He was. Jovial and businesslike, Alan Dancer had a short chubby body and a round rosy face. When he bounced into the room he reminded Dave of a wobbly-man toy he used to play with as a child. His wife followed him in and stood by the window.

In ten seconds flat Dancer made clear that they would be Nancy, Alan and Dave with each other and no standing on ceremony. 'This is a bad situation,' he said, 'but all I can tell you is that Jonathan came over as arranged. We had a beer and talked about restoring the beams in the main hall and repairing the panelling on the stairs. This

41

place is listed so I have to watch my p's and q's all the time. Jonathan gave me a quote on the spot, detailed and in writing – very efficient. I said I'd ring him the next day but before I could do it his wife was on the phone and soon after that, on the doorstep. She was in a state, of course. Late that evening we had a phone call from the police, but it was more of a formality than anything.'

'I've been told you offered him a lift home?' Dave felt false and unreal to be questioning the older man, as if he were a bad actor impersonating a detective.

Alan Dancer seemed to see nothing odd about it. 'That's right. It was getting dark but he said he knows every path for miles around and he'd go back across the fields. We said goodnight and that was it.'

'Did you see him off your land?'

'No, we said goodnight at the door, then I closed it and went back inside.'

'Alan, my brother and I used to play in your outbuildings when we were young; in fact, we messed about here whenever the house was unoccupied. Jonny knew the place well, as he might have told you, so has anyone searched your grounds?'

'Yes, half the men of Porthmenna – twenty-odd of them, I'd say. You're welcome to search the place yourself, though, if it will make you feel easier.'

That was what he wanted. 'Thanks, I'll do it now, if that's all right. Will anybody want to know what I'm up to?'

'Only the old chap who does odd jobs for me. At the moment he's in the stables. We're turning them into overnight accommodation – a sort of motel that can be run in harness with the hotel itself. The old chap's called Ludcott – lives in Porthmenna.'

'Sam Ludcott? I've known him for years. One last question. I've been told that my brother has worked for you before, so you must know what sort of man he is. Did he seem his usual self on Monday night?'

'Yes, as far as I could tell. I don't know him intimately, of course, but he didn't seem to be on edge, or very tired, or unwell. Look, Dave, I'd like you to feel that you can call round at any time, or give me a ring if there's anything at all I can do to help.'

Pleasantly, reasonably, Alan Dancer was telling him that their conversation was at an end. Behind her husband's back, Nancy was telling him something else: eyes fixed on his, the tip of her tongue between her teeth, she casually unfastened the top two buttons of her shirt.

Dave swallowed. Was he imagining it? She looked the sort of woman to put on an apron and start labelling pots of jam, or something. *Did* women of her age do this sort of thing? Married women? Those who'd come on to him so far had been young and a bit wild – the free spirits of surfing communities around the Pacific – whereas this one must be knocking on for fifty and had a husband. Alan here seemed a decent enough little guy, if not quite enough of a guy for his wife; and right now he was waiting for a reply to his offer.

'Right, Alan, I'll remember that,' he said hurriedly, 'thanks a lot.' In front of Nancy he tried

43

to look unaware; he simply said, 'Thanks again,' and made his escape.

He found Sam Ludcott in the stable yard, sawing a length of wood. 'Hello, Uncle Sam,' he said.

The old man straightened up and eyed him without surprise. 'I was wondering when you'd turn up,' he said. Hair more silvered, face more lined than when they said goodbye, this was the man who had been like an uncle or even a grandfather to him and Jonny. Always ready for adult male company, they often climbed the steps to the former net-loft where he lived, and they'd always been welcome. Now, though, there was distance between them – the distance of long absence and Sam's disapproval, because he'd made it very plain what he thought of Dave leaving home.

'I'm trying to find out what's happened to Jonny, Uncle Sam. Alan Dancer says I can search the outbuildings and the grounds.'

The old man waved a sinewy arm. 'Go ahead, I only work here. I've searched the place myself, mind – in, out, up, down; every hay-loft, every stall, the old ice-house, the cellars at the end of the walled garden. You name it, I've looked there.' The arm flapped again. 'Still, look again if you must.'

'Uncle Sam, when did *you* last see Jonny?'

'Monday afternoon. I'd been helping him with some plain carpentry. Not your specialist stuff – he always did that himself. I worked for him two or three afternoons a week, depending on how much work he had in.'

'Did he have any other help?'

Sam Ludcott eyed him with impatience. 'If you'd

44

been interested I reckon you'd a'known about his business. Did you and Jonny never exchange letters nor talk on the phone?'

'No. Frances wrote whenever she had my address. Sometimes she telephoned.'

'Not your brother, though? Not ever?'

'No, not my brother,' said Dave shortly. He was in no mood to explain himself to Sam Ludcott, so with a nod of farewell he went inside the stables. It was only then that the implication of what he was doing hit him. Searching for a man who'd been missing for four days, in the very place he was last seen, was as good as shouting out loud that he was looking for a body – that he believed his brother to be dead.

At that moment Dave Tregenza didn't know what he believed – only what he hoped for.

'That was the DCI. I'm to ring him from the car,' said Bowles as they made for the cobbled road fronting the harbour. 'It sounds urgent.'

Yates's chest tightened. 'What d'you reckon, sarge?'

Bowles shook his head. 'Maybe Tregenza's been found. If he has, I wouldn't bet on him being able to tell us much.' In the car he rang Channon. 'It's me, sir.'

'We have a body,' said Channon grimly. 'Young, male, it doesn't sound good.'

'Where?'

'In a creek of the Helford River. Some birdwatchers spotted it. I'm on my way over – we're just coming into Helston as I speak. Wait for me in the car park of the pub at Mawgan Cross and

45

we'll go on together from there. I've got a driver who knows the area.'

That was more than he and Yates did, thought Bowles. Give him a motorway and a junction number any day, rather than this patchwork quilt of a landscape. To Channon he said, 'Right sir, I've got that. We'll see you,' and to Yates, 'Check the map. We're to meet the DCI at a place called Mawgan Cross near the Helford River, and I'd like to go past Goonhilly on the way.'

He switched on the engine and concealed a smile. He wasn't going to relinquish *that* little line of enquiry without a struggle.

Chapter Three

On a hillside overlooking the Helford River a farmer was checking one of his dairy herd. Dolly was a fine milker, but she was off her feed again. Another visit from the vet was going to cost him, but on the other hand he couldn't afford to lose her.

With an affectionate hand on the cow's rump he stared down his middle pasture, pondering on what he should do. Then against the glint of the river he saw movement, and what looked like a police car in the lane above the creek. Eyes narrowed, he watched as two uniformed men rammed poles into the silt of the creek bed, tying white tapes to them around a shape that was lying there – a covered shape. God above – it was a body!

Giving Dolly a farewell pat he headed home to ring the vet and to ask his wife exactly what her Cousin Mildred in Cury had been telling her about that young chap who'd gone missing. Within fifteen minutes Cousin Mildred in her turn had telephoned her husband's sister in Porthmenna, and soon everyone in the vicinity of the harbour knew that a body had been found on the banks of the Helford River.

Concern brought caution as the close-knit community gathered itself together. They were all aware that two plain-clothes policemen had called on Delphi Tregenza earlier that afternoon. It was agreed that the men couldn't have brought news, because Frances had promised that if she heard anything at all she would let everyone know through the shop.

It was a unanimous decision that nothing must be said about the body to either Delphi, Frances or young Dave, who had come from the other side of the world to help look for his brother. Lizzie Bannon spoke for everybody when she announced to a full shop that nobody must say a word until there was an official announcement.

But a ten-year-old girl called Lucy Bedize was listening as the mothers talked together after meeting the school bus. She wanted to cry at what she heard, because she liked Mr Tregenza. He'd made her a swing and put it up in the yard, because her dad had been off work for weeks with a bad back and couldn't do it himself. Then she'd heard her mum telling somebody that Mr Tregenza wouldn't accept any money for doing it...

Well, now *she* would do something for him – or at least, for his wife. She'd pick some flowers and tie them up with that pink ribbon she'd put away in her drawer, and write a note saying something grown-up, like *In Loving Memory of Mr Tregenza*. No, when somebody had only just died, didn't people say *With Deepest Sympathy?* Yes, that sounded better. She'd put *With Deepest Sympathy, from Lucy.*

It was still and very quiet now that the wind had dropped. DCI Channon descended the track fol-

48

lowed by Bowles, Yates and the police photographer. A young WPC, Honor Bennett, was leading the way because this was her home territory and she knew the river. In the car coming over Channon had been intrigued to see her striving to appear solemn and responsible, when more than likely she was on edge at playing the native guide to a DCI and being one of the first at the scene of a death.

He surveyed what lay below them and wondered why awful things so often happened in the midst of beauty. In his case it could only be because he was a policeman who worked in a beautiful county. That was his good fortune – he acknowledged it every day of his life – but even after years in the force it could still shake him to see ugly death in a lovely setting.

Right now they were on a steep hillside leading down to a creek, at the mouth of which the Helford River flowed like blue-grey silk. Up on the bank a single strip of sand fronted trees in new leaf, but down in the creek it was all mud and silt; a grim resting place for the thing that was covered by waterproofs. It lay inside a circle of police tapes, and two local constables were standing guard over it.

'I'm Channon,' said the DCI without ceremony, 'so you can relax for a bit, lads. The police surgeon not arrived yet?'

'He's been and gone, sir. He said to tell you that you hardly need him to certify death and you'll know what he means when you see the body. As soon as he arrived he got a message about an accident on the A394. He went off right away, but

49

said he'd be in touch within the hour. Oh, and he said Mr Hunter knows about – about this.'

Channon nodded. 'He knows because I told him – he'll be here before long.' He stepped back and observed their surroundings. 'Nothing's been touched?'

'No, sir, except that the two men who spotted the body walked right up to it. They say they didn't touch it, though. We've got their details if you want to question them or take a statement.'

Already the photographer was clicking away, so Bowles unpacked protective clothing. He couldn't wait to get to the body. All this fiddling around to safeguard evidence got on his nerves. OK, he'd admit that advances with DNA had changed police work for ever, but he could count on the fingers of one hand the number of times it had solved local crimes. You still needed tip-offs, for crying out loud; you still needed confessions. Grunting in frustration he joined the others in getting all dressed up.

The body was a mess. Starting to decompose, soaked with the previous night's rain and maybe sea or river water, half-buried in mud, it seemed as if it had never even been human, let alone a living, breathing man. For two or three seconds Channon stared but saw nothing of the dark, discoloured flesh, the gaping mouth. All he could think was that this pathetic creature mustn't – it must *not* be Jonathan Tregenza, not with a wife at home and two little girls.

Bowles was crouching next to him, and as if granting the DCI's earnest request, said flatly, 'It's not Tregenza.'

Channon let out a sigh of relief. 'Why not? We can check against his photograph.'

The sergeant sat back on his heels. 'Well, I'm not sure about the clothes because of all the mud, though I admit it looks like he's wearing a shirt and jeans, the same as Tregenza. In spite of the gunge, though, you can see that this one has dark hair – Tregenza's is fair to light brown, and his eyes are blue. This one's eyes are a mess, but I'd say they were dark, and his teeth are poor – a couple missing and several fillings – Tregenza's are perfect.' He touched the corpse's thigh with a gloved finger. 'He's swelled up a bit, I know, but even so I'd say he was a bit overweight, whereas Tregenza's in good trim.'

He met Channon's dark gaze and thought he saw disbelief. 'It's no more than an hour since I talked to his wife!' he protested. 'I don't need a photograph!'

'All right, Bowles. I believe you.'

Then to his own embarrassment the sergeant said, 'I'm relieved for Mrs Tregenza, but it'll be bad news for somebody else.'

At the opposite side of the body Honor Bennett had been watching and listening. The sergeant was known as an awkward devil and something of a bully, but right now she couldn't fault him. Neither, judging by his expression, could Yates.

Then all was bustle as George Hunter arrived, puffing and blowing after scrambling down the track, while behind him came men from the mortuary with a stretcher. Hunter concentrated on the body, Channon examined the surround-ings, dictating notes to Yates and taking measurements with Bowles. Already he was sure that this was no crime scene. If it had been he would have had to call in the scene-of-crime officers, and that would have ruled out any trampling around near the body, any interference of any sort, come to that.

At last Hunter stood up. 'What d'you reckon, George?' asked Channon.

'It's too soon for an estimate and too late for accuracy, but it's probable that death was between three and five days ago. No visible signs of violence, but he's spent some time in water, so if there was any blood it'll have been washed away. We'll bag him up and take him back for the full monty, then I'll be in touch.'

As Hunter's men dealt with the body bag Channon beckoned to Honor Bennett. 'Do you happen to know if this creek is subject to the tide? I take it this mud and stuff comes from the river?'

'Yes, sir. When there's a really high tide it backs the river right up. I've seen it bring trees and bits of wreckage as far as this.'

'Could it have brought the body?'

'I'd have to ask my dad's opinion about a man's body, sir. I once saw it bring up a dead sheep, though. It just swirled in on the water and got tossed up on the bank like a bit of driftwood.'

Channon stared thoughtfully into the distance, then gave her the benefit of his rare smile. 'Thanks,' he said, 'that's really helpful. It's good to have somebody who knows about these things on the team.' Honor glowed at the praise, but Bowles, hearing it, told himself that Channon was still an old softie.

Within minutes they were heading back to the cars. When they had gone the little creek looked much the same as usual, except for the hollow in the mud.

Dave climbed the stone steps from the harbour to Lookout Cottage, reminding himself that it was closer to the open sea than any other house in Porthmenna. Not only that, the little tower in its roof really was a lookout, originally used to watch for shoals of mackerel approaching, but still with views far out to sea and down the coast towards Predannack Head.

It was a clear evening with a bright, sinking sun, but in spite of that there was a light in the window of the tower. Dave stared upwards and knew at once that the light was for Jonny, to show that his family were waiting for him. It was local custom to knock on a door and walk straight in. He did just that and was met by chaos. Two very small girls in patterned pyjamas were making an astounding amount of noise – it was bedlam. One was stamping her feet and yelling with rage, the other was crying bitterly and being cuddled by Frances. Their mother was on the phone, one hand over her ear.

At the sight of Dave both girls at once fell silent, staring at him with identical dark blue eyes drenched with tears. As a first meeting with his nieces it wasn't what he'd anticipated, except that they were so alike it was if he were seeing double. 'Daddy?' asked one uncertainly. 'Uncle Dave,' said the other – the one who'd been stamping; adding as if she'd learnt it by heart, 'Daddy will come back soon.'

This was awful, he thought, but managed a smile. 'Yes, I'm your Uncle Dave,' he said.

'They're tired and ready for bed,' Frances told him, drying their tears. 'This one's Dorcas and this is Sophie.'

'How can you tell?'

She smiled wearily. 'Sometimes I can't, but if they keep still for a minute and you look closely, you'll see that Sophie has a little blemish on her neck, just under her right ear. Tonight, though, all you need to know is that she's got butterflies on her pyjamas and Dorcas has hedgehogs. Girls, say hello to your uncle.'

All at once friends again, they stood in front of him hand in hand. 'Hello, Uncle Dave,' they said in unison. 'Will you read us our story?' asked Sophie. 'Have you seen our daddy?' asked Dorcas.

Delphi was saying goodbye to whoever was on the phone, so he looked enquiringly at Frances. 'We've told them he's away for a few days and that he'll be back soon,' she said, and to Delphi, 'Who *was* that?'

'A detective – a chief inspector. I'll tell you later.' Delphi looked at Dave, smiled slightly and bundled the girls towards the stairs. 'Time for bed,' she said firmly.

By now Dorcas was holding tight to her uncle's hand, while Sophie, foot lifted, was ready for more stamping. 'I want Uncle Dave to read our story,' she announced, pouting ferociously.

'Uncle Dave,' echoed Dorcas, 'he can read our story.'

It didn't seem to occur to any of them that he

might refuse. 'Come on, then,' said Delphi, 'and I'll show you the drill, Dave. We always carry them up to bed.' She picked up one of the girls, clearly expecting him to do the same with the other. He had no option.

So, within minutes of meeting his nieces, he was sitting on a narrow bed with a small girl cuddled on either side of him, reading a story called *The Bluebird who Danced*, to the evident satisfaction of his listeners. Behind the words part of his mind was telling him that having children was clearly nothing but a life sentence to hard labour. Why did people do it? One at a time must be bad enough, but two! A third one didn't even bear thinking about.

Saying she'd be back to tuck them in, Delphi had left the three of them to it, but from a gold picture frame nearby someone was watching. A blown-up snapshot showed Jonny Tregenza on a sunlit beach, smiling at the camera as he built a sandcastle. Dave wasn't even surprised when two sleepy little girls took turns at kissing the picture goodnight.

Delphi came downstairs and sank into a chair. 'The girls aren't usually like they were when you arrived,' she said in apology, 'but they were tired, and a couple of hours earlier we'd had an upset.'

Dave looked from her to Frances and back again. 'What sort of upset?'

'A posy of flowers was left on the doorstep and a message saying "With deepest sympathy". I thought – well – you can guess what I thought.'

Frances took up the story, her voice almost

55

toneless from exhaustion. 'It could have meant sympathy that Jonny was missing, of course, but that wasn't how either of us saw it. Then we realized that the note had been written and signed by a child, Lucy Bedize. You'll remember her parents – they live in Downalong near the old fish cellars. I rushed round there to have a word with her mother, and found that Lucy had heard grown-ups talking about a body that had been found near the river, and that it might be Jonny's. Lucy took it as definite and decided to do something kind for Delphi.'

Dave stared at her. Before he arrived he'd thought things were bad enough. How much worse could they get? Frances went on, 'Apparently everyone in Porthmenna – except us – had heard about the body. They decided that we weren't to be told until it was official, and then only by the police. Delphi was in a state so I rang the midwife and asked her to call and check on her, then talked to the local police. They were amazed that anyone knew about the body, but said it wasn't – isn't – Jonny, and they don't yet know who it is. So that's it. We were under stress, it affected the girls and they played up – especially Sophie.'

'And that phone call just now was from a detective chief inspector over in Truro,' said Delphi. 'It was his sergeant who came to see us earlier. He said they've both seen the body and it's definitely not Jonny. He said if there's any news of any kind he, personally, will tell me, and to pay no attention to rumour, or the local grapevine, or anyone at all, except him or Sergeant Bowles. His

56

name is Channon.'

'Well, thank you for that, at least, Mr Channon,' said Frances with a sigh. 'Now, does anybody want some beef casserole?'

Dave gazed down from the lookout and saw the lights of Porthmenna strung like pearls against the darkening night. In a minute he would go through Jonny's order book to check on the work in hand, but first he needed to think about what he'd seen and heard since opening the door of Seaspray House that morning.

The reality was that in the eight or nine hours since then nothing he'd seen and nobody he'd spoken to had shed any light whatsoever on Jonny's disappearance. He'd searched the Dancers' grounds, the old copper mine, the serpentine diggings and even the cave on 'their' beach, though why he'd done that he didn't know. The only good thing of the entire day was what he'd heard before the meal: at last the police were getting involved.

The meal itself had been an ordeal. The food was lovely, of course, because Frances was a good cook, but she'd been very quiet, which was hardly surprising in view of the day she'd had. He'd been on edge, watching every word so as not to alert either of them to his fears, but Delphi had seemed almost light-hearted. At first it had baffled him, but now he could see that it had been some sort of reaction to the events of the afternoon. And then as he and Frances drank coffee, Delphi had fixed him with those eyes of hers and asked, 'Dave, what do *you* think has

57

happened to Jonny?'

What should he have said? Not what he was actually thinking, that was for sure. He'd hedged and come out with things like: 'I haven't seen him for years ... I don't know the state of mind he was in ... I simply don't know...'

'I've told you his state of mind,' she said doggedly. 'He was all right; looking forward to the baby, happy because he expected more work from Alan Dancer. Oh, and that's another thing – his business. I've had two calls from clients today. I had to fob them off.'

That, at least, was something he could do to help. 'Show me where he keeps his records and I'll see to it,' he said, 'and if there's any sort of problem with cash-flow, I'll deal with that as well. I can put my hands on a lump sum that will keep you going until he gets home.'

If either of them were surprised that he had money, they concealed it well. Delphi thanked him earnestly, said she hoped she wouldn't have to take up his offer, and told him that Jonny's office was up here, in the tower. Now, he sat down at the desk, which was organized and orderly, like its owner, except for a stack of surfing magazines in front of the computer. The cover of the top one was a picture of himself, barrelling a vast wave and laughing as he did it.

He recognized the shot as one taken several months earlier. He'd been proud of it at the time, it had earned him good money from a sponsor; but now, in this house of fear and exhaustion and overwrought children, it seemed out of place. He didn't like to see himself laughing as he rode a giant wave at the other side of the world. If he'd been here at home he could have looked after his brother – the brother who cared enough to collect magazines to try and find out what he, Dave, was doing with his life.

For long moments Dave forgot all his rules about keeping strictly to the mental and physical aspects of life. Emotions poured into his heart: fear, regret, remorse, guilt; they were all there, wild and undisciplined. So was the one that had gnawed at him since he was nine years old. Oh yes, the daddy of them all – resentment. With his head in his hands he sat at Jonny's desk and let them all run riot.

Frances cleared the kitchen automatically, yearning to spend just five minutes without thinking. Ever since Monday night her mind had been like a washing machine that was never switched off, with thoughts swirling round and round inside it. Now, for the first time, some of the thoughts were pleasant. One was that David had money, which confirmed what she'd deduced from reading about him. She'd long since stopped torturing herself about him throwing away his A levels and his future, but at least it seemed he was no beach bum.

Another thought was that if she could get him to spend time with the girls it might help them to adjust to Jonny's absence. Yet another was that she must start thinking about wearing support stockings, because her legs were creasing her. And should she go up to the tower room right now to talk to him? For years she'd longed for the chance to speak face to face, to gauge his reactions; but right now she simply hadn't the energy.

He was back. He was worried sick about Jonny. He was going to help them. What more could she ask? She flopped into Delphi's big rocking chair and fell fast asleep.

'Nothing yet on the body from the river,' said Channon when Bowles and Yates came to see him. 'I doubt whether it has anything to do with Tregenza, so I've asked for normal identification procedures.' Then he tapped their report. 'This is good, but you haven't mentioned the brother.'

'We never saw him,' said Bowles. 'We heard he was all over the place searching.'

'Never mind, we'll get hold of him if we need him. You've given me the facts, but fill me in with a few personal impressions, will you? Alan and Nancy Dancer, for instance. You dealt with Tregenza's visit to them, but how did you read the Dancers themselves? Did you sense lying or evasion?'

'No,' said Bowles promptly, 'but the wife's a nympho.' At his side Yates squirmed slightly but nodded in agreement.

'Evidence of it?' asked Channon, aware that Bowles saw himself as an expert on women.

'You could spot it a mile off. She doesn't look the part, mind. She's like any well-off wife who'd put on a dinner party for eight and cook posh nosh, but it was there all right.'

This might be an angle, thought Channon. 'Could she have made a play for Tregenza?'

Yates spoke up. 'From his picture he's a good-

60

looking bloke, sir. I'd say she'd have a go.'

'Right. Make enquiries on the pair of them – routine channels from now on – no local gossip. Check both their backgrounds. It is possible that he attacked Tregenza on seeing his wife fancying him, but hardly likely. If she's a nympho, as you call it, he'll be used to it. Still, check on him – where he got his money, whether they've ever lived abroad.' He fixed Bowles with a thoughtful eye. 'Whether they've ever been embroiled in any kind of radical movement.'

Bowles knew at once what he meant, but restrained his wolfish grin. Goonhilly... If the name of Bowles didn't go down for something spectacular in this dead-alive authority it wouldn't be his fault.

Now the DCI was saying, 'Where did you get the local reactions you mentioned?'

That had been Yates. 'From folk round the harbour and in the village shop,' he said. 'The general feeling was that young Jonny, as they call him, is as happy as Larry. One old girl in the shop said maybe he'd gone off on purpose but the rest of them wouldn't have it. He's well liked and respected.'

'Mm. Now, Bowles, anything to add to what you've said about the harbourmaster – this Sandry fella – Howard Sandry?'

'Not really. He's a dyed in the wool old salt who's on top of his job. He's known Tregenza since he was a boy. Says he can handle a boat, but isn't likely to tackle anything more difficult than the waters he knows – close to the shores of the Lizard. He says if he did leave by sea it wasn't

61

from the harbour. He's cut up about it – they all are. We didn't see his son, who was out fishing; in the holiday season he runs pleasure trips and so forth.'

'Right. Tregenza's father-in-law, Terence Pennant. You say he wondered openly whether Tregenza was having an affair. Did you sense animosity between the two?'

Bowles rolled his eyes and kept silent. Let the little white hen – or cockerel – answer this one. 'I'd say there was no love lost,' said Yates, 'but it was more a touch of the cynic – you know – man of the world stuff. He spoke of his daughter as if she's a bit gullible, but certainly didn't come up with any evidence to back his idea. His place has got class, so I'd say he makes a bit, even though it's not on a recognized tourist route. He has the nose and cheeks of a drinker and I had the feeling he's been a bit of a drifter in his day. His wife – Mrs Tregenza's mother – was Greek. She went back there several years ago and died of cancer.'

'What about his art work?'

Yates shrugged. 'We saw some signed work and it looked pretty good to me, but I'm no art critic.'

'Did either of you find Mrs Tregenza gullible when you interviewed her?'

'No,' they said as one. 'She's worried to death, but she's no fool,' Bowles assured him. 'She's also some looker. I bet she's a peach when she's not in the pudding club.'

Channon was silent for a moment. He was getting a feeling about Tregenza, and he hoped he was wrong. 'I'll give it thought,' he told them. 'Make enquiries about the Dancers but don't spend too long on it. I can't sanction the time for what might be simply another missing person. Oh, one last thing. Nobody – I repeat nobody – is to pass on any news, good or bad, to Delphi Tregenza except me. If I'm away and you can't reach me you can do it, Bowles. In person – take Yates with you.'

'Yes, boss,' said Bowles, and thought, Thanks a million. You know I can't stand weeping and wailing.

Back at Seaspray House, Dave faced the window and stared out at the night. All was black and silver and gold. To his left lay the void of their little beach, black apart from the silver-edged waves; above was the black sky hung with stars, and far to his right were the lights of Porth-menna, gold and twinkly and horribly cheerful.

Around him the room was unlit, but he was well aware that it hadn't changed. He was sitting on the squashy sofa where he'd sprawled as a teenager; the same sand-coloured carpet was under his feet, the same copper-based lamps were there for when he chose to light them.

It had been some day, from the moment he arrived here at Seaspray to leaving Frances fast asleep in the rocking chair, with Delphi and the twins in bed. He had come down from the tower room to discuss Jonny's business. His books, his records were in good order, he'd expected no less, but he needed to find out more about the work in hand.

With nobody to ask, he'd decided to see Sam Ludcott next morning, and then stood looking down at his aunt. The grey streaks in her hair were new to him and she had more lines on her face, but the ring on her right hand was still there, he had never seen her without it. He used to scorn it as a tasteless fake until, in that final confrontation between them, she'd told him what it was. Oh yes, that had been an exchange of home truths...

As for Jonny's business, he couldn't understand why he didn't find it tame and uninspired. After all, he himself gained satisfaction from a high-risk sport that demanded rigorous training and was only just beginning to edge him into a luxury lifestyle. He was only twenty-five, but top surfers didn't reach their peak in expertise and experience until their mid-thirties – if they survived that long. Compare the exhilaration of it to the work of a jobbing carpenter – a family man who lived in a modest house in a Cornish fishing village.

OK, so he was comparing it – here in an unlit room in another modest house that happened to be his old home. Less than a week ago he'd believed that surfing was his life – that and his hard-won skills in predicting the movements of the oceans – but all at once he was unsure of what mattered and what didn't. He was unsure of everything.

Chapter Four

'Now, now! You did say to contact you direct if there was so much as a smidgen that seemed odd!' George Hunter was all tongue-in-cheek injured innocence.

Bogged down with paperwork, Channon hadn't wanted to hear about the body from the creek. Still edgy, he said, 'I thought you delegated identification of remains, George?'

'I do. I've got a young wizard over here who liaises with your lot in Forensic and comes up with answers. The point is – do you want to hear the questions?'

'You know my special angle. If it has any bearing on that then of course I want to hear – I have no choice. What have you got?'

'Age – early thirties. Fingerprints still intact, so your boys have confirmed that he doesn't have a record. We've taken blood from deep muscle that's not contaminated by river water; no news on it so far, but the least we'll get is a grouping and his DNA. Circumcised, though that's not conclusive of anything. Stomach contents a light meal with no animal protein or alcohol, and not completely digested at death. X-rays of bone structure in hand, *but*, and this is why I'm ringing you direct, oh master, his skin pigmentation is not native UK. Could be Mediterranean or even Middle Eastern, though as you know skin tones can vary. Dental work – expensive treatment in the past but total neglect in the last few years, which could indicate poverty or even badly supervised captivity.'

By now Channon was hunched over the phone. 'But how long has he been dead? How did he die? Was he dead when he hit the water?'

'I don't think so. The water in the lungs must have been inhaled – it's too soon for natural seepage and saturation. He might have been unconscious – there's a blow to the head but I can't say yet if it was deliberate or from rocks or debris in the water. I think about five days since death. My young wizard is organizing botanists and scientists from the Rivers Authority to suss out whether he went into the river or the sea. Oh – a good pointer – a pulpy mess in his pocket could have been a cheap copy of the Koran. Your boys in Forensic have got his clothes, so they'll deal with that if you want it confirming.'

'Yes, I do,' said Channon heavily. World events were making clear that nobody in authority could cut corners, not even in deepest Cornwall. 'I must watch terrorism – it's my responsibility and in any case we get extra funding for it. Don't bother to reel off about not all Muslims being terrorists – we already know it. We also know that religious, nationalist and political groups spawn terrorists by the cartload. So tell them to check it, will you?'

'Your wish is my command. All details later.'

'Thanks, George, I'll see you.' Channon tipped back his chair. Was it a coincidence that an unknown man had died by drowning only a few miles from where another man – a local man –

had gone missing, and within twenty-four hours of each other? He gazed at the ceiling. If there was one thing lacking in the life of a DCI, it was thinking time. So just this once, he would devote ten precious minutes to the sheer, unadulterated bliss of analytical thought.

'Come up!' It was Sam Ludcott's usual method of admitting visitors. People calling on him rang the ship's bell by the outside door; he looked out of the window to see who it was and bellowed down to them. It was rare for anyone to be turned away.

Following the usual procedure, Dave Tregenza climbed the wooden stairs to the net-loft. One of a row of four, Sam's was the only one used as a permanent home. The rest were holiday lets owned by outsiders.

The old man eyed Dave as he stood in the doorway of the long, raftered room. 'You fill the door a bit more than when you were last here,' he acknowledged. 'There's still no news?'

Dave shook his head. 'The police went to see Delphi yesterday. They asked a lot of questions but didn't say they'd search the downs, or anywhere else for that matter. I don't think they could hope to find any actual clues up there because of the rain in the last few days, and in any case the local folk have looked high and low for a – for Jonny himself.'

'Look, lad, come and sit down for a spell.' Sam led the way to his ancient basket chairs. 'As a matter of fact, I'm glad of the chance for a word. I'd even thought of walking along Sands End to

67

see you.'

'Oh?' Recalling the other's cool greeting the previous day, Dave wasn't prepared to show pleasure at that. Sam hadn't approved when he went away, but even so he'd expected to find some of the old warmth still there.

'I want to say maybe I was a bit brisk with you yesterday. I'm glad to see you – you young so-and-so.'

Dave flipped a hand at the implied apology. 'It's good to be back,' he admitted, looking around him. The same wood-burning stove, the same glass-fronted cupboard that held the maps and charts for Sam's hobby of tracing the countless past shipwrecks round the Lizard, the narrow bed in one corner with its crocheted quilt, and behind him the counter top that divided the room from the long galley kitchen.

All very nostalgic, but nothing to do with the matter in hand. 'Uncle Sam,' he said urgently, 'this just doesn't make sense. Something's happened to Jonny. I know it, so does Delphi and so does Frances. I can see it in their eyes, in their manner, in the things they're not saying.'

'It's a bad do,' agreed the old man, 'but Dave, you read it in the papers all the time, and folk with televisions see it on their news reports. People do go missing, and at least some of 'em must come back.'

'I know,' said Dave, 'but he's disappeared without the slightest trace. The reason I'm here now, though, is that I've promised Delphi I'll get in touch with his customers to explain delays. His computer listings are fine – accounts all in order, estimates noted and so forth – but I need to know about the actual work in hand. I can't find the details.'

'That's because they're all in his head,' said Sam. 'He didn't need no fancy screen and such to list 'em. Have you been to his workshop? There's drawings pinned up of all his orders. We could soon make out a list. You'll not need to get in touch with many of his customers, mind.'

'Oh? Why not?'

'Because they all know, that's why not. Here in the village it's the shop, the chapel and the pub that are the news centres; outside Porthmenna there's what you might call the grapevine of the Lizard. I've always thought it funny that old Marconi should have transmitted his messages to America from here, because it's a place where you don't need no wireless. News travels faster than light on the Lizard.

'Having said that, there's a chap the other side of Penzance waiting for an oak surround for his fireplace, and a village school over near Zennor wanting some desks repaired. Maybe you should talk to them?'

'All right, but first, will you come to the workshop with me?'

'Of course I will. I've got a key – let's go now.'

So the old sailor in his battered seaman's cap and the blond, suntanned young man walked together along the cobbled road that fronted the harbour. Passers-by greeted them but didn't stop to talk. Perhaps they thought there was nothing more to say when a hardworking young father had vanished into thin air.

Frances was feeling better than at any time since Jonny went missing. At first she hadn't wanted to admit the reason for it because it sounded ridiculous, even pathetic, but having made her vow to be completely honest with herself she'd had to do it. She'd made herself admit why her spirits had lifted.

Dead tired the previous evening, she'd fallen fast asleep in the rocking chair. Waking cramped and stiff at three in the morning, she'd found herself covered by a blanket – the one they used for the twins when they had a nap on the sofa, the one with the baby elephants on it.

Hearing Delphi moving about upstairs she'd gone up to check on her, giving her a kiss as she came out of the bathroom. 'Thanks for putting the blanket over me, love,' she'd said, 'I would have wakened all shivery without it.'

Eyes dark-ringed, Delphi had stared at her in puzzlement. 'I didn't cover you up. For once I fell asleep as soon as I got into bed, and I haven't been up until just now. I'm going downstairs to make a cup of tea. Do you want one?'

'No, I think I'll get undressed and try to go back to sleep. Are you all right?'

'What's all right?' asked Delphi, fastening her dressing gown. 'I've forgotten the meaning of it. We're both living on hold, Frances, so go and get settled down again, if you can.'

In a daze she'd put on her nightie. Nobody could have covered her with the blanket except David. He must have come down from the tower room, found her asleep and *covered her up!* For the first time in sixteen years he had shown concern for her. She knew she should be thinking, Not before time, or Better late than never, but instead she could only rejoice that the hurt and resentment that had blighted his life must at last have started to heal. Heal, maybe, but for what? To be replaced by another hurt that was every bit as bad?

God, she prayed from the heart, don't *do* this to him! Don't let him lose his brother as well as his parents!

More an instruction than a prayer, she'd thought ruefully as she got into bed, but the sense of well-being was such that she fell asleep again and didn't waken until seven o'clock. She could hear the twins talking together in the next room, no doubt cuddled together in the same bed. Sometime during every night one of them would join the other to sleep entwined. They were so very sweet, she thought, and it would be good for them to have each other when the baby arrived.

While Delphi was in the bath after breakfast she took them out on the beach. At low tide they liked to run around on the stretch of firm sand in front of the boats and mooring ropes. This was the first morning they hadn't asked for their daddy, she told herself, and wondered what exactly was the extent of their memory. If – she would say it, in her mind if not out loud – if he didn't come back, would they forget him? Yes they would, she decided, in time. She stood and watched the two small figures racing around and wondered how long it would take.

'No news, then?' said a voice behind her. She turned to see a stocky, grey-haired man wearing a reefer jacket. It was Howard Sandry, heading for the jetty.

'Oh, hello, Howard. No, we've heard nothing, but the police are making enquiries, so we're living in hope.' The trite, optimistic words sounded unutterably false.

From a network of weathered creases the harbour-master's eyes met hers. He said simply, 'Me and the lad are right upset about it.'

If she'd been less on edge Frances might have smiled at his description of his son. Reuben Sandry was no 'lad', but well turned thirty, a surly, uncommunicative man who didn't mix easily, and so made full use of his genial, good-natured father when he took holidaymakers out on boating trips.

Now Howard said, 'If there's anything I can do to help you must let me know. I can always call on a boat or two if the police should need 'em to go searching. They've already checked with me who sailed out of the harbour on – uh – earlier in the week.'

That was his way of saying 'on Monday when Jonny went missing'. Frances felt a familiar warmth easing its way round her heart. Porthmenna was populated by ordinary, hardworking Cornish folk; few of them well off, few of them educated beyond what was obligatory, but in tact and sheer, down-to-earth kindness, they were in a class of their own.

'I'll have to be going,' she said. 'The girls are booked in for the three-year-olds' session on the bouncy castle, so I mustn't let them miss their slot.'

Howard looked at the rosy-cheeked twins. 'They're a lively pair and no mistake,' he said. 'Now you know where I am if you need me.'

With the girls running ahead Frances made for the village hall. She planned to join the helpers there in order to let Delphi have some time to herself. She had slept late and been heavy-eyed and lethargic over breakfast, causing Frances to wonder for the hundredth time if the stress of the last few days would affect her pregnancy, even at so late a stage. The midwife had said that her blood pressure was a bit high, which was hardly surprising, but that there were no other signs of anything amiss, and that she would call again on Monday.

On that day she, Frances, would be away from Porthmenna. It was her regular day to take language classes at a private school near Carbis Bay. She found it a doddle, actually; one-to-one sessions with a series of girls, all well-behaved, all motivated, and the pay was excellent. She was reluctant to leave Delphi, though. Suppose the police arrived with news? Suppose she went into labour? The women of the village would take over, of course, but they weren't family. Maybe she should ask David to be around, just in case. He could at least drive her to the hospital...

Dave locked up the workshop, pleased with what he and Sam Ludcott had been able to sort out. Now, he could see no option but to call on Delphi to discuss money.

Almost as if their minds were in tune – which in itself was hardly likely, he told himself – he found her at the kitchen table counting out money. Her hair was in long damp straggles round her shoulders, her skin was pale, almost waxen, but there were two red blotches high on her cheeks. She looked awful.

He'd been hoping to find Frances with her, or the girls, but clearly she was on her own. Awkwardly he faced her. 'I've been to Jonny's workshop with Uncle Sam, Delphi. On Monday I'll deal with those customers who're getting impatient, if that's OK with you?'

'Yes, thank you,' she said politely. 'Won't you sit down? Can I get you a coffee?'

'No thanks. About what I was saying last night – you know, about money. Do you think you'll be all right?'

'I'm going through our finances now. As a start I'm checking my housekeeping money. We have a current account that's topped up each month from Jonny's business. I'm not sure how much there is in hand, though, nor what he owes to his suppliers or what's owing to him. For days I've been telling myself to look at his books and computer records, but – well – I haven't got round to it.'

Unthinkingly she laid a hand against her stomach. Dave looked away, oddly put out to find they couldn't even talk business without one or other of her children putting the mockers on it. Last night he'd been embroiled with the twins as soon as he came through the door; now it was the one who hadn't even been born who was encroaching. Then it dawned that she might need to talk about it, so he cudgelled his unwilling brain to come up with a question. 'Do you know whether it will be a boy or a girl?' he managed.

She gave a weary little smile. 'No. We didn't want to be told.'

'Oh. Right. When exactly will it – arrive?' That was a close one – he'd almost said 'come out'! His knowledge of childbirth was minimal; it came from biology lessons at school and films or TV dramas where women sweated and screamed and bared their teeth, with people they didn't even know peering and prodding at their genitals. It was pretty unnerving.

No more unnerving, though, than being alone with the girl he would once have died for. Oh yes, he'd never done things by halves in his youth. Quite simply, he would have died for her if the need had been there. When she first appeared in Porthmenna at the age of sixteen, she'd seemed like a creature from another world, another age; like a maiden from a Greek legend. Her mother *was* Greek, actually, but her father was Cornish, an arty type who trailed his wife and daughter all over the county and was often drunk.

They were an outlandish pair: the father a good-looking drifter, the mother thin, dark and intense. They had spectacular rows when the mother threw stuff around the place, crockery and ornaments and plant pots. Delphi herself had been beautiful and dreamlike and, somehow, very sad. He and Jonny had been drawn to her from the day she first boarded the school bus in Porthmenna.

It was pure relief that she now looked so different – apart from the eyes, and maybe the mouth, and of course the hair. Yesterday it had been bundled on top of her head, dark and cloudy and fastened with combs, just as he remembered it.

'Nobody knows exactly when a baby will arrive,' she told him, 'unless it's to be delivered by surgery or induced – that's when they hurry it up artificially. This one is due in two weeks' time on 8th May. Do you recall why that day is special?'

'It's the date of the Flora Dance, if that's what you mean?' Everybody in Cornwall knew that the age-old Dance in Helston was always on that date unless it fell on a Sunday.

Delphi smiled, the first real smile he'd seen since coming home. 'So if it's a girl we're going to call her Flora.'

'Hey, that's really good. And what if it's a boy?'

She looked down at her hands. 'Jonny insists on David.'

For the second time in less than a day his heart paused, then took up its rhythm with a single, heavy stroke. The brother he had left and never, ever contacted direct, wanted to call his son David. He knew he should say something, anything, to fill the silence between them, but what came out was more than a silence-filler.

'Delphi,' he said hoarsely, 'when I went away it wasn't just because I was jealous of Jonny having you.'

She put up her hands in front of her chest, palms outward, as if to push him away – him or his words. 'You don't have to explain yourself to me,' she said.

'I must. I see now that it might have seemed

76

like pique – like wounded pride.'

She shook her head. 'You were only eighteen, Dave, but if it wasn't jealousy and it wasn't wounded pride, what was it?'

Tell her, said his heart, tell her how you felt. But his head was saying, You vowed to steer clear of emotion, you'll only tie yourself in knots and get hurt. He knew he was starting to sweat; his upper lip felt damp and the back of his neck was clammy.

'I might have been only eighteen, Delphi, but I loved you – truly loved you. The trouble was I loved Jonny as well. He was my big brother. I used to cry in his bed when Mum and Dad died.'

She clutched at her head. 'Don't tell me this now! I don't want to hear it!'

'I have to,' he insisted, then fell silent. What was he *doing*, burdening her with his teenage hang-ups when she was almost ready to give birth and didn't know where the father was?

'You're trying to justify yourself,' she said flatly. 'Well, for your information Frances was devastated when you left – she was heartbroken. As for Jonny, he missed you every day of his life. We've been happy together but we would have been even happier if he hadn't been so desperate to see you and I hadn't felt guilty at coming between you. So think about *that*, will you, and leave me alone!'

He walked away from her and stared out at the steep back garden. Two little bikes with giant stabilizers were there, close to each other like the children who rode them, and next to a wooden shed were two dolls' prams, one pink, one yellow.

Deep in thought he looked at them, then turned back to Delphi. 'You'll hear no more about the past from me,' he assured her. 'Give me your bank statements, your cheque books, everything you can lay your hands on and I'll go through the lot. If Jonny has an accountant give me his name. We can keep everything ticking over until we have news of him.'

Dark blue eyes, heavy with resentment, met lighter ones that were shamed and defensive. 'Wait here,' she said tightly, 'and I'll see what I can find. I'll put it all on his desk in the tower room, then you can either deal with it there or take it back to Seaspray.' Damp hair swinging, she marched from the room.

Chapter Five

Relishing the sensation of waking up in his own bed, in his own room, Dave stretched in pleasure for all of ten seconds before reality kicked in. The sick dread that had gripped him for the past week clamped its vice on his innards and wouldn't let go.

Throughout his youth his first act on getting up had been to go and look at the ocean. This he did now, to see a gentle swell under heavy cloud; there was little wind and it was no longer raining. He watched the sullen grey waves and for an instant thought of his friends riding the dazzling blue-green rollers of the Pacific, then his mind clicked back into gear. This was Cornwall. Jonny was missing. Frances was going to work.

He himself had to be at Lookout Cottage in case Delphi needed him. If she did it could be awkward, because they were barely on speaking terms. He would try to be civil, but if she didn't respond – tough. He could always go up to the tower room and work on the computer.

Under the shower he reviewed what he, personally, had done about finding his brother. The answer to that could only be 'not much'. No, more accurately he'd done a lot, but without much result. On Friday he had scoured the terrain between Trevant and Porthmenna; most of Saturday and yesterday had been spent working his way through the gullies and ravines that scored the coastal cliffs on either side of the village. Even as he did it he'd known it was futile. Jonny would never have roamed the Trevant fields in the dark, he wouldn't have scrambled down the beds of streams to the seashore, or walked the morrops – the sheep-grazing grounds on the cliff-tops – not if he'd been in his right mind.

When Delphi first reported his disappearance to the police they'd told her that more than two hundred thousand people went missing each year in Britain. Surely anybody leaving a happy home without so much as a farewell had to be mentally disturbed? Even if they were, they still needed money to survive.

He had examined Jonny's cheque books, his bank statements, his building society records; he'd examined them minutely and found them perfectly normal. They revealed a married couple who were solvent and sensible; not well off, perhaps, but the wolf wasn't exactly howling at the door. There was no evidence of money being siphoned off to a secret account, either, though perhaps actual cash could have been stashed away over a period of time.

Still thinking about finance, he was at the table eating toast and honey when Frances rushed in. 'Oh, hello,' she said, 'I didn't take anything across to Delphi's to wear to school today. I'm apt to forget they don't like female staff to wear trousers.' With that she hurried upstairs.

Two minutes later she was down wearing a dark suit and cream shirt. 'About today – the midwife will call this morning, sometime soon after nine.

Bozena – Delphi's friend who helps run the play-group – is going to have the girls for the morning, to play with her boys, so will you take them round there? She'll give them their lunch and bring them back about one thirty. Delphi will decide what she wants them to do in the afternoon. Maybe you'd like to take them out for a bit, or play with them. And here's my mobile number, just in case.'

She gave him a slip of paper and at the door turned and said, 'It is *good* to have you back, David!' Then she hurried out to her car.

He was at Lookout Cottage just before nine and found the girls ready to go to Bozena's. They looked uncannily alike in blue denim skirts and identical pink tops, the only difference being that one of them had a lilac scrunchie in her hair and the other a white one. Today they were wearing name badges, probably for Bozena's benefit – or her sons'. When he came through the door they ran to him and each clasped a thigh. It was a habit they'd developed; he found it a bit strange but what was new? He found everything about them strange.

'They know the way, so they'll show you,' said Delphi, 'and will you give this to Bozena?' She handed him a plastic bag containing small items of underwear. 'Just in case of accidents,' Dorcas informed him solemnly.

Delphi helped them on with their jackets and the three of them headed for the steps down to the harbour. Once there, they clearly expected him to hold on to them, so with a small hand in each of his, he walked along the cobbles, having to bend over like an old man in order to listen to

81

their non-stop chatter.

He couldn't understand why he didn't feel completely ridiculous.

When he got back the midwife had arrived and was in the sitting room with Delphi. A small, brisk woman with cheeks like two rosy apples, she came into the kitchen ahead of her patient and gave him a keen look. 'You'll be Dave, then? I'm Mollie. Now listen, will you tell Frances that I say Delphi's all right? Her blood pressure's still up – it's borderline actually, but I'm not really worried at this stage. In fact, she's in good shape considering what's going on in her life. I've told her to keep near home and not to use public transport, but I can't see her wanting to go far under the circumstances. I'm really sorry about Jonny, but at least you're all part of a community that'll look after you. I'll pop in again tomorrow just to check on her.'

When she'd gone Delphi appeared, looking quite composed. It was the first time they'd been alone together since her outburst, so he was wondering what to say when there was a knock at the door and a familiar figure strolled in. Faded good looks, pot belly, wispy brown hair and a drinker's complexion: it was Delphi's father, Terence Pennant.

'Dad,' she said flatly, 'I didn't expect you.'

'Always the keen welcome,' he said drily. 'I didn't intend to come, actually, after being shown the door last time, but I thought I'd better see that you're all right.' Dark blue eyes swivelled from one to the other and rested on Dave. 'I heard you were back,' Pennant said. 'Is it a case of "duty

82

calls" or "pockets empty"?'

'That's my business,' retorted Dave. He'd never liked the man and he liked him even less after hearing what he'd suggested about Jonny.

Pennant tweaked uneasily at his cravat. 'All right, Dave, sorry. I just wondered what's brought you back after so many years.'

'My brother is missing,' said Dave. 'I think that's reason enough, don't you?'

'Of course – absolutely! Delphi, I'm going into Helston. Do you want anything from the shops?'

'No thanks. We have all we need.'

Pennant looked around him. 'I take it there's no news?'

Delphi shook her head. 'We'll let you know as soon as we hear anything.'

'*If* you hear anything,' he corrected, and left the house.

Delphi was mortified. 'I'm sorry,' she said, close to tears, 'but you know what he's like.'

Dave knew. He'd never been able to fathom how Delphi could be the offspring of a peevish drunk and the excitable, self-centred woman who was her mother. Now, with her back to him, she was fiddling around making coffee, taking longer than she needed on a decaff for herself and a rich strong brew for him. She turned with his mug in her hand and looked him in the eye. 'You're being really helpful,' she said. 'Having you here has made it easier for the girls to stop worrying about Jonny.'

He wriggled his shoulders. 'Is that right? I'm glad.'

'About the other day, I'm sorry I said what I

did. I was a bit on edge.'

'You had the right to say it.'

'I get tensed up, you see, in the house all the time, waiting for the phone to ring. Then when it does it's always something trivial.'

'You need a change of scene.'

'I suppose I do. Look, can we go for a walk somewhere? Not here in the village, though; people will keep stopping me.'

He was a bit stunned. One minute he'd had to go out in public holding hands with two little girls, bent double to hear their prattle; now he was being asked to walk out with a hugely pregnant woman! At once he was ashamed. This was Delphi – she was carrying Jonny's baby. If she wanted him to parade her through the streets of Helston on his shoulders he would have to do it.

'We could go somewhere quiet in the car,' he suggested, 'then stroll around for a while. Have the police got your mobile number?'

'Yes, I gave it to that sergeant.'

'Well then, we'll go if you like. Just as long as we don't walk any distance.'

Delphi tried to smile. 'Mollie's been laying down the law to you as well, has she?' They fell silent as they drank their coffee. He wondered what she was feeling, what she was thinking, but couldn't ask. There wasn't enough ease between them for that. Maybe there never would be. Ten minutes later they left the house.

He'd known better weekends than the one just gone, thought Channon as he settled behind his desk. His daily housekeeper had been diagnosed as terminally ill and had given notice; the high winds had lifted slates off his roof and within hours a downpour had ruined a bedroom ceiling.

As if that wasn't enough, he'd been called out during Saturday night to supervise a missing baby case. Men had been deployed, the child welfare people alerted, the mother demented with worry. Then they found out that she really was demented, and had hidden her baby in a derelict hen house two miles from her home. The child had survived for twenty hours with neither nourishment nor warmth, but was now safe and sound. The mother, poor woman, was having a psychiatric assessment.

It had been a costly affair in man hours; a lot of sleep had been lost, including his own, but that went with the job. Now it was back to the standard format of new week, new challenges, banish your problems and get on with it. For years he had cherished his ability to block out personal issues, even personal anguish. Being able to do it had kept him sane; that, and his work.

When his life fell apart four years ago it hurt too much even to think about Claire and Danny, let alone speak about them. He had loved his wife and son more than life itself and all at once they were gone. One minute talking and laughing, waving him off to work, the next being cut from the wreckage of a car. 'Another nasty accident,' people probably said, 'so very sad – a mother and her seven-year-old boy.' In the space of a minute his life became black and hollow and unendurable.

Except that he *had* endured it. Friends and colleagues were kind; they learned not to mention his wife and child. Then in time – a long time – he found he could manage to say a few words about them; sometimes even a sentence.

One occasion in particular had remained in his memory. It was so clear it seemed to him like a picture in oils that had stayed as vivid as the day it was painted; a picture of a woman who lived in a round house, a mother herself, whose husband and son were entangled in murder. He barely knew her when one night she asked him if he had children of his own. When he managed a strangled explanation her eyes filled with tears and she wiped them away with the cloth she was using to do her dishes.

Her life was in turmoil but she had cried for Claire and Danny. She had cared about them, about him, and he had cared about her. He had solved the case and exposed the killer. Her family were cleared, but by then her marriage was in trouble.

Since then he had seen her only once, in winter, walking along a frost-touched street in Falmouth with all three of her children. If she'd been alone he would have approached her, asked how she was, but he couldn't bring himself to confront the young ones. Seeing him would have brought back past trauma; after all, he'd had to take the older son in as a murder suspect, then do the same with the father.

So he stayed in the shadow of a doorway and watched them. He could see she'd lost weight, but persuaded himself that she seemed content. The four of them walked away in the winter sunshine and he stood there alone, remembering the day she cried at the door of her round, beautiful house.

That was then, this was now, life went on. He reached for a pile of reports and told Jenny, who monitored his calls, to put nobody through unless it was urgent. Twenty minutes passed before she disturbed him. 'Sorry, sir, but I have a training officer from Culdrose on the line. He insists on speaking to you.'

'Put him through,' said Channon, not sure whether he would be speaking to the navy or the air force.

It was both. 'At last,' said a voice with strong hints of Geordie. '771 Naval Air Squadron, RNAS Culdrose, Lieutenant Trencher speaking. I've been passed all over South Cornwall and been told you're the man.'

'Glad to hear it,' said Channon mildly. 'What's the problem?'

'I train personnel for our Search and Rescue Service. The recent high winds have eased, so first thing today I took lads out to practise winching off close in to the cliffs.'

At once Channon was wary. 'And?'

'We all saw what we thought was a body.'

'Where?'

'On rocks at the foot of Proudie Steep – that's one of the highest cliffs on the Lizard, not far from Porthmenna.'

Channon almost groaned. 'You say you *thought* it was a body. Was nobody sure?'

'Off the record, *I* was sure. After years on the job, you get the feeling.'

'You didn't see it up close?'

'No. We were behind schedule after a busy session winching off, but flying fairly close in. It's pretty wild at Proudy, you know; no access whatsoever except possibly by abseiling, by sea or by air. We carried on back here and reported in. The next thing was my commanding officer coming up against a memo from the Anti-Terrorist people, saying you're the man to talk to about suspicious deaths near sensitive sites. So ... I'm talking.'

'I appreciate that,' said Channon diplomatically. 'Tell me, what was your first thought on seeing the body?'

'That you're going to end up very dead if you throw yourself off a two-hundred-foot cliff and land on rocks.'

'You think it was suicide?'

'It's as good a way as any and better than most. If the impact doesn't get you, the tide will bash you around and then drag you away.'

'So the body might have been above the high water line or it wouldn't have stayed where it fell?'

'I'd say so, if it's been there longer than the last high tide.'

'What's the best way of recovering it?'

'If you want to examine it before it's moved, then by boat.'

'You're talking about the lifeboat?'

'No, I don't think we need call on them, not even the inshore. After all it's not an emergency. A small power boat will get you right in there. Watch the tide, though, or it'll be tricky. The next couple of hours should be safe enough.'

Channon's mind was in top gear. The police helicopter was based in Exeter, but 771 Squadron was right on the Lizard. 'I can organize the boat, but can you fly me out over the exact spot?'

'No probs,' said Trencher confidently. 'My lads are all experienced pilots and I've been given clearance to offer you every assistance. Maybe not *precisely* over the spot, though, as it's so near the cliff face, but we can hover pretty close.'

'That'll do. I just want to get the overall view. I'll ring you back with arrangements.'

'Always ready to oblige a bigwig,' said Trencher cheerfully. 'I'll see you.'

'Just a minute. If it's who I think it is I don't want the family alerted until I'm sure.'

'Staff at the base know how to button their lips,' Trencher assured him, 'and the locals are used to us being out and about all the time.'

'Good,' said Channon, almost convinced. 'I'll see you later.'

The wind was increasing again as Dave drove along the narrow coastal road, slowing the car to look down on the little cove he'd remembered. He was pleased to see it unchanged, unspoiled, and at that moment deserted; an ideal place to bring this tired, familiar stranger for a therapeutic stroll.

He parked on tussocky grass behind an ancient sea-wall and helped Delphi from her seat. She emerged clumsily with one hand to her back. 'Oh,' she gasped, 'my back. I'd got myself wedged in too tight. There's more room in our old banger.' Dark clouds were blowing in from the sea but they found themselves sheltered by the headland, cocooned in a grey and gold seascape with not a soul to disturb them.

It seemed strange to be walking at her side as if they were accustomed to each other's company. She was smaller than he remembered – either that or he was taller. Of course, he'd grown in the last seven years, lots of people had remarked on it, but perhaps she had stayed the same size – apart from that gargantuan bulge. She was wearing the clingy gear that all pregnant women seemed to go for: stretch pants and a tight knitted top that shouted out loud, 'Hey, look at me, I'm pregnant and it's great!'

That would have been fine had it not been so terribly at odds with the tension in her bearing and the white, young-old face beneath its mass of bundled-up hair. She put him in mind of a picture he'd once seen of a fisherman's wife, waiting in vain for her husband's ship to come home.

They moved on like two painted cut-outs against the sombre backdrop of the sea, but on the rising green bank behind them were drifts of pale pink thrift, the countless flowers seeming to watch them like so many eyes as they walked the empty sands.

'This is lovely, Dave,' she said. 'Thank you.'

He found himself riled by her constant, ultra-polite gratitude. 'There's no need to keep on thanking me,' he told her.

'Why shouldn't I?' she protested. 'You're being a comfort to me.'

What could he say to that? Uneasily he shifted

his shoulders inside the baggy old sweater he'd put on over his T-shirt. Long ago it had been a favourite; he'd found it wrapped in tissue paper in his drawer at home, smelling of the lavender Frances must have put with it to keep the moths away. He couldn't think of a reply to what Delphi had said so they walked on in silence, until a deafening clatter of rotor blades made them look up at a helicopter flying low and fast along the coast.

Suddenly alert, Delphi's eyes met his, then she shrugged. To her, as to everyone else on the Lizard, the red and grey machines of the Search and Rescue Service were simply a familiar, reassuring presence. Dave watched it fly out of sight and knew it was heading back to base. Where had it been? What had it seen? It could have been out on a routine flight, of course – that, or something else.

He decided they had walked as far as was safe, and was about to suggest they turned back when Delphi gasped and clutched at her abdomen. 'Ugh,' she grunted, bending at the waist. 'Something's happening – let's get back!'

God *above!* What had possessed him to bring her out here? 'Is it–' he began, and broke off to stare at her legs in puzzlement. Her blue stretch pants were wet from the groin down; the sand at her feet was dark. Horror and embarrassment made him gape.

'My waters have broken,' she said. 'It's all right, it's perfectly normal, but let's get to the car.'

The two hundred yards seemed an immense distance for her to walk. He bent to pick her up in his arms but with a strangled howl she fell to her knees. 'Get my mobile!' she gasped. 'Quick, tell Mollie it's urgent!'

He struggled to drag the phone from her pants pocket, then remembered he'd brought his own, along with the midwife's number. This was weird, he thought wildly; babies could come quickly, he knew that, but not this quickly. What about labour? What about all that sweating and gritting of teeth? He was fumbling the numbers, making a complete mess of it.

But Delphi was trying to crawl to where two rocks jutted close to each other over a hollow in the sand. 'Take my pants off,' she said.

Fear was gripping him as he heard the number ring out. When Mollie answered it seemed like the voice of an angel. 'It's me, Dave Tregenza,' he gabbled. 'The baby's coming. Delphi says it's urgent. What? We're out for a walk. No – only two or three miles from home – we came in the car. Uh – I've got to help her. Stay on the line!'

Delphi was now bent double, almost on all fours. He'd thought that labour pains came at spaced intervals, but she seemed obsessed by speed, wrenching at her pants until they were round her knees. 'Mollie – stay on the line,' he bellowed. 'Get the ambulance! We're on the beach!'

He pulled his sweater off and laid it on the sand. 'Delphi,' he said wildly, 'take some deep breaths or something. Don't worry, I've got Mollie on the mobile.'

For an instant she was still. 'I'll try and tell you what to do,' she said between her teeth. 'Aah!'

God in heaven, what had he done to deserve

this? He looked around but there wasn't a living soul in sight. Not a person, not a house. Delphi had started to thresh around. He couldn't see what was happening between her legs. 'You'll have to lie back,' he told her.

Mollie's voice was quacking from the mobile. 'I'm speaking from Coverack, but where are you? Where are you?' she was asking, her tone high and very clear. 'Dave. Tell me *where you are!*'

'We're on the beach. She's lying on my sweater. There's nobody around. Get somebody quick. The baby's coming. She says she'll tell me what to do.'

'Dave, where *are* you? The ambulance is just leaving Helston, but they don't know where to go.'

He was gasping, too tensed up to be ashamed that he wasn't handling things right. 'We're at Proudy Cove,' he said, 'the locals call it Proudy Low. Mollie, don't go! Stay on the line!'

'I'm here,' came her voice, loud and reassuring. 'Listen to me, Dave. Delphi might not be able to help you much – you'll have to help her. Now – look at her vagina. How wide is it dilated? Tell me as near as you can.'

Desperately he pushed Delphi's knees together so as to take down her wet panties, bending one of her legs to pull them over an ankle. She bucked and threshed as he bent closer. He could smell lavender and sea salt and something new to him that must be to do with the baby.

'It's very wide,' he said, amazed. 'I can see a damp, greasy thing bulging out – ugh – is it the head? It's trying to come out!'

Delphi's lips were drawn back, her teeth bared. 'I have to push,' she gasped. 'Hand, Dave, give me your hand!'

He was stunned by the power of her grip. It seemed as if she would crush his very bones. In the space of a second it registered that his face was inches away from a part of her that he'd once dreamed about, but never touched, not even at the height of his passion for her. There was no time for regret about that, nor for envy of the man who'd been welcome there and had fathered this impatient child.

'Dave, listen to me!' commanded Mollie, and almost as if that one brief thought of his brother had changed things, he became calm. He had to do this. He *could* do it if Mollie would help him. He bent close to Delphi's ear. 'It's all right,' he said firmly. 'I'm here. I'll look after you.' He wrenched his hand from her grip and tucked the mobile between his neck and his shoulder. 'Right,' he said to Mollie. 'I'm ready. I'm listening.'

Gaze intent, Channon observed the face of Proudy Steep from twenty yards seaward. At times like this he felt as if he had a computer inside his head, rather than a mere brain; it was seeing, evaluating, comparing, remembering. Analysis came later, and then, with luck, his old friend intuition would step in; sometimes interrupting the computer, sometimes stopping it altogether, and when that happened, things moved.

He had asked to view the scene from the sea and then go in closer. It was clear that only a skilled mountaineer or a practised abseiler could descend from the top of the cliff to the jumble of rocks at its base. Now, with the aircraft at the hover, he could see what Trencher and his men had spotted only at speed. Something crumpled, like a discarded doll; something that blended with the grey and seaweed-green of the rocks.

Wait – by all accounts the brother had spent hours searching the area, yet he hadn't found it, had he? Mouthing against the noise, he asked Trencher, 'Could it have been seen from up top?'

Trencher rolled his eyes. 'Not unless somebody with a neck six foot long peered over the edge. Maybe not even then.'

Channon tried to estimate the angle of the body's fall. Could it have struck an outcrop of the cliff face that would have altered its line of descent, or had it fallen direct, like an object dropped from a bridge into a river?

'Can you work out which spot he fell from?' he asked. 'We'll need to mark it out for examination.'

Trencher nodded. 'I can give you a good idea. I have charts of the cliffs with me. Just say the word when you want to move in closer.'

When Channon nodded they went lower and closed in. This was invaluable, he thought, the force could do with using a helicopter for every outdoor death. The lie of the land was revealed in panorama; the position of the body was shown in relation to its surroundings.

Behind him was the duty police surgeon – now known as 'forensic physician' after the latest renaming – summoned from his morning surgery

95

and no doubt already thinking that it was somewhat superfluous to be asked to certify death in this case. Next to him was Bowles, who was far from happy. At first he'd been impressed by Channon's calm commandeering of a Sea King. In fact, he'd only just managed to control a swagger as they crossed the field to get aboard. Then it had been all chaotic scuttling beneath the draught of the blades, followed by instant queasiness as they banked and turned out to the coast.

He hadn't liked flying in this deafening contraption. OK, it might be the last word in technology, but give him a Boeing any day rather than this bare little crate with its sliding door and webbing seats, not to mention the stretchers and paramedic gear.

The best thing so far about the whole shebang had been the view of Goonhilly to the east of them as they set off. Seen from the air it was some place, the vast dishes as high as their flight path, looking like something out of a science fiction film against the bare damp fields of the downs. Resentfully he eyed the DCI, who seemed unperturbed by the flight, observing the scene below as calmly as some egg-head scientist peering at a specimen in his laboratory

Channon sensed that his sergeant was watching him and wondered why he'd brought him along. Clearly, he was so ill at ease his deductive and observational powers must be at zero. Didn't he realize they were being given a brilliant view of a death scene, whether it was accident, suicide, manslaughter or murder?

They were now incredibly close to the cliff face

96

and almost over the body. It didn't stand out against its jagged bed; it looked faded, almost indistinguishable. The head was at an impossible angle, so was one leg. The hands were palm down at the ends of outstretched arms. He could see the glint of a wristwatch.

His gaze scanned the immediate area but could detect nothing untoward, while next to him Trencher studied his chart of Proudy and the cliff-top. When at last he gave the signal, the pilot backed them out to sea and flew to the next cove, landing close to where a big police launch rocked at a stone jetty.

Channon might be a softie, thought Bowles, but boy, could he move when he wanted to. Of course, that was what came with rank; he pulled the strings and everybody danced. The under-lings would dance, right enough, when *he* got to Inspector, and they wouldn't call him 'boss', as he now called Channon. Sourly he watched as the helicopter went off on its rising course, head-ing for the cliff-top to leave a marker at the spot from which Trencher judged the body to have fallen. Thank goodness that little ride was over. A Sea King might be high on public appeal, on glamour, high on usefulness in a crisis, but it was rock-bottom on passenger comfort.

As for this ghastly little tub that was rocking and rolling at the jetty – no thanks! Let Channon do the Captain Bligh on the briny, let him suss out the corpse. Good old terra firma – you couldn't beat it.

He took out Jonathan Tregenza's details as supplied by his wife, ready to pass them to

Channon for use in initial identification. This one *had* to be him – body number two within four miles of the world's biggest satellite earth station – *and* he'd found out something of interest about Dancer. He was going to chew on that for an hour or two before he told Channon.

In less than ten minutes they were with the body. 'No doubts about this one,' said the physician heavily. 'Broken neck, broken leg, broken arm – in fact, multiple impact injuries.' Each wearing gloves but not the full white suits, he crouched with Channon over the body. Above them reared Proudy, dark and sheer and forbidding. Channon felt it was brooding over the broken man at its base.

'He wasn't dead before he fell, then?'

'I don't think so, but you'll have to see what Hunter says. What I can say is he's been dead for several days, maybe as long as a week.' The doctor shot a glance at their surroundings. 'D'you reckon you'll need the SOCOs?'

Channon shook his head. 'Not down here. If it is a crime it took place up on the top.'

The doctor hesitated. 'All the Lizard's talking about this young chap Tregenza who's gone missing. Could this be him?'

'I'm about to find out,' said Channon. Face set, he checked the corpse's clothing against Bowles's list, the wristwatch, the colour of hair and eyes. With one gloved finger he lifted a bloated lip to look at the teeth, then felt in the back pocket of the jeans. A wallet was there, damp but not pulpy Inside it was paper money, credit cards belonging to J.R. Tregenza and a small, laminated photograph. It showed two identical little girls in swimsuits, cuddling on either side of a beautiful, bare-shouldered young woman. All three were smiling at the camera.

Channon replaced the picture in the wallet. 'This is him,' he said quietly, 'subject of course to final ID.' He turned to the uniformed men. 'Bag him up with extreme care, stretcher him and put him in the boat, then give me a minute to examine the spot where he's lying.' There would be nothing to see, he was certain of it, but it would give him the chance to compose himself.

Then, as if the heavens understood that a man in his position must never be seen to weep, rain started to fall, gentle as tears. Channon lifted his face to it. Who'd have the job? he asked himself in despair.

He wasn't to know that less than half a mile away real tears were about to be shed, by another, younger man.

Chapter Six

Face wet with tears and rain, Dave Tregenza looked up at the sky. There ought to be fireworks bursting up there, angels singing, trumpets sounding, sunbeams dancing – because the baby was here. He was alive. He had cried. He was gnawing his fist right now, held fast in his mother's arms. It hadn't been gruesome at all – it had been amazing, magical, and now rain was falling, soft and gentle, rinsing the blood from his hands.

He couldn't stop his tears, though; they were almost choking him as he looked at Delphi and her son: tears of relief and reaction, of triumph and some other emotion that he didn't want to recognize. He could hardly believe that he'd delivered a whole, live baby with no help apart from a voice at the other end of a phone line.

Delphi had been brilliant, brave and unself-conscious about him touching the most private parts of her body, though it had all happened so quickly there'd been no time for modesty. When he said, 'It's a boy! Clever girl!' she had simply answered, 'Clever Dave,' looking at that moment just as she used to look in the days when he'd loved her – young and fresh and unlined. Now, though, her mouth was tight with tension again as she held the messy little creature who was her son.

He must take care of them. 'Keep them warm,' Mollie had said. 'I have to stay here in Coverack with my colleague. We have a young mum who's almost ready to give birth. When the paramedics get to you they'll probably take Delphi to the Royal Cornwall to give her the once-over after such a quick delivery. Give her my love. I'll talk to you both later, and Dave – well done!'

As he leaned over mother and baby to keep off the rain, something made him check the place where the baby had come from. He stared, and felt his face grow cold as the colour left it. She was bleeding. Not the sticky ooze of a few minutes ago, but a steady flow of bright red blood. Fear gripped him. Women died in childbirth. Was it loss of blood that killed them? Haemorrhage?

Mollie had said that everything sounded all right, but it wasn't all right now, it couldn't be. Wildly he pawed at the sand for his mobile, and at that moment heard the sound of a vehicle on the road. 'Delphi,' he said urgently, 'listen to me. You're bleeding – uh – just a bit. Give me the baby. Now, put your hands here and press to try and stop it. The ambulance is nearly here. I'm going to show them where you are and hurry them up.'

The baby was wrapped in his T-shirt, so he pressed the bundle to his chest and raced up to the road. To his horror there was no sign of an ambulance coming from Helston – there was nothing at all. From the opposite direction, though, came a car – a police car. 'Thank you, thank you, God,' he was gabbling, then saw a second car following close behind. He held the child close – perhaps too close, because he let out a cry like the single bleat of a lamb.

Then he stepped out into the road. Both cars

screeched to a stop. 'Quick!' he yelled. 'A woman's given birth – she's bleeding to death! Help me!'

Next to the driver was a broad-shouldered man in plain clothes. He jumped out and ran to the car behind, leaving a younger man staring from the back seat as if mesmerized. Then a miracle: the man from the second car announced that he was a doctor.

'She's over here!' He ran ahead of them to Delphi, and in seconds the doctor took charge. Almost sick with relief, Dave put the baby back in Delphi's outstretched arms and stood there, watching.

The other man took him to one side. 'It looks as if you've been having a busy time,' he said gently, 'but you can let go now. Just leave her in the doctor's hands.'

'She's losing blood – a lot of blood. The ambulance is on its way.'

'Yes, yes. The doctor's in charge now. Tell me, is the mother by any chance a Mrs Tregenza?'

'Yes, she is. I'm Dave Tregenza, her brother-in-law.' All at once he was wary. Two cars, three policemen and a doctor? 'Why?' he asked weakly.

Dark eyes looked into his. 'I spoke to her on the phone a few days ago, that's all. My name's Channon, by the way – Detective Chief Inspector. That's my sergeant still in the car. I think he's a bit squeamish about childbirth.'

'So was I until half an hour ago. Oh, here's the ambulance.'

'I expect you'll want to go along with your sister-in-law?'

'Of course. I must.'

'We'll have a chat sometime soon,' promised Channon. 'Is it a boy or a girl?'

'A boy,' said Dave. 'I delivered him. On my own.' His voice broke on the last three words. Half ashamed, he looked into the detective's eyes but they revealed nothing, nothing at all.

He'd seen it all now, thought Bowles. Producing a child on a rain-washed beach with Mr Universe as the midwife – who'd credit it? And how was it that some men had the lot? Looks, physique, an expensive tan, though this one was minus a shirt and one of his trainers, and his chest was streaked with blood. Talk about a Viking out on the kill.

Channon got back in the car looking grim. 'Carry on to the mortuary,' he told the driver, then turned to Bowles. 'Well, have you worked that lot out?'

The sergeant wasn't keen on being questioned in front of a PC, so he said coolly, 'It's not rocket science, sir. Mr Universe can only be the brother from Hawaii – the surfer. That sort of tan comes from living it up in the sun long-term.' He took a last look at the paramedics bending over the mother. 'Therefore it follows that the baby is Jonathan Tregenza's.'

Even as he said it Bowles lost his hard-boiled edge and shivered. There was something pretty creepy about the birth of a baby and the finding of its father's body so close to each other, both in place and in time. He'd been taken with Delphi Tregenza when he met her, seeing at once that she'd be some looker if she wasn't nine months gone with a missing husband. He was glad it

103

wouldn't be him who would have to tell her he was missing no longer.

He looked at the back of Channon's grey-streaked head and heard himself say, 'I'm really sorry about it, sir. Count on me to help in any way I can.'

Unusual words from Bowles. 'Thanks,' said Channon, and meant it. 'If we can confirm ID with certainty we might be able to spare the wife or the brother having to do it, but before that we must decide how to tell her. Maybe through the brother, or the aunt. First of all, though, I want to have a closer look at his body.'

Bowles was all attention. 'You're not taking it as read that it's suicide, then.'

'Do I usually take things as read?'

'No.'

'Well, then, there's your answer. As a matter of fact, in this particular case, I'm getting curious.'

Bowles kept a straight face. If the DCI was curious, it meant that something interesting might happen. He'd been known to discuss his ideas with the lower ranks, so Bowles must make sure he stayed close at hand.

No need to look at the face again, thought Channon, the body was more than enough: broken, discoloured, swollen, it bore no resemblance whatsoever to the photograph of the lean, healthy young Tregenza.

Tape primed for his commentary, camera at the ready, Hunter and his young assistant were deftly removing the clothes, closely watched by the two detectives. 'Are you in a hurry for any particular aspect?' asked the pathologist. 'If so, say the word and I'll look at it first. Otherwise I'll follow the old T&T.'

Opposite him Bowles raised a pale eyebrow and Hunter saw it. 'T&T – tried and tested routine,' he explained. 'We follow it because it works, but it can be sidetracked in case of urgent necessity.'

'This is urgent *and* necessary,' said Channon. 'First, a confirmed ID against our details. It'll spare the family doing it right away, because things are pretty fraught with them at the moment. Second, I need to know whether it was suicide or if he was attacked and then thrown over the cliff.'

Hunter was unperturbed. 'As you wish, oh master. For your first query we'll start with the easiest and most obvious – have you been told of any identifying marks?'

Bowles had kept it to himself, but with a show of earnest innocence, said promptly, 'One large mole, left hip.'

Five pairs of eyes observed the mottled mauve flesh above the left buttock. 'One mole,' announced Hunter, reaching for his measure. 'Almost one centimetre in diameter.'

'That's confirmation enough,' conceded Channon, and feeling the need to give more sense of urgency, added, 'His wife gave birth to their third child less than an hour ago.'

Hunter shook his head in sympathy but didn't lose concentration. 'As for your second point ... fractures clearly apparent are those of neck, arm and leg, but there may be others, of course. Impact injuries are multiple, many of them to the head – in fact, very many. Do you know if it was

105

a direct drop or whether he could have crashed against rocks or vegetation on the way down?'

Channon nodded. 'He could. I've confirmed it.'

'In that case, I'll need time, lots of time, before I can say whether he was attacked first, or if he died on impact, or both. It might not be conclusive.'

Channon, however, had watched the clothes being removed, including the footwear. 'May I see the back of his heels?' he asked, and when Hunter lifted the legs he studied the feet and heels closely. 'And the shoes? The right sock?'

Silently the assistant produced them. A grey cotton sock, snagged into a rough hole at the heel; leather slip-on shoes, once well-polished, now damp and salt-stained, but with scuff marks from the base of the heels to the upper edges.

'What do you make of it?' asked Channon.

Bowles was on a high. This was the business, he told himself – this was what he liked about working with Channon. 'He was dragged, sir.'

'Yes, dragged along with his shoes still on, until the right one came off. Then dragged some more, maybe for only seconds, before it was noticed, damaging the sock and inside it, the heel.'

'It's grass on the top above where he landed, with a bit of gravel here and there. It's cordoned off for inspection with a couple of plods standing guard.'

'Get the SOCOs out there. Tell them I want to know exactly where he was dragged, and if he was transported to the cliff-top from elsewhere. I know the ground's been rained on time and again, but they can match samples and make impressions of tracks. Now – the Dancers at

Trevant. How far are they from Proudy? A mile? A mile and a half?'

'No more, probably less.'

'Right. Warn the SOCOs I'll be asking them to look at Trevant for soil specimens, samples of gravel and so forth. Now, George...'

Hunter looked over his glasses. 'Yes? I am still here. I suppose you'll be wanting examination of the flesh of the heels?'

'Correct. Bowles, on your way. Go and see the Forensic lads in person. Tell them I want the full monty on all the clothes, anything at all that will back Mr Hunter's conclusions on whether it's suicide or foul play. Oh, before you go, give me the aunt's mobile number. I've already got Dave's.'

He turned to Hunter. 'Proceed at your own pace, George. Detailed reports on your findings, and will you liaise with Forensic? I want anything, however microscopic, that will help sort this lot out.' His mind was moving faster than his words, which now came out staccato, like some sort of memo. 'Family next. The wife must be told.'

Hunter pursed his lips. 'Watch it, Bill. It's too soon to say for certain,' and as Channon gave him a look, 'Oops, sorry! I'm apt to forget it's naughty to try and teach your grandmother to suck the old ovoids.'

The DCI was too tense to smile. 'Ring me if anything turns up that we haven't thought of, and I'll talk to you later about our friend from the Helford River.'

Hunter was still noting impact injuries, and he nodded at the body. 'You reckon they're connected?'

'I'll be working on it,' answered Channon. And how, he added silently.

Frances drove along Sands End feeling what she described to herself as 'halfway normal'. Not that anything had changed; life was still awful, it was just that she'd needed to get away from Porthmenna and the anguished dread of life in Lookout Cottage.

As for her teaching session, she'd tried to enjoy it as much as usual, but it had been for only half the day, with afternoon lessons cancelled to allow the girls to take part in the final of an inter-school quiz. She'd stayed for lunch, though, purely for the pleasure of eating a meal that she hadn't prepared.

That was then, in Carbis Bay, this was now in Porthmenna, where she lived in two different homes and hadn't yet found time to talk at length with her nephew. She planned to change back into casual clothes and spend some time catching up on housework before going across to join Delphi and the children.

Delphi... Lord, her mobile was still switched off! What an idiot, what a fool to forget about it when the poor girl was waiting for news of Jonny and only days away from producing her offspring. Still, she was almost home; she would listen to any messages as soon as she walked through the door. She swung the car from Sands End to the track that fronted the house and stopped with a jolt. Looking dazzlingly clean and efficient, a police car was reversing out of the drive towards her.

She leapt out and ran to the front of it. A fair-haired woman was at the wheel, next to a broad, dark-haired man. Both were in plain clothes. Questions were tumbling around in her head but she couldn't make them come out of her mouth. She simply stared in silence as the man emerged and faced her. 'Miss Lyne?' he asked. 'We've been trying to contact you.'

At that, nerves jangling, she started to gabble. 'I've been teaching over in Carbis Bay. I can't use my mobile in the school, they don't allow it – they're a bit old-fashioned, you see. I usually leave it in the car and check it for messages during break. But today I left early and forgot to switch it back on...' She sighed, and the outgoing breath felt as heavy as lead. 'Have you brought news?'

'Yes,' he said quietly, 'we have. My name is Channon – Detective Chief Inspector. This is DC Donald. Should we have a word indoors?'

Channon – that was the name of the man who telephoned Delphi. She went ahead of them to the sitting room and turned in the doorway. 'I thought you'd have contacted my nephew's wife – Mrs Tregenza.'

'She's otherwise engaged at present. Her baby arrived two hours ago. A healthy boy. I've seen him.'

Frances gaped. 'The baby's *arrived?* She showed no signs of going into labour when I left at eight o'clock this morning. The midwife was due to visit her because of her blood pressure. Did she decide to admit her?'

Channon thought of the golden, bare-chested young fellow who was so proud to have delivered the baby. No doubt he would want to tell her about it himself, but time was pressing. 'No, your nephew Dave took her for a walk. The birth was sudden and very quick. I happened to be passing soon after. I spoke to Dave and when I left the scene the paramedics were with her. I'm told she's now in hospital in Treliske for a few hours, being checked over. Both she and the baby are well.'

It was as if someone was pulling a rug from under her feet, thought Frances. She felt off balance, uncertain, stunned to have missed the birth but at the same time glad that it was all over. 'I must see her,' she said. 'And what about the children?'

DC Donald spoke up. 'They're still with a Mrs Bozena Dabner who says she'll keep them with her for as long as needed. Everything's under control. Now, why don't you just sit down for a minute and we'll have a chat?'

Obediently Frances sat, her mind clearing and preparing itself. 'Just tell me,' she said, her head jerking backwards like that of someone being slapped in the face. 'Don't wrap it up – tell me everything.'

Channon's dark eyes met hers. 'I'm afraid it's bad news. Your nephew's body was found a few hours ago at the foot of a cliff called Proudy Steep. He didn't survive the fall.'

Frances felt her jaw go slack. 'Proudy Steep? Jonny wouldn't go near Proudy in the dark! He knows the coast – he knows Proudy.' Something in the stillness of the man facing her told her that he was assessing her reaction, and at once she felt false and unreal, like an actress playing a part beyond her capabilities. Behind the unreality, though, something was surfacing, something that both astounded and shamed her. It wasn't pain, it wasn't sadness, it wasn't shock – it was *relief.* Relief that the waiting was over, that she wouldn't have to pretend to be optimistic any longer. She'd suspected he was dead; known it, almost, and now it was confirmed. 'I'm sorry I interrupted,' she said evenly. 'Please carry on.'

'An examination of Jonathan's body is under way as we speak. We'll have a better idea of what happened when we have the results of that. My men are inspecting land at the top of Proudy and elsewhere. You can rest assured that we're trying to establish exactly how he died.'

'He didn't throw himself off Proudy, inspector.'

'Maybe not. Forensic evidence will help decide that. We're keeping an open mind at this stage. I've come to see you in person because I told Mrs Tregenza to pay no attention to what anyone said apart from me and my sergeant, DS Bowles.'

'So Delphi doesn't know?'

'I'm afraid not. I often have to deliver bad news, but I was reluctant to tell Mrs Tregenza about this so soon after the birth of her baby Dave is with her, so he doesn't know, either.'

Frances was silent as bitterness seeped into her soul, sour as acid. *She* would have to tell them. She would have to help with deciding what to tell the twins, she would have to care for Delphi and the baby. God in heaven, what a future, it could almost be a replay of sixteen years ago – looking after someone else whilst her own heart was breaking.

111

Channon watched her with compassion. He'd read her history and now he was reading her face. Early fifties, he guessed, and still good-looking, with a firm, full-lipped mouth, a strong jaw and very direct grey eyes. A good woman, he judged, an honest woman, one who wouldn't fool herself or anyone else. The fact that she had seemed unsurprised, hadn't shed tears, counted for little. In his time he had seen all kinds of reactions to news of a death, and hers was no stranger than many. At the moment her shoulders were drooping, as if weighed down by the burdens that lay ahead. Even as he watched, they straightened and she lifted her chin.

He exchanged a glance with Mary Donald and, as one, they nodded. Frances Lyne would be all right. He said, 'We can drive you to the hospital at once if you wish, Miss Lyne. DC Donald is free to stay with you and your family to help in any way she can. She has wide experience of this sort of thing.'

Frances almost smiled. He was offering her somebody to lean on. There was no way he could know that people leaned on her, not the other way round. 'Thank you, both,' she said. 'I'll take a couple of minutes to gather my wits and sort some clothes for Delphi and the baby, then I'll go in my own car.'

'And perhaps a shirt or sweater for Dave? I'm sure he'll explain.'

'Right. Oh – there is one thing you could do for me, if you can spare the time – something important. Could you tell everyone in the village about Jonny? They have to be told. I promised to

112

let them know as soon as there's news.'

'I'm sorry, but we can't tell anyone at all until his wife knows. I would have informed her myself if she hadn't just given birth. If you ring me on my mobile when Mrs Tregenza knows, I'll be more than willing to break the news to them in the village.' And observe their reactions, he added silently. 'Would the village shop be the best place?'

'Yes, the Harbour Stores. The owner is Lizzie Bannon, she's a good woman, she'll spread the word and let them know at the pub. As for the twins, Bozena will protect them from hearing anything.' She looked at the two detectives and thought that she was leaning on them, after all, and they were more than willing to let her. 'Thank you,' she said, 'I appreciate your kindness. Perhaps I should ring Dave to tell him I'm on my way.'

'Perhaps you should,' agreed Channon gently. 'We'll be in touch as soon as there's anything further to report.'

When they had gone Frances stood at the window and looked out over the limitless expanse of the sea. If I started to weep, she thought, my tears would outmeasure all the oceans of the world. Tears for my lovely Jonny, tears for David – first his parents, now his brother; tears for Delphi and the girls, for a baby who will never know his father; tears for myself, tears for all Porthmenna.

It was all unreal, thought Frances, like a far-fetched play staged against a realistic backdrop. Carefully, with Dave at her side, she had just told Delphi the news. Now, deathly pale but dry-eyed, the new mother was sitting up in the hospital bed with her son in a cot at her side. She and Dave were facing her, not sure what to say or what to do next.

Warned by her phone call to the ward, Dave had been waiting for her at the hospital entrance. 'They've found him,' he announced, as if he were the one bringing news, not her. 'He's dead.'

'Yes,' she agreed, 'he is. We both knew it, didn't we? It's not a shock, it's not even a surprise. A helicopter from Culdrose was out on a training exercise and spotted his body.'

'Where?'

'At the foot of Proudy Steep.' Brief, concise words that confirmed the end of a life. She and Dave didn't touch each other. They were each separate, self-contained, unemotional.

'Proudy,' he repeated, 'that figures. I couldn't get down there to search. I was going to go in from the sea as soon as I could, just – just in case he was there. So where is he now?'

'The mortuary. They're doing a post-mortem to try and find out if he killed himself.'

'Do you think he did?'

'I know he didn't.'

'So do I. What happened?'

'Nobody knows – yet.'

'Frances, what must we tell Delphi?'

'The truth.'

'What, now?'

'Yes. I think she already knows it, in her heart.'

Question, answer, question, answer, all unreal. Jonny was dead. Her Jonny, Delphi's Jonny – yes, even David's Jonny. The daddy of those little girls, the daddy of a newborn baby boy...

114

Now it was even more unreal, here with Delphi. She hadn't cried. All she had said was, 'We'll have to decide how to tell the girls.' Silence lay between the three of them. It was confirmed he was dead – each in their own way had known it to be so. Why, then, did the very air they were breathing seem heavy with disbelief?

They were still silent when the doctor walked in. He was young, newly qualified in obstetrics and highly uncomfortable. 'Delphi, we're all so very, very sorry,' he said awkwardly. 'If you weren't newly delivered I'd prescribe a strong sedative to see you through the next twenty-four hours. As it is, with you so set on breast-feeding, I'd rather not.'

Clever, well-meaning, but at that moment out of his depth, he looked at Frances and Dave. 'Physically, Mrs Tregenza is fit to leave, and we give permission for that. She can go home and the community midwife will call daily, as already arranged. If it's what you all want, you can take her home as soon as you like. Delphi – I'll give you details of the area's trained post-natal counsellor, should you wish to see her. She has wide experience in dealing with new mothers suffering trauma.'

Delphi looked at him with her vast, shadowed eyes. 'Thanks,' she said simply, 'we'll think about it.'

And that was it. Within twenty minutes they were on their way back to Porthmenna and lives that were changed for ever.

Chapter Seven

Channon had worked late on Monday, but by seven thirty next morning was back in his office. 'Clearing the decks' was how he thought of it: sorting paperwork, preparing reports, dictating summaries. Outstanding work would hinder his concentration if a demanding case lay ahead, and he doubted whether the death of Jonathan Tregenza was simply an open and shut suicide.

The people in the village shop the previous day hadn't thought so, either. There were four of them, the owner and three customers, but none seemed to consider suicide as even a remote possibility. 'We know the lad,' Lizzie Bannon had insisted. 'He's not one of them "still waters run deep" types – more of a "fresh waters run clear". He's straight as they come, inspector, and he loves his family – loved them, I suppose I should say. He would never, ever, have killed himself with the baby nearly due.'

The others had agreed; they were good, decent people who had known the dead man, even if they knew little of the complexities of mental illness. In his work Channon had seen how an apparently carefree man or woman could be revealed as having a mind in chaos. Debt, drugs, alcohol, illicit affairs, terminal illness, they could all tip a person over the edge – maybe over the edge of a cliff – but what was the point in saying as much? Instead, he told them that the baby was no longer 'nearly due', but already born and doing well.

It hadn't taken them long to work out that the birth and the body had been less than half a mile apart, and then the questions began. 'You'll be investigating how he got to the foot of Proudy?' asked a woman in a red cardigan. 'And what he was doin' at the top in the first place,' added another, eyes intent in her wrinkled walnut of a face. Belligerence was there. These people weren't fools, they wanted answers. Not only did they know the dead man, they knew the flow of the sea, the lie of the land, the rocks, the very earth of the Lizard. Local knowledge, he reminded himself, could be gold, pure gold, to a detective.

He looked at them and felt the depth of their affection for Jonathan Tregenza, their concern for his family, but they were waiting for his answer. 'We'll do our best to get at the truth,' he said simply. 'You can trust me on it.'

Mary Donald was watching with interest. The DCI made no grand gestures, uttered no eloquent speeches, but he had a certain quality: when he said something, people believed him. She'd seen it time and again, she was seeing it now as his words brought a sense of calm and reassurance to these people of Porthmenna. Still on edge, but for the time being willing to leave things to the police, it was a sad and silent foursome who stood at the shop door to see them off.

Now, early sun was striping his desk with gold as Channon finished clearing his trays, all the time wondering how soon he would hear from George Hunter. There was no point in pestering him. In the past the pathologist had been known to work straight through the night on an urgent case, and would have done the same with this one if he'd found it necessary.

Not only that, he would be giving more details on the body from the river. Channon found he had to stifle resentment at being landed with two bodies from two different sites, and told himself that an unknown man without a single possession deserved as much attention and expertise as a husband and father with a village full of friends.

Now suppose, just suppose, that the river man with his unusual skin pigmentation and his neglected teeth did have something to do with terrorism? Bowles was clearly agog to link him to an attempt on Goonhilly, and the sergeant wasn't exactly gullible. Admittedly he was drawn to high profile stuff, but that went with his ambition and thrusting, abrasive nature.

Whatever his faults, and there were plenty – the malicious streak, the bullying of underlings, the deep-seated inferiority that could lead to envy and even victimization of a well-heeled suspect – in spite of them all, Bowles was a good detective. Channon had mentioned it in reports more than once, so it would be prudent to at least pay attention to his views. Which brought him to wondering why the sergeant hadn't got back to him with the information he'd asked for on the Dancers.

Forgetting how early it was, he reached for the phone to ring him, but before he could press the number the man himself appeared, looking remarkably spruce and good-humoured. 'Morning, sergeant,' said Channon. 'Had trouble sleeping?'

'No, sir. I was here at six thirty finishing my report on the Dancers.'

Great minds ... thought Channon wryly, but merely said, 'Well done. Take a seat and let's hear it.'

After hanging on to the information for hours, Bowles had formed conclusions of his own and was feeling a trifle smug. 'Wait for it,' he said, eyes glinting. 'They've lived in Afghanistan and had long spells in Saudi.'

Channon was all attention. 'Have they indeed?'

'Yes. Nancy the nympho must have had to watch her step with the sheikhs.'

'More like the sheikhs would have had to watch their step with Nancy, from what you and Yates told me,' retorted Channon. 'What's his line of work, then?'

'IT, and pretty high-powered – he's an infrastructure consultant or something of the sort. Worthy, government-backed stuff in Afghanistan, mega-money contracts in Saudi, though some years ago he taught there. Apparently he's a brain, not your average hands-on screwdriver wallah.'

'Well, well. He speaks Arabic?'

'Fluent in it. Lived in Iraq as a child and took a degree in Middle Eastern languages at London University in his youth.'

'His youth? How old is he now?'

Bowles shrugged. 'Forty-five, fifty.'

Channon tipped his chair back. 'Right, so if our river man is Middle Eastern he could be connected to the Dancers both by his race and the proximity of the Helford to Trevant. When you called on them did you by any chance ask if they'd had any recent visitors in addition to Tregenza?'

Bowles studied his hands and tried not to grind his teeth. 'No, we didn't,' he said tightly. 'On Friday afternoon it wasn't an issue. We were enquiring about a local man who'd gone missing. We didn't know the river man might not be British, nor that Dancer had Muslim connections.'

'True,' conceded Channon. 'Did you get all this stuff on him from the Anti-Terrorist Branch?'

'Yes, you know they have pretty exhaustive records on Brits living and working out there.'

'And is he in the clear with them?'

'They haven't got him listed in any category of suspect whatsoever, so yes, he's in the clear. Les Jolly is still working on whether or not he has any other Middle Eastern contacts.'

'Good. I'm waiting for more info on the river man. When we've got it we'll call on Mr and Mrs Dancer.'

'There's more,' said Bowles, pursing his lips to prevent a smile.

'Such as?'

'Dancer had a spell at Goonhilly in 2002.'

'A spell? You mean he worked there?'

'No, a few weeks observing and fact-finding for a series of lectures he was preparing. Maybe that was when he decided to retire to the Lizard and open a hotel.'

DCI and sergeant each knew what the other was thinking. A hotel could be good cover. People stayed in hotels without questions being asked – people of all nationalities. 'My contact at Goonhilly can fill me in on his time there,' said Channon, 'and the fact remains that two men have died in the area within days of each other – maybe within hours. We'll have to see what George Hunter and Forensic come up with before we proceed. I'm clearing my outstanding work and I advise you to do the same.'

'You want me with you full-time?' Bowles was no modest violet but he was only too aware that he wasn't well liked.

'Yes,' said Channon. 'We've had our differences, but we've cracked a few cases. Clear your outstanding work and I'll be in touch. In the meantime, leave the report with me and see if you can dig up any more on Dancer.'

Highly pleased, the sergeant went off, leaving Channon staring thoughtfully into space. What, he wondered, was Delphi Tregenza doing? How were her little girls?

Frances stared at the clock in Delphi's kitchen. It was almost noon; twenty-four hours since the birth and slightly more since Jonny was found dead.

After he went missing the days had passed so slowly – no, they hadn't passed, they had crawled, crept, inched along in a vacuum of tension and dread. Now, though, each hour was racing, so crammed with unreal happenings it seemed there was no time to mourn; grief was being pushed aside by the relentless march of events. She kept rearranging things in her mind, as if that might make them more acceptable.

There had been Channon's visit to Seaspray with the news, followed by breaking that news first to David, then to Delphi. Then bringing her

121

home, helping with the baby, dealing with grief-stricken friends, answering the phone, receiving flowers, informing Jonny's customers... Worst of all, though, the very worst, had been coping with Sophie and Dorcas.

When they arrived back from the hospital, Delphi had put the baby in his waiting crib, where he went to sleep at once, as if making up for the speed and turmoil of his birth. Brushing aside the suggestion of a spell in bed, she then sat herself at the table and said firmly, 'We'll have to bring the girls home in a minute, so I have to decide right now what they must be told about Jonny. Bozena will spread the word and everyone in Porthmenna will go along with it.'

Frances exchanged a look with Dave, who seemed every bit as baffled as she was. Delphi had given birth with amazing speed – on a beach; she'd been in hospital, learned that her husband was dead, come home again and was now facing a vital decision, all with no visible sign that she found the situation unbearable. Surely she should be weeping, wailing, questioning, or at least, resting?

'Look, my pet,' she said gently, 'don't you think you could do with a few hours in bed while you adjust? Your emotions are on hold, your body has had an upheaval.'

Delphi stared at them both. 'Rest?' she echoed. 'How can I rest until I've seen the girls meet their brother? I hope they'll be thrilled with him, but they'll want to know why their daddy isn't here to see him and help look after him. They know he's Jonny's baby just as much as mine.'

Dave spoke up, eyes first on one woman, then

the other. 'Could you let them get intrigued by the baby, really attached to him, and then feed it to them gradually that – that he won't be back?' He sat down abruptly. 'He won't be back, he won't be back.' The phrase rattled and clacked in his head, seeming to him like the rhythm of a train at high speed. He and Jonny used to play at trains, back in the shining childhood days, racing around the big room at Seaspray or on the pale firm sands next to the house.

Watch it, he told himself grimly. You can't wallow in the past – the present needs all your attention. That was an understatement. Jonny was dead. He would never see his baby, his little girls would grow up without him, yet here was Delphi, deathly pale but quite composed, discussing their possible reactions as if it were an academic exercise.

'How I handle the next hour is crucial to their emotional well-being,' she said doggedly. 'I've got to get it right.'

'Do you want to tell them that he's had to go away for a while,' asked Frances, 'and let them realize gradually that he won't be coming back? They're only little – their memories of him won't last for ever.'

'Or...' The words were sticking in Dave's throat, but he made them come out. 'Or just tell them the truth?' Frances laid her hand on his, and for the very first time in his life he took hold of it and held it tight. He felt her fingers stiffen for an instant, then relax inside his.

'I don't know if I can do it,' whispered Delphi, 'but if we don't tell them, somebody else might, by accident or carelessness. Or it could be a child. Think of Lucy Bedize and the flowers.'

And so it went on: to and fro, for and against. In the end they had gone for the easy, the obvious: they would take their lead from how the girls reacted when they saw the baby.

They were both dancing with impatience as Bozena handed them over at the top of the steps outside Lookout. Tall, bosomy and normally serene, Bozena was red-eyed and on edge, her abundant hair escaping from its plait. 'They're a bit wound up,' she warned. 'The rain's kept them indoors a lot and they've been fighting with the boys. I think they're frustrated that they were with me when the baby came. All they've been told is that it's a boy.'

Frances gave her a quick hug. 'We can't thank you enough. It's made things less awful, knowing that you were looking after them.'

'And how's Delphi?'

'At present she's strong.'

'Come *on*,' squealed Sophie, pulling at Frances. 'We want to see our brother!' Dorcas remained silent, but was poised to run home.

'We'll be in touch,' said Frances, allowing herself to be dragged away.

'Just a minute!' Bozena grabbed her arm. 'There is one thing I must mention,' she whispered. 'I'm really sorry, Frances, but I heard Sophie telling the boys that her daddy will be with the baby when they get back.'

Frances let out a long, weary breath. 'And what about Dorcas?'

'She can't fathom it out. For once they aren't thinking alike. She keeps asking me why the baby

124

decided to be born before his daddy comes home.'

'The three of us have talked and talked about it,' Frances told her. 'In the end we decided we'll just have to see how things go. Thanks for telling me, though. We'll ring you tonight.'

The girls were racing for the door, so she hurried after them and took them inside. They hurled themselves on their mother and each clasped one of Dave's thighs, then Sophie said, 'Where's our baby?'

Delphi took them to the sitting room where he was in his crib on the sofa. They observed him closely but Sophie wasn't impressed. 'He's ugly,' she said, 'and he's got no hair. Why is he asleep? I want him to look at me.'

Delphi almost smiled. 'New babies sleep a lot, my precious, except when they're hungry or uncomfortable. Dorcas, what do you think of him?'

Dorcas twisted one ankle round the other but didn't answer. All at once she grabbed her twin and pulled her behind the sofa. The three grownups watched warily. The space behind the sofa was where the girls held secret conversations, communicating in a strange blend of ordinary speech and gibberish while wiggling their fingers at each other. After a minute they emerged hand in hand.

'Where's our daddy?' asked Sophie, lips thrust out aggressively. 'He said he'd love this baby to pieces, but he'd always love us.'

In spite of their discussion it seemed that Dorcas was still thinking things through. She went for first things first. 'Has my baby got a name?' she demanded, eyes narrowed intently.

Delphi gave her a squeeze. 'Not yet, love. We'll

decide what to call him very soon.'

'Daddy says if it's a baby boy his name will be David, like Uncle Dave.'

'Yes, I know, but we're not absolutely sure about it just yet.'

Sophie stamped her foot. 'But we like Uncle Dave.'

'I know you do. We all do.'

'Uncle Dave is Daddy's brother,' Dorcas informed everybody. 'People know where their brothers are.' She lifted her eyes to Dave and gave him the beguiling little smile that both girls used when they wanted to get their own way. 'You must know,' she said. 'Tell us where he is.'

Dave shot a glance at Delphi, who gave the smallest of nods. Acting purely on an instinct he didn't even know he possessed, he squatted down and held them both close. 'Your daddy loved you to pieces, but he's gone. He had an accident. He's gone for ever and he won't be coming back.'

Two pairs of eyes looked disbelievingly into his. 'Not ever?' asked Dorcas, her mouth turning down.

'Not for our birthday when we're four?' asked Sophie, lifting her foot.

'Not ever,' confirmed Dave. 'He had an accident.'

'We used to have accidents when we couldn't wait to wee,' Dorcas pointed out reasonably, 'but Daddy's grown up. He can always wait to wee.'

'Of course he can, but it wasn't that sort of accident. He had a very big fall. In the dark. The police found him.'

Sophie beamed. 'They found my daddy? Where

126

is he, then?'

Dave couldn't manage any more and looked at the women. It was left to Frances. 'Your daddy died,' she told them gently. 'You remember Amy Tresillian's grandma, and Velvet, your little rabbit. They died, didn't they?'

Dorcas frowned in puzzlement. 'We put Velvet in a blue box,' she said. 'We put him in a hole in the garden. Mummy and Daddy said he'd gone to heaven. Has Daddy gone to heaven?'

'Yes, my love. He was a very good man, and only good people go to heaven.'

Sophie fiddled with her brother's blanket. 'So he won't see this baby?'

They were getting deep, thought Frances. It was their mother who would have to tell them what to believe, as soon as she was up to it. At that moment she was sitting next to the crib, white-faced and silent. 'Mummy is very sad,' Frances told them. 'She'll talk to you about it later. For now you can look at baby's hands. See how tiny they are. Can you see his little fingernails? Shall I show you his toes? Let's see if you can count them.'

The girls exchanged a look. Curiosity about the baby fought with questions about their daddy – and won, but incomprehension shrouded them both like sea mist. Frances saw it and prepared herself for more explanations in the hours to come. She uncovered the baby's feet, showed his toes to his sisters, and hoped that for a short time the delights of a baby brother would outweigh the loss of a father.

After a minute Sophie ran off and came back with Jonny's gold-framed photograph from the bedroom. With a satisfied little smile she propped it at the foot of the crib. 'When he wakes up we'll tell him this is his daddy,' she said.

The kitchen clock showed that twenty minutes had gone past as Frances looked back on the previous day. She was late in preparing the vegetables for the girls' lunch, and Bozena would soon be dropping them off from nursery. When they arrived would it be more questions, more tears or more tantrums? Or all three?

She told herself it was a close thing which period of her life was worse: the time she took charge of her two orphaned nephews, or the here and now.

It was mid-afternoon before George Hunter made contact. 'Interim report only,' he told Channon. 'Print-out of everything we've got first thing in the morning. Final details on both bodies ASAP.'

'That's great, George. I need your input before we take things further. Fire away – I'm taping you so I won't have to brush up my shorthand.'

'I'd manage a chuckle at that if I wasn't worn out,' said Hunter. 'Right, oh master, body number one – the Helford River man. A few clarifications on what I told you earlier. He was unconscious when he hit the water – one powerful blow to the base of the skull, an interval of, say, twenty or thirty minutes and then – splatoosh! My little wizard and her friends can't say whether he went into the river or the sea. The water he took in was a mixture of fresh and salt, but that fits with it being a tidal river. They've studied the tides and

128

the flows and on balance think he was thrown in the river downstream from where he was found. No signs of being bound or gagged, so if he was transported to the Helford from elsewhere he must have been out of it and away with the fairies. No jewellery, tattoos, birthmarks, body-piercing – nothing at all to identify him, but Forensic have confirmed that the pulped-up mess in his pocket is a copy of the Koran, so that says Muslim. Can't do time of death with accuracy but let's say four or five days before he was found.'

'What, all spent in the water?'

'Probably.'

'If he was in the Helford as long as that it's a wonder he wasn't swept out to sea.'

'We think he got caught up in vegetation near a bank or outcrop. When heavy rain increased the flow he was swept away, then maybe came back on a high tide to be finally deposited in the creek. We've checked and the water alone could have swept him in and left him there. Stomach contents I've told you, and fingerprints. Now, ethnic origins ... nothing conclusive on skin pigmentation, but we think Middle Eastern. I doubt whether Forensic will come up with anything from nail scrapings and such, but we'll get his DNA if you need to match samples from anybody.'

'Brilliant. Now how about Tregenza?'

'Ah, your young father. We've done extensive tests on the cranium – on the whole body, come to that – to establish what happened before he went over the edge.'

'And?'

Hunter's matter-of-fact tone changed. 'I'm

sorry, Bill, but it was no accident, nor was it suicide. Manslaughter or murder, I'd say. At the very least you'll be classing it as suspicious death, and that's definite enough to inform next of kin and the media. There were multiple injuries and fractures, but we've been able to suss out which of them occurred before death and which after. I'll give full chapter and verse in writing, but for now take it that there were blows to the head, two moderate, one more severe, well before death. He was bound at the wrists with something soft – say a scarf or even a shirt. Whatever it was, it didn't leave much evidence. I think his head was covered and he *was* dragged, we've checked on that, but probably for only a short distance.

'Then, we think he was thrown bodily over the cliff. If one man on his own did it he was some weightlifter, but it's possible Tregenza was tipped out of a cart or even a wheelbarrow. The terrific drop broke his limbs and his neck and killed him – I'd say roughly six days ago but we're trying to be more accurate. There's been at least one tide in the past week high enough to soak him but not take him away, probably because he was jammed among the rocks.'

Channon was hunched over the phone. 'But it's almost a carbon copy of the other!' he protested. 'Don't say we've got a copy-cat killer, George!'

'You tell me,' retorted Hunter. 'You're the detective.'

'You can say that again,' Channon replied grimly. 'So what about his heels?'

'Forensic are on with it. They'll be in touch.'

'Anything from what was put over his head?'

130

'Ditto.'

'Stomach contents?'

'Nothing sinister. A substantial hot meal, and then sometime later, beer, but I can't give you the menu.'

'I don't need it,' said Channon hastily, 'but thanks a million, George.'

After a day of sunshine the air over the Lizard was so bright and sparkling it was as if two weeks of wind and rain had laundered it, ready for summer. Bowles was at the wheel as they skirted Helston and then drove past Culdrose Airfield. He glanced to his left and felt relieved that he didn't have to face another flight in a helicopter. 'Where to first?' he asked Channon.

'I'd say the Dancers at Trevant as it's on the way to Porthmenna, but I can't have Mrs Tregenza seeing our lot descend on the place until I've told her the reason for it.'

'Well, how soon will they arrive?'

'Soon after we do, I hope. I've managed to get Inspector Meade as office manager for the incident room.' John Meade was an old friend and solid as a rock on routine administration.

'Oh, great,' said Bowles heartily, well aware that it sounded false. Meade was a pain, one of the old school, who sometimes said things like, 'Less mouth, sergeant,' or 'Time to talk when you're in charge of an enquiry, if that day ever dawns.' Cocky old fool! Still, he only had a couple more years to go. He'd never get past Inspector, so who was he to come the heavy? Out loud he said, 'Anybody else I know on the team?'

131

'A few familiar faces on IT and door-to-door, and that good young DC from Falmouth on statement-reading. They'll all be on their way over here, and so will the incident room.'

Bowles rolled his eyes. He didn't like prefab incident rooms, however well-equipped, but a grotty little dump like Porthmenna probably hadn't got a room big enough to commandeer.

'The Tregenzas, now,' continued Channon. 'We'll have to start by checking the family, of course.' They both knew that murder and manslaughter were most often committed by a family member or someone close to the victim.

'How about Mr Universe?' suggested Bowles. 'When Yates was chatting up the old biddies last week they all seemed to dote on "young Dave" as they called him, but we mentioned in our report that it came out he went abroad in a huff when his brother got engaged to Delphi. There could have been bad blood between the two of them.'

'It's more than odd that he arrived back when he did,' agreed Channon, 'but if there was bad blood why did he wait seven years before coming home to take revenge?'

'Money? Opportunity? Seven years – the mystic number seven? Don't some weirdos believe that seven is, you know, special? Seventh son of a seventh son, seventy times seven, the seven-year itch and all that guff.'

Channon didn't reply He was thinking of a bronzed, overwrought young man clutching a baby to his chest; of the young man's aunt, lifting her chin as she faced a grim future. No, surely not the family ... but it wouldn't be the first time that seemingly decent people had tried to deceive him. 'We'll check on him,' he said, 'and on the aunt and the father-in-law. As for the wife, I really can't see a woman so near her time bashing her husband – the breadwinner of the family – and tossing him over a cliff.'

'No, maybe not her,' conceded Bowles, 'unless of course the baby isn't Tregenza's and she has a lover-boy waiting in the wings. It could be one of the others, though.'

'It could be anybody,' said Channon, 'so we follow procedure until we get answers. We have two separate cases, so we treat them as separate until, or unless, we find evidence that they're connected.'

'But they must be! What about the timing? What about being so close to each other – so close to–' Bowles stopped short. You could press your point only so far with the DCI.

'So close to Goonhilly,' finished Channon wearily. 'Don't worry, I'm not forgetting that. I'm senior investigating officer on both cases simply because they're in the vicinity of a sensitive site.'

Bowles picked up speed. Channon might be a softie but his special responsibility covered the whole of South Cornwall, and he'd chosen him, Bowles, to be his right-hand man. A PoT case was the chance of a lifetime, so hey, hey, promotion was beckoning.

They drove on beneath a sky streaked with the first flames of sunset, but he was in no mood to admire the glories of nature. He needed a right turn and had no intention of losing face by missing it.

Chapter Eight

Channon was so intent on seeing the Tregenzas he took the steps to Lookout Cottage two at a time. Behind him Bowles was less eager, telling himself that though the family knew the man was dead, they might not want to accept that he'd been killed and probably murdered. He himself was no good at giving bad news, so he wouldn't even open his mouth. It was Channon who was revered for his 'people skills', so let him do the talking.

Frances opened the door, her eyes widening at the sight of the two detectives. 'Inspector,' she said warily, 'and Sergeant Bowles. Come in.'

Once inside Channon was polite and very serious. 'We'd like a word with all of you, Miss Lyne. Is Mrs Tregenza here, and your nephew?'

Clearly this was to be no informal chat. 'David is upstairs reading a story to the children. He'll be down in a minute, but Delphi's in bed. We've persuaded her to have a rest, so if she's asleep I don't want to wake her.'

'I can understand that,' said Channon, 'but I must see all three of you together. I wouldn't ask if I didn't think it necessary.'

He doesn't want us to talk except in front of him, thought Frances. He wants to see our reactions to something. 'You've brought news,' she said.

'Yes, we have.'

134

She looked into his eyes, but they revealed nothing. 'Take a seat,' she said, leading them into the sitting room. 'I'll see what I can do.'

She was reluctant to disturb the girls and their uncle, but Dave met her on the landing outside their room. 'They're asleep,' he said. 'Delphi's kissed them goodnight.'

'She's awake? Good. The police are here – Channon and the sergeant. He wants to talk to the three of us.'

'Did he say why?'

She lifted her hands, palms upwards. 'I think he wants to tell us something and maybe ask questions. I'll get Delphi.'

The three of them entered the room to find the detectives standing by the window in the glow of the sunset. Channon looked at Delphi, the woman he had last seen bleeding on a beach. 'Mrs Tregenza,' he said gently, 'we've spoken on the phone, haven't we? I'm DCI Channon, in charge of investigations into your husband's death. I think you already know Sergeant Bowles.'

Delphi nodded but didn't reply. 'Please sit down, all of you,' said Channon firmly, then addressed himself to Delphi. 'I'm so very sorry about your husband, Mrs Tregenza. I'm here to tell you officially that extensive tests have been carried out on his body. All three of you were right – he did not commit suicide by throwing himself off Proudy Steep. We're treating the death as suspicious.'

They had known that such a thing was possible, even probable, but hearing it put into words seemed to stun the three of them. Two pairs of

135

eyes, one dark and one pale, observed every detail of their reactions. Delphi was the first to speak. 'You think somebody attacked him?' Her voice rose incredulously on the last two words.

'Yes, we do.'

'But who would want to do that? Why should they? Everybody likes him – liked, I mean.'

Questions were ranking themselves in Dave's mind like an army going to battle. 'You're saying it was murder?'

'Yes. Murder or manslaughter.'

They all gaped at him, Frances with her jaw slack and a hand to her chest. She was telling herself that the word 'unreal' had swamped her brain in the last week, but she hadn't even known the meaning of it. *This* was unreal – not Jonny missing, but murdered! Murder happened to other people, in newspapers and on television. It was committed by villains and thieves and – and–

'Where was he attacked?' It was Dave again. 'We don't think he would have walked the clifftops in the dark, and he wouldn't have headed for home by way of Proudy.'

'We do realize that,' Channon assured him. 'We'll be investigating in depth. From first thing tomorrow you'll see a lot of police activity in the village as we check with everyone. Our incident room is being set up at any moment in a central location. About your little girls, Mrs Tregenza, I don't know how much you've told them but maybe you'd like to consider whether they'd be better off away from the upheaval of our enquiry?'

'I'll think about it,' Delphi agreed.

'Also, the media will have to be informed as

there's already been interest when your husband went missing. It will be newspapers and regional television at the very least, so be prepared. My men will fend off reporters whenever possible.'

When Frances spoke there was steel in her tone. 'You must wish that so much time hadn't elapsed since my nephew went missing, inspector?'

'Yes, I do,' admitted Channon, knowing what was coming. 'Investigations are always harder with the passing of time.'

'Then why didn't you take action sooner? We told you and told you that it wasn't a routine missing person case.'

'According to the reports you also told us that Mr Tregenza had no enemies and no worries,' retorted Channon. 'The local police followed normal procedure for the disappearance of a blameless person. But of course—' he paused for long seconds – 'it may well be that he wasn't blameless.'

Bowles blinked. That was a slap with a red herring, but the stillness of Channon told him that the remark had been deliberate. It had the desired effect: first, blank astonishment, then both women started talking at once: Frances in fury and Delphi in defence of her husband. Only Dave kept silent, as if he knew they'd been goaded, but intended to reveal nothing.

'You're scratching around, aren't you?' Frances asked derisively 'What are you saying, that he was some sort of criminal? He was a carpenter, for heaven's sake – a specialist woodworker, not a self-made millionaire snorting coke.'

'My husband has never done a dishonest thing in his life,' said Delphi at the same time, her voice

137

rising to match that of Frances. 'He hadn't an enemy in the world.'

'In that case you won't mind if my men pick up his business records, including his computer. We'll safeguard all data, I assure you.'

Frances was still enraged. 'You're saying all this about his business to cover your refusal to take us seriously,' she accused.

'No, madam, that is not the case. It isn't unknown for a man to be killed because of shady business dealings. We want to rule it out, that's all. We'll be talking to his customers and suppliers tomorrow.'

She glared at him. 'I don't think you'd have made the slightest move about Jonny if it hadn't been for that other body!' Even as she said it she knew it sounded callous. 'That other body' was some woman's son, maybe some woman's husband. She ran a hand through her hair and flopped back on the sofa, breathing hard.

Channon smothered compassion. He was after impressions if he couldn't get anything else. Sympathy would only muddy the waters. 'As a matter of fact, Miss Lyne, I sanctioned work on Mr Tregenza's case some time before the Helford River body was found. Surely you recall that my men visited you here before we even knew about it?'

Frances dragged the days and the times from her mind and put them in sequence. He was right. Belatedly she remembered that she liked this man. She had even told herself that she trusted him, but she wasn't going to apologize. 'I'm a bit wound up,' she said stiffly. 'We all are.'

'That's not surprising,' said Channon quietly.

'Now, just a few questions before we leave you in peace. Could you tell us your movements last Monday evening, Miss Lyne?'

She let out a disbelieving sigh. 'We're his *family*,' she said wearily. 'All *right* ... I was here at home, marking some work from pupils and generally messing about.'

'You were alone?'

'Yes. I watched the news at ten o'clock and I was having a drink before bed when Delphi phoned me.'

'What time would that be?'

'I think just after eleven. She was worried that Jonny wasn't home because he'd told her that he wouldn't be gone for long. She'd already telephoned the Dancers and she wanted me to come over here to stay with the girls while she went up to Trevant to see them in person. I drove across at once and stayed the night.'

'Thank you. You're a linguist, I believe, Miss Lyne. Could you tell me which are your particular languages?'

'French, Italian and Spanish. I'm competent but less able in a few others.'

'Thank you,' said Channon again, then turned to Delphi. 'You've already told the sergeant here what happened. Do you wish to change what you said, or have you remembered anything else?'

She shook her head. 'No I told him everything I could think of. What *is* all this, inspector?'

'Bear with me,' said Channon. 'It's merely a routine formality that has to be followed when we have a suspicious death. We need to eliminate everyone, including family.' He turned to Dave.

'Now, Mr Tregenza. When exactly did you arrive back in the UK?'

Dave had been expecting it. 'Late Tuesday evening,' he said, and as one, both women turned and looked at him. 'I stayed the night in London and came to Cornwall on the early train on Wednesday morning. I hired a car in Penzance and I'm still using it.'

Channon's voice was silky-soft. 'But I understood that you first arrived at Seaspray House on Friday morning? Your aunt and Mrs Tregenza have confirmed it. Are they mistaken?'

'No, they're right. I'd come rushing back and then, when I got here, I found I couldn't just roll up at the house.'

'Why was that?'

This was mad, explaining his hesitations and hang-ups to a detective in front of Delphi and Frances, not to mention the sergeant scribbling in the background. 'I'd been away for seven years,' he said. 'When I was eighteen I chose to go abroad against everyone's wishes and advice.'

Pin him down, thought Bowles in irritation, make him admit there was a rift between him and his brother. But he knew the DCI would do no such thing. He was well under way with his 'iron hand in the velvet glove' routine, well aware that if people were upset, gentle handling could tempt them to reveal more than putting them under pressure. 'You'd been away for seven years, living a new life, yet you've just said you'd come rushing home. Why the hurry, Mr Tregenza?'

For a moment Dave couldn't answer. It would sound far-fetched, over the top, like some

140

second-rate psychodrama. Then he shrugged. 'I was in Hawaii when I got an overpowering urge to come back. It was only when I was booking my flight that I recognized it for what it was.'

'And that was?'

'A feeling – a premonition that things weren't right with my brother.'

It was so way-out it could only be true, thought Channon. This was no glib cover-up. 'Could you enlarge on that, Mr Tregenza?'

Dave flexed his shoulders and stretched his neck. He glanced at Frances, who nodded and gave him the smallest of smiles. He knew she was encouraging him to tell Channon everything. Maybe she was right.

'Since Jonny and I were very young I've – only sometimes, of course, not very often – known when things weren't right with him or when he was in danger. It happened a few times at school, and when we were playing.' To his relief Channon remained grave and attentive. 'The last time was several years ago, before I left home.'

'Does anyone else know of this?'

'I do,' said Frances. 'It was always a bit un-canny, but believe me it happened. Six times that I know of in the nine years I lived with them. At least once he saved Jonny's life.'

Bowles curled a lip but kept his eyes on his notes, because Channon was still asking questions. 'So how did you spend the two days?' he was saying.

'Visiting old haunts, travelling round the Lizard. I stayed in a small hotel in Helston because I didn't want anybody to recognize me.'

141

'But Mr Tregenza, if you had that premonition why did you wait two whole days before going home to check on your brother?'

'I can't really explain it,' said Dave awkwardly. 'I was still uneasy, but the urgency had gone.'

'Do you know why?'

The brilliant eyes blazed. 'Of course I do! He was already dead!'

Channon shot a glance at Delphi and said calmly, 'I think that's enough questions for now. Tomorrow Sergeant Bowles will call to take official statements from each of you, which he will then ask you to sign. Mr Tregenza, perhaps you'd also give him details of your flight from Hawaii, and documentation for the hire of your car.'

Dave stared at him. 'There's no need to check it,' he said blankly.

'Oh, I think there is,' said Channon. 'We check everything that anyone tells us – always.'

They said their farewells and left the house. 'Well, what do you make of that?' asked Channon at the top of the steps.

'The women didn't know he reached Cornwall on Wednesday'

'Agreed.'

'But if he'd wanted to lie about his return, surely he'd have said he got back on Friday?'

'Yes, but suppose we find that he actually got back on Monday?'

'If he did, then he's our man. But if he did it, why didn't he go back to the wide blue yonder right away, before anybody knew he'd been here? In any case, where does he fit in with the river man?'

They stood side by side, gazing down from

their vantage point. Police cars were arriving at the harbour, dropping off a night shift to set up phones and computers and office gear, while on the cobbles leading to the jetty men were unloading prefabricated sections of a building. Beyond the harbour wall it was very still: the sea flat calm, the sky rose-pink and without cloud, the sun sliding from sight behind the two pointed rocks known as the Eye Teeth. Nature was tranquil; the police were not.

Channon eyed the scene but made no move. 'Did you notice anything about their reaction to Jonathan being attacked?'

'Delphi didn't want to believe it.'

'True, but I found it very odd that none of them asked what had been done to him in the attack, nor whether he was dead or alive when he went over Proudy.'

Bowles gritted his teeth. That hadn't registered with him. Channon knew it but didn't comment. 'So,' he said now, 'we have no option but to check on all three of them – in detail.'

A less vital issue was bugging Bowles, however. 'One thing puzzles me, sir. Mr Universe was born and bred here, but he doesn't look like a Cornishman.'

'Neither did his brother, though he was less blond. Scandinavian genes still surface down here, Bowles. Swedes, Danes, Norwegians, they all came this way in the past and some of them stayed. Their bloodlines are still active.'

So he'd been right when he first saw Dave Tregenza and classed him as a Viking. Bowles thought of his own lanky physique with distaste.

143

'The guy's some looker,' he muttered.

It had been a long day and Channon was edgy. 'If he looks like the Archangel Gabriel it'll do him no good unless he's in the clear! Now, I'll have a quick word with John Meade then we'll go and see the Dancers.'

Frances, Dave and Delphi faced each other in silence when the detectives had gone. Delphi spoke first. 'I simply can't believe that somebody killed him,' she said quietly. 'He can't have been involved in anything crooked, anything illegal. Dave – have you found anything suspicious in his business records?'

'Nothing.' Dave was conscious of a strange feeling in his innards. He wondered if it could be nausea but, as he'd never been nauseous since childhood, wasn't sure he'd recognize it. What he *was* sure of was that he must get away from the women. He needed to be alone – to think, to adjust to the confirming of what he'd suspected but never allowed himself to contemplate. 'I'm going upstairs to look through Jonny's computer before the police take it away,' he told them. 'Then if you don't need me here I'll go back to Seaspray for the night.'

We do need you! Don't go! The words were so clear in her head Frances wondered if she'd said them out loud, but the others gave no sign of hearing anything. She tried for a sensible remark. 'If you want to go back to bed I'll bring you a drink,' she told Delphi. 'Maybe you'll be able to sleep for an hour or two before he wakes again.'

The baby was still 'he', unnamed but not

unheard. The high, nerve-stretching 'wah-wah-wah' of a hungry infant was already dominating their lives. As if on cue, it started up again and Delphi went off in response to what Dave told himself must be the worst sound on earth. He turned to Frances. 'Do they all carry on like this?'

'Some do, I think, if they're not getting enough food to satisfy them, or they haven't settled in a feeding routine. You see, Delphi is determined to breast-feed him. I think, and so does Mollie, that in view of the stress she's under she'd be better to supplement her breast milk with a bottle now and again, but she won't hear of it.'

Dave tried to look as if he understood, but had already accepted that delivering a baby didn't automatically bestow knowledge of how to deal with one. He escaped to the tower room at speed, and once there immersed himself in Jonny's computer files.

As before, he found no bad debts, no unexplained deposits, nothing remotely suspicious. Then he went through paperwork: written correspondence, print-outs of bank statements, cheque stubs, invoices, receipts; but before long pushed them all to one side and went to stand at the window. He could see activity down below as the police worked on establishing their headquarters, and asked himself grimly whether Channon was up to the job of finding out what had happened to his brother. He recalled the man's dark, steady gaze, his calm, decisive tones. Yes, he decided, he *was* up to it, and what was more, he–

There was a tap at the door and Frances came in. 'I know you want to be on your own,' she said, 'but I have to ask what you think about what Channon told us.' She sat tensely in the window seat and ran her fingers through her hair.

Dave was conscious of something shifting inside his chest. It was as if a piece of furniture that had obscured the light was being dragged to one side. He could almost feel a grating sensation, like a heavy weight being pulled across floorboards. What was going on? He shook his head and eyed Frances closely. Clearly, she was exhausted.

He said abruptly, 'Frances, why don't you go to bed? You need sleep.'

Tired grey eyes looked into his. 'I can't,' she said, 'I have to go out in a minute to see Lizzie at the shop. I must tell her why there's all this to-do by the harbour, and what Channon says about Jonny, so she can tell her customers and Donald at the pub. I want all our friends to know before the police start questioning them in the morning. I'll have to ring Terence, as well. He has to know that his son-in-law was mur – was killed. But David, most of all I want to know what *you* think about it.'

'I think Channon must be right. Jonny was murdered.' He had never in his life said anything that sounded so false. 'We all know he wouldn't have killed himself, don't we? Therefore somebody else must have done it. It's all so incredibly hard to believe.'

'Do you think he saw something he shouldn't have seen as he walked home from Trevant?'

'Perhaps – I don't know. We can all help Channon – we can do whatever he says, but in the end we'll have to leave it to him and his men to sort out.'

She let out breath in a long, relieved sigh. 'That's what I think, as well,' she said, staring down at her clasped hands. 'But there's something else. I don't want to pressure you, but how long do you think you'll be able to stay with us?'

'For as long as it takes,' he said simply. 'As long as it takes to find out who did it, and why.'

He watched in dismay as two large tears slid very slowly down her cheeks. He knew he should do something, but for the life of him could offer her no comfort. The habit of years was too ingrained, and in any case he was trying to cope with the strange feeling in his guts and the shifting of weights inside his chest. He knew what was causing it. In spite of his fine resolves, his old enemy emotion was at work again, this time causing physical symptoms. But what did he expect? Life was hell and the brother he'd ignored for seven years was gone for ever. He looked again at Frances's tears. She wasn't wiping them away Did she know they were there?

'I'll stay here until you're back from Lizzie's,' he offered.

'Thanks,' she said, and left the room.

Channon turned to the sergeant as they headed for Trevant. 'As you're so keen on the Goonhilly angle I thought you'd have wanted to know what they had to tell me about Dancer.'

At that moment the only thing Bowles wanted to know was how soon he could have a hot meal, but he kept quiet about it. 'Of course I want to know,' he protested, 'but you have to admit we've been a bit busy. Did you get anything out of them?'

'Yes. He's highly regarded, ultra-respectable, extremely clever, above suspicion – you name it,' Channon told him drily. 'But then, if he does have some sort of secret agenda that's how he'll aim to come over.'

Bowles switched on his stock expression of earnest, helpful assistant. 'So how do you plan to handle him, sir?'

'Straight enquiries concentrating on the river man, then take it from there.'

'And what about Nancy the nympho?'

'The same with her. We'll follow the old instinct, Bowles.'

'Right,' said the sergeant gloomily He didn't like talking about instinct. He knew it existed, that he himself had it, though to nothing like the degree that Channon did. The DCI had both instinct and intuition, and when he brought inspiration to the mix he raised detection to the heights. Reflecting on this, Bowles stayed silent as they approached the sprawling stone mass of Trevant House, knowing but not wanting to admit that he could learn something every time he watched Channon in action.

Nancy Dancer opened the door, looking neat and trim in tailored slacks and a silky sweater, the amber eyes glinting behind her glasses as Channon introduced himself. He watched her rear view as she led them across the hall, and thought she seemed no different from many a middle-class wife: well-preserved, attractive, decent figure; looking as if she'd be quite at home in a shiny kitchen making a sponge cake.

'It's the police, Alan,' she announced as they

148

reached a small office. 'They want a word with us.' She turned and gestured to them to enter the room ahead of her, then stood half-blocking the doorway so that they had to brush against her as they passed. Here we go, thought Channon; Bowles and Yates were right. It was like edging past a radiator turned on at full blast. He fancied he could feel heat from her body.

Cheerful, rotund, energetic, Alan Dancer gave no sign that he knew his wife was sending out a come-on. Maybe he didn't want to know, thought Channon, or maybe he was so used to it he didn't even notice. Whatever the man knew, they'd come to Trevant on more important matters than assessing Nancy's pulling power.

'Just a few enquiries, sir, madam,' he said with practised politeness. 'No doubt you're aware that Jonathan Tregenza's body has been found. I have to tell you that we're treating his death as suspicious, and that some of my men will be calling on you tomorrow to take an official statement regarding his visit here last Monday evening. Also, you'll see a forensic team removing earth samples and possibly specimens of vegetation from the immediate area.'

Both the Dancers stared at him. 'You're saying you think that Jonathan's death was deliberate?' asked Dancer, the eyes in his chubby face all at once chilly and careful.

'Yes sir, I do think that, but my questions just now concern the whereabouts of another man with whom you might possibly have come into contact. Did you have a visitor here at Trevant on, say, Monday or Tuesday of last week?'

'It was Monday when Jonathan was here,' said Dancer impatiently. 'We've already talked to your sergeant about it.'

'I'm aware of that. I'm asking if anyone else called on you.'

Dancer looked at his wife. 'Didn't a man call to ask about parking his caravan?'

'Yes,' she agreed, 'but he went off when we refused.'

'The man I'm thinking of was Middle Eastern,' said Channon blandly. 'I believe you have connections in that part of the world, Mr Dancer?'

'What? Yes, yes I do. I grew up there and I've worked there – lived there, both of us have – from time to time. Inspector, what exactly are you asking me?'

'Whether or not you had a visitor, or saw someone in the vicinity of your house, just over a week ago – a man of Middle Eastern appearance and origins. We're trying to trace his movements.'

At that Dancer's jaw tightened. Channon almost missed it; he'd been watching Nancy pushing her hands deep into the pockets of her slacks – an innocent enough gesture, but one that was almost impossible to ignore when inside the fine fabric her fingers moved visibly against her crotch. Bowles was staring at her as if hypnotized.

'What has this chap done?' asked Dancer curiously. 'Robbed a bank?'

'It's a case of what's been done to him,' answered Channon gravely. 'He's been murdered.'

Nancy's oversized glasses slid down her nose a fraction, while Dancer's ruddy features took on a patchy appearance, as if blood was draining from

150

behind random patches of skin. He shot a single look at his wife, then asked, 'Are you saying that you're investigating two different murders?'

'Yes, I am.'

'By the same hand?'

'We don't yet know.'

'And this Middle Eastern man – is he the one everybody's talking about – the one who was found in the Helford River?'

'Yes,' said Channon again.

Just for an instant Dancer's shoulders sagged, then he straightened them and braced his short legs. Behind him, eager and intent, Bowles stood to attention gripping his notebook. 'We did have a visitor here last week,' Dancer said heavily. 'I didn't want to tell you about it because he's on the run – he's in a bit of trouble. He came to me on Monday for help and advice.'

'And did he get it?'

'Yes. I knew him when he was in his early twenties and a student of mine. He's – he was – Saudi Arabian. A good lad – very bright, well-off family, his future assured.'

'And then?'

'I moved on and we lost touch. Much later I heard from acquaintances that he'd quarrelled with his family and left home. Somebody said he was in Afghanistan, but that was some years ago.'

'So why was he in the UK, Mr Dancer?'

'He didn't tell us. I suppose he was trying to make a living.'

'But you said he was in trouble – on the run.'

'Yes, he was. He believed that an extremist Islamic group were intent on recruiting him. He

151

was frightened and had decided to return to the safety of home and try to make up with his family Also, I think he'd had enough of being poor. He wanted to borrow money for his air fare.'

'And did you let him have it?'

'Yes.'

'How much?'

'Six hundred. I don't keep much cash in the house. He refused a lift and went off on foot.'

'So he'd been living within walking distance?'

'I don't know. He never got round to telling us.'

'So he didn't stay long?'

'Uh – no.'

Channon raised his eyebrows. 'You didn't share a meal, then?'

Dancer tightened his lips. 'As a matter of fact, we did. We had a light supper together. Then he left.'

'What time would that be?'

'About eight, I think.'

'And when did you see him again?'

'We didn't,' said Dancer flatly. 'We haven't seen him since.' He was shaking his head repeatedly. It put Bowles in mind of an old-fashioned clockwork toy. Channon, however, had been observing the little man closely, noting the fast-blinking eyes, the clenched hands, the restless feet. Dancer might be clever, he thought, but he was too on edge to watch his body language. He was frightened of revealing something.

'Did you notice any change in his appearance since you last saw him?'

'He didn't look too fit – a bit overweight and somewhat unkempt. He was wearing Western

152

clothes, of course.'

'What, exactly?'

'Jeans and a checked shirt. Cheap casual shoes.'

'You haven't yet given us a name for your visitor, Mr Dancer,' said Channon gently.

'It's – it was Abdurrahman al-Makki.'

'Thank you. From what you've told us I think it highly likely that the body found in the Helford River is that of your former student. Would you be willing to attempt an identification for us?'

Dancer stretched his neck out of his collar. 'Of course,' he said briskly.

'Thank you. A car will be here at eight thirty tomorrow morning to take you to the mortuary and bring you back again. As I said, I'll need a full signed statement from you both, which I think will be better done at our temporary head-quarters in Porthmenna. That way, you'll both be on hand for further official questioning. Perhaps you'd be so good as to keep yourselves free for the entire morning?'

'But I've told you all I know,' protested Dancer.

'Oh, I don't think so, sir. I need to know a great deal more about this man's contacts, his origins, where he's been living. I assure you that I have authority to question whoever I choose on matters that could have even a remote bearing on terrorism. Add to that the fact that you and your wife have very close connections to two violent deaths and I think it abundantly clear that we need to talk in much more detail.'

Dancer's quick, clever eyes slid away from Channon's dark implacable ones. 'Whatever you say, chief inspector.'

'Thank you both for your time,' said Channon soberly.

Nancy moistened her lips and patted her hair. 'Don't mention it,' she said.

Channon couldn't fathom her. She sent signals that were belied by her appearance. In his time he'd seen life in the raw: he'd had more than one spell on Vice, he'd seen predatory females in action, put pimps behind bars, even lectured on prostitution, but this woman was from a different world – a different era. She was like an old-fashioned sex-pot from the sixties. Was it some kind of exhibitionism with no real back-up, or was it simply that she saw the genuine article as having no need of modern trappings? That could be it...

They went out to the car beneath a sky that had darkened to purple. Bowles was on a high because of the terrorist link, but Channon was morose, staring grimly across the velvety lawns to the distant sea. 'What's up, sir?' asked Bowles. 'Aren't you satisfied?'

'Far from it. It doesn't add up. A man who might have naughty connections ends up conveniently dead. There was no money on him, though he'd been given a sizeable handout from Dancer. He didn't get around to telling Dancer much about his life, even though he felt enough at ease with him to ask for a loan, and to sit down for a meal with him. He had no car keys and no car's been found, so did he arrive on foot? From where? There was no identification on him, so it was either removed or he didn't have any in the first place. Does somebody want us to believe he was killed for what he had on him? An impulse

154

robbery? Late on a Monday evening in the middle of nowhere?'

'And not far from Goonhilly,' added Bowles innocently. That crummy little incident room by the harbour would soon need upgrading by one four times the size, or he was a Dutchman.

Chapter Nine

Lizzie Bannon had opened her shop early, and by seven thirty had dealt with the baker's man, filled her bread shelf and stacked extra milk in the cabinet. She was reluctant to make money out of poor Jonny, but told herself that Porthmenna would be swarming with police, and some of them might conceivably call in for a drink or something to eat.

'Standing to make a bit, then, Lizzie?' Sam Ludcott had come in and was eyeing the shelves as if he expected them to be groaning with extra provisions.

'No, I'm not,' she said tartly, 'but if any of them police want a quick snack, better they get it close at hand than go a-wandering elsewhere and wasting time that could be spent on catching criminals.'

A brown loaf in one hand and a carton of milk in the other, Sam wriggled his shoulders. 'It's bad, then, is it? They're saying it was deliberate?'

'Yes, they seem sure of it. Frances came down last night to let me know the police had been to see them. It's murder or manslaughter, they said, though she wasn't sure what they thought about that fella in the river. She wants me to spread the word so folks'll know why there's police all over the place. I went and told Donald at closing time, so he'll tell his regulars. I can hardly believe it,

156

Sam, not here – not in our village. Frances says it's some high-up detective in charge – a chief inspector. She says he seems to know what he's doing.'

'A pity he didn't do it a bit sooner, then.'

'I know, but I've heard there's a hundred thousand or more go missing in a year. They can't spend time on 'em all, now can they, unless it's a child or there's what they call cause for concern.'

The bell pinged and two women came in. One made straight for the bread shelf but the other made no pretence of buying. 'What's going on, Lizzie?' she asked. 'Is all this to-do outside on account of young Jonny?'

Sam handed over money for his goods and leaned across the counter. 'You'll be doing a roaring trade till word gets round,' he said soberly. 'I'll tell a few folk, if you like, or you'll be hoarse by the day's end.'

'Thanks, Sam, that'll be a help.' Lizzie turned to the women. 'I'll tell you what I know,' she said, 'but it won't make pleasant hearing.'

Channon felt a twist of distaste as he entered the incident room. He never liked to see the trappings of violent crime in a beautiful setting, and this was surely the ultimate – an incident room for two murders right on the harbour front of this lovely little village.

Grey-haired and solid, John Meade gave him a quick smile. 'Red-carpet treatment, Bill – you've got an office all to yourself this time. Surprising what a hint of terrorism can do for funding. Do you want to see the set-up?'

157

Channon nodded but lingered by a window. Outside was the ancient stone jetty with a couple of fishing boats tied up, a stretch of yellow sand left bare at low tide overlooked by stone cottages, the pub and the shop. Then, seeming out of time and place, a line of police cars parked on the cobbled road that led to the start of the jetty; all under a cloudless blue sky more suited to midsummer than late April.

John Meade knew his old friend. 'Don't tell me,' he said. 'It would be more fitting if we had to work in a concrete high-rise under low cloud and drizzle.'

'Got it in one,' answered Channon.

'It's a bad do is this, Bill,' acknowledged Meade. 'What's your feeling? *Are* they connected?'

'I think they must be. Near enough the same time, not to mention the same area and the same method. All we need now is the motive and the perpetrators.'

'More than one?'

'I'm not sure yet, but our two dead men were well-built types who were attacked, transported and then chucked round. We both know that unconscious men aren't easy to shift. Now, have the Anti-Terrorist people been on?'

'Need you ask? They have extra men champing at the bit if you need them.'

'Have they indeed? We'll have to arrange a Middle Eastern corpse on every case, won't we? If we get a definite link they'll take it out of our hands, anyway, which will suit me, if not Bowles.'

John Meade rolled his eyes. 'He's a glory-hunter, is that one. He thinks his promotion's overdue.'

Channon shrugged. 'Promotion has to be earned. He's good on the basics, but if he gets a fixation on something he'll let it affect his judgement.'

'You're too charitable,' Meades warned. 'He's an awkward bugger if you ask me.'

'Aren't we all when we're pushed? Time will tell with Bowles. Now, let's have a look at what you've got sorted out.'

Together they examined the ranked computers, the phone tables ready for manning, the big blown-up photograph of a smiling Jonathan Tregenza and next to it a large sketch – an artist's impression of how the river man might have looked before time, water, animal life and mud took their toll. Channon eyed it curiously. 'Dancer should be able to tell us if this is accurate.'

Meade nodded. 'Bowles and Steve Soker are already on their way to pick him up to identify the body. Do you still want him back here for his statement?'

'The statements can be taken anywhere – and from both Mr and Mrs, don't forget. The thing is, I'm pretty sure that Dancer knows more than he told us last night, therefore I want to question him here, officially and on the record. So what time have you fixed for the briefing?'

Meade knew that Channon set great store by his briefings. He liked the lowliest man or woman on the team to know the score, with the consequence that the rank and file would work their guts out for him. 'I thought you'd want Bowles here for it,' he said, 'so I've arranged it for nine thirty after they get back. Until then there's

159

plenty for everybody to do.'

Channon looked round at the mix of plain-clothes and uniformed personnel. 'Don't let me delay things,' he said.

'All done and dusted,' said Bowles as he reported in to Channon. 'Dancer hesitated at first, then he vomited. After that he refocused and recognized the missing tooth lower front left.'

'Without being prompted?'

'Yes. He said he'd noticed it when the guy first arrived and then when he sat opposite him at the supper table. He was a bit cut-up at seeing the body and I think it was genuine. He said he was ninety-five per cent sure it was him. Then we showed him the clothes – a hundred per cent on those, and the same on the artist's impression, though he said it should have been a bit chubbier. We picked up Nancy-dancy on the way back here and they're both outside in the big room.'

'Well done. Tell Inspector Meade I say to put them somewhere comfortable until we've had the briefing. Get your thoughts together for that and we'll start in – let's see – in eight minutes flat.'

'You're not dealing with the Dancers first?'

'No. I'll want longer than eight minutes with them, Bowles.'

Bowles zoomed off, telling himself he could question the Yorkshire Ripper in five and Bin Laden himself in seven. Sometimes Channon needed a rocket up his backside.

The incident room by the harbour was crowded, with those who hadn't got a chair perched on

160

tables or standing at the back. All were eager and intent. Nobody liked murder, but it was a rare enough event in the Devon and Cornwall force to generate excitement among the rank and file.

Channon was listing a few dos and don'ts in his introduction. 'We're starting off cold and late on these two cases,' he told them, 'so what we've lost in time we must make up in effort. Try not to antagonize the local population – the people of the Lizard are an independent lot and we want them with us all the way. Do not dismiss any information as of no consequence, though I don't need a note of what somebody's uncle had for his dinner the day before yesterday. Use your judgement on what's relevant to the enquiry and put it in writing.

'Remember this is a very close community – everybody knows everybody else. You'll come across resentment that we didn't take action sooner when Jonathan Tregenza went missing. If you're tackled about it your line must be that police reaction was in accordance with laid-down procedure, but it won't hurt to point out that work was put in hand on Jonathan's case before the body was found in the Helford. The reason for my doing that was partly due to the immense local regard for the man, but mainly because of his family situation, which you're all aware of.

'Now, you'll know that there's talk of the threat of a terrorist attack on Goonhilly.' Channon's gaze rested briefly on his sergeant, who was standing, eyes narrowed, directly beneath a huge and atmospheric poster of the satellite station. Trust Bowles – he'd got hold of that from some-

161

where and was standing guard on it like a mother hen with one spectacular chick.

'At this stage,' went on Channon, 'I want you to remember that such an attack is only a possibility. Nevertheless, the Anti-Terrorist Branch is watching all we do with close attention. You must not discuss Goonhilly with members of the public, even if you're asked a direct question. Give the standard response – "I can't comment because all aspects of the enquiry are in the hands of my superior officers." Now, hands up anybody who actually lives in this part of the Lizard, or who knows it well?'

Four hands went up, among them that of Honor Bennett, the young WPC who had led the way down to the body in the creek. Channon nodded and smiled at her. 'Honor here knows the Helford,' he said, 'and she's helped us already, but does anyone actually come from this village?' There was no response. 'A pity. Local knowledge is invaluable: beaches, gullies, rockfalls, mineshafts, tides, shipping, weather conditions, they can all have a bearing on our investigations. Any local knowledge that comes up from your questioning must be noted in reports, which must be clear and accurate. I can't have sloppy reporting. Inspector Meade will give you briefing sheets and sample questionnaires showing what will be of most use to us.

'Now, you four locals – the inspector will give you your areas. The rest of you will be in two main groups. First, house-by-house in Porthmenna itself. Every single dwelling must be visited and all members of each household must

162

give their whereabouts for the entire evening. People might not like this. Don't offend them. Use the old get-out – "to eliminate you from our enquiries".

'Your line must be that we have two suspicious deaths that might, only might at this stage, be connected. Ask the usual – did they see anyone they didn't know, anyone acting suspiciously or out of character; anyone they *did* know who was missing from their usual haunt or was somewhere unusual. I don't want you to press the foreigner angle, but if anything comes from them, get full details.

'The second group will be visiting outlying farms, smallholdings and isolated cottages. You may think that this part of the Lizard is pretty deserted, but that isn't the case. There are lots of tiny hamlets and dozens of remote houses. We aim to cover a swathe of land three miles deep from here to the Helford River, and to find out if anyone saw strangers that evening, especially in the vicinity of Trevant and the Helford. The inspector has the area mapped out and allocated in sections. Now, any questions?'

A dark-haired DC spoke up. 'Sir, what about statements?'

'Get your reports in first and we'll decide who must make a statement. If you consider one is urgent, come back in person, tell us about it and we'll take it from there.'

'Sir, somebody was asking why Mrs Tregenza hasn't been allocated a personal support officer.'

'Tell "somebody" not to worry. Mrs Tregenza has been offered one, but has declined. She's well

163

supported by Jonathan's aunt and by his brother, not to mention everyone in this village.'

DC Soker spoke up from his place at the back. 'What about folk going to sea, sir?'

Somebody sniggered and Soker coloured up. 'You said all members of every household must say where they were all evening. Suppose some of them were out in their boats?'

Channon eyed the youngster thoughtfully. This was a good lad who never raised a point that wasn't valid. 'What exactly are you getting at, Steve?'

Soker rubbed his shoulders against the wall behind him. 'I'm thinking that somebody who knows the coast, who owns a boat, could say that they were at sea that evening, or even all night, when in reality they could have put out, then come in again along the coast, beached their boat and gone inland on foot to attack either of the victims.'

Channon was always ready to give credit where it was due. 'An excellent point,' he said, 'well done! Everybody take note. All households with access to a seagoing craft to be listed. Anyone who was at sea that evening to say why and where and produce witnesses.

'Now, get your stuff from Inspector Meade and off you go. Reports in by six this evening. They'll have been examined by morning, so we'll all meet here at eight thirty tomorrow to have another chat, and good luck!'

Bowles had been paying close attention and was cudgelling his brains to come up with something that Channon had missed. Unable to think of anything, he listened to John Meade allocating areas of enquiry and looked forward to sharing in the grilling of the Dancers.

Arms full of children's clothes and toys, Frances hurried down the steps to her car. She wasn't sure if what she and Delphi were doing was right, but she was working on a principle that had served her well in the past: 'You can only do what you think is right at any particular time. If, in retrospect, it turns out to have been wrong, then too bad – at least you've tried, you've done your best.' How often had she comforted herself with that?

Now, after a tense discussion by Delphi's bed, she was in the midst of moving mother, baby and twins to live at Seaspray House for a while. Neither of them knew how much the police activity would register with the girls. At times they seemed almost babyish, cocooned in their twin-ship, sending and receiving their secret signals and talking their gibberish behind the sofa. At other times they were like six- or seven-year-olds, assessing and reasoning to an unnerving degree.

Propped against pillows and picking at her breakfast, Delphi had been tearful and heavy-eyed after a bad night. 'Frances,' she said desperately, 'I don't want the girls to find out that the police are looking for somebody who hurt their daddy. Sometimes they're so mature for their age, asking questions, coming up with the answers and homing in on the truth – especially Dorcas. I simply can't bear it if they find out that somebody killed him.'

God above, thought Frances, what have we done to deserve this? 'I know you can't bear it, my precious,' she said gently, 'neither can I.' She added silently, But they'll find out one day.

Then she said out loud, 'Look, as I see it we'll have to take it one day at a time with them, dealing with each problem as it arises, but trying to be consistent in what we tell them. Let's just get them away from all this lot outside, if only for a week.'

'They'll want to know the reason for moving to your place.'

'We'll make one up. Tell them there's something wrong with the boiler, or that workmen are coming in to take up the floor. They like it at Seaspray and they love playing on our beach.'

And so it was fixed, without even telling Terence. Delphi kept the girls occupied while Frances went in and out stacking the car. Then a quick drive across to deliver the load, a breathless explanation to Dave, and back again to pick up mother and children.

Once inside Seaspray and with their brother in his crib on the kitchen table, the girls clasped Dave around the thighs and then ran around the sitting room, which they preferred to that at home because it was bigger and closer to the sea.

Dave cleared out his room and shifted beds and furniture as Frances decreed. The big swap, he told himself as he prepared to go and spend his nights at Lookout Cottage. Leaving the sanctuary of his room was a small price to pay if it helped the girls. OK, they were still pretty weird, but the thought of them getting to know that

166

Jonny had been murdered was more than he could stomach – it had tormented him ever since Channon delivered the news.

He paused as he piled his pillows and duvet into the car. No, the thought of it hadn't merely tormented him, it had been a knife between his ribs. Yeah – emotion again, worse than anything in his entire life – except, of course, for *that*. But 'that' was sixteen years in the past; this was the present, and the present was a black, anguished hole too deep to climb out of.

Chapter Ten

Alan Dancer was tapping the table with his fingers and shifting his feet as he faced Channon and Bowles. 'My wife and I kept our morning free as you requested, chief inspector, but we didn't expect to be kept waiting once we'd been brought here.'

'No, I'm sorry about that,' said Channon mildly. 'It's amazing where the time goes when you're investigating two brutal murders.'

Dancer clamped his teeth together and eyed the DCI intently. Channon switched on the tape. This, he thought, was a man used to dishing out the irony, not being at the receiving end. Well, there was always a first time, wasn't there? But hey ... softly, softly...

'Now, Mr Dancer,' he began gently, 'your statements are being printed out and when we've had our little chat you and your wife will be asked to sign them.'

Bowles kept his head lowered. Not so much of the 'little chat', he seethed silently. Grill him like a pork chop until he's cooked to a frazzle. Bowles didn't like Dancer. The little bladder of lard had been stroppy as hell when he and Jolly took the statements; he'd been annoyed that he was separated from his wife and barely civil when asked to clarify anything, making it clear that he considered the combined intellect of a DC and

DS unequal to the task of recording his words. As for Nancy, she'd been polite but subdued, with never a hint of come-on, even though her husband was out of the room. She had recited the events of that evening with such precision she must have learned them off by heart.

'What I'm after, Mr Dancer,' Channon was saying, 'is background on your time in the Middle East, when Mr al-Makki was your student. I'd like to hear about his family situation and, in particular, everything you know about his recent whereabouts and activities.'

'I've told you what I know about that – next to nothing! I hadn't seen him for about ten years until that night. He asked for help. I gave it. End of story.'

Channon shook his head. 'I don't think so, Mr Dancer. You're an intelligent man with wide knowledge of Islam and the Middle East. Given the proximity of your house to a sensitive site and the fact that your Saudi Arabian visitor was probably murdered, you must have known we'd be asking questions and expecting answers. Even as I speak your friend's name and likeness are being checked by the Anti-Terrorist people in London.'

'That may be so,' said Dancer coolly. 'The fact remains that I did not invite him to Trevant.'

'You've made that very clear. So a man you hadn't seen for ten years turned up out of the blue, asked you for a loan, and you handed over six hundred pounds. Just like that?'

'Just like that,' agreed Dancer, eyes hard as pebbles.

'Even for someone comfortably off, such as

169

yourself, surely that was very generous?'

'Maybe it was. Saudi ideas on friendship and hospitality are different from ours.'

'That being the case, I would have thought you would offer him a bed for the night.'

'As a matter of fact, I did. He couldn't stay.'

'What a pity, it might have saved his life, mightn't it? But let me make this clear, Mr Dancer, you and your wife were the last people to see al-Makki alive and now he's dead, we believe murdered, so whether you like it or not you and your wife are suspects.'

But Dancer was having none of it. 'Don't threaten me, Channon,' he said between his teeth. 'I have connections in high places.'

Oh, back to the 1920s, thought Bowles, but Channon was unperturbed, smiling grimly. 'High places? You mean the mountains of Afghanistan? Mr Dancer, I'm doing an awful lot of spelling out and making clear, but I do assure you I have authority to ask you anything I choose, and if I'm not satisfied I'll hand you over to the experts on counter-terrorism. You were visited by a Saudi Arabian who had spent time in Afghanistan, who told you that an extremist group was trying to recruit him. He left your home and soon afterwards was murdered. Even you must see that you are in an unfortunate position, and so is your wife.'

'Leave her out of it.'

'But just as you were al-Makki's host, so your wife was his hostess. Why should I leave out anyone even remotely connected to murder and terrorism?'

Dancer folded his arms. Now, thought Channon, he'll ask for a lawyer. But he made no such demand. Was he confident that he could handle anything a Cornish DCI could throw at him? If so, a gentle frightener wouldn't come amiss. 'Perhaps I should remind you that the rights of the individual in police custody can be somewhat curtailed in matters pertaining to attempted terrorism.'

'Prove I'm attempting it, then. Prove I'm attempting anything, for that matter.'

'I don't have to. Reasonable suspicion is enough.'

'Reasonable? The whole country is paranoid about terrorism.'

Some might agree with him there, thought Channon, but not him – he had a job to do. 'Mr Dancer, things will be easier for you if you simply answer my questions to the best of your ability. If you gave money to this man and shared a meal with him, he must have revealed something of his life.'

Dancer sighed impatiently. 'It doesn't work like that,' he said, his tone reminiscent of a teacher with a dim pupil. 'The male Arab is proud and rather reticent. He wouldn't launch forth into his life history in the first moments of meeting me after many years, nor would he share a confidence until we were alone together. The presence of my wife would have put a stop to any serious talk for much of the time he was with us. But when she was out of the room seeing to a quick meal he did confide that he wanted to get back to the safety of his home and family. I suspect it wasn't easy for him to tell me that.'

'Do you recall anything about his family? They'll have to be informed of his death.'

'Ten or eleven years ago they were well established and well respected in Jeddah. I think Abdurrahman was the second son of several children. They lived in north Jeddah – the al-Andalus district. I'm not sure of the actual address – it might have been on the street Mahmud Nasif.'

'And in what subject was he your student?'

'IT – global communications, which at that time was in its infancy compared to now. He was good – an ideal student, that's why I remembered him at once.'

'When did he leave home?'

'I think about '98 or '99. I heard on the grapevine that he'd gone to Afghanistan and was in an area of deprivation worse than the norm.'

'Doing what?'

'I don't know. Humanitarian work, perhaps. As a student he had a strong social conscience.'

'Did he tell you why he was in the UK?'

'He said he was visiting, but to me he seemed semi-destitute. He didn't say where he was living or how he was supporting himself. I did wonder if he was tangled up with illegal immigrants.'

'What about the extremists who had tried to recruit him?'

'I think he was too scared to say much, though he wouldn't have admitted it. He never said who they were or where they were based, and frankly, I didn't want to know. I was sorry for him, but glad when he refused to stay the night. I didn't expect to hear from him again, though I wouldn't have been surprised to have my money returned at some future date. And that's all I can tell you.'

Channon didn't quibble. He closed the interview and switched off the tape. 'Thank you,' he said. 'That wasn't so very difficult, was it?'

'It wasn't difficult at all. I protested because I simply didn't see the point.'

'But I did, Mr Dancer, and I may have to ask more questions before I'm satisfied. One last word: don't leave Trevant for any length of time without informing us here at the incident room, just in case we need to get hold of you in a hurry. The constable will see you out and then I'll speak to your wife.'

They watched him stump from the room and Bowles said, 'Nancy-dancy next – she was subdued and non-nympho when we took her statement. She was also well primed.'

Sure enough Nancy was restrained and apparently calm, but the bright eyes blinked warily behind her glasses. 'I don't know what I can tell you that my husband can't have said more clearly, inspector. If you want to know about poor Mr al-Makki, he was very polite and grateful for the meal. I would have liked to offer him a hot bath and a change of clothes but of course that wouldn't have been proper.'

'Oh? Why not?'

'He could have taken it as a reflection on his personal cleanliness. One must respect the men of Saudi Arabia.'

'Mrs Dancer, did he give you any information about himself, or did you form any opinions about how he'd been living?'

Nancy dabbed her mouth with a lace handkerchief. 'He spoke mainly to my husband, but of course that's to be expected with his background.' She was twisting her thumbs together as she spoke, one scratching the skin of the other. Clearly, she wasn't as calm as she hoped to appear.

All at once Bowles broke in. 'Mrs Dancer, the chief inspector and I have both remarked on how you seem to be a woman of character and intelligence.' The flattery was blatant but Nancy didn't seem to notice. 'Did anything strike you about your visitor that you think might help us in our investigations?'

'He was nervous,' she said. 'He was uncomfortable to be needing help. He had walked some distance – his clothes were damp and very grubby, his shoes were filthy. He was hungry. He treated my husband with great respect.'

'Thank you,' said Channon. 'Did you notice if he was wearing a watch or any jewellery?'

'No jewellery and no watch.'

'You said he was hungry, Mrs Dancer. What did you think of his physical state? Did he seem badly nourished?'

'No. He was a trifle overweight, if anything, but that didn't stop him being – didn't make him look unhealthy. He was a fine figure of a man, well built, you know. He looked – I suppose you would say he looked tough.'

'Thank you, Mrs Dancer. I've asked your husband to let us know if either of you need to leave Trevant for longer than a couple of hours, just so we'll be able to contact you if we need you. The constable here will take you back to your husband.'

When she had gone Channon leaned back in his chair. 'Both wary,' he said, 'but I didn't get any vibes that they'd done him harm. Did you?'

'No. Dancer's a cocky little sod, though. Thinks he's too clever to need a brief.'

Channon smiled grimly. 'Nobody's too clever for that, but perhaps in his case he really doesn't need one. Let's get on. I want the Tregenzas' statements, and will you check with the family whether Jonathan had any dealings with Middle Eastern types? Then I want you to go and talk to the father-in-law – Pennant. See if you can find out more than he told you last time. Detailed statement from him, as well.'

'We'll have statements coming out of our ears,' warned Bowles.

'I know, but one or two of them might tell us something we didn't know. I have a load of admin to sanction with Inspector Meade now, so off you go. Report to me when you get back. I want to know what you think of Pennant and I might have something else lined up for you.'

'But about Dancer, sir, do you think he's connected to Tregenza as well as our friend from the river?'

'He was the last to see both of them alive, but apart from that I simply don't know – yet. On your way, sergeant. Take Yates or Soker with you.'

This was a place he loved, Dave told himself: Lizard Point, the most southerly tip of the British Isles. In front of him was one of the world's busiest shipping lanes, behind him the great

175

lighthouse that warned ships far out at sea to keep their distance from this wild and dangerous coast.

At that moment, though, everything was tranquil: the waves slapping lazily over the rocks, the sky without cloud, the steep grasses carpeted with spring flowers. This was Cornwall at its best, this was home.

Home. He'd come here to escape from home – from Seaspray House, needing to gather his wits and think his thoughts. He would never have believed how little time there was for thinking when you were looking after children. They invaded your space, your liberty, your mind. No doubt they would invade your heart as well, given the chance, but that wouldn't happen with him. He wouldn't allow it.

All morning he'd been in and out of Seaspray with the girls; actually, more out than in because the baby's crying was a pain, and out of doors they had their little beach all to themselves. He had built them a sandcastle and then watched as, heads together, they whispered over it. After a minute they had sidled up to him. 'Uncle Dave,' said Sophie, wrinkling her nose, 'we think that baby's boring.'

He would have laughed if things had been less grim, and wondered if they even knew what boring meant. Apparently they did. 'All he does is cry and have his nappy changed,' Dorcas told him gloomily.

'And have feeds,' added Sophie. 'We thought he'd play with us but he's not big enough, and anyway, he's always lying down.' She bashed a bucket with her spade, tipped out a wobbly sand pie and sighed gustily.

'Auntie Frances says he'll grow big,' Dorcas reminded her. 'She said we used to be babies, and we've grown big enough to play.'

'We'll have to love him even if he's boring,' said her twin with foreboding. 'Daddy said we must all love this baby.'

'Daddy was grown up,' Dorcas pointed out. 'He was a man.'

Once again they had come round to the subject of Jonny. 'Uncle Dave,' said Dorcas, reaching for his hand, 'does my baby keep crying because he hasn't got a daddy?'

What should he have said to that? He had sat down on the sand and cuddled them both on his lap. 'I think he cries because he's hungry,' he said. 'New babies are always hungry. They're like baby lambs and baby cows. They always want their mother's milk.'

They both thought about that, then their minds must have moved on and they'd asked how long it would be before their dinner was ready. The moment had passed and now, sitting beneath the lighthouse, he wondered how many more such moments there would be, how long it would be before they stopped asking questions. Would it be weeks? Would it be months?

And what about him? He would have to ring the gang in Hawaii very soon; he would have to ring Olly, his coach. What was he going to tell them? 'Sorry, lads, I won't be back for a while – my brother's been murdered and I want to know who did it, and why?' or 'I have to stay here for a while to help look after my nieces and nephew,' or what about a real shaker – 'I won't be coming back, ever. My family need me here.'

He simply couldn't look that far ahead. He tried to capture a mental image of the awesome Hawaiian surf, of the exhilarating sessions with Olly, of the sun-kissed little blonde he'd been seeing and the photographer who could sell pictures of him at the drop of a hat. It was very odd, but he couldn't seem to bring such images from his memory. Just as moisture clouds the lens of a camera, something was clouding the lens of his mind's eye.

And then his mobile rang. It was Frances. 'David, we forgot to tell the police that we wouldn't be at Lookout to give those statements. Sergeant Bowles has just rung me to say he wants them. Can you come back?'

'I'm on my way,' he said. So much for getting away, so much for thinking his thoughts, but maybe the sergeant had news. Hawaiian surf forgotten, the sun-kissed little blonde wiped from his mind, he found himself clambering over rocks and then racing up to the car park behind the lighthouse. Nothing, he thought, nothing mattered except making things right regarding his brother, and the only way he could do that was to help find out who had killed him, and to look after his family.

Bowles was on his mobile as soon as the door of Seaspray closed behind them. Once in the car he said to Yates, 'Right, I've put somebody on to checking Dave's flights from Hawaii. Now, let's head for Poldhu and Terence Pennant.'

They were silent for a while, both thinking of the Tregenzas: Yates with compassion, Bowles in analytical mode. 'I can't see any of them having a motive for murder,' he said, 'not even Mr Universe. He simply doesn't ring the bells.'

Yates made no reply. Bowles usually pulled rank when they were together, never giving a hint of what he was thinking; so he, Yates, wasn't going to be a sounding board just because he'd softened up and verbalized for once.

'What the aunt said at the door,' Bowles went on, '–you know, about whether Delphi and the kids are at risk if there's a killer about. I reckon I'll mention it to the DCI.'

Yates tried not to goggle. 'He'll already have thought of that, sarge. Not much gets past him.'

'Maybe not, but I'll talk to him. Now, this Pennant guy – we have to suss him out some more and take a statement.'

'Anything you say,' agreed Yates, wondering if he was imagining that the dynamic and hard-boiled Bowles was losing his edge.

Once at the gallery the sergeant's opening words dispelled that idea. 'Mr Pennant, I believe you know that your son-in-law was murdered. We're here on the orders of Detective Chief Inspector Channon to check your movements the night he went missing.'

'Don't phrase it gently to spare my feelings,' said Pennant with sarcasm. 'You'd better come in, I suppose, and I'll close the gallery for ten minutes.'

'We'll need at least that, sir,' agreed Bowles,

179

strictly polite but exuding aggression. Yates swallowed a sigh. It was to be intimidation, then? To what end? The man's daughter had lost her husband, for crying out loud; his grandchildren their father.

Still abrupt, Bowles said, 'We want to know the date and time you last saw your son-in-law, sir.'

Pennant spoke with careful patience. 'I'd seen him only the day before he went missing. Delphi invited me to Sunday tea. We shared a meal – the three of us and the children.'

'Was that a usual occurrence, sir?'

Pennant hesitated. 'Not really. I find the children a bit wearing. All that chatter and I can never tell which of them is which. It doesn't matter to me but they set such store by it. Delphi knows how I feel. I call round there now and again and I have a meal with them every couple of months or so.'

'I see. Would you say you were on good terms with Jonathan?'

Pennant observed him with thinly veiled amusement. 'We were civil to each other, but not exactly bosom pals. I didn't dislike him enough to kill him.'

'I'm glad to hear it,' said Bowles tightly. Another cocky devil, he thought. They were thick on the ground in these parts. 'So you did dislike him to a certain extent? Why was that, sir?'

'We'd had our differences in the past. He didn't approve of the way I'd raised my daughter.'

'I see. Presumably he approved of the end result, as he married her?'

'Oh yes, he approved. He was head over heels,

180

was Jonathan – apparently.'

'Apparently? Did you have doubts?'

'Doubts but no evidence,' said Pennant, his lips thinning. 'Jonathan was a handsome young fellow. I know from experience that good looks bring on the women.'

Not any more in your case, thought Bowles, have you looked in a mirror lately? 'So do you know of any females in the area who might have an eye for a good-looking man, Mr Pennant?'

'I've no doubt you've come across one already. We've got our own local man-eater on this side of the Lizard.'

'And who might that be?'

'Mrs Nancy Dancer. She's only been here four or five months but it's common talk she's up for it.'

Yates was squirming, unsure whether this line of talk was allowed, then telling himself that in a murder enquiry anything goes.

'I'll bear that in mind, sir. Now, did you notice anything unusual about Jonathan over tea that Sunday?'

'No, nothing at all. He was the doting papa, as usual, and he tried to be civil to me. I left before the children went to bed.'

'Did he mention where he would be going the next evening?'

'No, I don't think so.'

'And so how did you spend that Sunday evening?'

'I worked on a painting for a while and then watched television. At about eight thirty I walked to the pub along the road here and stayed until

181

closing time. I told you all that on your last visit, sergeant.'

'Just checking,' said Bowles blandly. 'We'll need the names of the other customers in the pub when we take your statement in a minute. Tell me, Mr Pennant, how long is it since you lost your wife?'

'Two years ago. She had cancer.'

'I'm sorry to hear that, sir.'

Pennant merely shrugged and Yates eyed him closely. There was something repellent about the man – not just the sagging, drinker's face but the dismissive tone when he spoke of both his dead wife and his dead son-in-law. That said, he was no fool. He'd expected this visit and openly admitted to not liking Jonathan, so he knew he was in the clear with a watertight alibi.

'One last question,' Bowles was saying, 'do you know whether your son-in-law had any contacts with foreigners?'

'You mean visitors? Tourists?'

'Anyone at all, but in particular someone from the Middle East – the Muslim community?'

Pennant rolled his eyes. 'We're on the terrorist bandwagon, are we? Any fool could link Jonathan's death to Goonhilly, sergeant. It's the talk of the Lizard. No, I do not know of Jonathan being linked to any Middle Eastern type. Bin Laden didn't join us for tea at Lookout Cottage.'

Bowles's pale eyes were hard as glass. He'd pin this one down if it was the last thing he did. He signalled to Yates and watched as he switched on the laptop. 'Now, sir, let's get it all down,' he said politely.

Chapter Eleven

'Jonathan!' said Delphi. 'That's his name – Jonathan David Tregenza. What else could it be? I don't know why I've taken two whole days to make up my mind.'

Frances smiled, which in itself was unusual. Her facial muscles felt stiff and unused, as if it were years since they'd stretched to a smile. 'It's a lovely name,' she said gently. 'The only one you could have chosen.'

They were sitting out in the sun, watching the children having a dolls' tea-party, with the baby in view through the open window, for once fast asleep in his crib. Frances thought if it hadn't been for Delphi's white, young-old face, they could have been any normal mother and her aunt enjoying a quiet afternoon, rather than two fraught women in the middle of a nightmare.

It was so lovely to have this spell of what seemed like ordinary life. She must take hold of it, cherish it, make it last ... but it didn't. The sound of a car on the drive and the slam of its door put an end to normality. She jumped up and rushed round the side of the house to be faced by Channon, arriving alone. 'Oh, it's you!' she said in relief. 'I thought – that is – I wasn't sure who it might be. Do you want to see Delphi?'

'Yes, but first, a quick word. My sergeant tells me that you're concerned about the safety of

Delphi and the children?'

'I can't help it. That's why I was worried when I heard somebody arrive.'

'It's understandable. I just want you to know that ever since I got the results of the post-mortem I've had somebody keeping guard – unobtrusively, as I didn't want to alarm the children. For as long as it's necessary you and your family will be protected.'

Frances felt her knees go slack. This was what people meant when they talked of going weak at the knees, she thought in confusion. In her case they were weak with relief. 'I should have known you'd do something,' she said, 'but I was frightened for them.'

'Don't be,' he said. 'You may not see a uniformed policeman but somebody will be there, watching over you. I doubt it's necessary, but we'll take no chances. 'Now, I'll just have a word with Delphi.'

Like Frances he was struck by the peaceful normality of the garden, and watched in fascination as the identical little girls poured tea from a plastic teapot. It was the first time he had seen them, and in that instant he asked himself whether anyone who knew them could possibly have killed their father. Experience gave the answer to that one. Human nature was what it was – it could rise to the heights or sink to uncharted depths.

Frances told him which twin was which, and said to them, 'This is Mr Channon, a friend of ours.'

He got the message. For the time being at least, they were being sheltered from the knowledge that police were involved with the family. Delphi said quietly, 'We're trying to keep it from them that somebody hurt Jonny.'

But the twins were all set to welcome this dark and serious friend. Even Delphi didn't know if they turned on their charm deliberately. Eyeing him over their shoulders they ran back to their table, then with a beguiling smile Dorcas brought him a fairy cake on a plastic plate, while Sophie poured cold tea into a little cup, added milk and carried it carefully across the grass to him. 'Will you stay to tea, Channon?' she asked.

Dorcas nudged her and whispered loudly, 'Say Mister! You have to say Mister.'

And so DCI Channon sat in the garden of Seaspray House, eating one of Frances's fairy cakes and drinking cold tea from a very small cup. 'How's your baby?' he asked the girls.

Dorcas twisted one foot around the other and shook her head. 'He's sad 'cos he hasn't got a daddy.'

Sophie started to shake her head as well. 'It's because he's hungry,' she explained carefully. 'He's like a lamb or a baby cow.'

'Is that so?' Channon was bemused. He finished his tea and stood up. 'Thank you, that was delicious,' he said heartily, 'but now I have to go.' To Delphi he said, 'May I see your son?'

The girls beamed at him and ran back to their teacups. Delphi led him indoors and they stood beside the crib. 'He's a fine boy,' said Channon awkwardly.

'We're calling him Jonathan,' she told him. 'Jonathan David.'

185

He nodded, and gave her his rare smile. 'That's good,' he said. 'It's right. Delphi, I just want to say that we're doing everything in our power to find out what happened to Jonny. Will you bear with us if we have to ask you questions that you may not want to answer?'

She looked down at the crib. 'Ask anything you like,' she said.

'Just one small point for now. Did he ever mention that Mrs Dancer was interested in him – that she – er – flirted with him?'

Delphi said drily, 'She *is* old enough to be his mother, inspector. As a matter of fact, he thought she was a bit weird. He said she was an old saddo who would give the come-on to anything in trousers.'

'To him in particular?'

'No, I don't think in particular, but she tried it with him. He told me the only way he could deal with it was to pretend it wasn't happening. I think he was sorry for her husband.'

'Thanks,' said Channon, 'that's all I want to know. Oh, one more thing. Reports of Jonathan's death will be on regional news – probably this evening. I think only a mention at this stage. There might be something in the press as well, though I doubt it will reach the nationals.'

Delphi thought about that. 'And the other one? The man in the river?'

'At this stage he'll just be reported as an un-identified drowning. If there's to be anything more detailed about Jonathan either my sergeant or I will let you know. I'll be off now, and remember, we're doing our best.'

By six that evening the incident room was calmer, though Channon himself was in the tense, ultra-alert state that was usual with him as an enquiry got under way. Earlier that day he had detailed Bowles and Yates to interview three key locals and now, knowing that the sergeant was busy with SOCOs and Forensic, he had sent for Yates. 'I want a word,' he told the younger man. 'I know your report's in hand, but I could do with knowing right now if you and Sergeant Bowles got anything of interest from Ludcott and the Sandrys. I want your feeling on them.'

Yates shifted his feet uneasily. 'Sir, the sarge might want to tell you himself. Old Ludcott – well – he was a bit awkward.'

'Relax,' said Channon. 'I'll talk to the sergeant later. Just tell me your impressions.'

Yates swallowed. 'Well, Ludcott's an independent old fella. He challenged us at once about not taking action earlier when Jonathan went missing. As for what we asked him, he says he worked for Jonathan a couple of days a week doing plain carpentry He knows all the customers and says Dave has already contacted them. It's clear Ludcott thought a lot of Jonathan and of Dave, though he admits to being angry when he left home seven years back. He said the brothers were very close in their younger days and that he became a sort of grandad to them when their parents died. He says he'll do anything that's needed to help us. As for the Dancers, he's done quite a bit for them up at Trevant. He says Dancer wants good work and is prepared to pay for it.'

'Did he mention Mrs Dancer?'

'Yes. He was disapproving – says she's always after the men and she should be ashamed of herself. He didn't say much about the husband's reactions to the way she is, but I got the impression he thinks Dancer should make her behave herself.'

'Does Ludcott own a boat?'

'Yes, we've got details of it. He says if it was a car it would be called an old banger, but it's seaworthy, and he *was* out in it that Monday evening. He knows the waters round here. He keeps complicated charts that he updates and adjusts from time to time, locating all the ships wrecked around the Lizard. He sails in and out of the danger spots. It's his hobby.'

'Is it indeed? What's his place like?'

'Clean, tidy, quite cosy but pretty basic – much as you'd expect for an old sailor.'

'And the man himself? How did he strike you?'

'Straight as they come, but a bit wary – you know what people are like when we call on them.'

Channon knew. The most open and innocent citizen could become cautious and uptight under the mildest questioning. Even the cleverest of them rarely behaved normally. 'You've said he was awkward, though. Why was that?'

Yates chewed his lips. The truth was that Bowles had bullied the old fella, been a bit sarky, and Ludcott hadn't liked it. 'I reckon he wasn't keen on being questioned,' he said diplomatically.

Channon nodded. Bowles doing the metal rasp rather than the fine sandpaper again. Would he

188

never learn? 'And what about Howard Sandry and the son – Reuben, is it?'

'You remember we've already spoken to the father, sir? This time we had them both, and for longer. Howard is making a list for us of all those in Porthmenna and district who own a seagoing craft. He knows all the locals who use the harbour and takes details of any visiting vessels. They have two boats themselves, but he himself wasn't out that evening. Reuben was, though, giving the small boat a trial run after doing some work on the engine. They both say it was for about an hour between eight and nine.'

'So what about Reuben? What did you make of him?'

'Quiet, almost surly. A big fella, well set-up and sort of weather-beaten. His dad calls him "the lad", but he must be well turned thirty. He answered our questions openly enough, but he was a bit wary. They both seem cut up about Jonathan.'

'Do they live on their own?'

'Yes. It's an old house – that one right on the harbour with a yellow door. Pretty comfortable inside, but not luxurious. They do a bit of fishing but most of their income is from running pleasure trips in the bigger boat.'

'So how do you see them both?'

'Reuben's a bit withdrawn, but he didn't seem uneasy. He's no dumbo – his vocabulary says he's intelligent. The father's more of a charmer – a confident type, but I'd say honest as the day and also a bit of a softie. He said he wasn't happy that some of our men had been laughing and joking

189

in public view when they had a break and a smoke on the jetty. He said the locals are so upset about Jonathan they wouldn't have liked to see us taking it lightly and would we mention it to our superior officers.'

Channon thought about that. 'He has a point there. I'll speak to the men. Thanks, Yates, I'm glad to get your impressions. Look, you can come to me direct, you know, if anything strikes you at any time. Don't feel it would be disloyal to Bowles. You both have your strengths and weaknesses and different ways of seeing things.'

As Yates went off the phone rang. It was Bowles, clearly on a high. 'Sir – things have been moving with the SOCOs. There were traces of wheel tracks at the top of Proudy, and after a search they found an old hand cart at the edge of a field about a quarter of a mile away. It had been used at one time for animal feed – hay and so forth – but it was a wreck and overgrown with weeds and stuff. Closer examination showed that the wheels had been oiled and it had been moved, then returned to its original position. Some care had been taken to cover it again with the original vegetation.'

Channon was hunched over the phone. 'And the wheel tracks?'

'Preliminary match to those on Proudy, but that's to be confirmed.'

Channon felt, and welcomed, the stirrings of his instincts. This could mean that one person only could have dealt with Jonathan – but a person who knew those fields or at the very least had searched them and found the cart. 'I'll go up there in the morning to have a look at things for

190

myself. In the meantime tell the SOCOs well done from me, and keep Forensic on their toes. They'll know what to do next: full examination of the cart, forensic match of the wheels to the tracks, etc.'

'They're pessimistic on footprints,' Bowles warned him, 'what with the rain and the length of time that passed, but it's a sure bet the wheel tracks will meet up with the path Jonathan took going home from Trevant.'

'Is there any such thing as a sure bet, Bowles?'

'There is when you win,' was the reply.

When Dave arrived at Seaspray the girls were pink-cheeked and sleepy after their baths. As usual they clasped his thighs then demanded that he carry them up to bed both at once. 'Daddy can do it,' Dorcas informed him. 'Daddy's strong.'

'So am I,' said Dave, picking one of them up on each arm and heading for the stairs. Five days ago he would have laughed in disbelief if anybody had told him he would enjoy doing any such thing. But now, well, it was – it was OK. They were still a bit weird, of course; they still took up your thinking time when you were with them, but they sort of got to you.

The ritual of reading the story over and Jonny's photograph kissed, he came downstairs and Delphi went to tuck them up for the night. For a moment he was alone with Frances. 'Did they say much about Jonny?' she asked.

'Sophie said she'd rather kiss her real daddy than his picture,' he told her, 'but Dorcas said they couldn't do that because he had to go in a box like their rabbit.'

Frances looked bleak. 'We'll have to give them time to adjust.'

Dave wriggled his shoulders. 'I've been thinking, Frances. There's a lot of mail round at Lookout.'

'I suppose there is. What about it?'

'It's mostly cards and letters of sympathy.'

'That's not surprising, surely. Everybody for miles around knew Jonny. We'll look at them tomorrow.'

'The postman brought them in a sack. He said he and his wife send their love. Frances, you might think this mad, but would it be an idea to bring the cards round here and put them all up so the girls can see them?'

She stared at him. 'Of course! It's a brilliant idea. They love cards at birthdays and Christmas. I think they'd like to see that lots and lots of people loved him. It might help them to accept that – that he's gone. We'll see what Delphi says.'

The three of them sat down to a home-cooked meal sent over by Bozena's mother and Frances put the suggestion to Delphi.

She thought about it and said quietly. 'We'll do it. It might make them feel that their daddy dying is special rather than horrible – it might help them. They'll see how many people are thinking of him – and of us.'

And so it was arranged that Dave would bring all the mail across as soon as they finished eating.

Channon left his office and headed for Lookout Cottage by way of the beach, partly as a short cut, partly for the sheer pleasure of walking the firm, damp sand. The case wasn't making much progress, he thought grimly. Already it was fifty-five hours since Jonathan's body was found and much longer since finding al-Makki, so things needed speeding up. He wasn't sure if he'd find Dave Tregenza at the house, but it was worth walking a couple of hundred yards to arrive unannounced. If people knew you were coming they prepared themselves; innocent or not they put up a protective smokescreen. He wanted to talk to Dave without any kind of screen and he hoped he would find him in.

He was in but on his way out, with a postal sack over his shoulder and about to close the door behind him. His eyes widened when he was faced by the DCI. 'I'm afraid the family have gone to live at Seaspray,' he said.

'I know. I was over there this afternoon. I just want a word with you on your own. Can you spare a minute or two?'

'I was just going back over there with this load of mail,' said Dave, 'but come in.' He led the way to the sitting room, where he stood with his back to the amazing view. 'How can I help you?' he asked.

Channon observed him carefully. This was a spectacular young man, though that didn't necessarily make him an innocent one. The instinct that was almost infallible was screaming at him that Dave Tregenza was being eaten up by guilt. He could let that lie for now, though. 'Dave,' he said, 'I'd like to go deeper into the matter of your premonition about Jonny.'

'Oh,' said Dave flatly. Thank the Lord they were alone. He wouldn't have wanted to talk about it with that abrasive sergeant present, nor in front of Delphi for that matter.

'You see,' went on Channon, 'it would help our enquiries to have an exact time for the attack on your brother. We're pretty sure there was an interval between the first attack and – and what happened later.'

Dave tried to swallow to relieve the tightness in his throat, but all he could manage was a strangled gulp. His mind was crowded with visions of some-body creeping up on Jonny, hitting him, dragging him along like an animal carcass...

'I'm sorry,' said Channon, 'I know this is awful. Can you tell me whether you think you got the first warning when he was actually attacked or – or later?' Faced with those sad, dazzling eyes, he simply couldn't say, 'or when he was killed'.

Dave sat down and waved at Channon to do the same. 'It was the first time it had happened for years,' he said quietly, 'but I've thought about it a lot. I don't know for certain but I have the feeling that I got the warning when he was first attacked. He was knocked unconscious, wasn't he? Was he struck more than once?'

'Yes,' said Channon.

'Do you think he felt the subsequent blows?'

'We don't know.'

'I think I knew then – when he was first hit. I didn't analyse it at the time. I was sort of galvan-ized, you see, by instinct. I just made excuses to my friends and went off to ring the airline.'

'Do you know what time that was?'

194

'I've tried to remember exactly. I think it was between ten thirty and ten forty in the morning.'

'That fits. Jonny left the Dancers at about nine thirty that evening. Hawaiian time is eleven hours behind the UK, so he could have been attacked within minutes of leaving Trevant.'

Dave sat hunched forward with his hands clenched. 'So you believe it? About me knowing something was wrong?'

'I believe it,' said Channon. This was the root of Dave's guilt, he told himself – that he was at the other side of the world when it happened. 'You took action, you came back,' he pointed out. 'Try not to feel guilty.'

Dave looked at him. So much for trying to crush the old enemy, emotion. 'I don't feel guilty about coming back too late,' he told the older man. 'I feel guilty that I went away in the first place.'

This was remorse, genuine remorse, thought Channon. 'You were still in your teens,' he said, 'still a boy. We all do things that we later regret.'

To his astonishment Dave found that it didn't feel odd to be unburdening himself to this grave-eyed policeman. 'I was in love with Delphi,' he admitted. 'I was mad about her. People think I left because I couldn't bear to see her marry my brother, but that was only part of it. Jonny was my big brother and I – uh – I was very fond of him. I thought that if I stayed I'd lose him – that when I saw him married to Delphi I'd start to hate him. I had this mad idea that by going away I was saving what was between us. And then, the awful thing was, I tried to wipe him from my

195

mind. It hurt, you see, leaving him, and it was easier to try and forget him.'

'And did you?'

'No.'

There was such an emptiness in that one word, such desolation, that Channon knew with certainty that this young man had never wished harm on his brother, never conspired in his murder. He asked himself if he was seeing something very rare: a man with a broken heart. He searched his mind for words of comfort, but all he could find was a single sentence. 'Perhaps Jonny understood you better than you think.'

Dave made no reply. The empty blue eyes were fixed on a photograph on the mantelpiece – a photograph of Jonny and Delphi on their wedding day.

It was Thursday morning. The room by the harbour was packed and noisy, but when Channon walked in all became quiet. 'Well done yesterday, everybody!' he said. 'Your stuff is recorded and it's being analysed right now. Soon we'll have a clearer picture of what was going on that evening, but for now just one or two questions. First, about the woman who knew Delphi Tregenza's mother when she lived here. Which of you dealt with her?'

A constable spoke up. 'Me, sir.'

'Did she specify the violence that Pennant inflicted on his wife? There's nothing on record.'

'No, sir, I don't think it was ever reported. The witness just said she knew Pennant knocked his wife about when he'd had a few. The wife had a temper and threw things around, whereas he liked the drink, so I think the witness saw it as tit for tat stuff.'

'Right. I might ask for more on that. Now, I wanted special attention given to the three people who have their fingers on the pulse of Porthmenna: the landlord of the Fisherman's Rest, Mrs Bannon at the shop and the minister at the Methodist chapel. The landlord, Donald Tull, said there were a couple of strangers in the pub that evening.'

Steve Soker raised a hand. 'He said it wouldn't have registered later in the season when they're always busy, but it was noted that night because they were so quiet. The men left about nine after putting away a fair amount.'

Channon nodded. 'You got good descriptions so we'll work on it, and we're double-checking on a couple of regulars who were missing from their usual seats. I specified you, Blamey, and Mary Donald for the shop, didn't I? Your report is the longest of all but I can't fault it – it's all relevant. I'll see you two and those who did the pub and the minister in a few minutes.

'For now, I want to remind you all of what I said yesterday. This is a close community. People here know things they don't even know they know. We must deal gently with them – respect them. And that reminds me – I'm aware that you all need a break now and again from stress and hard work – a smoke or a bit of a laugh together. *Do not* laugh and joke in public view! It will offend those who knew and loved Jonathan. Now, a few questions for those who visited outlying dwellings...'

And so it went on, with both uniformed and plain-clothed men and women speaking out, contradicting each other and making comments. Bowles thought of it as undisciplined chaos, Channon as pure gold.

Later, in his office with the sergeant and John Meade, he went through a preliminary print-out of information. 'Bowles, you'll work with the inspector and the computer boys on weeding out and eliminating. At this moment the computers are idle. That's one thing to be said for a rural patch – the sheer volume of stuff that comes with a metropolitan crime simply isn't there.'

Bowles kept quiet. Volume or not, they were getting bogged down with what all these mackerel-chasers were doing and saying. What about the big boys who masterminded the suicide bombers? What about al-Makki? What about security at Goonhilly?

'You found the Sandry son a bit surly and withdrawn, didn't you?' Channon was asking him. 'A snippet's come through that in his teens Reuben was badly affected by the death of his mother. He had some sort of breakdown and it's left him a bit odd. He can't hold down a job and that's why he works with his dad on casual stuff like their pleasure trips.'

Bowles dredged up a show of interest. He didn't share Channon's belief in the importance of family ties. After all, his own had been non-existent and he'd survived. But all at once old Meade was grunting and leafing through his print-outs.

'Reuben Sandry?' he asked. 'I have a cross-reference for him here. He's listed as a boat-owner, a source of info about users of the harbour, and also because a witness – an old man from near Cury – made a sour remark about Nancy Dancer making a play for him. For Reuben, that is, not the old fella. He saw them in a remote spot, just talking as if they'd met by accident, but the old fella suspected more because of the talk about her.'

Bloody hell, thought Bowles, news of even a fifty-plus nympho got around. Evidently there was more to 'the lad' than met the eye. Though if the eye in question belonged to Nancy, Reuben might attract. He was male, he wasn't repulsive, he was a robust specimen...

'Bowles, get more on that,' ordered Channon, then he turned to John Meade, his mouth twisting in distaste. 'I hope I don't have to talk to the husband about it.'

Meade turned up his palms in sympathy, but Bowles felt like saying that he himself would be more than willing to tackle Dancer. It would be pure pleasure to make the cocky little brainbox admit that he couldn't satisfy his wife.

When Channon's phone rang the DCI answered it in irritation. He'd given orders that he wasn't to be contacted unless the matter was urgent, but the earnest young operator was well aware of that. 'Sir,' she said, 'there's an Alan Dancer on the line. He's in a state, sir. He says his wife is dead. He says she's been murdered.'

Chapter Twelve

With Bowles at the wheel they were soon at Trevant, leaving the car at the gate and approaching the house on foot. All was still, all was silent apart from the far-off sound of more police cars coming up from Porthmenna. Bowles rang the bell while Channon observed their surroundings. Another lovely setting for another ugly crime, he thought, but please God don't let us have a serial killer on our hands – preserve us from that.

The door was opened by Alan Dancer, red-eyed and blotchy, his hair standing on end. 'I haven't touched her,' he said tonelessly. 'I just – saw her. Then I rang you – no, no I didn't – I dialled 999 and they transferred me.'

'We got the message right away,' Channon assured him. 'Mr Dancer, may we see your wife?'

Dancer didn't ask them in; instead he pushed past them and headed for the side of the house, where a door in a tall granite wall was open to a yard. There he stopped and pointed, finger and arm outstretched.

Next to him Channon stood immobile, only his eyes moving, while Bowles stared at the two shiny new wheelie bins. Aw, no, he thought, suddenly queasy; Nancy-dancy couldn't be in one of those...

Already Channon was clicking his fingers for a protective suit, and for once Bowles could see the

200

point of such a covering. This yard, this bin would be littered with clues, with traces, with evidence. Nothing must be allowed to contaminate what was ready and waiting to be gathered.

Footsteps behind them announced the arrival of more officers: Yates, Soker and Mary Donald, followed by the lugubrious Jolly. 'Mr Dancer,' said Channon firmly, 'would you go back indoors with my men? Leave this to us and we'll be with you in a minute.'

Without his confident ebullience Dancer seemed to have shrunk. Looking shorter than ever between the two DCs he allowed himself to be led to the door of his house, but Channon followed and took Yates to one side. 'Keep him in your line of vision at all times,' he said quietly. 'Don't let him do anything or go anywhere without telling me first.'

Yates blinked. 'Can't I even give him a cuppa, sir?'

'Yes, yes, but make it yourself or let Soker do it. Don't ask him any questions, and make a note of anything he says to you.'

Yates went off and the DCI looked at Jolly. 'Where are the uniforms?'

'Right behind us, sir, and so are the SOCOs. They'll be here in a minute and so will the doc.'

'Mary, go and wait for them at the gates. The usual drill with the cordon, but tell them I say it's to be outside the gates, and make them leave their cars out there, as well.' Then he turned to Bowles and said, 'Right.'

The first wheelie bin was full of neatly tied bags of household rubbish. Channon lowered the lid and said over his shoulder to Jolly, 'These to be saved for examination.' With a plastic-covered foot he touched a stack of similar bags on the floor. 'And these.'

The second bin was different. Doubled up inside it was the body of Nancy Dancer, her bare legs and feet tucked to one side of the bloodied mess that had been her face. One open eye was visible, its bright amber colour clashing with the purple bruising and the red-brown of congealed blood. Something black and silky was covering her hair, slanting jauntily across what was left of her forehead. Frowning, Channon touched whatever it was with a gloved finger.

'A pair of knickers, sir,' muttered Bowles.

A gesture, Channon told himself grimly, a gesture deriding her obsession. His eyes met those of Bowles and each knew what the other was thinking. 'We don't know whether she was touched in *that* way,' said Channon. 'Hunter's the one to tell us that.'

A smell of blood and urine rose from the bin, but he continued to stare into it. The upper torso was clothed in what appeared to be daywear, but the whole body was surrounded by stones – smooth stones in assorted sizes, similar to pebbles on a beach. Some of them were dark with blood; a large one, sticky with it, was wedged next to the head. Well, well, well.

He closed the lid. 'Jolly, stand guard over this bin and this body until the others get here. Don't let the duty doctor go off without me seeing him. We'll be indoors talking to Mr Dancer.'

They found him in the little room called the

snug. Yates was with him. Soker, presumably, was making the tea. 'I'm very, very sorry about what's happened, Mr Dancer,' began Channon. 'I regret I have no option but to ask you some questions.'

Dancer looked at him but made no reply.

'When did you last see your wife alive?'

'Last night at about ten thirty. We'd had a wearing day so I locked up and went to bed – we have separate rooms because my wife is – was a light sleeper. She was watching television and said she'd follow me in a while.'

'Did you hear her come up to bed?'

'No.'

'And this morning?'

'I thought she was sleeping late like she sometimes does. I had breakfast, watched the news on TV and came in here to go through my notes on what I had planned for the day I saw my reminder that it was dustbin day, so I went to the yard to put them out ready for collection.

'I tried to wheel the first one but it was too heavy to shift, even though I knew it hadn't been full. Then I saw that its contents had been tipped on the floor. I – I lifted the lid. I think I lost control. Then Ludcott appeared. I grabbed him by the collar and bundled him into the old laundry. Then I locked him in.'

'You locked Mr Ludcott up? Why did you do that?'

'I thought he'd done it.'

'And where is he now?'

'Still in there, I suppose – it's opposite the bins.' He felt in his pocket. 'Here's the key.'

Channon jerked his head at Bowles. 'Go and

get him. Make a note of what he says. Bring him indoors – keep him in the hall. As soon as the others arrive leave him with somebody and come back here.'

Bowles went off, his mind racing. The little bladder of lard might be distraught – but he might not. He might look awful, but anyone could inflame their own eyes and make their hair stand on end. OK, he'd stammered and stuttered a bit at first, but he was pretty lucid now for a man who'd discovered his wife's corpse less than half an hour ago.

He unlocked the door of the low stone building and found Ludcott sitting on an ancient wicker chest. 'The arrival of the cavalry,' said the old man heavily. 'I heard you all talking, so I didn't interrupt. I knew I could get out when I wanted to.'

Bowles wasn't going to bandy words with a senile old twit. 'Follow me,' he said briskly. 'We're to wait in the house until the DCI can talk to you.'

Minutes later, he went back to the snug, to find Channon still deep in talk with Dancer. 'We have to move fast,' the DCI was explaining. 'The first day, the first hours after a murder are crucial, so we can't let the fact that your main hall is under repair prevent our scene-of-crime officers doing their job. They'll need time.'

'Workmen from Truro are due to arrive at mid-day,' protested Dancer. 'Specialist woodworkers who have replaced Tregenza. This is a listed building.'

'Give my men their details and they'll cancel

them,' said Channon calmly. 'All work on this building – listed though it may be – stops as from now. The house and grounds will be sealed and examined minutely.'

Dancer's previous hostility was surfacing. 'Why the house? It happened outside, inspector. Or do you think I killed my wife indoors, then put her out with the rubbish?'

'I don't think anything without cause, Mr Dancer. At this stage I must follow laid-down procedure for a violent crime. I appreciate your distress, but I have no option but to remove you from these premises.'

Dancer's eyes swivelled from Channon to Bowles. 'For what?'

'To let the SOCOs do their job, but also for forensic technicians to examine your person; for your clothes to be removed under supervision and for you to help us with our enquiries in an official recorded interview.'

Yates and Soker exchanged looks. Yates saw this as brutal and far too quick; Soker, younger and a fervent admirer of Channon, was in full agreement. Bowles was simply wondering how soon he himself would have the chance to get a word in.

Dancer's red-rimmed eyes stared challengingly into Channon's. 'Are you saying that my wife's murder is part and parcel of the al-Makki affair – al-Makki and Tregenza?'

'I'll be surprised if it isn't,' said Channon. 'I'm sorry about this, but take a complete change of clothing with you. My men will ensure that you do not wash, or take a bath or shower.'

'But I've showered already.'

205

'Maybe so, but at this stage we at least do not know the time of Mrs Dancer's death. It may be very recent.'

'You can only see as far as the end of your nose, can't you? My wife is battered to death by a maniac – a triple murderer – and you plump for me – *me!*'

'Yes, I do, as a preliminary to further enquiries. We have three suspicious deaths in a row. You are closely connected to all of them. In fact, we believe that you are the last person to see each of them alive. I ask you now, will you come with us voluntarily to answer questions and help us with our enquiries?'

'No, I will not.'

'Then I'm afraid I'll have to insist.'

Dancer stared at him incredulously. 'You'll arrest me?'

'Yes.'

Dancer's skin was now more blotchy than ever. 'Very well, then. I agree. Where do I go afterwards if I'm not allowed back here?'

'Do you have family or friends nearby?'

'No.'

'In that case we'll discuss it further. We can put you in a house or hotel of our choice.'

'I don't believe this,' Dancer muttered thickly.

'You will, Mr Dancer, you will. Now, please go with my men to select a change of clothes. They'll pack them for you and then take you to Porthmenna. I'll see you there.'

'I want my solicitor present.'

'That is your right. The inspector in charge of our incident room will arrange it.'

When the three of them had gone upstairs, Channon sighed. 'I'll have Headquarters on my back now we've got a third one. What do you make of Dancer?'

'He's pretty cool, considering. He's clever, but if he's all that clever, why kill her on his own doorstep?'

'Perhaps he'd had enough of her going after the men and he just snapped.'

'That would explain the knickers,' agreed Bowles. 'I thought it a bit weird the way he went on about the work on the house when Nancy's been bashed to a pulp.'

'I haven't got his measure yet,' admitted Channon. 'We'll let him stew for a while before we tackle him.'

'Sir – you'll have to grill him about Nancy being a nympho.'

Channon gave him a look. 'I am aware of that, Bowles, but thanks for the reminder. As to how long she's been dead ... she was wearing day clothes, wasn't she, so it could have been hours ago, probably last night. As for Dancer, he might have showered and changed and scrubbed his nails, but we'll still have to do checks on him. Anything else strike you in the bin?'

'The stones, you mean?'

'I do mean. I think she was stoned to death, Bowles – either that or we're meant to think she was.'

Bowles swallowed. This was sick, he thought, really sick. It was alien, it was primitive, and wasn't stoning to death an Arab way of– But Channon wasn't prepared to linger. 'We'll have a quick word with the doc. Then we must find out if Ludcott was simply arriving for work. If he was we'll want witnesses who saw him either setting off or on his way here – and the times they saw him. As for Mr Hunter's contribution – the SOCOs will have to tell him when he can have the body and I'll make myself available for when I'm needed at the mortuary. For now, Bowles, I want to go and see the top of Proudy. Don't look so surprised. There are two others besides Nancy, you know.'

Lizzie Bannon had done a roaring trade the previous day: snacks and soft drinks, ice-cream, hot pasties at lunch-time – she'd had her work cut out to keep up with demand. Increased trade was all very well, she'd told herself, but what about the reason for it? She'd rather be twiddling her thumbs in retirement than making money hand over fist because young Jonny had been murdered.

Right now there were four of her regulars in the shop and the atmosphere was tense. Word was going round that something was happening and as always the locals had turned to her. It was one of her functions to pass on news, to make announcements, but she couldn't announce anything this time – not until she was sure of the facts.

'What's going on, Lizzie?' asked a mother with a toddler.

'I don't know,' she admitted, 'but I can tell you what we've seen and heard in this shop and you can draw your own conclusions. Bozena was in just after nine, having a chat, when we saw the inspector and his sergeant go running to their car. They drove off at speed and within minutes more cars went after them. Bozena and me – well – we thought something had happened, but no police came in the shop and we could hardly go across to the room and start asking questions, now could we?

'A bit later Doris came in and said her husband had just driven down past Trevant and the place was swarming with police – he said they were taping it off. Then when Howard came in a few minutes ago for his milk both of us saw Mr Dancer arrive in a police car and go into the room between two policemen. Then to cap it all, who should they bring in next but Sam – *Sam!* They took him in, as well.'

'You mean Sam Ludcott?' asked a woman in disbelief.

'He's the only Sam I know of in Porthmenna,' said Lizzie. 'So – something's wrong. Me and Howard – well – we don't know what to make of it.'

For long seconds there was silence in the shop, but from outside came the everyday sounds of the village: the rhythmic thud of waves behind the harbour wall, the cry of the gulls, the rattle of a winch on a boat moored at the jetty. Then a car door slammed and Frances rushed in.

Five pairs of eyes observed her with concern. 'Frances, I've told you before you only need to pick up the phone if you want anything,' said Lizzie gently. 'There's enough folk ready and able to deliver anything you might need.'

Frances looked at them all and tried to smile. 'I know, Lizzie, and thanks. Everybody's being lovely, and we do appreciate it, but I haven't come to buy. A few minutes ago DCI Channon called on Delphi and me. He came to tell us...' She hesitated, all at once conscious that what she was about to say might seem ghoulish. These were her friends, though – her good, loyal friends. 'I did promise to keep you all informed about what's happening,' she muttered.

'And you did, my precious,' said Lizzie, coming round the counter and giving her a squeeze. 'You've kept your promise. So tell us – have they got somebody for it?'

'No, it's worse than that, much worse,' said Frances unsteadily. 'It's awful. There's been another murder.'

They all stared at her. The toddler whimpered uneasily as his mother gripped his hand too hard. 'It's Mrs Dancer,' she told them. 'Her husband found her body up at the house less than an hour ago. Channon says we must be prepared for reporters and camera crews and so forth. He says they'll be here in a matter of hours.'

As if a cold wind was blowing around them, those listening to her moved closer together. The mother picked up her toddler. 'We're not safe!' she declared. 'There must be a madman on the loose. Channon will have to put men to patrolling the village – they'll have to set up road blocks or something, won't they? Mr Sandry, what about the harbour? Are you keeping watch on who sails in and out?'

Howard Sandry shook his grey head reprovingly. 'Don't I always? It's part of my job. I was over in the room first thing this morning with a list of who was in and out the day Jonny – I'm sorry, Frances – the day Jonny was killed.'

Frances gave an awkward little nod. 'Well, that's all I came to say I'll see you later.'

'Before you go, how's Delphi?' asked Lizzie.

'She's bearing up and looking after the baby. David's being a big help with the girls.' For the life of her she couldn't say any more to these good, caring people. 'I must get back to her,' she said, and left the shop.

She was about to start the car when across the beach she saw Dave's tall, familiar figure running down the steps from Lookout Cottage. Her heart leapt as it did every time she saw him. He would be heading for Seaspray and it looked as if he was carrying more mail. She could tell him about Nancy Dancer now, rather than in front of Delphi. For speed she cut across the beach towards him.

They faced each other and he said, 'Frances, what are you doing here? I'm just on my way to see you all.'

'I know. I saw you from the other side of the harbour. I wanted to catch you.'

She looked awful, he thought. There was no trace of colour in her face apart from the purple of the rings around her eyes. 'What's the matter?' he asked. 'Has something else happened?'

'Yes. That is – no – not to us. I just want to tell you now, without Delphi around. There's been another murder. Nancy Dancer. Her husband found her this morning.'

Dave's jaw went slack with disbelief. Weird, man-hungry Nancy murdered? Confident, bouncy little Alan without a wife? He stared down at a tangle of mooring ropes snaking across the sand. 'How did

211

she die?'

'I don't know. Channon called in briefly to tell us – he didn't give details, but then, they don't, do they?'

'Does Delphi know?'

'Yes. She didn't say very much. I've got to get back to her.'

Deep in thought, Dave shifted the mail bag from his shoulder and swung it back and forth at arm's length. 'What do you make of it, Frances?'

She didn't stop to weigh her words. 'I simply don't know. I can't see how it can be connected to Jonny, but it makes it better for us.' Oh! – she gaped at him in horror. What had she just said? How could she have come out with something so callous? She wiggled her hands in the air and gabbled, 'I didn't mean – what I meant was–'

To her astonishment he took both her hands in his. 'It's all right, Frances. I think I know what you meant. You're saying that if somebody has murdered three people who're so very different, then they weren't after Jonny in particular – he was caught up in something.'

Relief surged through her like an incoming tide. 'That's it exactly,' she said in amazement. 'You understand!'

'It has been known,' he assured her wryly, 'though not very often.'

She couldn't think what to say to that, and edged her fingers from his. 'Not very often.' As far as the past was concerned, that should be 'never'. In the nine years she looked after him he'd been so antagonistic, so wrapped up in resentment, he hadn't understood himself, let alone anyone else... but now?

They faced each other in silence. 'I have to go,' she said. 'Were you about to walk to Seaspray?'

'No, I was going to go in the car. Later on, if you don't need me, I want to go over to Proudy and have a look round the top.'

'Bozena's going to pick up the girls to take them round to her place to play, so if you want to go to Proudy – go now.' Her brain must be in reverse, she told herself. She'd been longing to have an in-depth talk with him, yet with the opportunity for it in front of her, she wanted to get away from him. Wait – she'd made a vow to be honest with herself, hadn't she? Right, then, the truth was that her brain wasn't in reverse, it was on overdrive: too full of horror, suspicion and dread to do justice to a lengthy sorting-out with David.

And, yes, admit it ... she was frightened of what each of them might say. After that horrendous scene seven years ago when he told her he was leaving home, that unearthing of every feeling, every thought she'd concealed for nine whole years, she simply couldn't risk saying or hearing anything that might make things worse between them. She couldn't – she wouldn't risk it.

Still in awkward silence, they left each other and she walked back across the firm, damp gold of the sands.

'Wasn't that Dave Tregenza's car?' asked Channon as they drove back from Proudy.

'Mr Universe himself,' confirmed Bowles. 'Perhaps he's on his way to do what we've just done – survey the scene of the crime.'

'If that's the case he can do it to his heart's content, now the men have finished up there.'

Bowles merely grunted. He was edgy after half an hour of tramping the rough grasses of the cliff-top fields. Channon had been in his silent mode, eyes observant but with the oddly blank expression that told the sergeant he was in that other world – the world of the victim and the villain. It was a world that he, Bowles, rarely entered. Give him facts, not intuition; an interview room and a tape, not some airy-fairy imagining; a bit of forensic, with blood, fingerprints and human hair – that was what was needed to sort this lot out. Whoa ... steady ... his experience with Channon here had shown that intuition and imagination were worth at least as much as all the rest put together. He'd better remember that.

John Meade was waiting when they got back. Channon asked him, 'Has Dancer's lawyer arrived?'

'He's on his way. Dancer says he won't speak without him.'

'Fair enough. We can talk to Ludcott while we're waiting. Did you put somebody on to finding witnesses for when he went up to Trevant to start work?'

'Men are on with it now.'

'Right. Let me know as soon as we have anything.' Channon headed for the interview room trailed by a reluctant Bowles, who was telling himself he could do with a bit of nosh. He'd been up at six and all he'd had since then had been a slice of toast. Tomorrow, he resolved, he'd have a decent breakfast before he left the flat – if he

214

remembered to buy some food. And he would throw out that mouldy cheese that was lurking in the fridge, and sort out all the half-bottles of iffy milk. Maybe he should go mad and visit a supermarket? The trouble with that was there'd be no option but to buy ready meals. He could never see the point of laying out good money on anything that would need cooking when he was no good at it and in any case hadn't the time.

He wondered what Channon did for food. Somebody had said he had a daily housekeeper who cleaned the house and saw to his meals. Bully for him! He probably ate meat and two veg every night, with fresh fruit to follow. But right now he was saying something...

'Ah, Bowles, you *are* with us, then? Were you doing a bit of mental detection?'

'No, I was wondering how soon I could go for a snack, sir.'

'You can go now if you like. Dancer's cooling his heels in my office, so I've changed my mind. I'm going to have a private word with him right away.'

'Why private?'

'To spare his feelings,' said Channon shortly. 'If it wasn't just top show with Nancy – if she followed up her come-ons to the logical, or biological conclusion, then he won't want to talk about it on the record.'

'Maybe not,' conceded the sergeant. He wasn't going to see the little brain-box brought low, then. Well, he could live without that pleasure if he could have a quiet half-hour on his own with a hot cuppa and a sandwich from that old biddy

215

at the Harbour Stores.

Dancer was sitting with his head in his hands. When he looked up his expression held both misery and resentment. Channon perched on the edge of the desk. 'Mr Dancer, I think it might be helpful for us both if we have an informal little chat before we get down to an official interview.'

'Oh?' From his tone it was clear that being helpful was not Dancer's intention.

'Even as I speak enquiries are under way into your wife's death, and I want to say that we're going to have to look into the question of her friends and acquaintances.'

'So?'

Rather than stare into the red-rimmed eyes in that blotchy face Channon gazed at the wall above Dancer's head. 'So I want you to tell me whether you know of anyone with whom she was particularly friendly.'

'What makes you think she was friendly with anybody?'

'Common talk,' said Channon bluntly. 'Before her death our enquiries had already revealed that she had a keen interest in men.'

Dancer breathed in, expanding his chest until he reminded Channon of an overfed pigeon. 'My wife, chief inspector, suffered from a hormone imbalance. She'd been receiving treatment for it over a period of many years.'

Not a bad line to take... 'It must have been difficult for you both. If you could possibly be completely frank with me it would help me with investigations. The fact that we're about to question you doesn't mean that, at present, we see you as a prime suspect.'

'I'm glad to hear it,' said Dancer. Then he leaned forward in Channon's chair. 'But as you want me to be completely frank I will say one thing – I appreciate you trying to spare me embarrassment.'

Progress, thought Channon with relief. 'I'm glad you see it like that. I have wide experience, Mr Dancer. I assure you that whatever you feel able to tell me, I'll have heard worse. I'm unshockable.' To his dismay he saw the glint of tears in Dancer's eyes, and recognized the prelude to the other man's unburdening. He'd told Bowles that he hadn't yet got Dancer's measure, but now it looked as if he was going to get it down to the last centimetre.

And then it came; fast and very low. 'I knew before I married her that she was a bit – different,' muttered Dancer, 'but even so she seemed so normal, so neat and tidy and attractive. I persuaded myself that it was a passing phase. I soon realized how wrong I was. I was no use to her sexually. She had – unusual tastes, you see. My biggest mistake was to take her to the Middle East. I'd grown up there, been happy; I spoke the languages, but above all I thought that the strict Muslim ethos would allow her no leeway in her obsession with other men.

'If anything, it inflamed her, and because she was neither a Muslim herself nor married to one, she was seen by some of the men as easy – an infidel not deserving of respect. She simply couldn't help being provocative, though she was

217

choosy as to who she took as an actual sexual partner. I had to accept it, but it made life very difficult. We left Saudi because of it and I had to turn down several lucrative offers from other Muslim countries. Our time in Afghanistan was disastrous, but I won't bore you with details.'

With a home life like that, no wonder the man was awkward as hell, thought Channon. 'Did neither of you think of leaving the other?'

'I thought of it for years, but I don't think Nancy did. She liked the façade of being a respectable married woman – I think it added spice to everything. I provided security, stability, the sort of life she wanted.'

'And you?'

'I loved her.' There was an emptiness to the words. 'But at times I admit I hated her. Whatever – the years went past and I began to hope it wouldn't last for ever. She was getting older – I hoped she would quieten down. Then we came here on holiday and saw Trevant up for sale. We bought it. Nancy was brilliant at ideas for converting the place.'

'And what about the visit from al-Makki?'

Dancer's lips twisted. 'You've guessed, of course,' he said bitterly. 'Nancy tried her tactics on him, tired and hungry as he was. She did it in front of me, as usual, and I had to pretend I didn't see it. He was embarrassed and affronted and left the house. I never saw him again.'

'He took your money?'

'Yes. We had a difference about it and an unpleasant scene. He threw it on the floor and said it would be an offence to accept it. I picked it up.

I could see he was desperately in need of it. I asked him to take it for old times' sake. He left the house with the money and without saying a farewell. Nancy and I had an argument. She cried. Soon after that Jonathan Tregenza arrived. Nancy and I put up a front for him – we were quite good at that.'

Channon needed a breath of fresh air, but he could hardly call a halt. 'What about any local men? Was there anyone she'd been seeing?'

'There would be somebody,' said Dancer with certainty, 'but I don't know of anyone in particular. We had an understanding, you see.'

'You let her have what relationships she chose?'

'Not exactly "let" her. I had little choice. It was a compulsion with her – a sickness. I went along with it.'

Channon was forced to admire the other man's honesty. It was as if the relief of talking about it was allowing him to discard subterfuge. The strange thing was that the more he revealed of their travesty of a marriage, the more he seemed to salvage his own dignity and self-respect. Channon fancied he could see it, this self-respect, wrapping itself around Dancer's chubby body like bright and steely armour. But he must get on.

'Thank you for being so open,' he said. 'I'm sorry but I must ask you this, and then we'll leave it. After you went to bed last night, is it possible that Nancy went outside the house to meet somebody?'

Dancer stared at his clasped hands. When he looked up his eyes were dead as stones. 'It's possible,' he said through gritted teeth. 'She'd done

219

it before. Many times.'

'And you have no idea who it could have been?'

'No. No idea whatsoever.'

'Thank you. Somebody will come to fetch you when your solicitor arrives. I'll try to phrase my questions appropriately.'

With a flash of the old aggression Dancer gave a harsh bark of a laugh. 'Save your pity!' he said dismissively. 'I've had enough of it – pity and scorn. I've lived with it and I can tell you *I don't need it!*'

Chapter Thirteen

A constable brought in the sinewy old man and Channon said, 'I'm sorry to have kept you waiting, Mr Ludcott. Things are a bit busy, as you can imagine.'

From their network of lines, Sam Ludcott's sharp blue eyes looked back at him. 'With three folk dead, what's a bit of time spent waiting?'

'Exactly.' Channon sat down and didn't miss the other's glance of pure dislike as Bowles took his place behind him. 'As far as you're concerned, Mr Ludcott,' he began, 'I'd like you to tell us in your own words all that you saw and heard this morning, from leaving your house until the sergeant here let you out of the old laundry. Give me times as far as you can recall them.'

Ludcott looked at the tape. 'On that?'

'No, not at this stage. We use a recording when we're questioning a suspect, but with you we'll just go through what you did, what you saw, when and where. We'll print it out as a statement and when it's correct we'll get you to sign it. I already have details of your employment at Trevant, so what time did you leave home this morning?'

'Knocking on for seven thirty. Within a minute I saw Lizzie through her shop window and then Lem Hazlitt starting to clean the chapel windows. I walked up to Trevant like I always do. I might have passed a car or two but I didn't pay

221

any attention. Nobody was about when I arrived so I went round to the stables to carry on with work on the doors – I was taking 'em off.'

'Did you see anyone near the house? Did you hear anything?'

'No. It was quiet. Later on I went past the room that's to be their new sitting room and I saw the flicker of the television, so I knew somebody was up and about. That'd have been around half past eight.'

'So what took you to the yard where the bins are kept?'

'That was later. There's good tools in the workshop there from years back. I needed the big screwdriver to take the old door hinges off.'

'And what time was that?'

'It must have been about ten past nine. I checked my watch after Mr D shoved me in the laundry, because I know times are important in a crime. It was twelve minutes past nine when he turned the lock on me.'

'Did you see what had upset Mr Dancer?'

Ludcott's lips turned down and he wrinkled his nose. 'I saw a woman's legs in the bin, feet upwards but no shoes on, and what could have been a head – all bloody with something black laid on it. Little Mr D was in a bad way. He was sort of gabbling and sobbing.'

'Where did you appear from?'

'The back entrance to the yard.'

'What exactly was Mr Dancer doing when you first saw him?'

'He was standing with one hand gripping the rim of the wheelie bin and the other holding up the lid. He was staring into the bin. He looked pretty bad. His face was a sort of greyish-white with red blotches on his cheeks. He didn't see me at first, or maybe I just didn't register with him. When I moved he looked up and let out a – a sort of yowl. Then he bared his teeth at me.'

'What happened then?'

'My dear life, he had the strength of ten! I'm no weakling but he frog-marched me into the laundry and locked the door on me.'

'Were you surprised?'

'What do you think? I'd been all set to calm him down – to have a look in the bin for myself and then ring you lot, but I didn't get the chance.'

'Did you recognize who it was in the bin?'

'No, but there was only one woman lived at Trevant. Mrs D.'

'Did it shock you that she'd been murdered?'

Ludcott raised bushy white eyebrows. 'Well, strange to say murder wasn't an everyday occurrence up there. She might have been no angel, inspector, but you can say that about a lot of folk and they don't all get killed and dumped in a bin.'

'Of course they don't, but it's possible that she was attacked by somebody she knew who also had connections with Jonathan. We have to consider that these three deaths are linked. I'm sorry to have to ask you this, but do you know who Mrs Dancer was – seeing?'

'Talk about the wages of sin,' said Ludcott grimly. 'Now listen – I go in the pub, you know, and chat to old mates on the jetty, so I do hear things now and again without having to resort to gossiping about a man who pays me good money.'

'What things do you hear?'

Ludcott breathed out loudly through his nose. 'I reckon you know already. She had a name for going after the men. I heard she'd been seen with Reuben – Howard Sandry's lad. I know – in fact I witnessed that she tried to tempt young Jonny. You'll appreciate I say "tried"? She was old enough to be his mother and he had a lovely young wife at home. Then there was Delphi's dad, Terence – though I think it was fifty-fifty in his case – he was as keen as she was, but he hadn't got youth on his side.

'I daresay there's more... Oh, yes – she was seen chatting up them two chaps who sailed into harbour in their big posh Hanse – lovely craft it was, mind. She wasn't fool enough to do it in the pub and cause offence to the regulars, but she was seen with them just before opening time, and she might have been with them later, for all I know. She was a strange woman, but she didn't deserve murdering and cramming in a dustbin.'

Channon shot a glance at Bowles, who was intent on every word. He was good at statements, he wouldn't have missed a trick. As for the old man, he was looking pretty sick. 'I know this is distasteful for you, Mr Ludcott, but do you think Mr Dancer knew of his wife's interest in Jonny?'

'It's my belief he knew about 'em all. He was too soft with her. She made him a laughing stock – he made himself one. Now can I go? I feel the need to get home and have a tot of rum.'

'Yes, off you go, Mr Ludcott, but sometime soon we might need to ask you a few questions about your boat and your knowledge of the waters hereabouts.'

'Ask me anything you like, inspector.'

'Maybe I'll have to,' replied Channon. 'Perhaps I could call on you sometime and we can have a chat?'

Ludcott gave a twitch of the lips that might have been a smile. 'Perhaps you could,' he agreed, 'and let me say this – I'll do all in my power to help you.'

Both detectives were silent as they drove back from the mortuary: Channon because, hardened though he was, the savagery of Nancy's injuries had sickened him; Bowles simply because he'd found that he wasn't as tough as he'd thought himself to be. Images kept invading his mind: of Nancy's body, folded double and crammed in the bin, of her one open eye staring from that bloody pulp, of her broken body on the slab.

Not only that, this stoning business was getting to him. *Was* it that, or was it *meant* to be that? If it was a stoning it brought Islam to centre stage, didn't it? He negotiated a steep turn and below them lay the vastness of the sea, the waves white-capped and racing for land under a cloudless sky.

A strengthening wind was of no interest to Bowles at that moment, nor at any other time, come to that, and his mind went back to Nancy. Would a terrorist embroiled in planning an attack on a sensitive site bother to follow ancient tradition when killing an adulterous woman? Would he *know* she was adulterous? 'I don't get it,' he said out loud. 'How could a terrorist know she

225

was sex-mad?'

'You're leaping ahead a bit, aren't you?' asked Channon wearily. 'But since you ask, he could know from personal experience if he'd come across her when she was out in Saudi. Or he could know of her solely by reputation.'

'But why wait until now to polish her off?'

'Maybe she'd found out something he wanted to keep secret.'

'Well, I don't know what Dancer told you in your private talk, but in the actual interview he said she'd had no contact with Middle Eastern types since they left Saudi – except for when our friend the river man called on them. I noticed you didn't ask too much about that, sir?'

'Dancer had already told me all I wanted to know. He was pretty open about her. I think the shock of it, the horror, had loosened his tongue. She was promiscuous and had been for years. He said it was a hormone imbalance.'

'He was aware of what was going on, then? He accepted it?' Scorn dripped from Bowles's tongue like acid, making Channon recall how Dancer had said, 'Pity and scorn? I've lived with it.'

He said quietly, 'He might not have killed her, Bowles. He'd put up with her all their married life – he'd got used to it, he'd chosen not to leave her. He was hoping that as she got older she would quieten down.'

Bowles thought about that. What a pathetic little bladder of lard. Maybe the DCI was right and he'd never laid a finger on her. Well, then, he should have done! Had it never occurred to him that a bit of a smack might have made her behave

226

herself? But that image of her on the slab kept creeping into his mind... 'Another thing, sir. I thought Fred Jordan and his SOCOs were a bit officious in the mortuary. Even old Hunter had to watch his step with them.'

'*Mr* Hunter to you, Bowles. In a tricky case like this the SOCOs have precedence in order to protect their samples and specimens. They can't afford to miss anything, and neither can we. What with Fred and his team, Hunter and his AP technicians and the entire Forensic Unit champing at the bit, we won't have a hair or a nail clipping unexamined. If we do, the defence will have a field day exploring the holes in our case.'

Bowles tried not to sneer. 'Case?' he said. 'We haven't got a suspect yet, never mind somebody who can be brought to trial.'

Channon didn't reply. This affair was snowballing, getting more complicated. Not to put too fine a point on it, he himself was floundering. Added to that his superiors were getting edgy and breathing down his neck; and as for the media... 'I've got to say a few words on camera later today for the evening news on TV,' he said gloomily. 'Do you want to be in on it?'

Hey, hey! This was more like it! With an effort Bowles kept his tone low and thoughtful. 'To say something, you mean?'

'No, as SIO they'll insist on me doing the talking. I could make it clear without spelling it out that you're my right-hand man, though, and you'd be noticed by the big-wigs.'

His promotion to DI was getting closer, Bowles told himself, but with a nice show of modesty all he said was, 'That would be fine by me, sir. Thanks.'

Dave left Proudy with his spirits at rock bottom. It had been lovely up there in the fresh clean wind: remote, undisturbed, to him an unbelievable place for the murder of his brother. He had felt like an actor playing a detective as he trod the rough terrain, touching outcrops of rock between the flowered grasses, searching for he didn't know what.

He had tried to envisage where his brother was attacked, going back over ground that he'd examined just once, before dismissing the place because he'd reasoned that Jonny would never have gone there. Now, he knew he hadn't gone, he'd been taken. On that one visit he'd noticed an old metal cart in a field some distance from the cliff-top. It was no longer there. Only grooves remained where the wheels had rested. Had Channon's men removed it – or someone else?

Ten minutes later he was parking on the cobbles by the incident room, all set to ask if he could speak to Channon, when the man himself came out and stood at the door talking to a grey-haired officer. Dave headed across to them. 'Hello,' said Channon. 'Meet Inspector Meade, in charge of admin. John – you'll have realized this is Dave Tregenza, Jonathan's brother. What's on your mind, Dave?'

'I've been walking the tops over at Proudy – you know, just looking at everything. There was a cart in the corner of a field when I was last up there, but now it's gone.'

'We know about it,' said Channon gently. 'Our scene-of-crime team have removed it for forensic examination.'

Dave swallowed. 'It had been used? For – for Jonny?'

'We think so. It had been rearranged to look undisturbed. Dave, we've had men up there for days and now they've finished their investigations. We're trying to establish what happened, when it happened and exactly where.'

Dave gritted his teeth and rubbed the back of them with his tongue. The police were doing all the vital stuff, while he was playing nursemaid to his nieces. He could almost taste the bitterness of it. But John Meade was muttering to Channon, who said, 'Like me, the inspector recognizes that you need to see some action. Would you like him to show you round the room so you can see how we're dealing with everything? The sergeant and I have to go off somewhere or I'd give you a conducted tour myself.'

So for ten minutes Dave was given an insight into the running of a murder enquiry. John Meade was a good guide: knowledgeable, informative and sympathetic. He had three lads of his own at home and kept asking himself how any of them would react if they lost a brother to murder.

Impressed and reassured, Dave went back to Lookout Cottage knowing that every conceivable electronic device was in use on the case – computers, fax machines, video screens, illuminated maps, banks of telephones – the place was buzzing with up-to-the-minute stuff. Unreality was

229

kicking in again, because right outside all the modernity was the ancient harbour, the granite cottages, the whitewashed old pub. But he told himself that the contrast was as it should be. No matter how traditional the setting, modern technology was being used to track a killer. What more could he ask?

Opening the door of the cottage, he realized that he was getting used to being there on his own. At first it had seemed weird, intrusive; having breakfast in Delphi's kitchen, opening her cupboards, sleeping – yes, sleeping in the bed she had shared with Jonny – something else that was unreal, but it had to be done and he'd tried not to let it get to him.

He made himself a coffee and sat at the big table staring at the silky-smooth oak kitchen units. Jonny had been a wizard with wood, his work was all over this house ... and what of *his* work, the riding of giant waves, the hours of training, the exercises with his breathing? Like all professional surfers he worked on preparing his lungs against the times when he was dragged under water and tossed around like an item of laundry in a washing machine. When he wasn't exercising his body he was on line with the oceanography boys – the experts who could read the movements of the oceans like an astronomer reads the heavens.

He'd been away from it all for how long? Ten days? Had he missed it? No, but his body had. His muscles were accustomed to strenuous daily use. As soon as he had time he must set up some sort of regime to keep himself in trim, but for now he had to get across to Seaspray to join Delphi and Frances and the girls for a meal. He would go on foot. No more using the car for short distances, in fact he might return it to the hire people. Maybe he would buy a second-hand motorbike, purely for pleasure.

Even as the word entered his mind he recognized it as false. Pleasure? In the Tregenza family?

'More cards!' Sophie and Dorcas shrieked with delight and clasped Dave's thighs in excitement. Pink-cheeked and slightly hyper after a morning playing with Bozena's boys, they rearranged the massed cards of sympathy to make room for this latest delivery.

Dorcas tugged at his hand. 'Uncle Dave,' she whispered, 'we've got all these cards 'cos everybody's sad about our daddy.'

'Everybody!' chimed in Sophie. 'Everybody loves him – not just us.'

It caught at Dave and for a moment he couldn't answer. He blinked and turned his head away, but not quickly enough. 'You can cry if you want,' Sophie told him generously. 'Mummy says it's all right to cry.'

'When you cry it stops hurting in here,' said Dorcas, patting her chest. Then she gave him her bewitching smile. 'When we've had our rest will you make us another sandcastle?'

From the kitchen door Frances was watching. Thank you, God, she breathed silently. Thank you, thank you for David.

In a deep armchair by the window Delphi was feeding baby Jonathan from a bottle. Mollie had called earlier and uttered strong words, with the result that the baby had started his feed at the breast and was now being topped up from a bottle. 'Purely as a temporary measure,' Delphi had agreed defiantly.

'Whatever you want to call it,' said Mollie, and went on her way.

Frances went back to dishing up the meal. She couldn't understand it, but for some reason she felt ever so slightly better.

'Come in, come in!' Forewarned of their visit, the Reverend Jim Dowson had the door of the manse open before the two detectives could ring the bell.

Bowles eyed him warily. Judging by the earth-stained cord trousers and the ancient shirt, they'd interrupted a gardening session. As a breed, bible-thumpers gave him a pain, and he doubted whether this one would be any different from the rest. Channon, however, was at his most affable, introducing them both, apologizing for taking up the man's time and refusing a cup of tea without so much as a blink in Bowles's direction.

'I know you've already spoken to two of our officers,' began the DCI. 'They described you as a man who has his finger on the pulse of Porthmenna, so I thought if we had a chat you could give us a bit of general background to fill in any gaps in our knowledge of the people here.'

Jim Dowson nodded. 'I'll try to help, of course. I've been in this area for less than three years, so I'm no expert, but I do know most of the folk in Porthmenna. It's only one of my churches – I have five others dotted around the area.'

'I believe you know the Tregenzas?'

'Oh yes. Frances attends worship regularly, so does Delphi. The twins are in the beginners' section of our junior church and they come to the playgroup run by Mrs Dabner. I knew Jonny well – he often did repairs on the fabric of the chapel building.'

'What about Jonny's brother, Dave?'

'We met for the first time a couple of days ago. I've been told that he and Jonny went through our Sunday School as young boys. I think Frances is glad to have him back home, even for so terrible a reason.'

'Reverend, if I ask any questions that seem to you to be bordering on tittle-tattle, please rest assured that I never ask anything out of idle curiosity. We have three murders on our hands, with extra men being drafted in from other areas even as I speak. Now, do you know of anyone who might not have been on good terms with Jonathan Tregenza?'

'No,' said Jim Dowson, 'I really don't. He was a good, decent young fellow, devoted to his family and honest as the day. I doubt you'll find a soul in Porthmenna or further afield who would say any different. People here are heartbroken, the church family are devastated. I'm arranging a special service tomorrow evening so that everybody can show their support. Nobody can remember anything as awful as this since the accident that killed the boys' parents.'

'That was years ago, surely?'

'Yes, in 1989. I looked it up in the church

records a few days ago. The whole village, the whole area was united then in trying to help, just as they are now. You probably know that Frances was their legal guardian. She was living abroad at the time, following her career as a linguist. She gave it up and came back to look after them, and since then has worked as a private tutor and supply teacher and so forth.'

'What about Mrs Dancer? Was she a member of your church?'

'No, I'm afraid not.'

'You'll have heard that she had a certain reputation?'

'Yes. I hear most things, inspector. I'm not a hellfire and damnation man. I follow the precept, "Judge not, that you be not judged." None of us are perfect, are we? We'll all have to face a final judgement, one day.'

'Have you, in your ministry, come across anyone who might resent – even hate – Mrs Dancer or her husband?'

Jim Dowson pulled thoughtfully at the collar of his faded denim shirt. 'People talked about her,' he admitted, 'but simply with shock and embarrassment. Some might have resented them, because they had more money than many of the local folk have seen in a lifetime of hard work, but I don't know of anyone who hated them. If anything, they were admired for restoring that lovely old house. Sam Ludcott, in particular, didn't like to hear anything against them, but then, Alan Dancer paid him a wage.'

'Have you yourself ever visited Trevant?'

Jim Dowson smiled. 'Oh yes. Cornwall is still a

stronghold of Methodism, but we haven't got so many members we can neglect trying to add to their number. I visited them a couple of times since they took on Trevant.'

'What did you think of Mrs Dancer?'

The minister shrugged. 'As I said, inspector, I don't judge. I saw her simply as one of God's strange people.'

'Reverend, can I come back to you if I need advice or more information?'

'You'll be welcome. Oh – I've had a few calls from the press, and a request to say a few words for radio and television. Is there any particular line you think I should take?'

Channon shook his head. 'Speak as you see fit,' he replied. 'I needn't tell you to say nothing that would lead to fear and panic among the population?'

'There's quite a bit of that already,' said the minister, 'so you can rest assured I won't add to it. I'm here if you want me.'

The media had descended in force on Porthmenna: reporters hanging around the harbour or waylaying passers-by, cameramen waiting on the jetty to get dramatic pictures at high water or backing across the sands for a distance shot of Lookout Cottage.

Channon had been his usual self for the television interview: calm, lucid, serious; inspiring confidence when in truth he was feeling distinctly lacking in it. He told himself that there were too many loose ends fluttering around on these three murders for anybody to feel con-

235

fident, except perhaps the killer. But with modern technology and the Devon and Cornwall force in action, he or she wouldn't be confident for long – at least, he hoped not.

Bowles had savoured the brief spell in front of the cameras, and looking back had to admit that Channon had done his best for him, once referring to him as 'my sergeant – my right-hand man', and turning to include him when he spoke of 'the work of the entire force'.

Actually Bowles had felt more self-conscious on camera than he'd anticipated, but at least his face had been seen. The full interview and a commentary would go out on the regional network and a shorter version on the national news. Channon had put a block on any mention of the terrorist angle, but that could wait. What mattered to Bowles personally was that the big noises in London had seen him as a capable second-in-command on the triple murder in Cornwall.

By seven that evening most of the staff were still hard at work: computers humming, foot-sloggers reporting in, phones ringing, car doors slamming out on the cobbles. Bowles went into Channon's office and found him behind a pile of paperwork. The DCI waved a couple of sheets at him. 'Hunter's report on Nancy! Only the preliminary, and subject to forensic checks.'

Bowles was wary. He couldn't get his head round Nancy-dancy and the stones. 'So?'

'So I'll talk to the rank and file about it tomorrow morning. For now, reflect on this – Hunter's confirmed the time he gave when he first saw her – not this morning but several hours earlier. He thinks last night – lateish.'

'That explains the door key in her pocket. She locked the front door behind her as she left the house. She must have arranged to meet somebody.'

'It looks like it. We'll be seeing Reuben Sandry first thing tomorrow, and anybody else she'd had her eye on. Hunter also says there'd been no sexual assault – no sexual contact at all.'

'That wouldn't be through lack of her trying,' said Bowles cynically. 'We're still doing a trace on the two sailor-boys who spent time with her.'

'Let me know as soon as there's news on it – wherever I am, wherever you are.'

'OK. So what about Nancy, then – what killed her? The stones? The head injuries?'

'No. Hunter says she was already dying when she was battered with the stones. They weren't thrown at her in the traditional way – they were hand-held and used as blunt instruments.'

'So she was already dying? Of what?'

'Of a stab wound under the right shoulder blade – your legendary stiletto or something similar, slanting up between her ribs and into the heart.'

'Well, well. But if that was enough to finish her, why the stones?'

'To make sure? To make a point? To emphasize her loose morals? To bring in Islam? To make such a mess of her that no clues could be gathered?'

Many questions and Bowles considered them all. 'We'll find out which it was,' he said with certainty. 'Do we know where the stones came from?'

'They're large pebbles from a beach. We've checked with Dancer and they were already at Trevant – in a pile at the side of the house, ready to surround a fountain. He was put out that we thought he'd simply taken them from a local beach. He's into conservation and knows it's dis-couraged.'

'So if the pebbles just happened to be there it was an opportunist thing?'

Channon pursed his lips dubiously. 'Maybe, but listen to what Mr Hunter says.' Channon riffled through the report and quoted: '"I'd say the attack was ruthless and calculated rather than spur-of-the-moment and frenzied." Did some-body know the stones were at Trevant and plan in advance how to use them?'

You're the clever-clogs, thought Bowles, you sort it. And then he pulled himself up short. What was he on about? He was desperate for pro-motion, wasn't he? When he was a DI, and later on a DCI, he would have to do his own sorting, wouldn't he? This business of the stones must be addling his brain.

Channon eyed him thoughtfully. 'Look, Bowles, we've had a long day. I'm going to call in on the Tregenzas, then I'm off home. I suggest you get off as well, ready for an early start tomorrow. I'll see you here at seven thirty so we can have an update with John Meade before the briefing.'

It was almost nine when Channon reached the cream-washed house outside a village near St Mawes. He opened the door and wrinkled his nose. Things were no longer in immaculate order since his housekeeper left. He hated muddle and

238

detested grime, so before long he would have no option but to either replace her or do all the chores himself.

Tonight he couldn't wait to get in the bath. That was his favourite thinking place. A deep hot soak, a glass of whisky and uninterrupted thought. Three murders were enough to exercise his mind for a week, not just half an hour among the soap-suds.

Chapter Fourteen

Frances woke when early sunbeams touched her bed. It was six o'clock. For the first time since Jonny went missing she had slept through the night. Mental turmoil kept her awake – that and the baby – but last night exhaustion must have taken over. Now she could hear the rhythmic thud of the waves, the scream of the gulls, but the house itself was silent: no baby crying, no early-morning chatter from the girls, just precious, precious silence.

Silence! She shot out of bed. How could she have slept all night without checking that every-body was safe? A murderer was on the loose. No matter what Channon had told her about some-one watching over them she simply had to see for herself. She rushed to the twins' room. They were entwined in the same bed, fast asleep; a muddle of pink cheeks, dark hair, patterned pyjamas and teddy bears. Thank God! Delphi and the baby were in the next room. Quietly she opened the door to see him gnawing a fist and stretching before tuning up for a full-scale cry. As for his mother, she was sleeping with one hand stretched out and resting on the crib. Even in sleep she was looking after her son.

Calm again, Frances decided to have ten more minutes in bed, planning the day ahead. Her teaching was cancelled for a couple of weeks; she couldn't have coped with it and hadn't been expected to, but one more week without it was as much as she could afford. No teaching meant no income. Her work consisted of private tuition, supply teaching when it was available and her one day a week at the school in Carbis Bay. It was an arrangement that suited her, giving her enough to live on without the stress of full-time teaching. Now, though, with Jonny gone, she might have to change her lifestyle.

She hadn't even mentioned money to Delphi, but clearly she and the children would need financial support. She wondered whether the government gave help to the families of murder victims, or whether Delphi would qualify for some sort of widowed mother's allowance. Days ago Channon had offered them a personal support officer. They'd thought about it and declined. Now she wished they'd accepted. Such a person could probably advise on financial help.

She didn't even know about the mortgage arrangements on Lookout Cottage, but wait – there was someone who did – David! How could she have overlooked him? He'd been going through Jonny's finances, his business accounts, the household bills. Relief eased its way round her heart. It wasn't that she'd forgotten David, how could she? It was just that she'd never been able to turn to him for help in the past. He'd gone away a boy and come back a man – a man who had told her only days ago: 'I'll stay for as long as it takes to find out who did it, and why.'

That promise had been sweet music to her ears, but would he, could he stay even longer? Long enough to see Delphi and the children financially secure? Probably not, but the next time they were alone she would have to talk to him about money.

Channon sat down at his desk and asked, 'Did anything come in during the night?'

John Meade consulted his papers. 'A lot of stuff from your TV spot. Men have been working on it but nothing significant has come up so far. Apart from that we've had more reports, print-outs of statements made yesterday and a load of bumf on our two unknown sailor-boys. So far we haven't got them.'

'Unknown? I thought Howard Sandry gave us names and addresses?'

'He did. The Hampshire force is on with it now. The two men are on the electoral roll, but there's nobody at home. We're contacting the Small Ships Registration people to check that Sandry got their details right.'

Channon had lived by the sea all his life. 'It's not obligatory to register with them.'

'No, but they had an SSR number on their boat and Sandry made a note of it.'

Channon was thoughtful. 'If they were planning murder I can't see them sailing openly into harbour in a registered vessel and then spending the evening boozing in a public bar.'

'They could have done it as a blind,' suggested Bowles.

'I suppose so,' said Channon reluctantly, and to Meade, 'Have we asked Dancer if he knows them?'

'No,' admitted Meade.

242

'Do it, then. No – I'll have a word with him myself after the briefing. Did he accept a support officer?'

Meade shook his head. 'He says he has enough intelligence to handle things without the help of the lower ranks.'

Channon looked grim. 'Nobody's doubting his brain power, merely his common sense. What about emotional trauma? What about his position in this enquiry? About keeping abreast of what's going on? Has he got all that sewn up as well?'

'Probably. He's a strange little fella.'

Channon grunted irritably. 'How about the SOCOs at Trevant? Have they found anything?'

'Indoors, you mean? They're still taking the place apart. You know what Fred Jordan's like. He says they'll need until midday today, maybe longer because of all the building stuff that's being used in the restoration. As for the yard and the bin, they've got enough specimens and samples to sink a ship. Forensic are dealing with it now.'

Channon was in no mood for delay. 'Keep chasing them,' he ordered. 'Nancy's the hot one of the three. The other killings are old and cold compared to her.'

Listening, Bowles was feeling alert and good-humoured. Yesterday he'd spent ten minutes with Mary Donald, getting the low-down on break-fasts, and this morning he'd got up at the crack of dawn and following her instructions made himself scrambled eggs on toast. Lo and behold, it had been halfway decent! A bit stiff and solid, per-haps, with a faint flavour of burnt pan, but dis-tinctly eatable. Now, with some nosh inside him

243

he was all set to be helpful. 'About the two men, sir. Would you like me to coordinate the trace?'

'Yes, I would, but only if we get no joy from Dancer. John – we've got a time of death for Nancy so we'll need people available to check on what everybody was doing late on Wednesday.'

'They'll be ready and raring to go when you say the word,' promised Meade.

'And are we checking the phone calls to and from Trevant before it happened?'

'It's in hand,' Meade assured him, 'and we're checking if she spoke to anybody else besides the sailor-boys that evening.'

Channon was still edgy. He was bogged down by detail when he felt the urge to work on a broader canvas, to step back and contemplate the wider issues, the main one being whether or not the three deaths were related to terrorism. The bath and the whisky last night hadn't clarified that one; in fact, nothing new had come to him among the soapsuds, but he was determined on one thing – this afternoon he was going some-where, on his own.

Out of all the information they'd gathered so far, one indisputable fact had emerged: Dancer was the only one with a finger in each pie – Jonny, al-Makki and Nancy. Not only that – he was connected to Goonhilly by the position of his house, his past dealings with the place and his links to a possible – only a possible – terrorist. Furthermore, one of the two sailor-boys was black-haired and swarthy, even if his name was either Meredith or Bellwood, and even if he'd put away plenty of alcohol... 'What did the two men drink in the Fisherman's Rest?' he asked.

John Meade didn't have to check. 'The fair one was on Boddington's, the other on Stella. They each had a pasty. One was the usual, with meat, the other was cheese and onion.'

'Which was which, do you know?'

'No, but maybe the girl who served them will remember.'

'Tell somebody to ask her. Now, let's get the briefing over and then we'll start work.'

Meade and Bowles exchanged a look. For once they were in accord. Start work? What did he think they'd been doing since they arrived? Twiddling their thumbs?

The briefing was finished. As always Channon had enjoyed it while Bowles had seen it as chaos. They went to see Dancer, and found him standing by the window of his room in the Fisherman's Rest, a place chosen both for his comfort and for its closeness to the centre of activity. Channon noted the shadows under the little man's eyes, the bitten lips, the naked aggression as he eyed them both. Pity softened his approach. 'Mr Dancer, our colleagues should have finished their work at Trevant later today. All being well you'll be able to return home this evening.'

'I'm glad to hear it,' said Dancer shortly. 'Now – are you going to do me the elementary courtesy of telling me the outcome of my wife's autopsy?'

'Not at this stage, Mr Dancer. The autopsy has been carried out according to the requirements of the law, and we need reveal the findings only at our discretion. What I can tell you is that she died

245

quickly – we believe without too much pain.' That was stretching a bit, but what was the harm?

Eyes that were red-rimmed but still shrewd ignored Bowles and stared at the DCI. 'She didn't die of the battering? She was dead before the stones were used on her?'

'She was dying, that's as much as I can say. I do assure you that it's normal procedure not to reveal details of the method used in a case of murder.'

'What, not even to the next of kin?'

'Not until the next of kin is eliminated – if then,' confirmed Channon. 'Mr Dancer, we're trying to trace two men who sailed into harbour on Wednesday evening. They were strangers to the locals but it occurs to me that you might know who they are.'

'Why should I?'

'Because your wife was seen talking to them before they came into this pub for the evening, that's why.'

Dancer let out breath with a drooping of his shoulders. 'You think she invited two strangers up to Trevant late that night and they just happened to kill her and cram her in the bin?'

'No. I don't think anybody "just happened" to kill her. We're trying to trace these men to eliminate them from our enquiries. If you can tell us something about them it could save both time and money.'

'Why should I save you time and money?'

'Because, Mr Dancer, we're trying to find your wife's murderer.'

'And finding him will bring her back to life, of course.'

246

With an effort Channon kept his patience. 'You know the answer to that one.'

'All right, all right. Have you got their names?'

'James Meredith and Martin Bellwood, from Hampshire.'

'Never heard of them.'

'Do you recognize their descriptions?' Channon nodded to Bowles, who read from his notes briskly and without expression.

'One of them was tall, about six foot, with fair straight hair. Broad and a bit tubby round the middle. Light eyes – blue or green. Good casual clothes. The other shorter, slim build, blue-black wavy hair and swarthy skin. Dark eyes, excellent teeth. Again, stylish casual clothes.'

Dancer pursed his lips. 'I don't know them.'

Channon eyed him carefully. 'Do you have any idea why your wife was by the harbour that evening?'

'She certainly didn't announce that she was coming down here to meet two men, if that's what you mean. She simply liked to feel part of the local community.' Bowles raised his eyebrows but Dancer didn't see it, and went on, 'She once told me that in the summer she was going to sit at a table outside the pub here, sipping wine and watching the sun go down.'

'If she'd been alive to do that, would you have sat here with her, Mr Dancer?'

For a moment anguish surfaced from beneath the aggression. 'You must remember our conversation yesterday,' said Dancer bitterly. 'Form your own conclusions.'

'I will,' Channon told him. 'I think that's all we

247

need to bother you with at the moment. Somebody will let you know when you can go home. A
police car will take you.'

They left him standing where they had found
him, and walked back together past the Harbour
Stores. 'He isn't falling over himself to be helpful,
is he?' asked Bowles. 'You'd think he'd want us to
find Nancy's killer.'

'Not if it's him,' said Channon grimly, 'though
I don't think it is. I suspect he's cagey because
Nancy was promiscuous. Maybe he doesn't want
us to find out who killed her, in case it opens a
can of worms. Whatever he wants or doesn't
want, we carry on. Theories are all very well, but
we need evidence. It'll be at least tomorrow
before Forensic give us much from the house.'

'How long before they report on the body and
the bin?'

'Maybe later today,' conceded Channon. 'Did
the inspector say if anybody saw the sailor-boys
leave?'

'Nobody saw them go. People took it that they
slept on the boat then upped anchor and left as
soon as the tide was high enough. Sandry didn't
see them leave and he was up and around by
seven.'

Channon stopped in his tracks and eyed the
long granite house with the yellow door. 'He lives
in a prime position for seeing what goes on,' he
said thoughtfully. 'Would you say he misses
much?'

'I'd say as harbourmaster he tries not to miss
anything at all.'

'Well, three people have died in the area, so he

must have missed something,' said Channon heavily, 'and so must everybody else. We'll do more on the sailor-boys later. For now, I want to check the Sandrys' original statements and then we'll go and have a word. I'll be interested to meet Reuben.'

'You mean "the lad"?' asked Bowles derisively. 'He was man enough for Nancy, by all accounts. I don't know who finished it between the two of them, but that could be significant.'

Half eager, half reluctant, Frances climbed the steps to Lookout Cottage. Bozena had called round with her boys to see Delphi and the children, so she had seized the moment, telephoned David and was now hoping to talk to him uninterrupted.

He opened the door and was struck yet again by the lack of colour in her face. It was as if all warmth, all blood had been sucked out of it, but what did he expect, that she'd be radiant? 'Sit down, Frances,' he said awkwardly. 'I have coffee on the go. Can I get you some?'

Bemused, she looked up at him. He was being considerate – again. 'Thanks,' she said, and sank down on the familiar sofa. Gather your wits, she warned herself. Stop goggling when he behaves like a normal human being instead of the awkward-as-hell teenager you remember.

'Is something else wrong?' he asked when they were settled with the coffee.

She shook her head. 'No, nothing new. I just have to talk.'

He told himself she'd always been keen on

249

pinning him down for discussions he didn't want. The strange thing now was that he did want it. On impulse he said, 'Frances, I need to talk, as well.'

She stared at him warily. Had he changed as much as he seemed to have changed? 'The first thing I need to ask you about is finance,' she said. 'I feel it's too soon to worry Delphi about it, but I need to know if you have any idea of what there will be for her and the children to live on.'

'Is it so urgent? I've told you already that I can come up with enough to keep things going for a while.'

'I know you have, and it's lovely of you, but yes, it is urgent. I need to know in case I have to change my job so I can earn more to help support them.'

For a moment he didn't reply. Things were moving round inside his chest again: heavy doors were being dragged open; bulky, oppressive weights were being pushed aside. Watch it, he warned himself grimly.

'You see,' she was saying, 'I don't know yet if Delphi will get a pension as a widowed mother, or if she might be entitled to some sort of compensation for Jonny. I thought you might have some idea how her finances will work out.'

'I do have some idea,' he said, 'I have a very good idea. I've spoken to a police adviser and to the DSS. Also, I know exactly how much is in the business and how much in the family account, and I've checked Jonny's life insurance.'

'Oh.'

'She'll be OK, Frances. Not well off, but

enough to live on. The mortgage on the house is protected, so it will be paid off. You know what's happening to house prices in Cornwall. If necessary she could sell this place, buy something cheaper not so near the sea and make a profit. You mustn't even think of taking on more paid work. I've been preparing a chart showing exactly how she'll be fixed. I'll do a copy for you, as well.'

All she could find to say was, 'You've changed so much.'

Maybe I needed to, he thought. 'I've grown up a bit.'

'David, you say you have some capital. Have you got a regular job? Do you earn money from surfing, or what?'

How she used to bend his ear back about 'his career' – and how it used to infuriate him... 'I've qualified in oceanography,' he told her. 'Surfers and sailing clubs and communities in vulnerable areas use my skills and sometimes pay me. Apart from that I win prize money from time to time and get paid pretty well for action shots.'

Even as he said it he was swept by longing for the thrill of riding the great waves, for the laid-back comradeship of the surfers, the long, golden days of life around the Pacific. It was another world from the nightmare he was having back here, embroiled in three murders on a windswept stretch of land.

But Frances was reflecting on what he had said. 'You mean you take pictures of surfers in action?' she asked.

'No, I mean somebody takes pictures of me in action, then they sell them and I get paid. I do all right financially, Frances.'

She stared at her coffee. All the anguish she'd suffered when he tossed aside his A levels and relinquished his place at university... He'd made a life for himself, earned a living; he was fulfilling his potential, which was all she'd ever wanted for him. 'I'm glad,' she said, 'oh, I'm glad to hear that. But there's something else, David. I have to say this – it's important. You're so very good with the girls. Because they have you they've been able to cope with not having Jonny. They love you.'

'Hey,' he said uneasily. He knew they liked him as a sort of substitute, but loved him? He could feel warmth building up inside him. *Love?*

'I think because of you they'll adjust to losing their daddy.'

'Uh? That's good,' he said lamely.

'But the thing is, David, if they get used to having you and then you go away, they'll have lost somebody they love twice over.'

The vivid eyes stared into hers. 'What are you saying?'

God, how could she cut off an arm or a leg? She looked away from him. 'I'm saying that if you plan to leave, you must give them warning of it and then go away soon. Please, *please* don't let them get the idea you'll be here for ever.' The relief of having said it made her weep; hard, rib-shaking sobs that seemed to tear her heart apart.

So much for shutting out emotion, thought Dave. He was being swept by it, battered, bruised. He could hardly bear to look at her rocking back and forth in pain. She'd told him to leave, and soon, but she didn't want him to go. He knew that

252

as surely as he knew that the moon governs the waves.

What she had said was no revelation. It had been creeping into his mind, into his – yes, he might as well admit it – his heart, that the twins were accepting him as a replacement for Jonny. He had encouraged it, even, in order to help in their loss. But he'd been so devastated himself, so taken up with remorse and guilt that he'd pushed aside the looming problem of their reliance on him.

'Frances,' he said, kneeling in front of her. 'Frances? I hear what you say. I understand why you say it, but I've told you already that I can't leave here until I know who killed Jonny, and why. I'll try not to let the girls get too used to – to having me around. If you think it best I'll leave Porthmenna for a few days at a time, but I won't leave the area – I can't – not until I know.'

Then, obeying some inner prompting that he didn't even recognize, he got to his feet, touched her hand for a second, and walked out of the room. A moment later she heard the front door close behind him.

The two detectives found the Sandrys subdued but eager to help; Howard serious but still talkative, Reuben with less to say and slightly on edge.

Channon had assessed the room in a single glance. It wasn't what he would have expected as a setting for two working seamen with no woman in the house. It was clear that loving care was lavished on the place: polished old furniture,

253

gleaming brasses, an immaculate carpet and bronze leather armchairs where they were sitting overlooking the windswept harbour. It was a beautiful room, old-established and very, very clean.

But he wasn't here to admire the decor. Polite as always, he began, 'I know my men have already been here, but as we're investigating another suspicious death – that of Mrs Nancy Dancer – I want to have a word with you myself. I take it you both knew the lady?'

'For my part,' said Howard, 'I didn't know any lady. I knew a woman, but only to pass the time of day or exchange the odd remark. Reuben here can speak for himself.'

Channon observed the younger man, from force of habit making a mental record of his appearance: curly dark hair, weather-beaten skin, a big frame but no surplus flesh, large hands backed by black hairs. The eyes, grey like his father's, were carefully unrevealing. He could sense intelligence in him, an awareness that he might face awkward questions, a calculating mind that was quite prepared to deal with them. This, he asked himself, was a man who couldn't hold down a job? There was no outward sign of instability. 'Mr Sandry,' he said mildly, 'I believe you knew Mrs Dancer quite well?'

'Yes,' said Reuben.

'There's always talk, isn't there, in a small village? Particularly about a married woman who has an eye for men other than her husband?'

Reuben's shoulders twitched, perhaps with relief that the subject was out in the open. 'Nancy was up for it,' he said bluntly. 'Her husband knew

254

she went with whoever she fancied. He accepted it.'

Channon shot a glance at the father. Lips tight, he looked pained and embarrassed. 'I'm sorry about this, sir, but we have to investigate everyone who was close to Mrs Dancer.' To Reuben he said, 'Mr Sandry, this would be simply a personal matter between you and Nancy Dancer – and maybe her husband – if she hadn't been brutally murdered. Now – were you lovers?'

Bowles sat up straighter. When push came to shove, the DCI didn't mince his words.

Reuben looked at his father with a touch of almost boyish defiance. 'Yes, we were,' he admitted, 'and she didn't need any persuading. Quite the reverse.'

'Did you visit her in the marital home?'

'No, I did not. We met four or five times in remote locations.'

Howard Sandry leaned forward. 'That woman,' he said tightly, 'that tart, had taken marriage vows. My lad is single.'

'Please, Mr Sandry, if I could just chat to your son?' Channon turned back to Reuben. 'Were you still in a sexual relationship with Mrs Dancer when she was killed?'

'No, we finished it a couple of weeks earlier.'

'Who finished it?' asked Channon gently.

'She did. She was sailing for new fishing grounds. Nancy liked variety.'

In his chair Howard Sandry clamped his teeth together and bared them in disgust. Bowles was watching both him and his son with attention. Would Channon get any more out of 'the lad'?

255

'Yes, I've heard she had a succession of partners,' he was saying. 'Do you know whether she'd started another relationship before she was killed?'

'I didn't know of one, but I reckon she'd have somebody in her sights.'

'Were you resentful when she dropped you?'

'Not resentful enough to kill her,' said Reuben drily. 'I wasn't pleased, but I'd never expected it to last. I was just one of a long, long line. For me, it was an interlude. In a way I was glad when it was over. It was all a bit – sordid.'

Not sordid enough to put you off shagging a married woman nearly old enough to be your mother, thought Bowles. But hey – he himself wouldn't have thrown her out of his bed. She might have taught him a few interesting variations, and at least he wouldn't have had to pay out good money for it. In fact, maybe *she* would have paid *him*? Wasn't that what old biddies did with their toy-boys? He eyed Reuben thoughtfully. Could this tough, leathery individual be described as a toy-boy? No, he decided. No way.

'I must make clear that this little chat is preparing the way for your statements,' Channon informed them. 'My sergeant here will call round later with a colleague to take an official statement from each of you, which he will ask you to sign as a correct record. Now, Mr Sandry, during your times with Mrs Dancer, did she give you any idea of who else she'd been interested in?'

'She didn't discuss her past conquests, but I knew – because he told me – that Terence Pennant was one. She dropped him as well. And it was common talk among the local men that she'd been asking about Dave Tregenza, though even Nancy must have seen that he had other things on his mind, and that he could get any gorgeous young thing he wanted if he so much as crooked his finger.'

'She'd been interested in his brother, so I hear?'

'Oh, yes, she'd tried it on with Jonny, as well, but he managed to resist her, which was hardly surprising when you look at Delphi.'

'Now, to Wednesday night. Could you both tell me your movements from, say, ten o'clock?'

'Ten o'clock at *night?*' said Howard in bafflement. 'Oh – I see – it's when that woman got her wages.'

'Her wages?'

'The wages of sin is death,' the other quoted.

They must be fundamentalists to a man round here, thought Channon. That was the second time this morning he'd heard that. 'After ten,' he prompted. 'Were you at home?'

'Well, by then I'd have done my round of the harbour – you know – seeing all was in order. Then me and the lad usually watch the news and maybe have a tot. Sometimes we'll play a bit of crib – yes, that's what we did on Wednesday. Is that right, lad? We got a bit carried away, didn't we? It was late when we finished – maybe half eleven when we went to bed.'

'Do you agree with that, Mr Sandry?'

Reuben was drumming his fingers on the arm of his chair. 'So was Nancy out and about when it happened? It was late on Wednesday? We heard she'd been found in the grounds of Trevant.'

'I can't discuss that, I'm afraid. Do you agree with your father on what you both did late that evening?'

'Yes. I'd been out earlier tinkering on the big 'un – that's our big boat. Then I called in the Fisherman's. I got home before ten, I think. Like my dad said, we got a bit carried away with the crib.'

'There were no witnesses to the two of you being here from ten onwards?'

'No. We were alone.'

'I see. Thank you,' said Channon, getting to his feet. 'If you need to change any details, or add anything you've forgotten, you'll have the opportunity. Oh, by the way, are either of you familiar with the alterations that are being done up at Trevant?'

They both stared at him. 'I've told you I never visited Nancy at home.' That was Reuben, while his father said, 'I don't know the place and I wasn't on what you'd call visiting terms.'

'That's what I thought,' said Channon. 'One last thing – if we find it necessary to take DNA samples from the local population, I take it you would both be available?'

'DNA?' echoed Howard, as if it were a formula from outer space. 'Whatever you want, you can have, inspector.'

'And you, Mr Sandry?'

'The same,' said Reuben.

They made their farewells and once outside Channon said wearily, 'They little know that so far there's no DNA to do a match on – except Nancy's. I should think there's enough of hers for fifty thousand samples. Whoever did it can't have escaped her blood.'

It was always the same old tale, thought Bowles indignantly, they were hampered by red tape. 'Why can't we take their place apart?' he asked. 'Why can't we examine Reuben's clothes?'

'Because, Bowles, we have no grounds for doing so – at the moment. And that is that. Now, we have an appointment with Terence Pennant at three this afternoon, and before then I have to go somewhere. The Anti-Terrorist people have promised to ring late this morning or early afternoon, so I've told them they can talk to you in my absence. If I'm not back – deal with them. Let me know what they say. Right?'

'Right,' agreed Bowles, concealing a grin. Even if they hadn't seen him on the box, the Anti-Terrorist bigwigs would soon know the name of Bowles. Things could be worse.

Chapter Fifteen

Rain was blowing on the wind as an expectant crowd left the visitors' centre at Goonhilly Satellite Earth Station and boarded the coach for a guided tour of the site.

There was a group of schoolboys, a noisy toddler with his parents, a foursome of trainspotting types, three matronly ladies on holiday, a group of teenage girls, and, wearing a sky-blue fleece, jeans and trainers, DCI Channon – incognito.

He told himself he hadn't needed to go for shades and a false moustache; nobody had recognized him as he paid his entrance fee and strolled around the busy visitors' centre. Nobody had the faintest idea that the policeman with special responsibility for the prevention of terrorism in South Cornwall was mixing with the tourists.

He was feeling a trifle foolish to be there unannounced, but he'd had to do it; not only for his own private risk assessment on public access, but also because he needed food – not for the body, but for the mind. His instinct, his intuition, had to be fed. He could never have said as much to anyone, it would have seemed self-indulgent and quite mad, but his instinct needed the nourishment of information, of observation and of atmosphere. No doubt of it, Goonhilly had atmosphere in abundance – a strange, compelling blend of the very old and the very new.

A five-thousand-year-old standing stone was in full view of satellite dishes that linked one side of the world to the other. There were dozens of Bronze Age burial mounds on Goonhilly Downs, six of them actually inside the perimeter of the site, lying there undisturbed among the sixty massive dishes that tracked satellites orbiting the earth. One of these Bronze Age barrows was up against the security fence, the ranked white propellers of the adjacent wind-farm seeming to stand guard oven the ancient green mound.

Such contrasts fascinated Channon. He could almost imagine the spirits of the clever, prehistoric men who once walked the Downs observing the marvels of Goonhilly, maybe even seeing them as a logical progression from their own skills in reading the heavens and moving immense stones in answer to the sun. Nobody knew what the heathland had been like in that long-gone age, but right now it was desolate and uninviting: a vast tract of heather roots still black from winter, stunted gorse and outcrops of rock. Word had it that locals avoided certain roads at night. A gibbet once stood at nearby Treboe Cross and there were tales of murder and mayhem in bygone days.

Murder still happened, thought Channon as the coach set off – mayhem still reigned in Porthmenna only a few miles away – nothing was new. Rain blew against the windows but the man giving the commentary was enjoying himself: clear, enthusiastic, knowledgeable, he was eager to paint an impressive picture of Goonhilly.

Channon barely listened. He knew all about the

261

wonders of science that made the station so captivating to visitors. The staff dealing with them were pleasant and well informed, no doubt with a tick against the 'good with people' boxes on their annual reports. Were they good with security, too?

His own security contact was nowhere to be seen. He would be in some other part of the vast site doing his job. The two of them kept in touch, meeting at intervals either in Helston or in Channon's home territory around Truro. He knew that the other man was satisfied with how Goonhilly was safeguarded. In any case the place didn't come under government jurisdiction – it was a business concern run by British Telecom, who were a very long way from being either careless or gullible.

Now, he eyed the great dishes as they drove past. He knew that CCTV coverage was everywhere, though so unobtrusive as to be almost invisible. The secure perimeter fence stretched for miles. Public access to the actual site was banned apart from the supervised tours; and in the hands of a company whose electronic skills were state-of-the-art, there would be safeguards that even he didn't know about.

So DCI Channon sat on the coach, outwardly a quiet man who was interested and impressed by what he was seeing; in reality a quiet man with eyes like lasers – a man who assessed, who noticed, and who tried to decide whether Goonhilly was a likely target for terrorists.

There would be no air attack, he thought. With RNAS Culdrose just up the road the airspace would be impregnable. It would have to be personal attack – probably one or more suicide bombers, and they wouldn't go for the widely spaced dishes. A single dish out of action would be inconvenient, maybe catastrophic for both the business and private sectors – but only in one part of the world; and in any case, the experts could soon align a different dish to the appropriate satellite.

No, a well-informed extremist organization would target the whole shebang – the control room. They would aim to take out the whole of the earth station, to cripple communications worldwide. Land-line and mobile telephones, faxes, internet connections, all would be put out of action. The tourist coach didn't call at the actual control room – there was a limit to where visitors were allowed – but that would be the target, if ever an attempt were made. The idea was improbable, implausible, impractical, but it wasn't impossible.

He stared out at the rain and thought of such an attempt. In spite of a small army of police working like mad to give him information, in spite of nourishing his instincts on this solitary, self-indulgent trip, he was no nearer to deciding whether a young father, a demoralized male Arab and an obsessive, man-mad woman had been murdered because of it.

Bowles came on the mobile as he drove away from the place. 'Boss? I've had a load of stuff from the Anti-Terrorist people.'

'Did you tape the call?' Channon was aware that the sergeant had been known to exaggerate information if it backed his current theory.

He was all injured innocence. 'Of course I did – it's all ready and waiting for you. I've been on the blower to the Hampshire force, as well.'

That could mean there was something on the sailor-boys. 'I'll be back inside half an hour,' said Channon. 'Be available when I get there.'

'I certainly will,' Bowles promised blithely. Things were moving. He'd talked to a big-wig who knew his name, and Channon would have to admit that he, Bowles, had been right all along.

Channon left the fleece and the trainers in the car, but kept the jeans on, causing Bowles to eye him with interest when he reached his office. So the mystery outing had called for casual gear? But there were more important things on hand. He tried hard not to look smug, but a hint of triumph was there as he waved papers and a tape at the DCI. 'Records of telephone conversation!'

'I'll go through them later,' said Channon. 'For now, just tell me everything in your own words.'

'First, they confirmed that the artist's impression we'd got from al-Makki's body matched up with their records, and backed by Dancer's ID they've informed his parents in Jeddah. It seems he came over here in midsummer 2001 on a genuine passport, arriving on a flight from Afghanistan, apparently to visit Muslim communities in the UK. That was before the twin towers, of course, so there was no general panic going on and only minimum caution concerning followers of Islam. He melted into the Muslim population in London.

'Then came 9/11, followed by a check on blameless Muslims and a drastic sorting-out of known extremists. A routine check was done on him and they found he'd travelled around a bit and then disappeared. Nothing against him then or in retrospect, but they think he got embroiled with illegals, probably in low-paid agricultural labouring. *But*, even before Jonathan Tregenza's death, the A-T people were sussing out a group of Islamics living on Exmoor under the banner of "Love and Peace to All", or some such stuff.

'Locals were wary of them, and last week reported that they'd seen menial types who might be there under duress. The A-Ts were doing backroom investigations and getting descriptions in preparation for a raid, but before they could make their move we contacted them about al-Makki. They think one of the downtrodden types might have been him.

'Yesterday they raided the place – it's an old farmhouse – to find one half-witted old guy left in charge. Everybody else had scarpered. They took the place apart and discovered maps and info on various sites. One of them was Goonhilly, with details of satellite timings and global communications. The old guy's in custody, but either he *is* a half-wit or he's coming it.'

'So there was stuff on other places?' asked Channon mildly. 'Buckingham Palace, maybe, or Canary Wharf, or the London Underground?'

'Well, yes,' admitted the sergeant reluctantly. 'All the places we've discussed, and more besides, but come on, boss, showpiece sites will all be better guarded than Goonhilly.'

That was true, but true or not, they had confirmation of something – at last. 'It looks as if you

265

were right all along, Bowles. Well done.'

Bowles attempted a modest shrug. 'It all fitted, didn't it?'

'Yes,' admitted Channon, 'but where does it leave us?'

'How do you mean?'

'Well, we have firm confirmation of a terrorist link to al-Makki, which also confirms what he told Dancer. We can assume at this stage that somebody from the Exmoor lot trailed him to Trevant yet allowed him to enter the house and possibly tell what he knew. Then when he came out they killed him, emptied his pockets and threw him in the Helford. We can even assume that they came back nine days later and killed Nancy, as well. Maybe they'd decided that al-Makki had confided in her, rather than her husband. It could even have been that the stones were for real because her killers were dyed-in-the-wool fundamentalists.

'All of that's possible, though stretching it a bit, but if it did happen like that where does Jonathan Tregenza fit in? Did he, as we thought at first, see something that night? Did he actually witness al-Makki's death?'

Bowles concealed his dismay. Trust clever-clogs here to muddy the waters with this analytical guff. Muddy or not, one thing was clear. Goonhilly was the target. The killings were a consequence of *that*.

Channon was pursuing his own chain of thought. 'It's a miracle HQ haven't been on, spelling out what *they* want me to do.'

Bowles noted the emphasis on 'they' and took it as a sign that the DCI would follow his own inclinations come hell or high water. No chance, he thought pityingly. In a conflict of priorities the A-Ts would call the tune and, no matter how clever, a rural DCI would have to dance to it.

By now morose as well as thoughtful, Channon observed his sergeant and regretted that he'd left him to take the call. Bowles would have asked no deep questions, seen no nuances in the conversation; in fact, he wouldn't recognize a nuance if he was slapped in the face with one. He should have dealt with the call himself. And was he going to be taken off the case to see it handed to the tough guys of the Anti-Terrorists? If so, it would spare him a few headaches. It might even help the Tregenzas if it were proved that Jonny had been murdered by somebody working against their country – against their home county, come to that.

He couldn't help remembering Dave Tregenza as he'd seen him on the beach that day, face streaked with tears and clutching a newborn baby to his chest; he thought of two adorable but confused little girls, of their sad-eyed mother and of Frances Lyne with her colourless, exhausted face. He didn't want to hand over the case to anyone else, however clever, however experienced. He simply wanted to do what he'd promised to do: his best – his very best... Wearily, he asked, 'So did the A-Ts give a hint of their next move?'

'They're going to liaise with Goonhilly. I reckon they'll make them jump to it.'

Maybe they would, thought Channon. Maybe the stylish visitors' centre and the tours of the site would be changed out of all recognition – but maybe they wouldn't. Goonhilly was a jewel in the crown of British technology, but it was also big business – and big money. With a sigh he changed the subject. 'What about the sailor-boys?'

'They're two businessmen who are neighbours and good friends – one a widower, the other divorced. They share a boat with a mooring on the Hamble and were known to be in south-western waters before going across to France.'

'So have they been questioned?'

'No, they're now in Brittany.'

'Presumably one or other of them owns a mobile?' asked Channon acidly.

Bowles shrugged. 'The Hampshire boys are dealing with it.'

'I'm glad to hear it.'

'There's no sign they're villains, boss.'

'That doesn't mean they're angels.'

'No,' agreed Bowles. 'I'll chase it up again.'

'Right, off you go, and don't forget we're seeing Pennant at three.'

Back to the grindstone, thought Bowles sourly. Why had he let himself get all excited?

Channon believed that much could be deduced from a person's home setting, and found that the room behind Terence Pennant's gallery echoed its owner exactly. There were expensive furnishings that were slightly grubby; decor that had been all the rage in the eighties; framed photographs of the man himself – outstandingly good-looking in younger days – and a portrait in oils, showing him as a brooding intellectual wearing scholarly clothes.

If it was a self-portrait he was no mean artist, decided Channon, who could recognize talent when he saw it. Perhaps he earned good money from his work? Perhaps, in spite of his gallery being off the tourist track and spending lavishly on drink, he was comfortably off? His living quarters might be dated, but there were no signs of shortage of money.

'Thanks for seeing us, Mr Pennant,' he began pleasantly. 'We need to talk to you as part of our enquiries into Nancy Dancer's death on Wednesday evening. We have you listed as a key witness and a man well informed on local affairs.'

Flattery, flattery, thought Bowles. Just the thing to get the old has-been talking.

'It's terrible, this murder,' said Pennant. 'I simply can't believe it. I expect you've decided that you're after a madman.'

'No, I wouldn't say that. We try not to decide anything at all until we have proof.'

'I see. So how can I help you?'

Channon said gently, 'By telling us something of your relationship with Nancy Dancer.'

A fleeting smile touched Pennant's lips. 'Nancy was Nancy, you know. She was sexually voracious.'

Tell us news, thought Bowles. So she was up for it – look where it got her.

'We've been receiving confirmation of that,' agreed Channon, 'and of course we're checking on the men she was involved with. I believe you and Mrs Dancer were lovers?'

'We were,' confirmed Pennant.

'For how long?'

'About ten weeks.'

'Mr Pennant,' said Channon, 'I'm sure we can talk man to man here. Did she make the first move?'

Again that fleeting little smile, hardly more than a twitch of the lips. 'Oh, yes. Nancy didn't mess about. She made it clear that her husband wouldn't object. She simply wouldn't take no for an answer. I merely obliged.'

'I see. Could you tell me where you used to see each other?'

'Round here. I could hardly take her to bed at Trevant, could I? Sometimes we used either her car or mine in the old serpentine diggings or the disused copper mine near their place. Nancy liked alfresco.'

Channon was feeling slightly nauseated. He had to block out a mental image of Alan Dancer's humiliated eyes. 'So was your relationship with her still flourishing at the time of her death?'

'No. We finished it about three weeks ago.'

'Why was that?'

Pennant sucked at one side of his mouth. His cheek puckered, giving him a wrinkled, lopsided look. 'If you must know, I became weary of being one of many.'

'You wanted to be the only one?'

'I didn't say that,' retorted Pennant. 'I had no hard feelings towards her. She was – a diversion.'

'So you wouldn't ever have considered doing her physical harm?'

Pennant shifted his shoulders uneasily. 'That isn't my style, inspector.'

'Oh? I have it on good authority that you used

physical violence on your late wife.'

Something flashed deep in Pennant's dark blue eyes: fury, fear or merely wariness. 'We had a tempestuous marriage,' he said, attempting a shrug. 'She was very excitable and I was younger then. Sometimes I would drink heavily.'

'But I hear that you still do, Mr Pennant.'

'Not by my past standards, I don't.'

'We'll be requiring you to make an official statement about your relationship with Mrs Dancer and how you spent Wednesday evening. This little chat is what I might call a preliminary. Could you tell me your movements on Wednesday evening?'

'I drove over to see Delphi and the children, but it was their bedtime and their uncle was doing his stuff.'

'You mean Dave Tregenza?'

'They only have one uncle, as far as I'm aware.'

'Quite. So you didn't stay?'

'No. I went to the Fisherman's for an hour or two.'

'How long exactly?'

'I don't know. Say seven thirty until about ten.'

'Two and a half hours in a pub and you managed to stay under the limit?'

'Of course. I'm not a fool.'

'And where did you go after ten o'clock?'

'I came back here.'

'You didn't call at Trevant?'

'No, I did not.'

'Did you take the road that passes Trevant to join the one that leads here?'

'Yes, I did. And before you tell me what your

271

spies have reported, I did stop the car and watch Nancy's house for a bit.'

'Why did you do that?'

Pennant shifted in his chair. 'Sometimes she would leave the house late at night.'

'To see somebody?'

'Yes.'

'She'd done it with you?'

'Yes.'

'So you didn't always meet well away from Trevant?

'No,' the other admitted. 'Once or twice we met outside the house. Late at night.'

'And did you see her do that on Wednesday?'

'No.'

'This is important, Mr Pennant. Did you see anyone outside the house? Anyone waiting?'

'No, I did not. I sat in the car, smoking. Then I came back here.'

'And what time did you get back?'

'Oh, after eleven. Eleven fifteen, perhaps – maybe later. I have no witnesses to that. As you can see I have no near neighbours.'

Channon stood up. 'Thank you, sir. We'll telephone you to say when somebody will come to take your statement. Please don't leave the area until we give you clearance, and arrange to make yourself available at short notice should we wish to question you further.'

Pennant brushed the front of his striped shirt with the flat of his hand and gave a strained little laugh. 'With a warning like that, how can I refuse? The next thing I hear you'll be after my DNA.'

'We'll let you know about that, Mr Pennant,' Channon replied blandly. 'Thank you for your time.'

'What do you make of him?' he asked as they drove back to Porthmenna.

'A self-satisfied old has-been,' said Bowles.

'We know that already. Anything else?'

'He said he finished it with Nancy, but Reuben said she'd dropped him. I think that's more likely.'

'So do I. I think he's a possible. Thwarted lust, wounded vanity, the capacity for violence – and he's devious.'

'A devious big-head. I'll get his times at the pub confirmed.'

Channon nodded. 'As for what comes next in the case – or cases – we can only wait to see what Forensic and the SOCOs have found, if anything. Oh – I'm going to the service in the chapel this evening. Occasions like that are worth observing. You must come with me.'

Bowles grunted in horror. He couldn't stand bible-thumpers, and weeping and wailing simply wasn't his scene. Shooting a glance at Channon he found the dark, steady gaze fixed on him. 'Uh – right,' he said lamely. 'We sit at the back, do we, and keep our eyes open?' When he got his DI he'd have to attend such affairs as routine, so he might as well get used to it.

'And you'd better call on Alan Dancer,' added Channon, 'just to assure him that we're pulling out all the stops, and so forth. And remind him not to leave the area without telling us.'

Thanks a million, thought Bowles. A cocky little brain-box who just might have murdered his wife was all he needed!

Both busy with their thoughts, they drove past fields that were all at once sunlit again, heading for the dazzling blue and gold of the coast.

The Harbour Stores was quiet and Lizzie was snatching five minutes on the old dining chair she kept tucked in a corner. This extra trade was taking its toll of her legs. She was worn out with making sandwiches and mugs of tea, selling hot pasties and loading her shelves with extra milk and soft drinks. She'd even trebled her sale of tea bags. It would all have been fine – extra in the kitty for her overdue retirement – except for the reason behind it.

The doorbell pinged, and putting her thoughts into words before the customer got through the door, she said, 'You know, Lily, my only comfort in all this lot is that what I sell might help the police do their jobs. There's talk now of 'em setting up a mobile canteen or some such, run by their own, and to tell you the truth I'll welcome it, and I expect Donald next door would say the same. It just doesn't feel right to be making profit out of young Jonny.'

Plump and placid, the other had known the shopkeeper all her life. 'Why torment yourself, Lizzie? You're running a business here, you're providing a service to all concerned. It'll all help in the end. I just popped in for my bread and to see if you've heard whether Frances and Dave are going to be at the service tonight? I got one of my lads to put a note in at the house saying I'd go round if Delphi isn't up to being left with the three children, though I daresay many another has offered.'

'I think they've got somebody. All being well the twins will be fast asleep, which is why Reverend Jim fixed the service for eight o'clock. Frances has told me she and Dave hope to be there and Delphi's insisting on going, even though it's only her fifth day since the baby. They want to show their appreciation of the way people have helped. She says they can hardly move round the house for flowers and cards and letters of sympathy. They have to have their mail delivered in a sack.'

'Well, it's a sad thing, but I can't see there being sacks of mail delivered to Trevant,' said Lily. 'That poor little man! I've left flowers and a card, but what can you say? We all know what she was.'

'Whatever she was or she wasn't,' said Lizzie, 'she didn't deserve to be murdered. Sam's in a right state about it. He won't tell what he saw, but he says it was bad. The scene-of-crime people were up there for a day and a half. As for that other poor fella in the river – we hear nothing about him, do we?'

'No, we don't,' agreed Lily, 'but what's worrying me is this – if we're having a service of support for Jonny's family, I don't see how we can ignore Alan Dancer.'

'We're not ignoring him. The Reverend Jim has asked him if he wants a joint service and he said no.'

'He probably can't face it so soon. But going back to Jonny's family – what do you make of Frances?'

'Well, she's strong, is Frances, but she looks just awful, and I can only think Delphi is even worse. As for young Dave, he's so grim I doubt he'll ever smile again.'

'He's seeing a lot of his nieces, though. Surely those two would make anybody smile.'

'Not when they can't understand why they haven't got a father,' said Lizzie shortly. 'About tonight, in case there isn't room for everybody in chapel, they're going to relay the sound to the church hall, and use it as a sort of overflow.'

Lily nodded. 'I think they'll have need of it.'

'I know they will,' agreed Lizzie.

Today was being quite a day. Channon let out breath and put down the phone after a call from Headquarters. He was still senior investigating officer on the case. The Anti-Terrorist Branch had taken on responsibility for al-Makki; they would carry out their own investigations on his death and liaise with Channon. He was *still in charge!*

He knew he'd been given a compliment. 'A free hand' had been mentioned; 'every confidence', 'this is from the highest level', 'confirmation in writing', and 'you may request PR assistance in dealing with the media'. It had all been official jargon for one huge pat on the back. But for what? He'd done nothing so far.

The phone rang again. 'It's Mr Platt from Regional Forensic,' said the girl. 'I've told him you might not be free.'

He had ordered his calls to be diverted, but Eddie Platt was different, just as George Hunter

276

was different, and Fred Jordan and his SOCOs. The rush of adrenalin banished his weariness.

Eddie Platt's cheerful baritone boomed across the line. 'Hey, Bill, long time no talkee-talkee. You're being a greedy boy, with three of 'em on your plate, aren't you? George tells me he's done most of his stuff and a full report is on its way. Fred's handed over to us as well, but you know what he's like – his list will be the length of *War and Peace*. This is just a quickie on the body and the bin, and it's not helpful. There'll be something, somewhere, but we haven't got it – yet.

'The attacker was extremely cautious. Not a print so far; not a hair, not even a particle of skin or a broken fingernail. Blood in abundance, of course, but only the victim's. Urine – you'll recall it was all too evident? For a moment we thought it was the final insult of the attacker to urinate on her, giving us his DNA, but no such luck, it was her own. She voided in her final moments – that's par for the course, as you know. As George and I see it she was failing from the stabbing when the first blow was used on her face. The systematic battering used a series of stones before she was put in the bin.'

'If that's so, why was there urine in the bin?'

'There wasn't – at least, not much. It was on her clothing – her undergarments, and on the flagstones of the yard.'

'Hah! There was blood and urine on the floor, so what about footprints? Shoes? Boots? He didn't do it all from the air.'

'No, Fred and I are sure he did it on his own two feet. There are Dancer's footprints, of course,

277

after the spillage of blood, and also those of the old man who came to the yard. Before the killing there are just those of workmen that match those in the house and grounds.'

'What, nothing else?'

'Oh yes, plenty! There are foot*marks*. The attacker's foot-gear – we don't think bare feet – was covered in cloth, some sort of canvas or strong linen, not hessian. Swathed in it, wrapped, bandaged, call it what you want. Personally, I'd guess he used sailcloth. There are minuscule fibres, and we're working on them. Full written reports as soon as we can – maybe Monday afternoon.' The deep tones were no longer bright and breezy. 'This is a bad do, Bill. There's a whiff of something very sick. It's evil. It's – I don't know – it's alien.'

'I know it is,' agreed Channon. 'I have to go somewhere in five minutes, Eddie. We'll talk again.' He looked out of the window and saw two small boys earnestly digging channels in the wet sand, with their father watching nearby. It was a delightful little scene in the soft glow of the evening sun; a scene so far removed from the Dancers' blood-clotted wheelie bin it was set in another world – a normal, happy, beautiful world.

Minutes later he set off for the Methodist chapel with Bowles and Yates, both of them clearly reluctant. He'd brought Yates to cover the church hall if it was needed for an overflow. People were arriving from far and wide – churchgoers and non-believers alike were making for the little chapel. He thought Porthmenna itself must have turned out to a man – or a woman. Sure enough,

278

the chapel was full, so Yates went and established himself next door in the hall.

A steward showed them to seats that had been saved for them. Bowles fidgeted in the pew but Channon was immobile. Rather him than me, he thought, as Jim Dowson took charge. How would he handle it? It wasn't a funeral, after all; it wasn't even a memorial service.

He could see the back view of Frances Lyne, and Dave Tregenza, big and blond and, even when seen from the back, clearly tense. Between them was Delphi, her dark cloud of hair bundled up by its combs above the slender neck and shoulders. A few days ago he had seen her lying on a lonely beach, losing blood after the birth of her son. Then later, at Seaspray House, she had looked as if a puff of wind would blow her away. But here she was, surviving physical, mental and emotional trauma – with the help of her husband's family. Where was her own family – her father? Oh, right behind her, wearing a black velvet jacket and a lilac shirt, his sparse hair slicked down across his skull.

And then it began. Jim Dowson's opening words were, 'Friends, thank you for coming to support Delphi and the children, and Frances and Dave – at the same time remembering the other two tragedies that have struck our community. We welcome you all, wherever you are from. This is the most difficult service of my entire ministry, so please bear with me while I do my best. We won't be raising the roof with hymns – none of us have much heart for singing, we're just going to have prayers and readings to show our love for the fine young husband and father who has been taken from us...'

And so began a short service that was dignified, reverent, and a clear declaration of sympathy, love and support. Channon watched everything. There was weeping – quiet sniffles, dabbing with handkerchiefs, but not from Delphi and Frances. Perhaps they could weep no more.

At his side Bowles was prepared to let his mind wander, but found to his amazement that something was getting to him. It wasn't the surroundings, which were plain and unadorned in the manner of Cornish Methodist chapels – apart from the massed wild flowers that filled every window ledge and garlanded every pillar, making the simple interior look like a meadow in the springtime of the year. No – it was the sense of togetherness, of joining one with the other. For a self-confessed loner with no close friends and no family background, the atmosphere in the chapel was a revelation.

So the two detectives sat there, watching and assessing, but all they could discern was simply the coming together of a devastated community. There was no great oratory, it was clearly beyond the minister to hold forth at length, but what he said kept the congregation in complete silence; not a sniffle could be heard now, not a handkerchief fluttered. At the close everybody was invited to go outside to join with those from the church hall and there, overlooking the amber-tinted harbour, they joined hands in a great circle that included Delphi and Frances and Dave, while Channon and the other two stood at one side; noting the attitudes and facial expressions of those who were present. In closing, the Reverend Jim said prayers that asked for strength and understanding and forgiveness of an unknown murderer.

Only Yates noticed the small, tense figure of a man watching from the shadows of the Fisherman's Rest. It was Alan Dancer, unwilling to attend, but clearly unable to stay away.

Then everybody wanted to speak to Delphi, to hug her and to kiss her. The three detectives left them all to it and walked away together; back to the computers and telephones of the incident room.

Chapter Sixteen

Dave was getting into the habit of eating his breakfast in the tower room. It wasn't remotely convenient, but it gave him a kind of comfort to sit in Jonny's chair, at Jonny's desk, looking at the view Jonny had looked at.

He ate cereal and some fruit, reflecting on the previous evening's service in the chapel – the first time he'd set foot in the place for eleven years. At the age of fourteen he had stopped going there – severed all connection with worship, the youth club and even the football team. To his amazement Frances hadn't objected. She'd said something like, 'It's your choice. You're growing up – you must make up your own mind about what you believe or don't believe.'

He hadn't wanted to tell her that it wasn't about belief in God, or lack of it – it was simply another instinctive 'no'. No to life, he realized now, to what life had handed him: a father, previously loved and admired, who had failed to ensure the safety of either his wife or himself when he took her out to sea; no to a woman who wanted to be a mother to her sister's sons when she *wasn't* their mother, she was only their aunt. Looking back it seemed that his life from the age of nine had been one long 'no' – an endless display of half-understood resentment.

He had expected to feel resentful in the chapel

282

last night, to feel embarrassed and out of place, but it hadn't been like that. He'd felt at home there with Frances and Delphi, surrounded by people he'd known all his life. Somehow, there had been no need to batten down his old enemy, emotion; he had been able to give it free rein in his heart and his mind. When he walked back across the sands of the harbour he had felt cool, rinsed out, as a wound feels after being cleaned and dressed.

Now he poured more coffee and stared across the harbour to where the police seemed to be swarming around like ants. All those men and women chasing about, yet it seemed they were no nearer to finding out who had committed three murders.

Impatiently he bundled his breakfast things together. Down in the kitchen the machine had finished its cycle, so he wanted to hang out his washing before going across to Seaspray with the mail. That had been some good idea, he thought – letting Sophie and Dorcas handle all the cards. He could hardly believe he'd been the one to think of it.

Coming in from the garden he went to put out the previous day's empty mail bag, just in time to greet the postman and accept another one. He emptied its contents on the kitchen table, putting aside bills and business letters to be dealt with later; and there, among the cards and letters of sympathy, was an envelope with an airmail sticker. It was addressed, forwarded and readdressed – to him, David Tregenza. He recognized the handwriting of his name.

Fumbling for a chair he sat down at the table. Then he picked up the envelope. It was rubber-stamped in black by some postal worker: *Gone Away – Return to Sender*. The sender was Jonathan Tregenza of Lookout Cottage, Porthmenna, The Lizard Peninsula, Cornwall, England.

He turned it back and forth as if he'd never seen anything like it – which, in truth, he hadn't. It was a letter addressed to him at Bells Beach, near Melbourne, Australia, and marked in the same hand – Jonny's: *Please Forward If Necessary*. Then it had been readdressed by someone else to Yallingup Beach in Western Australia, and then once again marked *Please Forward* and sent on to Hawaii.

The morning sun slanted across the little garden. It touched the line of washing and shone warmly through the kitchen window, but Dave felt cold – very cold. Before he was murdered Jonny had written to him, to *him* – for the first time since he left home. He didn't want to open the letter. He did not want to open it. Something was telling him that pain and grief were inside that grubby envelope.

Could he leave it on the table here until he came back from Seaspray? Of course not, it might be important. Might be? It was important, right enough, or Jonny wouldn't have written it in the first place. Deliberately he went to put the clothes pegs from his pocket into Delphi's peg basket. Then he emptied the coffee pot. Then he put his cereal bowl and mug in the sink. Then, when he could postpone it no longer, he opened the letter. It was dated Monday, 28th March, and it said:

Dear Davey,
I hope you're OK because I can't get hold of you. How am I supposed to get in touch? I have no email address for you. I've tried ringing your old numbers and I can't get you on your mobile.
Look, I need to talk to you. I don't want to tell this to Delphi or Frances – or to anyone else apart from you. You have to know. Something has come up that makes me think – no, makes me almost certain – that Mum and Dad's death wasn't an accident. I'm going to get the records of the inquest. I must talk to you. Ring me on my mobile (above) as soon as you get this letter.
Oh God I've missed you, Davey, I need to talk to you.
I love you – Jonny.

Reason and logic were banished as shock and remorse took their place. Dave gripped the letter and raced up two flights of stairs to the tower room. Dimly he knew he was acting like a madman as he grabbed the pile of surfing magazines from the desk and ripped them apart one after the other. Then he threw them on the floor and stamped on them. With his mouth wide open he let out a howl. He was in pain.

Then all at once quiet, he stood with his hands pressed flat on his brother's desk, and wept.

'What exactly are you asking?' Channon was edgy. Yesterday Bowles had played down the importance of the sailor-boys; today he was all agog to chase them up. Ah, but yesterday he'd had visions of fame as a buster of terrorist plots; today he knew that the Anti-Terrorist Branch had taken over all investigations relating to their own field. He also knew that they had given no notification of being interested in two English businessmen from Hampshire... That was it! The sergeant had thought about it and come up with his own agenda, no doubt because one of the men was black-haired and swarthy. Maybe he had an Italian grandma, for goodness sake, but Bowles would want to discover that for himself. If he was nothing else he was thorough.

Still, the dark-skinned one was a man, and so was his sailing partner. Nancy ate men for breakfast. It was a simple fact that she could have been deeply involved with the pair of them inside ten minutes. According to info neither of them had a woman at home, and she'd have been pre-pared to do more for them than their ironing.

But Bowles was making his point more clearly. 'As the two men are out of the country the Hamp-shire force have asked us to trace them ourselves.'

'Have they really?' retorted Channon. 'We've got three murders on the go, possibly tied up with a threat to national security, but of course we mustn't poach another force's manpower! But you were saying?'

'I want you to let me go across to Hampshire, to ask around Chandler's Ford and find out what I can on their backgrounds, their interests, their sources of income and so forth.'

Channon stared at him. 'They might have sailed off into the wide blue yonder but we do know their names and addresses. For crying out loud put somebody on to contacting them by radio, or failing that get their mobile numbers in the usual way. If they're hugging the Brittany coast there'll be a signal. If we get them by phone or radio we'll have a conversation. If we aren't satisfied we tell them to put into the nearest harbour and somebody can go across to interview them.' The three 'ifs' echoed mockingly in his head, but he went on, 'They were the only strangers we know of in the area that night. There are witnesses who confirm that they talked to Nancy – or she talked to them.'

Bowles's pale eyes were hard with resentment at being thwarted. 'All right, then,' said Channon, relenting. 'How's this? If anyone needs to go to Brittany, it can be you.'

Bowles squirmed a little. 'You mean, by *sea?*'

'Don't worry, not in a rowing boat. You can take a car and a good driver and go by ferry – say Plymouth–Roscoff, depending on whereabouts they are. You can put your travel pills on expenses.' That had been a cheap jibe, he thought uneasily, but the sergeant was being a pain.

'So you don't want me to ask around their contacts on the Hamble?' he persisted.

Channon gritted his teeth. Bowles had a surprising liking for doing the private investigator, and he had to admit he was quite good at it. 'Go and see what comes up about the mobiles or the radio,' he said. 'If we can't contact them and we can't get hold of them any other way you can have a free hand and if necessary some manpower, but I need action. It'll soon be three days since those two were talking to Nancy only a hundred yards from this office. Let's get moving!'

The sergeant hurried away and Channon started to go through a stack of print-outs that summarized recent information. The first one was based on Howard Sandry's list of all those in the area who either owned or had use of a seagoing vessel. Many more than he'd expected, they ranged from well-off second-homers to ordinary Cornish fisher-folk whose families had lived on the Lizard for generations.

Some enterprising person had included a potted biography of each owner and a description of their vessel. Sam Ludcott was listed, of course, with his ancient fishing boat, and a note said that he was a retired seaman who had never married and whose hobby was pinpointing past shipwrecks around the Lizard. Later in the list – and this was a surprise – came Terence Pennant. Channon wouldn't have thought of him as a sailor. Apparently he was from a seafaring family; hardworking types who could be traced back to his great-grandparents. His boat was a speedboat and pretty flash – a Benetaux Flyer 650. That figured. It fitted his personality just as his home surroundings did. Was it always the case that possessions reflected their owners?

'Bill?' It was John Meade at the door. 'Sorry to disturb you but young Tregenza wants a word with you – alone. He's not prepared to take no for an answer.'

'Then I won't give it,' said Channon. 'John, who did this work on Sandry's list of boat-owners?'

'One of our own lads – let's see – I think it was

288

Les Jolly. Yes, it was Les, helped by a WPC.'

Well, well, the mournful Jolly had talents... 'Tell him from me it's good and extremely helpful. I'll talk to him later. His people skills might be zero, but he has a flair for this sort of thing. Right, you can send our young friend in.'

Dave strode in and stood in front of Channon's desk. 'Can I close the door?' he asked.

'Feel free.' Channon eyed the younger man. He looked much as usual; radiantly healthy but with tension in every sinew. 'What's up, Dave?'

'I've had a letter from Jonny.'

Just for a second the hairs at the back of Channon's neck lifted. He rubbed a hand across them, went round the desk and pulled out a chair. 'Sit down, Dave,' he said quietly. 'Now – when did this letter arrive?'

'This morning, with the rest of the mail. I'd have to come to see you sooner, but they were expecting me round at Seaspray, and I didn't want to have to tell them why I was late.'

'So you haven't told anybody about it?'

'No.'

'Have you brought the letter with you?'

Silently Dave handed it over. He was amazed to see how small and insignificant it looked compared to the enormity of its contents.

Channon studied the envelope, then took out the letter and read it. He spread it flat on his desk and put a steel paperweight on it. 'How do you feel?' he asked.

'Terrible.' The relief of speaking about it made Dave's voice tremble.

Channon gave no sign that he'd noticed. He

289

simply said, 'That's understandable.' Then he hesitated, weighing what he was going to say. 'Dave, do you realize the significance of this letter? What it could mean?'

'Yes,' said Dave dully. 'It could be giving the reason for his murder.' What was the matter with him? His mind was grinding and clanking like a rusty winch, with the result that he was saying out loud something that was too awful for words. 'Do you think that's likely?'

Again Channon weighed his words. 'I see it as possible,' he said guardedly. 'Jonny mentions getting hold of details of the inquest. Has anything arrived at the house from the Coroner's Office or maybe the County Records?'

'No, and if it had arrived before I came back, Delphi would have told me. I'm handling all the paperwork.'

'Right. I'll deal with the Coroner, and I'll get my own records of the inquest. How much do you remember of what happened when your parents died, Dave?'

'Quite a lot,' Dave said grimly. 'Once a year they went off on their own. It was an anniversary – not of their wedding but of the day my dad asked my mum to marry him. It was June 15th. That year it fell on a Thursday.'

'So they always took time off work for this?'

'My dad did. My mum didn't go to work. If the anniversary fell at the weekend they got somebody to look after us for half a day. They didn't talk about it much – it was sort of their little secret. Jonny and I just thought it was one of the weird things that parents sometimes do. I sup-

290

pose you would say they were still – uh – very much in love.'

'Do you know where they went?'

'Not for certain. It was never confirmed officially, as far as I know, but Jonny and I decided between ourselves that it must be a certain beach near Lizard Point, because it's isolated and you can't get to it from land. They used to set off in that direction in our little Shipmate Senior and take a picnic and wine – just the two of them, of course. My dad had sailed since he was a boy.'

'So what happened on that particular day?'

'They didn't come back. People spoke of hearing an explosion out at sea, but nobody saw anything so they thought it must have been a maroon sent up to summon the lifeboat, though it was soon established there hadn't been a call-out that day. It's pretty wild down there, you know, not many people sail close in. A search was set up and flotsam from *Jemima* – that was the boat – was found over a wide area.'

'And was there any trace of your parents?'

'Some – uh – remains, fragments of clothing.' Dave still felt as if he were dragging replies from a mind that was grating and grinding like an engine starved of oil. 'It was pretty clear that *Jemima* had blown up. Nobody knew for certain but it was accepted that it was to do with the flares.'

'Do you mean your parents sent up a flare because they were in danger?'

'No – nobody really thought that. The police and the insurance people investigated, of course, and what was found among the wreckage suggested that flares on board accidentally ignited

291

the spare fuel.'

'What did you and your brother make of that?'

'We were only nine and eleven years old, and stunned by what had happened. I blamed my dad. I thought he should have been more careful.'

Channon's heart twisted with pity. The pain of that old loss was adding to the horror of the recent one. He must leave the subject of the parents' deaths for the time being. 'Dave, since you came back has anyone asked you if you kept in touch with Jonny?'

'I think people just took it that Frances heard from me now and again. As far as I know she never actually spelled it out that she rarely knew exactly where I was.'

Channon's high opinion of Frances Lyne went up another notch, but Dave was looking at him in sudden disbelief. 'What did you mean by that? Are you saying that somebody in Porthmenna was involved in my parents' deaths?'

'I'm not saying anything at this stage – I'm just asking.'

Dave shifted in his chair. 'As a matter of fact, one person asked very specifically whether Jonny and I kept in touch.'

'And who was that?'

'Uncle Sam. Sam Ludcott. The first time I saw him he was a bit short with me. He asked more than once if Jonny and I had ever communicated. I thought at the time he was going on about it.'

'Mm. Let me know if you think of anybody else who showed an interest.'

'You're way off the mark if you think anybody here had anything to do with my mum and dad

292

dying. They were all devastated. They all wanted to look after us.'

'I'm sure they did. It was just a thought. Now, listen, Dave. I want you to leave all this to me. I've got to make enquiries and I've got to think very carefully about what line to take. Something must have made Jonny doubt the verdict of accidental death. We don't know what it was, what he saw or what he found out. We don't know if he had any idea of who might be involved. I know it will be hard, but *don't talk about it* – to anyone. I'll set things in motion under a strict security ban. I'll need to speak to you again. Keep yourself available.'

But Dave wasn't convinced. 'Do you really think somebody in Porthmenna was involved?'

'I don't know what to think, as yet. We're exploring so many different avenues. We can't dismiss the possibility that these three deaths aren't linked at all – that it's some almost impossible coincidence.'

All at once Dave could talk no longer. He simply shook his head and held out his hand for the letter.

'Leave it with me for a while, Dave,' said Channon gently. 'I'll look after it, never fear. I'll be in touch.'

When Dave had gone Channon waited for all of three minutes before taking action, staring unseeingly through his window at a scatter of boats swaying and dipping at high water. Jonny, Nancy, al-Makki – they would have been an unlikely threesome in life, let alone death. How much more unlikely that they were connected to the deaths of a young married couple in 1989, to two well-off sailing types from the Hamble, to extremist Muslims in a hideout on Exmoor and to a clever, humiliated husband.

He sighed. Order, method, established procedure were what cracked cases, not a DCI gazing into space. He picked up the phone to contact the Coroner's Office.

Dave went back to Seaspray House, where Dorcas and Sophie were eager to make sand pies with their initials on top as soon as the tide turned. Delphi was nowhere to be seen and Frances was giving the girls their mid-morning milk and biscuits. Baby Jonathan was against her shoulder, screaming.

'Oh, you're back,' she said, and without even pausing held out the baby. 'Take him for a minute, will you? He's ready for his feed and Delphi's in the bathroom.' She put the child in his arms and went back to giving the girls their snack.

It was the first time Dave had held the baby since he ran from the beach with his newborn nephew clutched to his chest. He had never yearned to hold him, and no doubt Frances and Delphi had been too busy to wonder if he wanted to. Maybe they thought he would rather forget about delivering him, that he was trying to dismiss from his mind those frenzied and intimate moments.

He cradled the baby in his arms and took him to the sitting room, moving with the rhythmic, measured tread that he'd seen Delphi and

Frances use. For a moment Jonathan's outraged little body remained stiff, then he relaxed and stopped crying, his splayed fingers, each with its perfect little nail, pressed to his mouth. Two blue eyes looked earnestly into Dave's.

He felt his heart thud just once, and then open to receive this small human being whose father he had loved. Outside and below them lay the beach where he and Jonny had spent countless happy hours. Jonathan squirmed in his arms, opening his mouth to cry again and revealing bare pink gums. Dave found himself pressing his lips to the warm, bald little head. 'I'll look after him, Jonny,' he whispered out loud. 'Don't worry, I'm here – I'll help Delphi.'

Minutes later Frances was alone in her kitchen; Dave and the girls had gone down to the beach and Delphi was feeding the baby. All was silent, all was peaceful; sun was streaming through the window and for the space of a few seconds she felt better. She had seen David kiss the baby. That must have meant something, she told herself, but was she imagining that a new tightness gripped his mouth, that the dazzling eyes were concealing something? Earlier he had left the house with a brisk excuse and she had watched him head towards the harbour. It was hardly rocket science to deduce that he'd gone to the incident room.

She started to prepare the vegetables for lunch.

'No joy on the sailor-boys' mobiles,' announced Bowles as he came into Channon's office. 'I've put somebody on checking their radio and we're doing our best on their ethnic origins. The A-Ts have never even mentioned them, so can I check with them, as well?'

'What's happened to the urge to visit Hampshire?' asked Channon.

'It's still there,' Bowles assured him, 'but it's pretty clear that the action's right here at the moment.'

Channon eyed the sergeant. On a personal level, it would have been a relief to get rid of him for a couple of days, but on the other hand he needed him, both as a sounding board and as a keen brain. What was more, he would have to put him in the picture about the letter from Jonny, but it wasn't going to be made common knowledge on the force, not yet.

Saturday morning or not, the Coroner's Office and County Records were already unearthing details of a sixteen-year-old inquest, and those details would soon be on their way to him by special courier. Something was telling him that the deaths of Dave's parents were – as police jargon had it – relevant to the enquiry. Before he spoke to his superiors, to John Meade or to the sergeant, he wanted to study the inquest evidence for himself.

It was early afternoon and Dave had just delivered the girls to Bozena's house to play with her boys. Once he was alone his mind was filled by the contents of Jonny's letter, and by the time he reached the steps to Lookout Cottage he was so on edge he had to force himself to climb them normally rather than race up them at top speed.

Once indoors he rushed up to the tower room and there turned full circle, eyeing the desk – still without its computer – the loaded shelves and the filing cabinet that had all been at the heart of Jonny's business. What was he after, for heaven's sake? There was nothing to be found that he hadn't already examined in the searches he'd made since his return.

He sat tensely in Jonny's chair, his fingers drumming on the arm of it. It was all very well for Channon to warn him to keep silent about the letter, but if he wasn't allowed to discuss it, he doubted whether he could reason, analyse, imagine... He needed imagination to envisage what could have prompted his brother's urgent appeal; but even more than imagination he needed action – his muscles felt as if they were wasting away from lack of it.

By now Channon would be examining the evidence that had been put before the inquest; maybe ordering his minions to investigate people that Dave had never even heard of. The frustration of it was like an animal gnawing at his heart. It hurt – it was a pain in his chest.

His gaze fell on the ripped-apart surfing magazines on the floor. There, staring up at him was a torn picture of himself, riding a vast blue-green wave with his hair slicked back by wind and water. He was laughing, teeth gleaming against the wet gold skin. Looking at it, he became still. He might have been warned against talking about Jonny's letter, but Channon hadn't warned him to stay at home, he hadn't told him not to leave Porthmenna. Prudence, however, was urging him not to borrow a boat, not to sail openly down the Lizard to a certain beach that was inaccessible from land...

A moment later he left the house wearing swimming trunks under his clothes and with a rolled-up towel under his arm. It was time he went to the place which he and Jonny had visited secretly once a year throughout their teens.

Sam Ludcott was on the quay as he headed for the car. Awkwardly Dave waved to him. Why, why did he feel ill at ease to see the man who had been like a grandad to him and his brother? Evidently Sam's sharp eyes had spotted the towel, because he waved back and mimed drying himself. Then he called out something.

Dave just caught the words. 'Take care.' What did he mean? Of course he would take care. He never entered the water *without* taking care. With a nod to the distant old man and another one to the approaching figures of father and son Sandry he drove along the harbour front and headed down the Lizard.

Frances was checking provisions. They needed several items of food, so she decided to go to the shop herself rather than ringing to ask for a delivery. She needed to get out of the house for a while and Lizzie was an old friend, sensible, caring and down-to-earth, so if the shop wasn't busy they could have a bit of a chat.

Delphi was having a nap, with the baby in his crib at her side and the window open to the warm breeze from the sea. Wait! What was she thinking of? She couldn't leave them alone –

what about their safety? From force of habit she had looked out from every window in the house but seen no sign of police protection. It must be there somewhere because Channon had assured her of it, but even so, she would have to wait for David to come back.

On impulse she rang his mobile. 'David, I'm wondering how long you'll be. I need to go to the shop and now's a good time while Delphi and Jonathan are asleep, but I can't go out and leave them on their own.' Too late she realized that never before had she shared this particular fear with him.

Dave had almost missed her call. He was in a gully that cut down through a cliff to the sea, his mobile in the pocket of the jeans he'd just taken off and tossed aside. Another minute and he would have been in the sea, swimming to what he and his brother used to call 'Mum and Dad's place'.

Now, the phone at his ear, he sat on a rock and stared out to sea. 'You're worried about leaving them alone.' It was a statement, not a question.

'Yes, I am. I can't help it.' Frances knew she was gabbling. 'Channon says he's got somebody watching over us round the clock, but I've never, ever seen anybody – not from any of the windows. I keep getting up in the night to check that they're all safe.'

There was silence in the gully apart from the crash of waves on rock and the constant sigh of the wind. For the third time in his life Dave was feeling the sensation of heavy weights being shifted inside his chest. This was the woman he had pushed away for nine long years, the woman who had given up her career to look after two orphaned nephews – given up her man. Oh yes – it had come out in that final confrontation just why she always wore that amazing ring...

Now she was revealing that she was trying to protect his brother's widow, his brother's children from whatever evil surrounded Porthmenna, while he – who was so proud of his strength and fitness – slept in a different house and drifted in and out of Seaspray whenever he felt like it.

'David, are you there?' she was asking. 'Sorry about that – I'm going on a bit, aren't I?'

'No you're not, not at all. Frances, I'm some distance away at the moment, doing something I – I have to do. It'll be an hour or so before I can get back. Can you wait until then?'

All at once calm, she let out breath. He understood. 'Of course I can. I'll go later and then I can pick the girls up on my way back.'

'I'll be as quick as I can,' he told her, and switched off the phone. Then he climbed over a scatter of rocks and waded out to sea.

She was ironing when he got back. She had no idea where he'd been and she didn't ask. His hair was damp and he had an odd, fixed expression on his face. 'Oh,' she said, 'that was quick. It's less than an hour since I rang you.'

He found he was treading on the spot – one-two, one-two, as if marking time to the beat of an unheard drum. 'Frances,' he said hoarsely, 'I'm sorry.'

She managed not to say, 'What for?' and came

300

round the ironing board to face him. 'David,' she said gently, 'what exactly are you sorry for?'

'I'm sorry I was such a little swine during the years you looked after me.'

All the anguish, all the grief she'd suffered because of him was wiped out on the instant. She felt warmth and comfort enfolding her heart. 'You were very unhappy,' she said. 'I understood that, but I thought you hated me.'

'I did,' he admitted. 'I did hate you, but not because you were you. It was – it was because–' God above, he couldn't say it – he'd be weeping in a minute!

She said it for him. 'It was because I wasn't your mother.'

'You knew it?'

'Of course I did. I knew I was a poor substitute, but I was as near the real thing as you were likely to get.'

He looked at her colourless face and swallowed, hard. 'I want to say thank you, Frances.'

'There's no need,' she said. 'I love you, David, just as your mother did.'

'You'd never have put up with me, otherwise.' He reached out for her and for the very first time in his life, held her close. Then he put her away from him but held on to her hands. 'There's something else I must say. I tried to tell Delphi but she didn't want to listen. When I went away it wasn't only because Jonny had got Delphi – though that hurt. It was because I was frightened that if I stayed I would lose him.'

As he spoke surprise kindled in his mind; he'd said all this before – and to Channon of all

301

people. He finished in a rush. 'I thought if I kept seeing them together, saw them marry each other, I would start to hate him. I couldn't bear the thought of it.'

She hadn't known he felt like that, hadn't even guessed, or she might not have said as much as she did in that last horrendous argument. Now she looked up at him. 'I feel better for hearing that,' she said, 'it's made things easier.'

He held on to her hand. 'Delphi said that Jonny missed me every day of his life. Is that true?'

'Oh, yes,' she said, 'it's true.' She stood on tiptoe and kissed his cheek, then she switched off the iron and went to do her shopping.

Chapter Seventeen

Frances felt the need to talk to someone other than the family. David's apology had been balm to her rock-bottom spirits, it had been wonderful; but now she craved an outsider's concern, the comfort of an old friend's company.

She was hoping that Lizzie's shop would be free of customers, but it was no surprise to find someone about to enter just as she arrived. It was Terence Pennant, wearing one of his smart striped shirts and a primrose yellow tie. He wasn't one of her favourite people but he was Delphi's dad and he must be worried to death about her. 'Oh, hello, Terence,' she said. 'I've just popped out to stock up on a few odds and ends.'

'And I'm just on my way over to your place to see Delphi and my new grandson. How's everything?'

'The baby's settling down a bit,' she told him as they approached the counter, 'and Delphi – well – she's trying to adjust.'

Lizzie looked at them both and told herself she thanked the good Lord for young Dave. He might be only in his twenties but she'd back him in a crisis rather than this faded old dandy. That said, Delphi was his daughter and it cost nothing to be civil. 'So how are you both?' she asked.

'You must ask Frances, not me,' Terence told her. 'She's carrying more of the burden than I am.'

303

That was true, thought Frances, but at least he was having the decency to acknowledge it. For once she felt completely at ease with him as they faced Lizzie across the familiar counter. 'We're coping,' she told them. 'Dave's being a great help, both with the girls and with all Delphi's business affairs. The thing is, I have the feeling that there's something bothering him today – something new. He wasn't himself when he came round first thing, then this afternoon he went off on his own after he'd taken the girls to Bozena's. I think he went swimming.'

Terence was paying close attention. 'He'd have found it a touch colder than the Pacific! Did he say where he'd been?'

'No, he's not saying anything.'

'You'll have to try and have a bit of a chat with him,' said Lizzie comfortingly, 'and ask him–' She broke off and spoke to somebody behind her central unit of shelves. 'Mr Dancer, are you finding what you want?'

Alan Dancer, calm but rather pale, emerged from behind an array of tinned goods. Silence descended on the shop. 'Don't let me interrupt,' he said coolly. 'I'll just take these few items, Mrs Bannon, and some bread.'

The silence continued as he paid for his purchases, but Frances's conscience was screaming because she hadn't given this man more than a couple of thoughts since his wife was murdered two days ago. But he was saying to Terence, 'Could I trouble you to look outside to check if there are any reporters or photographers lurking? I don't want them to approach me again.'

304

Frances swallowed. There was something unutterably sad about this once-chubby little man. He couldn't have lost weight already, but surely he'd – what? Deflated? That was it – it was as if all the air, all the breath had been squeezed out of him. Terence hadn't moved, so she rushed to open the door and looked out. 'There's nobody to be seen,' she said awkwardly. 'Mr Dancer – I'm so sorry I haven't been in touch to see how you are. Life has been such hell, hasn't it? Even so – I'm sorry.'

Dancer stared at her. '*I* could have contacted *you,*' he pointed out, 'but thank you.' He gave an odd little bow, bending from the waist just for a second, then made for the door.

She touched his arm. 'I believe you're alone up at Trevant. If you should feel the need for company you're very welcome to call in at my house for a coffee – or a meal if you like. You may find it a bit noisy, but you'd be welcome.'

Once again there was silence, with Lizzie looking tearful and wondering if Alan Dancer knew he'd just spoken to one of his wife's lovers, and Terence gazing through the window as if he wanted no part in what was being said. Dancer said to Frances, 'I appreciate that, but as soon as the police give me clearance I'll be leaving Trevant – for good.' Without another word he left the shop and headed rapidly to the cobbles where his car was parked.

All at once Lizzie had had enough. She didn't want to serve the man who had humiliated little Mr Dancer by carrying on with his wife, but Terence was related to Frances by marriage, and she wasn't going to upset her. 'Mr Pennant,' she said briskly, 'should I serve you first so that Frances and I can have a bit of a chat? We go back a long way, don't we, Frances?'

Terence made a show of good humour. He bought his usual brand of cigarettes and said to Frances, 'I'll see you later,' then without a thank you to Lizzie or a word of farewell he left the shop.

'I'll put the kettle on, shall I?' said Lizzie. 'We'll see if we can manage ten minutes to ourselves.'

By late afternoon on Saturday the incident room had quietened down. Some of the staff had gone home and were hoping not to be needed next day; others were still working on cross-referencing and the routine analysis of information.

Bowles was in a corner with a couple of uniformed men still trying to contact the sailors Bellwood and Meredith, and establishing whether they had visited the Lizard at any time other than Wednesday evening. DCI Channon, protected by a 'do not disturb' instruction to the switchboard, was in his office attacking a mountain of printouts.

This was typical, he thought. For days he'd been hungry for the smallest snippet from Jordan, Hunter or Platt, and now everything had arrived at once – some of it even earlier than promised. Lying on his desk next to the printouts, however, was something possibly even more urgent – the details of a sixteen-year-old inquest. Clearly he would have to examine the reports first, in order to put in hand any necessary action. Only then could he give time to the inquest, only then would he make it known in the force, only then to a limited number of officers, and only then under a security blanket.

Rather pleased with all the 'only thens', he started to read. It was no surprise to find that samples of soil and vegetation on the wheels of the old cart from the top of Proudy matched those from the track linking Trevant to Porthmenna – rough terrain for the transporting of a well-built, unconscious man on a makeshift trolley. Then Jonathan's heels, his shoes and his socks had yielded minute particles from the same source. So he *had* been attacked not far from Trevant, just as Bowles had said ... it had been the 'sure bet' he'd prophesied.

As for confirmation of where al-Makki had been attacked – nothing definite; prolonged immersion had seen to that. Analysis of grit embedded in the soles of his shoes had matched the gravel fronting Trevant. Nothing startling there, considering they already knew he'd visited the place.

Nancy, though, was the most recent death, she was the hot one, and sure enough there were pages of scene-of-crime stuff on the house and the yard. No sign of the weapon used to stab her, but Channon hadn't expected there to be when the best hiding place in the world – the limitless ocean – was all around them. There was nothing whatsoever to link the inside of the house with her death and the wheelie bin, apart from the obvious traces when Dancer ran inside to the telephone after he found her.

The contents of her room were listed, including phone numbers of local men she'd been involved with, but all of them already known. Phone numbers! Channon leafed through the reports. No – no phone calls to or from Trevant in the days and hours before her death, apart from those to local shops and workmen linked to the renovation.

The murderer had used gloves, of course, so no real clues from the stones, none from anywhere except – ah! – three short fibres from the material used to swathe the footgear, found on the blood-soaked flagstones. Forensic had classified them as from strong canvas, almost certainly sailcloth – previously well-used and permeated with salt. Channon became still. Was this the murderer's first mistake? Used sailcloth pointed to a local man, rather than a fundamentalist Muslim, or someone pretending to be one.

He went through the details of Nancy's bedroom. Oh no – she'd been a bit old to play Juliet, hadn't she? Fred Jordan and his men had checked that a floor-length window in her bedroom opened to a wide ledge that joined the top of the wall fronting the yard. Oh, *please* ... the woman was a promiscuous juvenile in a fifty-year-old body! A stout wooden ladder was often propped at the rear of the wall with its foot in the yard. With nerve and agility she could have used it to climb down to meet the current man... Not on Wednesday night, she hadn't, Channon told himself briskly. She'd had the front door key in her pocket.

He leaned back in his chair and looked out. He could see the opposite side of the harbour, the steps up to Lookout Cottage, one end of the jetty

308

... his window was a vantage point. Slowly he sat upright. If his small window was a vantage point, how much more of one was Nancy's floor-length bedroom window at the front of Trevant – a house which was itself on rising ground above Porthmenna?

His staff had been busy investigating whether Jonny could have witnessed something unlawful before he was killed. How about Nancy witnessing something unlawful that same night? Had she seen what happened to al-Makki? How about her seeing a murder, or at least the preliminary to one? How about her seeing *two* murders? But if she did, why hadn't she told her husband? And if she had told him, why didn't they report it?

Closing the files he went out and said to John Meade, 'I won't be long. Get me on my mobile if you need me.' Inside ten minutes he was at Trevant. Alan Dancer opened the door and Channon was struck by the pallor of his once-ruddy complexion. 'Could you spare me a moment, Mr Dancer?'

Dancer stood aside to let him in. 'Have you brought news?' he asked flatly.

'No, I'm afraid not. I simply want to look at Mrs Dancer's bedroom.'

'Your men have already turned it upside down. I can't see them having missed anything.'

'Maybe not. May I go up?'

Dancer nodded. 'The second door on the left at the top of the stairs.'

Par for the course, thought Channon, when he was faced by a set of pictures of nude young men on the wall above the bed. Beneath them, in contrast, was a cuddly soft toy on the pillow – a well-worn pink rabbit with a ribbon bow around its neck. Channon eyed the rabbit thoughtfully, sympathy for Nancy pushing aside his distaste. Poor little woman. Perhaps she really was a victim of rogue hormones, as her husband had tried to insist.

Then he moved to the window, and stood there, observing. It opened like a door, but not on to a balcony; merely on to a wide stone ledge some sixteen feet above the ground, jutting from the house and stretching to the top of the yard wall. He could see the top of a sturdy, old-fashioned ladder, and knew that its base must rest not far from the bins. Had it been there when he and Bowles first saw her body? No, he was sure it hadn't. He would have a word with Dancer.

And what about the vantage point he'd come to inspect? He could see the front garden, and beyond the gates a further stretch of drive that joined the road. Further away still, beyond fields and hedges, there was the distant glint of the sea and the two dark shapes of the Eye Teeth, a stupendous view impeded only by a scatter of tall shrubs in new leaf inside the garden wall. Nancy *could* have seen Jonny attacked out there, but only if she had run up to her room as soon as he left the house.

He didn't relish asking what must be asked, but went down and found Dancer waiting with one hand on the newel post of the banisters. 'Mr Dancer, I wanted to see what was visible from your wife's bedroom window. Did she ever mention to you that she'd seen anything suspicious from there?'

'If you mean Jonathan Tregenza being killed – no, she didn't,' answered Dancer acidly. 'Nor did she mention seeing Abdurrahman al-Makki being carried off to be thrown in the Helford.'

Channon became still. 'So you think he was attacked right outside this house?'

'What? No. Yes – oh, I don't know. I'm getting muddled.'

Channon merely said, 'If there was something to see, she could have seen it, Mr Dancer. Do you recall whether she went up to her room immediately after the departure of either of them?'

Still clutching the newel post, Dancer shifted his feet. 'We had words as soon as al-Makki left the house,' he said. 'She – yes, I think she ran upstairs in tears. I can't remember what she did after Jonathan left. Look, Mr Channon, I am aware that I'm not co-operating very well. I want to say that it isn't deliberate. I can't help it.'

'I have dealt with murder before,' Channon assured him gravely. 'I'm accustomed to all sorts of reactions from the families of the victims. I know you don't want a support officer, but I can get someone to arrange counselling for you, if you wish, or even ask for an experienced trauma psychologist to visit you.'

A very small, strained smile touched Dancer's mouth. 'Thank you, but the time I should have seen a psychologist was when I first married her.'

'Maybe you should,' agreed Channon. 'Still, the offer is there if you change your mind. One last thing – the ladder in the corner of the yard. It wasn't there on Thursday morning.'

Dancer chewed his lower lip. 'You've worked out how she used to use it?'

'Yes, we have. Clearly she was an agile lady.'

'It wasn't there the night she was murdered because Ludcott had been using it in his work on the stables, but your scene-of-crime men soon noticed the signs of it being kept in the corner there. They examined it and I put it back when I was tidying up after they'd ransacked the place.'

'Thank you, Mr Dancer,' said Channon. 'I'll see myself out.'

When he got back Bowles was waiting for him, clutching a large buff envelope that had been delivered by police messenger. It was addressed to Channon and marked *Classified*. The DCI took it. 'Come on,' he said, heading for his office. 'I take it you've sussed out who it's from?'

'The Anti-Terrorist Branch,' said Bowles with certainty.

Channon settled to read. It was a lengthy report, crammed with officialese and confirming the A-Ts' liaison with him, as promised verbally by his superiors. Bowles sat opposite, trying not to chew his fingernails, until at last Channon looked up. 'You can go through this in a minute, but here on the cover it says for my eyes only and those of my assistant. That's you, Bowles, and when I tell you what it says, you can take a bow.

'It's an interim report only, confirming that the men who were in the farmhouse on Bodmin are still at large and are being traced as a matter of urgency. The apparently senile old man who was left there has been questioned at length and finally talked – *and* talked.' At Channon's next words Bowles moved up a notch from trying not to chew his nails to trying not to grin. 'Apparently it's now confirmed that they *are* a group of extremists – though an independent one rather than internationally backed – who were brainwashing a group of young men, of whom al-Makki was probably the eldest.

'They *had* been examining various targets for an attack, and – wait for it, Bowles – it's now definite that one of three scheduled for a full assessment was Goonhilly. Well done! You were convinced of that even before al-Makki's body was found, weren't you? I'll ensure that it goes on your record.'

'Thanks,' said Bowles, and meant it. 'So do they know who killed him?'

'No, they don't. They suspect he was tracked down by the extremists that evening, but they reached him too late to prevent him going inside Trevant. Later, when they got to him, they attacked him and emptied his pockets except for the Koran, before throwing him in the Helford. The A-Ts want us to pursue our own investigations into his death in tandem with them, so all is not lost as far as you're concerned.' Channon tapped the report. 'And then they come to the sailor-boys.'

'I thought they didn't want to know?'

'They do now,' said Channon grimly. 'They've found out that Bellwood – that's the dark one, they've enclosed a picture – was investigated as routine when he came up as having had contact with a suspect Muslim.'

313

Bowles was leaning with his elbows on the desk, and said eagerly, 'The waitress at the Fisherman's said it was the dark one who chose not to have the meat pasty, though he did put away the booze.'

'Whatever. He has Muslim connections, if not Muslim blood. So far they have nothing on him, but–'

'Don't tell me! They're taking him over as well!'

'It's their job,' said Channon. 'Accept it. No trips to Hampshire for you, no trips to Brittany. No trips anywhere unless it's in the immediate area.'

Bowles was so annoyed he was pacing back and forth in front of Channon. 'That's bloody good, that is,' he said. 'So can I read it for myself now?'

'Yes, but only in this room,' warned Channon. 'The A-Ts play everything close to their chest.'

They weren't the only ones, thought Bowles resentfully, and demanded, 'Why is Les Jolly in a huddle with Yates and that young bird?'

'Because I've given them a job to do.'

'Why them?'

'Because they're good at it.'

'At what?'

Channon's eyes were getting colder by the second. 'At something you see as a bore and a waste of time.'

Belatedly, Bowles realized he'd been pushing it. 'Sorry, boss, I just wondered why you hadn't done it through me.'

'Because – and I have no intention of keeping on explaining my every move to you, sergeant – because I wanted to brief them myself.'

'So what are they doing, boss?'

If Channon noticed the use of the word 'boss' twice in quick succession he made no comment on it. 'This is highly confidential. It must not get out – yet.' He unlocked a drawer and took out Jonathan Tregenza's letter to his brother, still in its airmail envelope.

Bowles read it and his heart plummeted. This would make old clever-clogs delve into the past. He was obsessed by how the past could affect the present, whereas for Bowles it was the here and now that mattered. But in more than one of Channon's cases, the past *had* affected the present. This letter, now, was dynamite, but it was no help on al-Makki, and hey – just a minute! All at once furious, he waved it in front of the DCI. 'It's highly confidential, is it? So why have you put Jolly and the other two in the picture before me?'

'God above!' said Channon, irritated beyond endurance. 'You're a bloody sergeant, not the Chief Constable! I've told nobody about it except you and John Meade.'

'Oh. So Jolly and the others don't know?'

'No, they do not – as yet. They simply happen to be very good on local stuff – families, events, friends, enemies. If – and I emphasize if – somebody local was concerned in these sixteen-year-old deaths I don't want them alerted. We have people analysing statements all the time, but looking for current stuff. I simply gave Jolly and Co. the job of extracting background information on the past in Porthmenna and district, using statements and remarks made by local people and put on record. And that's just for starters.'

'So what's for main course?'

315

'Me going home to study the records of the inquest.'

'Me as well?'

'No, Bowles, not you. Not yet. You can go home as well and think about al-Makki, as he's your favourite of the three. You're on call, and I want you in at the crack of dawn tomorrow. And Bowles,' the dark eyes were cold and very direct, 'don't ever try to give me the third degree again.'

'No, *sir!*'

With the twins and Frances not yet back and the baby for once asleep, silence enfolded Seaspray. Dave was on the sofa in the sitting room, questions assailing his mind like pirates boarding a merchantman, when Delphi came in and announced, 'I'm just going to bring in the washing.' He felt like saying, 'So what?' or 'Well done' and then it dawned. 'Delphi,' he asked, 'are you scared of being in the garden on your own?'

Clutching the basket in front of her she said, 'I just don't feel safe there. I know it's mad, but I can't help it.'

He took hold of the basket. 'Stay here – I'll see to the washing. As a matter of fact, when Frances comes back I'm going into Helston to get some extra bolts and a couple of better locks for the doors.' And I'm going to find out for sure whether there really is a police guard on the house, he added silently.

It had eased him so much to have had that in-depth talk with Frances that he longed to do the same with Delphi, but he didn't see how he could pester her again with his ancient hang-ups. He

316

felt a bit of a fool, actually, holding one handle of the basket while she still gripped the other. For seconds they faced each other, while he marvelled yet again that he had once been madly in love with her. Now, she was simply a once-beautiful new mother who just happened to be his dead brother's widow; a sad, frightened woman who deserved his protection.

Then, as if her mind was tuned into his, she blurted, 'When I said I'd marry Jonny it wasn't because I loved him more than you!'

'*What?*'

'I loved you both,' she said, turning her head away.

'*Uh?*'

'You were the exciting one – wild and unpredictable – you made my heart leap, but Jonny was so lovely, so warm and understanding – I felt safe with him. I'd never felt safe in my life, you see. You don't know what my childhood was like. We were always moving house. Once we lived in a tent for three months in the middle of winter, and I went to so many different schools. My mother and father had such rows – she threw things and shrieked and sometimes he hit her. Once he knocked her unconscious but he wouldn't let me get the doctor.'

Then she lifted the vast eyes to his. 'Sorry – I just felt I had to tell you that I didn't reject you. I simply chose Jonny instead and said I'd marry him quickly, even though we were both so young.'

So that was it. All that heartache, all that grief... This was being an afternoon of tell and be told, right enough, but he would have to think about it later. For now he would simply label it, put it in a little box in his mind, turn the key on it and get on with trying to find out about – about everything. And then he would have to talk to Channon.

He took the basket from her. 'I'm glad you've told me, and even though Jonny isn't here, you're still safe. I'll make sure of it.' With that he went out to the washing line and brought in what seemed like dozens of small items of clothing.

Half an hour later, with Frances and the girls back and Terence just arrived, he was out on foot, searching the roads and byways around Sands End, determined to satisfy himself that when Channon said they were being protected, he had meant it.

The evening sun striping his comfy old sweater with gold, DCI Channon was at home in his favourite chair, reading and rereading his copy of the inquest proceedings on Richard and Laura Tregenza, of Seaspray House, Porthmenna. It had been the usual format, the standard process. Witnesses had been local people who knew the young Tregenzas well.

What had marked this particular inquest as different was the manner of the deaths and the fact that nobody had seen the accident happen. Nor was there an exact pinpointing of the place of death, and very little in the way of evidence: a slick of fuel, burnt remnants of a boat, fragments of clothing, all swept hither and thither by wind and by tide.

Different also was that the whereabouts of the dead couple immediately before the accident had never been established. Timings indicated that they had been away for three hours; long enough to sail to their unknown destination, to linger over their anniversary picnic and set off for the return journey.

Channon stared unseeingly at the distant sea, then leafed back and forth through the evidence. As far as he could see the police investigations had been thorough, and, according to their specialist witness, so had those of the insurers. Experts on the coast of the Lizard had put forward possible sites for the anniversary venue. All had been examined by the police, who had found nothing whatsoever to point to two deaths by explosion at sea.

No suspicious vessels had been seen in surrounding waters, there had been no squalls, no freak tides, no evidence of the boat capsizing, nor had examination of the recovered parts of either body revealed sudden illness or heart failure. There had been a procession of witnesses saying ordinary things that formed the background to an extraordinary event.

'I'd have gone to sea with him any day of the week.' That had been Harbourmaster Sandry, robustly backing Richard Tregenza's skills as a sailor. 'I checked with him like I do with all local boat owners about the safety of his fuel being so near his flares, but he convinced me he knew a risk when he saw one and he didn't see one there.' Asked whether he judged Richard to be a man to take risks, Sandry had said, 'Never! He was a man

319

who loved his wife and family. He would never have taken risks.'

Sam Ludcott had paid similar tribute. 'He knew what he was doing, and what's more so did his wife. And he had the sense not to take risks with his flares and his fuel.'

And then – well, well! – a certain Terence William Pennant, boat owner and artist, of Lizard Point, who had been out in his sailing dinghy that afternoon. He had heard but not seen an explosion, somewhere between his boat and the coast just above Kynance. On his return he had reported it, giving the exact time of the explosion, which tallied with what others had heard.

And so it had proceeded: confirmation of timing, confirmation – from one Elizabeth Bannon of Porthmenna – of the date of the young Tregenzas' engagement and subsequent anniversaries of it; even the opinions of close friends on the state of their marriage... What had the authorities suspected there, wondered Channon in bemusement – a suicide pact?

In short, a stream of evidence that described a highly competent sailor and his equally capable wife: a happily married couple who were devoted parents and with no connections whatsoever to crime. The verdict had been unequivocal – Accidental Death.

So what, then, could Jonathan Tregenza have unearthed to make him doubt that verdict? Twenty-one days had elapsed between the date of the letter and his death. Had he made further enquiries during that time? If not, why not, and why had he not followed up his intention of getting hold of the inquest records? Had something happened to supersede his interest in the actual inquest? If so, what? And, more important, had that interest led to his death?

Still in his cloistered little world of analytical thought, Channon sat in silence, thinking, thinking, thinking. After a while he rang the incident room. 'John? You're still there, then? How about Jolly and Yates? I gave them some work earlier and it's more urgent than ever now. They are? Good. Get them to hang on, I'm coming back in to have a session with them. See if they have a room for me at the Fisherman's, will you, for tonight and maybe tomorrow night as well? See you later. And John, I thought you wanted to get off? Go, then, but I could do with having you in tomorrow.'

Sophie and Dorcas had almost grown out of having a daytime sleep, but they'd nodded off on the brief journey from Bozena's and in a moment of weakness Frances had let them sleep in their car seats for half an hour. The consequence of that had been that they were very late going to bed, and then only reluctantly.

By the time he had read an extra story and Delphi had tucked them in, Dave couldn't wait to be free of them. They were pretty good, he told himself; in fact, to spell it out, they were absolutely gorgeous, but he needed space, he needed to think. Sophie, though, hadn't finished with him. 'Another cuddle, Uncle Dave!' she pleaded, holding up her arms.

'Me too!' Dorcas was even more sleepy, but she

321

grabbed Jonny's photograph again. 'And Daddy!' she said, giving the glass a smacking kiss. Then she shot a sideways look at Dave. 'It's only a picture, you know,' she said, in the tone of an adult explaining something to a dim child, 'it isn't a real daddy.' If it hadn't been so sad he might have smiled.

Sophie kissed the picture as well and then they exchanged one of their looks. 'Why haven't we seen our daddy in his blue box?' she demanded, wrinkling her nose.

Dorcas pulled at her ear the way she always did when she was tired. 'Is it because nobody can find one big enough? Our rabbit, Velvet – his box was ever so big, but Daddy would need one as big – as big as–'

'The sky!' finished Sophie, stretching her arms wide. 'As big as the world.'

'As big as the world,' echoed Dorcas, eyelids drooping. 'He's very big, our daddy.'

A minute later Dave covered them up and crept from the room, then stood at the landing window looking down on the beach. It had been some day, he thought. There hadn't been a minute without a new problem, a new revelation, a new question to answer. And why hadn't he rung Channon? He'd said to ring him on his mobile at any time, and now it was Saturday evening. Did a DCI in charge of a triple murder have time off on Saturdays?

The truth of it was that he didn't *want* to ring Channon. He'd had it with being a wimp and taking no action towards nailing the murderer, and now, after going to the secret place, he had the first faint hint of a clue. All right, he should tell Channon about it, but if he could get five minutes to himself simply to think, he might conceivably come up with a line of action to take – on his own. *Action!* The word was like a peal of bells.

He ran downstairs to Frances and Delphi. 'They're asleep,' he announced, 'so now I can tell you that we *have* got a police guard. I found a man watching the house from behind Cantrell's old wall. He was concerned that I'd spotted him, because they're under instructions from Channon to keep out of sight. There's a round-the-clock rota keeping watch and he has a brilliant view of the house and garden. He says they come in closer as soon as it gets dark. And I've finished changing the locks and there's an extra bolt on each door.'

They both stared at him, and Frances asked herself why she hadn't told him earlier that she was worried about their safety. 'I don't know how we'd manage without you,' she said. Delphi clutched the baby more closely, and simply said, 'Thank you.'

'And now,' he told them, 'I think I'll go for a stroll on the beach. I feel like a breath of air. I won't be long. I'll take a key.' With a sense of escape he took the quick route down the granite steps at the edge of the garden; leaping the last few to land amid the flowers of the grassy bank above the beach.

Once pacing the cool firm sand he felt more at ease. It was almost dark, the sky still streaked with rose from the setting sun and a huge, yellowish moon hanging over the land. Wind was gusting behind the incoming tide and he walked at the water's edge, pushing aside memories of the times he and Jonny had danced in and out of the swirling waves and splashed in the rock pools. He needed to think, to plan, to decide whether or not to get in touch with Channon.

Why had Jonny let so long a time elapse after writing to him? Had he been waiting for a reply that never came? Had he been waiting for a brother who never arrived? Or had he been conducting his own investigation?

Deep in thought he leapt across the surge of a wave that was higher than the rest. Just as quickly it slid back, sucking at the sand with a gurgle and a hiss, making way for the next one. Tide almost on the turn, he noted absently; high water was due at about ten. So ... had Jonny visited the secret place? Once there, had he perhaps seen more than he, Dave, had seen? Or had he–

He felt the blow before it landed: a waft of displaced air swirled past his ear and a split second later something struck the back of his head, sending him down into the waves in a spiral of pain and sickness. Stars raced and wheeled, but he didn't know if they were in the heavens or his mind.

Something was tugging at his feet, not dragging him out of the sea but pulling him deeper into it. It wasn't the undertow, it was the grip of hands, strong hands, hard and merciless, trying to keep him under the water. *What? Why?* His senses were going, he was losing it. Salt was in his mouth, English salt from an English sea, but it was warm, almost sweet ... it was blood. Blood and sea water were in his mouth, in his chest, his life's breath was ebbing...

And then years of training came to his aid. Young lungs and strong airways closed against the water. His breathing slowed. For seconds he could see the starlit sky before the next wave crashed over him. But he had been under water more terrifying than this – *tons* of water had tossed him around like washing in a giant machine. He turned his head and took in air, and there, next to him, was a sinewy leg wearing rolled-up jeans, and another, braced against the waves. It was *him* – the man who killed Jonny!

Rage gave him enough power to lift his head and shoulders, but no, he wouldn't do it. Play dead, said his mind. Get out of the water, said his lungs. Deliberately he let himself float in on the next wave, face down in the water, arms limp, and seconds later let himself float out again. Only then did he risk moving his head. Waves were crashing, sand was hissing, his breath was louder than the banging and thumping inside his chest. It was no effort to go limp again, he was drifting, it was lovely, the water was warm to his mouth...

But no! One last, desperate effort helped him to lift himself from the water, his hands digging deep in the shifting sand. There was still noise, both inside and outside his head, but moonlight shone serenely on the chaos that engulfed him. He saw bare feet walking away from him, leaving him as dead meat to be swept out to sea. The man those legs belonged to thought he was dead. He was walking away, leaving footprints in the sand.

A burst of awareness galvanized his brain. Footprints! He must see them. He must remember them. He would tell Channon about them. He would describe them, describe the feet, the legs... He saw the feet pause, and then swivel. At once he submerged his head, knowing that the man was looking back to check on him. Then, as if satisfied, he walked away in the moonlight and his footprints walked behind him.

This was important, Dave thought hazily. This English sea was weird – it was warm and it was sweet... But it wasn't the sea that mattered, it was the *footprints* ... dark footprints in silver sand. For the last time he lifted his head, to see them touched by the incoming water; their edges blurred, their hollows filled. They were being washed away. Footprints, he thought dully; footprints in the sand. Evil footprints, footprints of the devil.

He knew he was losing consciousness. One stupendous heave moved him only inches. His breathing practice had never been as hard as this, but he was comfortable, he had always liked the water. It was lifting him, caressing him, he was going to see Jonny, he hadn't a care in the world...

Chapter Eighteen

There was screaming, high-pitched and desperate. Hands were pulling at him, at his shoulders. He could see bare legs with something wet and pale flapping around them. It was dark, so it must be night – it was a nightdress! He could see and he could hear, so he wasn't dead. The shock of it jerked him to full consciousness and the pain in his head became terrible.

Frances was bending over him, mouth gaping with horror and the need for breath. She was trying to pull him to dry sand, and somebody was running towards them – dark trousers, black shoes – was it the policeman? Frances shrieked at the man, 'Why weren't you watching? He's still alive! Help me pull him out!'

He *was* alive. Dave tried to lift a hand and was vaguely surprised when it didn't move. Nothing was moving. *He* wasn't moving, except when Frances and the policeman dragged him. They put him in the recovery position and more sweet salty water gushed from his mouth. That was good. Olly his coach always said, 'Get rid of what you've swallowed.'

Frances was still shrieking, 'Go back to the house! Watch them! Keep guard! Lock the doors! Get help! Get a doctor!'

Instructions were coming so fast Dave didn't know how she could think of them all, let alone

327

shout them at such speed. Everything was all a great big muddle, he thought feebly. His head felt terrible. The pain of it was stopping him from remembering something – something important. Then it came to him. 'Footprints!' he said hoarsely. 'Frances – footprints! Tell Channon!' He relaxed with his cheek on the sand. She would see to it. She always saw to things.

He knew he was smiling, but where was the moonlight? Where was Frances? One last thought came to him through the pain. 'Frances,' he groaned. 'Don't tell the girls. Don't let them know.'

Channon was in his room at the Fisherman's Rest, going through a catalogue of information unearthed by Jolly, Yates and Honor Bennett: unconnected snippets about the past, selected at Jolly's discretion. If he hadn't felt so on edge he would have enjoyed the memory of Jolly's face when he told him what he wanted him to do. If it were possible for a human being to resemble a highly pleased bloodhound, Jolly resembled one then.

When his mobile rang he grunted in dismay. He'd been on the job since seven that morning and it was now ten at night. 'Sir,' said a man's voice from the switchboard, 'we've got an SOS from PC Blamey on watch at Seaspray House. He needs reinforcements urgently, and a doctor. He says Dave Tregenza's been attacked and left for dead.'

Sheer horror robbed Channon of speech for all of ten seconds. 'He *isn't* dead?'

'No, sir, but Blamey says he has injuries to the head, and he nearly drowned.'

'Get Sergeant Bowles back in. Tell the officer in charge I say he's to send two men to Seaspray – more if he's got them – with lighting equipment. Get the doctor on call – that's probably in Mullion – and ring Helston to send an ambulance to take Dave to the Royal Cornwall. He'll need A&E at the very least.'

'Are you going across to Seaspray yourself, sir?'

Channon rolled his eyes. 'I'm SIO on three murders. This could have been the fourth, so what do you think? I'll be on my way inside a minute.' He thought but didn't say, And heaven help Blamey when I get there.

When he arrived they were still on the beach, with Delphi and the children locked inside the house. Dave was now minus some of his clothes and wrapped in blankets, Frances was wearing a coat and rubber boots, while Blamey was standing guard over the prostrate victim. Channon bent to check on him and felt sick with relief to find a steady pulse. 'It had better be good,' he warned the constable.

Clearly petrified, Blamey stood very straight. 'I was moving close in for the night, sir. It was nearly dark but I had the house in view even as I was shifting my gear. I knew Dave was inside but I didn't see him go out. It never even occurred to me that he'd go on the beach in the dark. This lady thinks he went through the garden and down the steps.'

'Why?' he asked Frances.

'He said he needed some air and he was going

329

for a stroll, but I think he needed space and the chance to think.'

'Well, he's got plenty to think about now,' Channon answered grimly. 'Did nobody see it as a bad idea to go on a deserted beach, in the dark, with a killer on the loose?'

'Yes, I did,' she retorted, glaring at him, 'but he'd made the house more secure for us and checked that you had a man on watch. He thought we were safe to leave and I thought we were *all* safe under your guard.'

Blamey grunted in embarrassment but Channon put a hand on his shoulder. 'It's as much Dave's fault as this officer's,' he told her abruptly. 'Who found him?'

'I did,' she said again. 'I was getting ready for bed and listening for him coming back. When he didn't come after ten minutes or so I put the light off and tried to see the beach from the window. I made out what looked like a low rock where there isn't one. I just knew it was him. I ran out and locked the door, then I came ... I came...' Her voice broke and she sank down on the damp sand with one hand on Dave's blankets. 'Your man arrived seconds later,' she said weakly.

'I saw her run out and then start screaming,' muttered Blamey.

Channon looked down at her. This woman had had as much – no, she'd had more than she could take. 'I'm sorry,' he said. 'I lost it for a minute. How is he?'

'Not good. He seems to be slipping in and out of consciousness, but I think he's stopped bleeding. I've put a pad of towels at the back of his head. I thought he needed to be kept warm, but he's so heavy the two of us couldn't move him any distance, so I ran for the blankets.'

'Was he able to speak? Did he say anything?'

'Yes. He said, "Footprints. Tell Channon."'

Hah! Channon whirled round to look at the beach. There wasn't a footprint to be seen. It was all black shadows and silver sand in the light of the moon; black sea rolling in and as quickly out again in a swirl of foam. It looked incredibly sinister and he felt the hairs lift at the back of his neck. This man, this devil had had the gall to try and kill Dave when there was a policeman only twenty yards away. Had he known that Blamey was there? Why had he done it? Did he have a reason for doing it? Was he a maniac?

A car door slammed and four men ran towards them carrying lamps and a searchlight. 'One of you stay here with Blamey and wait for the doctor,' ordered Channon. 'Check that the ambulance is on its way. Tape off the beach – it mustn't be touched until daylight, and I want one of you on the front door of the house and one on the side. Nobody is to enter on any pretext whatsoever. And be quiet – children are asleep inside.'

Leaving Frances crouched over Dave he went ahead of the men to tell Delphi what was happening...

Bowles was not pleased. He'd been dragged out of his flat as he was digesting a meal that had taken him ages to prepare. He'd used a recipe from a book called *Simple Meals for One* – a book he'd bought for hard cash. It had been pasta with a cheese sauce, and it had tasted pretty good, though the sauce was a bit lumpy. He was starting to get interested in this cooking lark, though he had to steel himself to do the washing up.

And why had he been dragged out like that? Because Mr Universe had gone walkabout with a lunatic on the prowl, that was why. They'd know more about it soon enough, because he and Channon were on their way to the hospital for a midnight pow-wow. Did old clever-clogs think he'd get any sense from Mr U when he'd been bashed on the head and half drowned?

The thing that really bugged him was that this latest attack put the sailor-boys in the clear. The A-Ts had sent a second message saying they'd contacted them at 8 p.m. near St Nazaire in Brittany, so unless they'd been flown back and dropped by parachute over the Lizard, there was no way they could have come back to waylay Mr U. It looked like goodbye Mr Meredith and goodbye Mr Bellwood, but at least he wouldn't have to face a journey by sea to interview them.

What he *would* have to face, though, was the fact that for him the terrorist angle was out of it – unless they found proof that al-Makki had been killed by one of his own. There were still pointers leading to that – the Koran left in his pocket, the stones in the bin with Nancy...

At midnight the hospital was very quiet, but they found Dave wide awake in a room to himself, with a uniformed constable on the door and Frances sitting by his bed, still wearing the rubber boots. This was a tough young man, Channon told himself. Propped against his pillows he looked much as usual, tanned and superbly fit, apart from a bandage round his head and the fact that he was linked up to a blood transfusion.

'I'm sorry,' was his greeting. 'I can see now I was reckless, but I never imagined for a second that he'd have the nerve to come near our beach. I'm afraid I've given you some trouble.'

Channon shook his head. 'Let's face it, you didn't give the trouble, someone else did, and I need to find out who, as soon as I can. The doctor told me earlier that I can ask you questions if you feel up to it.'

Frances broke in, still feeling sick with relief. 'They said if he hadn't trained in underwater survival he'd be dead, and they're surprised his skull isn't fractured. As it is they've simply stitched it. They say he lost a lot of blood, as well, so they're topping him up. He can go home in the morning.'

'Thank heavens,' said Channon. 'Dave, what happened on the beach, can you remember?'

Head still throbbing, Dave let Channon take him step by step through his time on the beach. After a minute the DCI said, 'So you think he turned to check that you were unconscious? And did he hurry away?'

'No, he just walked away as if he was quite calm.'

'And left his footprints?'

'Yeah. His feet were bare. I knew it was important to look at them, but they were just footprints, being washed away by the sea.'

'Old feet or young?'

'I'm not sure, but they were sinewy, so were the legs.'

'Suntanned?'

'I don't think so, but there was only the light of the moon.'

'Were the feet large or small?'

'Not as big as mine, but I don't think they were small. Things weren't registering.'

'Dave, your aunt tells me you went swimming somewhere this afternoon. Where did you go?'

'To Mum and Dad's secret place. I was going to tell you about it.'

'When?'

'As soon as I could make myself. I was trying to think of something I could do on my own.'

Channon said wearily, 'The days of the amateur sleuth are over, has nobody told you? So ... you swam to the beach which you believe to be the one your parents used to visit?'

Here we go, thought Bowles. It's always the past. Has he never heard of *Back to the Future?*

Channon went on, 'This is important, Dave. Does anyone else know that it's the beach your parents used?'

'I don't think so. Nobody knew for sure where they'd been when they died, and I don't think anyone knew that Jonny and I used to go there. We weren't even sure ourselves if it was the right place, so we never told anybody. We – uh – we thought that as they used to keep it secret, so would we.'

'Does anyone know you went there this afternoon?'

'No, there was nobody about. I swam round the headland like Jonny and I always did.'

'Did anyone see you set off?'

'Only Uncle Sam down by the harbour, and the Sandrys. They couldn't have known where I was going, though.'

Frances was looking uncomfortable. 'I did mention in the shop that Dave seemed on edge and had been swimming,' she said reluctantly. 'I was talking to Lizzie, who's an old friend and concerned for us all. A couple of people might have heard me, though of course I didn't say where David had been, because I didn't know.'

'Who heard you, Frances?' Nobody seemed to notice that Channon was using her first name. He himself wasn't aware of it. 'Who was in the shop?'

'Delphi's father and Alan Dancer,' she said, and wondered if things could get more awful than naming people who might be involved in attempted murder. She answered her own question. Yes, they could. Lots of things were more awful than that, such as telling two little girls that their daddy was dead.

Channon was still standing by the bed, dark eyes weary, his grey-streaked hair flopping across his forehead. 'One last question, Dave. Did you hear or see a vessel whilst you were at the beach?'

'As I went in the cave I heard a motorboat, but I thought it must be heading for Lizard Point or the hotel round at Housel. As for seeing anything – I wasn't really looking. Oh – I did see a fishing boat a long way out.'

'Did you recognize it?'

'No, it was too far away, but it was a Caledonian type, with the wheelhouse at the back. They're ex-Merchant Navy and there are a few of them about. Uncle Sam has one, though it's pretty ancient. I did see something on the beach, though, or rather, in the cave. That's what I knew I must tell you.'

'And what was it?'

'Not much,' admitted Dave, 'but we'd never seen anything there before. Two small wooden crates, up on a sort of shelf formed by the rock, right at the back of the cave. I don't think they'd been washed there by the tide.'

'Were they empty?' asked Bowles, breaking his self-imposed vow of silence whenever Channon was doing the questioning.

'Empty but not old. They looked pretty new to me. There was no name on them, no letters stamped, or anything.'

The eyes of the two detectives met. 'That might be very useful, Dave. I'm glad you didn't keep it to yourself for long. Now, we may need to visit this beach, and as we haven't got a police boat for the whole of Cornwall, could you pinpoint it for, say, the coastguard launch?'

'Yes, but it would be simpler to take you there myself. Do you think I was attacked just because I went there?'

'It's possible,' said Channon thoughtfully. 'And now we'll leave you in peace. Miss Lyne, can we give you a lift back home?'

'Yes,' said Dave, answering for her. 'Go home, Frances, and get some sleep. I'll ring you in the morning.'

Frances smiled at him, savouring the warmth of their new relationship, but her gaze was very direct when turned on Channon. 'Will your guard be on duty all night? Will David be safe here?'

'He will,' said Channon. 'You can trust me on it.'

'In that case, I'll come with you,' she said.

By seven thirty next morning Channon was walking to work along the waterfront, deep in thought. He almost bumped into Lizzie Bannon, out in front of her shop sweeping the cobbles. 'Better the day, better the deed,' she said defensively, as if she felt guilty to be doing such a thing on a Sunday. 'You're off to an early start, inspector.'

On impulse he stopped. This woman had her finger on the pulse of Porthmenna, if anybody did. 'Start early, finish late, that's the way it is on a murder enquiry,' he said briskly, adding deliberately, 'It was two o'clock when I got to bed, and Sunday or not, we have a full work force coming in today.'

Suddenly uneasy, Lizzie leaned on the handle of her broom, facing him. 'Nothing else has gone wrong, has it?'

His background of police procedure warned him not to reveal anything to a member of the public, but his own instinct was urging him to get information – fast. 'Things are bad, Mrs Bannon. I'm sorry to tell you that Dave was attacked on the beach at Seaspray last night. He was left for dead.'

Lizzie clutched at the broom to steady herself. 'What? He isn't...?'

'No, he was found in time.'

'And the others? Frances?'

'Delphi and the children are all right. It was

Frances who found him – in fact, she might have saved his life. She went to the hospital with him and we brought her home very late. Dave's all right now, but he almost drowned.'

Without a pause Lizzie went straight to the heart of it. 'If someone attacked him on that little beach, they'd been watching him – waiting their chance.'

'Perhaps. Mrs Bannon, could you spare a few moments for a confidential chat?'

'Come inside.' Still grim-faced with disbelief she took him up to her rooms over the shop, where she made him sit down and said, 'Donald's given you a good breakfast, I hope?'

'Donald? Oh, the landlord. Yes, I had an early breakfast and I hope my sergeant did the same. There was no room free at the Fisherman's, so they put him up at the bed-and-breakfast next door – at very short notice. They were really good about it.'

'Of course they were good,' she retorted. 'I'd expect 'em to be good when folk are being murdered right and left. As for this confidential chat you're after – I've already talked to your young detectives. They made notes of everything I told them.'

'I know, I've read their report. I just want a bit more. If I ask you about anybody in particular it won't mean I see them as a suspect, merely that I want to eliminate them from our enquiries.'

On my say-so? she asked herself. Did he think she was green? She could recognize police-speak when she heard it, but things were at such a pass she would go along with him and his questions.

All she needed to do was tell the truth, and she'd done that all her life.

'I can't go into my reasons for this,' Channon continued, 'but I'm in the process of delving into the past, when the Tregenzas were young boys. I need more background on what was happening in Porthmenna at that time – who lived here, who they were related to, what their jobs were and so forth. Anybody still living here who was here, say, at the time young Mr and Mrs Tregenza were killed in the accident, and who owns a boat.'

Lizzie eyed him thoughtfully. 'Well, there's Howard, of course. Even back then he was harbourmaster, along with his fishing and other bits and pieces. He was one of several at that time who went searching the seas for what was left of them both, and him with a poorly wife. I tell you, Porthmenna was heartbroken over Richard and Laura, and three weeks later Eileen – that was Howard's wife. He was devoted to her, and so was Reuben. In fact, Howard will tell you the lad hasn't been the same since she died. I don't think he's ever got over it – you can ask Donald next door. If Reuben's on his own in the pub he'll have more than he should, and go on about his mother. Many's the time Howard's had to bundle him off home, to spare customers having to listen to him.'

'Mrs Sandry's death was due to illness, though?'

'Oh, it was expected. She had a bad time – skin cancer that had spread. Now who else can I think of? There's Sam, he's always off somewhere in his boat. He's a funny old devil, Sam, but he's good at heart.'

339

'Was he always as close to the Tregenzas?'

'He was friendly enough when they were young, but after Richard and Laura died he could see the boys needed a man's company. He used to have them up in the loft, studying his maps and charts and listening to his yarns about shipwrecks. He always said Dave in particular knew the waters round here as well as he did himself. In recent times he's done work for many a one to make a bit extra, not just Jonny and Alan Dancer. He didn't like to hear a word against Mr Dancer, you know. Little Mr D, he called him. He liked him, but...'

Lizzie drew the line at gossiping about the dead, but Channon said it for her. 'He thought he was too soft with his wife?'

'Yes, but so did a lot of other folk, though some were sorry for him. I did hear she tried it on with young Jonny, and her old enough to be his mother. But I can't say much, because she spent money in my shop. She was a good customer.'

'What about Terence Pennant?'

'Well, Terence is Terence, and always has been. He's lived on the Lizard for years, but not always in Porthmenna. He's a vain man, is Terence – mind, he could have charmed the birds off the trees when he was young – and talk about good-looking! His wife was the same – pretty as a picture, but dark, you know, with being Greek. They do say he used to knock her about, but I've no doubt she gave as good as she got, because she had a temper on her. The trouble with him now is he doesn't like growing old and losing his looks.'

340

And so it went on, with Lizzie reminiscing freely, partly to please Channon, partly because she thought that if her memories would help nail the madman who was making a hell-hole of her village, then she'd do it until he told her to stop.

'So,' Channon persisted, 'is there anyone else who knew Jonny in his young days who is still here – and with a boat?'

He was going on a bit about boats, thought Lizzie curiously, but who was she to tell him his job? She thought for a minute. 'Well, not Mr Dancer, he doesn't have a boat now, though he used to sail like mad when he was younger. His uncle had money, you know.'

'Alan Dancer? I thought he'd only just arrived in Porthmenna.'

'In Porthmenna, yes, but he had an uncle who owned land on the other side of the Lizard. I did hear he spent his boyhood either there or in foreign parts. He knows about the Arabs and such, and speaks their languages. He lived in Eastern parts for years after he got married. I heard that when the uncle died he left his place to Mr D, but he never lived there, so I suppose it was sold.'

When Channon got up to go he was amazed to see he'd been with her for more than half an hour. Hurriedly he thanked her and went down the stairs. Had their talk been worth using up valuable time? He already knew some of the things she'd told him, because Jolly and the others had done a good job. As for the rest, he would reflect on what Lizzie Bannon had said.

'Oh, you're here, boss.' Bowles was clearly on

341

edge. 'I thought you were having a lie-in.'

'That'll be the day,' said Channon grimly.

'Loverack's on duty watch over at Seaspray, and Dave's going home from hospital at ten, so I've fixed up for two of the uniforms to fetch him.'

'Tell them not to use an official car, because of the children.'

Bowles picked up a phone and issued the order. 'Boss,' he asked thoughtfully, 'do you reckon that whoever did it will have sussed out that Dave hasn't drowned?'

'If he was watching what happened after the attack he'll have seen Frances with Blamey, and the paramedics on the scene. Unless he was cool enough to leave at once, then yes, he'll know. Are the SOCOs there yet?'

'Yes, and a couple of Forensic boys.'

'Good, we'll go and see them.'

'Can you call and have a word with Delphi at the same time? She's just been on the phone wanting to talk to you. She wouldn't say what it was about.'

Channon grunted. It was barely eight fifteen, so she had something on her mind. 'Right,' he agreed. 'We'll go and see what she wants. Come on.'

In the car he asked, 'Have you arranged a coast-guard launch to take us to this unknown beach?'

'Yes, they're standing by for when, and if, Dave's up to it.'

'I'm going whether he's up to it or not,' said Channon briskly. 'I want to see the lie of the land and what access there is to the cave.'

'So you're thinking it's smuggling?'

Channon shrugged. 'It's gone on for centuries. The locals know it, so do we, but these days it's more likely to be hard drugs than brandy.'

'So do you want me with you?' asked Bowles, carefully casual. The thought of tossing around on the briny made his stomach churn;

Channon took pity on him. 'No, I'll take one of the others. You can do some research for me – I'll talk it through with you when we go back. Tell Soker to help you and you'll need to put him in the picture about the letter from Jonny. In fact, I'll have to tell several others as well, but I won't have any loose talk about it.'

When they reached Seaspray House Delphi answered the door holding a squirming baby Jonathan. 'Frances is giving the girls their breakfast,' she said, facing them in the sitting room and keeping her voice low. 'What I have to know is this – when are you going to release Jonny's body?'

Bowles shifted uncomfortably and hoped she wouldn't start weeping. Channon, however, was unsurprised; in fact, he'd been expecting this days ago. 'Not yet, Delphi,' he said gently. 'I think we have everything we need from – from Jonny, but I can't say for certain that we've finished. I'm sorry.'

'I need to have a funeral,' she said doggedly. 'Not for me – for the girls. They've linked his death to when their rabbit died and we buried it in a blue box. They keep asking why they can't see their daddy in his blue box. None of us can get it through to them that they won't be able to see him.'

343

Channon thought of what he himself had seen of Jonathan Tregenza after his death. 'They couldn't possibly,' he agreed. 'I'm really very sorry. As I mentioned before, I could get hold of a counsellor for you – one with special training on dealing with families bereaved as a result of murder.'

Delphi chewed her lips. 'I'll think about it,' she said, 'though a counsellor won't know my girls like I do. I would never have thought it right for children so young to go to a funeral, but now we're beginning to think it might help them.'

'I'll let you know as soon as we can release Jonny's body,' promised Channon. 'Now, if you'll excuse us, we have to go and see the men on the beach.'

Standing next to the wheel as the launch dipped and swayed, and looking quite fit apart from his bandaged head, Dave and the coastguard helmsman manoeuvred until they were close in to a tiny beach. Dark cliffs spiked the sky, waves crashed over rocks; it seemed an unlikely setting for a proposal of marriage and a series of romantic visits.

Eyes narrowed in concentration, Channon assessed the approach from the sea. It was clear that Dave's father was a romantic. Among these rocks it would have been no mean feat to anchor even a small sailing boat and then row the two of them ashore. But anchor where? If his theory was correct, it could only have been behind the great rock to the right of the beach. He would check on that...

A minute later he was rowed ashore with the others to follow Dave across pale sand to a half-obscured cave. 'This is it,' he said simply, and beckoned them inside. It was cold and dark, and smelled of seaweed. Far back, and part of the cliff itself, was what Dave had termed a shelf – simply a low, horizontal layer of rock that was now quite empty.

Channon eyed it thoughtfully. Someone knew that Dave had been to this little anniversary beach. Maybe he watched from out at sea and saw him enter the cave, concluding that, like his brother, he was investigating his parents' deaths. Had the attacker then hoped that Dave would see nothing significant in two empty crates, but to make quite sure he would take it no further, removed the crates and within a matter of hours tried to kill him? A fourth murder, but this time a failed attempt. In each case – even with Nancy, where the stabbing had been what killed her – he had used a heavy blow to the head: no skill, no finesse, just brute force. A strong man, then, or simply a determined one? A frightened man, a vengeful man, or a madman?

With Dave delivered into Frances's care at Seaspray, Channon headed back to the incident room, where he found Bowles and Soker in front of a computer screen going through police records. 'How did it go, boss?' asked the sergeant. 'What's your thinking? Could the place have been used for smuggling?'

'Yes,' said Channon, sinking into a chair. 'How does this strike you as a scenario? Richard and Laura Tregenza went on their annual trip to their secret place, which Dave believes to be the one we visited today, the one where he saw the crates, which – surprise, surprise – have now disappeared. Right?'

'Right,' agreed Bowles. If there was one thing he liked about the DCI, it was his readiness to share his thoughts.

'Once there, they anchored their little sailing boat out of sight behind a huge rock and went ashore in their rowing dinghy, which they also pulled out of sight.'

'Why?' asked Bowles. 'Why the secrecy?'

'For the same reason they didn't tell anyone the whereabouts of the beach – it was their romantic little secret. Some time later they were annoyed to find their privacy invaded when a bigger boat heaves to and someone starts ferrying goods ashore, probably in a rowing boat, and maybe making more than one trip. Not knowing he's being watched, this person then proceeds to take the goods inside the cave – there was ample storage space above the water line.'

This had the ring of possibility, Bowles admitted to himself, but holes were gaping in the story. 'So the Tregenzas saw some smuggling,' he said dubiously. 'Records show it isn't exactly unknown in these parts even today, and no doubt the same was true sixteen years ago. Are you saying they were murdered because they happened to see something that people had turned a blind eye to for hundreds of years?'

'Yes, I am,' said Channon calmly, 'but only if the goods were special, or well known, or dangerous.' Or possibly, he thought but didn't say – if they knew the smuggler.

346

'Drugs?' asked Bowles, still dubious. 'OK, a prison sentence for dealing or possession or what have you – but would that warrant murder? Boss – we've gone back to '88 and come up with absolutely nothing on drugs or unsolved thefts of really valuable stuff – not in the whole of Cornwall. Steve here is bursting a boiler on it.'

Soker looked up from the screen. 'I've done print-outs of every crime for miles around during '88 and '89. There's nothing worth big money, let alone the risk of a double killing.'

'There is such a thing as road transport to Cornwall,' Channon pointed out. 'Try National, try London. The Lizard's a good UK exit for anything illegal, and it was '89 when there was that big gold robbery. I'm pretty sure it was in the summer.'

Soker turned back to the screen and concealed a smile. This was more like it. 'I'm to search the first six months of 1989, sir?'

'Just get details of the bullion job for now,' said Channon, 'while I make a phone call.'

He was getting carried away, wasn't he, thought Bowles, and followed the DCI to his office, where he stood at the door, fidgeting.

'Something on your mind, sergeant?'

'Yes. If the Tregenzas saw something that could have been illegal, wouldn't they simply have tried to find out what was going on?'

'Not if they were fobbed off by a plausible story.'

Bowles thought about that. 'But even if he did fob them off, you're saying he was so put out at being seen he decided to silence them for ever?'

'Yes, I am.'

'So how did he manage to make their boat explode way out at sea? With both of them on board?'

'That's what we have to find out, Bowles. We're detectives, in case you've forgotten. I've already checked that it's possible to rig an explosion if you first board the vessel to set it up.'

'So how would–'

'Sir.' It was Soker. 'Is this any good to you? The gold bullion job – it was stolen by fake security guards as it was delivered to a secure depot on 13th June 1989!'

'Where was the depot?'

'London, sir, one of the high-security bullion warehouses. I'll go and get full details.'

'Just a minute, Steve. What exactly was the value?'

'Five million sterling, sir. It's never been recovered.'

'Right, off you go. Bowles, give me a minute while I make this call, will you?'

Bowles sauntered off, clearly reluctant. He was looking over Soker's shoulder at the screen when Channon came in minutes later. 'Purely as a matter of interest,' the DCI said blandly, 'I've had a word with a contact of mine who has inside information on lots of things, including government finance. I asked him whether the gold was government property.'

'And was it?'

'No. It was Saudi gold.'

Bowles stared. 'Dancer!' he breathed. Who'd have thought the little runt would have been up

348

for the big time?

As if answering questions not yet asked, Channon said, 'He was on the Lizard in '89. He could sail a boat.'

Well, well, *well!* Bowles was so pleased he forgot himself and sat on Channon's desk, his wolf-grin much in evidence. Hadn't he sworn he'd make the cocky little blighter eat humble pie?

But Channon was in analytical mode. 'It isn't cut and dried, Bowles, far from it. Apparently the gold was surety against the purchase of property in West London by a Saudi Arabian – unnamed, and the full purchase price never revealed. Sorry to disappoint you, but no link to terrorist activities – not that anybody would be hot on that aspect sixteen years ago. It was taken to be simply a well-organized robbery by a close-knit gang – nationality unknown.'

'I'm doing the print-out of details, sir,' said Soker.

Channon's eyes had taken on a sombre, faraway look. 'I need the number and size of bars – include that,' he said. 'Also the total weight, and how it was packed.'

Soker nodded intently. 'I'll do it now.'

'Right,' said Channon. 'Good lad. Get Inspector Meade to come and see me, will you?'

Highly pleased, the good lad made his exit, leaving the DCI and his sergeant deep in discussion and waiting for John Meade to join them.

Chapter Nineteen

It was two o'clock on Sunday afternoon and Porthmenna lay peacefully in the sunshine, the tide on the ebb but still high enough to smack against the ancient stones of the jetty.

All at once four detectives came out of the incident room and headed for the parked police cars. The youngest, Soker, could hardly conceal his delight at being one of the foursome. Yates, older in years and experience, was more wary; not that he doubted Channon – it was simply that arrests always worried him in case they'd got it wrong.

As for Bowles, he was annoyed with himself. He wasn't sure whether Channon was right with his list of reasons and probabilities and eliminations. He himself would have preferred to bring in every possible suspect for a good grilling. But it wasn't only his doubts that troubled him, it was memories of the three bodies. The men had been bad enough, but as for Nancy in that blasted wheelie bin – he couldn't seem to block it from his mind, and that annoyed him. He was a sergeant, a tough nut, not some stressed-out neurotic.

Outwardly calm, Channon led the way. He was pretty sure of his ground, but tension was there. They were walking along the sand-streaked cobbles where people were messing about on their boats and children were running around.

Someone was listening to a band playing the famous Dance on Radio Cornwall; it seemed no different from any other day in the run-up to Helston Flora.

But the detectives didn't go to the cars. Channon took them on to the jetty itself, heading for a sturdy fishing boat – the smaller of the two vessels owned by Howard and Reuben Sandry. Howard had been watching their approach. 'Good afternoon,' he said, slightly puzzled. 'What's this, then? A deputation? When your constable checked we'd be here in harbour he said you just wanted a quiet word.'

'That's right,' said Channon pleasantly. 'With you and your son. Is he here?'

Reuben Sandry came out of the wheelhouse, wiping his hands on a piece of cloth. He looked at the four of them and his mouth tightened, but he said politely enough, 'There isn't room for six down below, so we'll have to talk here on deck.' He waved an arm at the orderly clutter of ropes and fish boxes.

Of necessity the six men stood centre deck in a small circle. Channon wasted no time. 'We want to question you both a little more closely about the murders of Abdurrahman al-Makki, Jonathan Tregenza and Nancy Dancer; and the attempted murder of David Tregenza.'

Father and son exchanged a look. Howard's was merely puzzled, Reuben's was unreadable – a mere sideways movement of the eyes in an unmoving face.

'In addition,' went on Channon, 'we have certain questions about the deaths of Richard and Laura

351

Tregenza, on 15th June 1989, and the handling of stolen goods on that date.'

Howard ran a hand through his curly hair. 'But that's long gone,' he said in bewilderment. 'It's all in the past.'

'Maybe, but I believe it's had an effect on the present.'

'Oh? In what way?'

'I think Jonathan Tregenza either saw or heard something which made him suspect that his parents' deaths were not accidental. I imagine he was probably alerted by a chance remark.' He turned to Reuben. 'Perhaps made by you, Mr Sandry.'

Reuben merely pursed his lips and let his cool grey gaze rest on the DCI. 'All right,' admitted Howard, sounding half indulgent and half annoyed like many a father with a wayward son. 'Maybe he has a drop too much now and again, but I don't see how whatever he said could have given young Jonny any wrong ideas.'

'Oh, I didn't say they were wrong,' Channon corrected gently. 'On the contrary, I think Jonny's suspicions were justified. We've visited the beach used by the Tregenzas on their secret trips all those years ago and found clear evidence of smuggling.' Which was stretching it, he thought, but he was after a breakthrough.

'You can't have! That is – I can't see there being signs of smuggling in this day and age, inspector.'

'But in your position as harbourmaster you must be aware that it still goes on, Mr Sandry. The trafficking of drugs, for instance; and in 1989 at least, the receiving and handling of stolen goods.'

Howard was gaping in perplexity and running a hand over his curly grey hair. Bowles told himself that this genial old guy was either innocent or a damned good actor. Either way, there was something pretty weird about Channon doing his 'softly, softly' routine in full view of half Porthmenna. He could see locals gathering at the rails along the waterfront, and next to them a couple of reporters eager to see action, while uniformed police were guarding the end of the jetty against an influx of watchers coming near the boat.

'Well,' said Howard, 'even if smuggling did go on in 1989, how can me and the lad help you on it?'

'First of all by telling me why, in June 1989, you were acting as receivers to stolen gold bullion, worth five million pounds at prices then current.'

Howard Sandry's neck was turning a dull red. He unfastened the top button of his shirt and drew in breath. 'You'd better get your facts sorted out, Mr Chief Inspector,' he said briskly. 'What would we be doing with a load of gold worth millions?'

'Receiving it from the people who stole it, then transporting it to a certain beach that was inaccessible by land, probably to store it there until it could be passed on to someone else for further transportation.'

The grey eyes that were so like his son's closed for a moment. 'You're saying that I was *paid* for this?'

'Yes, well paid. I've been looking into your family situation at the time, and I believe you needed the money to send your wife to America for expensive

353

treatment.' Quickly he looked at Reuben, whose strong dark face had slackened with some emotion or other. 'I think the Tregenzas saw you ferrying the gold ashore – no easy task in a small rowing boat in treacherous waters. As you must have found, gold isn't high on bulk, but it's high, very high on weight, and more than half a ton had to be shifted. It was fortunate that you had your strapping young son to help you.'

Howard Sandry tutted and jerked back his head as if dealing with a fool. 'Go on, go on,' he said wearily. 'You'll all feel a bit daft when you can't find proof of this.'

You can say that again, thought Bowles, but Channon was undeterred. 'If it had been a small item you could have passed it off as a naughty little earner in the Cornish tradition, couldn't you – a bit of sailing close to the wind with maybe a drop of liquor or a few thousand cigarettes – but most people know that gold bullion is very, very heavy, and a theft of it had been in the news only two days previously.

'The Tregenzas knew you. You couldn't risk them putting two and two together, so you rigged an explosion to silence them for ever – two young parents with sons only a few years younger than your own... And was it worth it? No. Your Eileen didn't live long enough to travel to America, did she? It was all for nothing. A double murder that made orphans of two young boys.'

'Prove it,' said Sandry through his teeth. *'Prove it!'*

At that Reuben uttered a cry. He leapt across the deck and stuck his face in front of his father's.

354

'He doesn't need to prove it because I confess!' he yelled. 'You crafty, domineering old swine! I went along with it for the sake of the mother you never let me have – I never got a look in with you round her neck all the time.

'I helped you with the gold because it was for *her* – to make her better. You made me board the Tregenzas' boat and knock them out. You made me help you rig the line to the flares. You lied and I had to lie too – for *her!* You let me take anti-depressants by the bucketload, you watched me go in and out of mental hospital, and all the time I had to pretend – to Jonny, to Dave, to psychiatrists – to everybody. All Porthmenna thought I was a sour-faced oddity to be the son of such a lovely outgoing father, didn't they? Well, they'll soon know different!'

He swung round on Channon. 'I told him you were clever but he wouldn't have it! I was half-cut when I dropped a hint or two to Jonny in the pub, but I knew what I was saying. I'd had enough. Do you hear me, you self-satisfied old devil? I'd had *enough!* I'll make a full statement. I'll tell how you've done your little deals on the side over the years, how you couldn't even murder the right man – you bashed the Arab by mistake.'

Channon exchanged a look with Bowles. 'Just a minute,' he said keenly. 'Were they so alike, then, Jonathan Tregenza and the Arab?'

'Not really,' said Reuben contemptuously. 'I said wait a minute, but no – he always knows best! They were both well built, though the Arab was more flabby. They were both wearing jeans and shirts, but the Arab was much darker than

355

Jonny. We both knew as he fell that it was the wrong man.'

The Anti-Terrorist people could stop their enquiries, thought Channon heavily. Poor al-Makki – he'd escaped a gang of extremists and sought help from a man he trusted, only to be targeted by the man's wife and then killed in mistake for somebody else...

'You emptied his pockets?' he asked quietly. 'Took his money?'

'Oh, yes,' said Reuben bitterly. 'We left his copy of the Koran to make clear he was a Muslim, and therefore a possible terrorist. Then who had to help load him in the van? Who had to chuck him in the Helford to finish him off? Reuben – the lad! Well, I'm not a lad, I'm thirty-four years old and I feel a hundred.'

With a thud he sat on a coil of rope and looked up at Channon. 'I'm going to salvage something from a life that's been hell. I might get a shred of self-respect if I make a full statement. It will tie in with what you've already worked out. Just let me say for now that both of us killed Richard and Laura. I helped with Jonny and the Arab, but he tried to drown Dave on his own.'

'I know you saw him setting off for his swim,' said Channon, 'but how did you know where he was going?'

'We didn't,' said Reuben, 'but Sam shouted, "Take care." I thought it was a joke, because everybody knows that Dave's an expert swimmer, but my father was worried – that's what being a murderer does, you know. He jumped in the van and followed him.'

'But he couldn't attack him there,' finished Channon. 'He couldn't get to the beach, and when Dave came back it was broad daylight and he might have been seen. So he watched Dave for the rest of the day and waited his chance.'

'That's it,' said Reuben wearily. 'I couldn't see he'd try to kill him, not after Jonny, but I should have known... As for Nancy – that was him alone, as well. He said she'd have to go because she'd threatened him – threatened both of us. She'd seen us near the house that night, and because I'd finished with her – yes, it was me, not the other way round; you'll be surprised to know that I do have a few principles, even if they're a bit twisted – she got worked up and said she'd tell the police. Oh, he was confident he'd have you baffled, wrapping his feet up and putting on his gloves before – before he did it... He hated her, you see. I think he actually enjoyed what he did to her. I'll tell you everything I know. What's more,' he shot a glance of pure triumph at the older man, 'I've saved a few bits of evidence for you – what you lot would probably call "forensic".'

Channon could have leapt up and down at that, but all he said was, 'Did you never hesitate when it came to Jonny Tregenza?'

Reuben's lips twisted, as if he were tasting something very bitter. 'I had what I thought were reasons,' he said reluctantly. 'I'd dropped hints to him and I knew I'd raised his suspicions, but nothing happened for weeks. Then at last he came to see us, chatting about this and that, but asking questions, probing. It's mad, I know, but he looked so sane, so healthy, so normal; he had a lovely wife and those little girls. I thought, why has he got everything and I've got nothing except a father I hate? I went along with the killing. I helped throw him off Proudy. God forgive me, I was jealous of him. But that's not the only reason.'

'Oh, what other reason did you have?'

Reuben said emptily, 'Once you've done murder, it's easier the next time.' He breathed out wearily. 'I'm quite prepared to rot in hell, as long as I don't have *him* next to me.'

For an instant there was silence, then Howard groaned, 'But lad...'

Reuben leapt at him, hands clawed, but Yates and Soker took his arms and controlled him.

Channon said, 'Cuff them both.' He looked at Reuben, grey-faced now as he held out his wrists; at his father, all at once a quavery old man instead of the burly, confident harbourmaster. Would he admit to anything? Would he try to justify killing five innocent people? A long, long interrogation lay ahead, and it might lead to another confession. One thing at least was clear: with Reuben's help Channon would have no trouble in putting together a case to hand to the prosecution.

He eyed the other three. Soker was grim-faced, Yates looked sickened but relieved, while Bowles was reluctantly admiring. 'Well done, boss,' he muttered.

Already Channon's mind was on the Tregenzas, on Alan Dancer, on the al-Makki family in Saudi Arabia. He felt slightly sick and very tired. 'You are both under arrest,' he said quietly, 'and your house and boathouse will shortly be searched. You will be taken to a recognized police station and there you will be questioned in detail.' To Bowles he said, 'Go ahead,' and listened as the familiar words of the caution rolled loudly from the sergeant's tongue. 'Take them in,' he ordered.

And so Howard and Reuben Sandry, each in handcuffs, were led from Porthmenna jetty to where the people of their village lined the cobbled slipway. It was completely silent apart from the distant slap of the waves and the sound of footsteps as the six men passed by. Behind the onlookers stood a small figure, shoulders hunched and fists clenched. By accident or design, Alan Dancer was there to see the man who had murdered his wife being taken into custody.

Three uniformed men stepped forward, and at Channon's nod joined Bowles, Yates and Soker. 'The usual procedure,' the DCI told them, 'and strictly by the book. I've spoken to the people in charge at the station. I'll follow you as soon as I can.' Then his eyes met those of Bowles. 'When we've got it on the record, would you like to be the one to tell the Anti-Terrorist Branch that we have a confession for al-Makki?'

'I certainly would!'

'Do it as soon as it's official, then,' said Channon, 'and sergeant – thanks.'

'Thank *you*, sir,' replied Bowles.

Channon saw John Meade at the door and went to him. 'It's nearly over, John. Reuben cracked up and confessed, but so far the father's admitted nothing. We have a long haul in front of us at the station, but there's no doubt about it.'

They went inside to find everyone waiting. Remembering his days as a young officer who never knew exactly what was happening, Channon addressed the lot of them. 'Well done, all of you. We've got our man – or rather, men – though nobody's been charged so far. Those of you scheduled to take the bank holiday tomorrow can enjoy it to the full, with the blessing of the Devon and Cornwall Constabulary!'

He looked around for Jolly and Honor Bennett. 'As soon as I have time I'll explain how your work helped me to sort things out,' he said. 'Thank you.' With a wave of the hand to everybody he left the incident room, but not yet to follow the others...

He could see the doors of Seaspray House wide open. They knew! Someone had beaten him to it.

Frances had seen his car approaching and was waiting by the gate. 'Come in, come in,' she said. 'Delphi won't be a minute – she's upstairs with the baby.'

Behind her the twins had stopped running around the garden and were staring at him, holding hands. 'It's the friend who came to tea,' hissed Dorcas. 'Hello, Channon.'

'*Mister* Channon,' corrected Sophie, sidling up to him. 'Hello, Mr Channon. I'm sorry you can't have a drink of tea. We're not having a party today.'

'Oh dear, what a pity, but I've only called in for a minute. You can carry on playing, if you like.'

They gave him looks over their shoulders as they ran off, and Frances said, 'Alan Dancer was here just a minute ago. He said you'd arrested Howard and Reuben. Is it true?'

360

'Yes, it's true.'

'Are you sure you're not mistaken?'

'Time will tell. They haven't been charged yet. I just called to tell you that you can feel safe again.'

'So you're pretty sure it's them?'

'The courts will decide that, Frances. Let's just say that I try very hard not to make mistakes when I arrest people. Is Dave here?'

'No. As soon as Mr Dancer had gone he gave me a hug and a kiss and went off on his own. Look – he's down there on the beach. Shall I call him?'

Channon watched the solitary figure walking the empty sands, the sunlight glinting on his hair. 'No, leave him alone for a while. We'll have a talk later – all of us will have a talk. Tell Delphi I'll see her tomorrow. I have to go now.'

Frances was remembering that once – she wasn't sure when – she had vowed that she would always be honest with herself. Now, she had to admit that she didn't feel better for knowing they'd caught the murderer – she felt worse. Worse because it was one of their own lovely little community, and she hadn't the faintest idea why he could have done it. She touched Channon's arm and said brokenly, 'Why, why did he do it?'

As he expected most people to do, she'd taken it that the killer was Reuben – odd, unstable Reuben... Would she feel better or worse when she knew it had been both of them? 'When I'm free to speak, I'll try to explain,' he said gently. 'For now, I have to go.' He laid his hand on her shoulder and went back to the car.

It was the morning of May Day bank holiday and Dave was at the window of Lookout, watching the far side of the harbour as police equipment was loaded into vans before the dismantling of the incident room. Clearly Channon could have no doubt of the Sandrys' guilt if he had ordered the withdrawing of the police presence in Porthmenna.

With all of them out of the way, Delphi might come back home with the children. Would she want to do that? Would Frances feel that she must offer to live with them, to help out either here or in the larger premises at Seaspray? That had been her role in life for years, after all: looking after other people's children.

And what was *his* role in life? He would have to ring Olly to tell him whether he'd be going back to Hawaii. The very thought of the Pacific surf made him tense his muscles and flex his shoulders. It would be months before the Sandrys were brought to trial – maybe as long as a year. Could he go away before then and come back to be with Frances and Delphi in court? No wonder he'd had a sleepless night...

Deep in thought, he ran down the steps and set off on foot for Seaspray House. He could hardly believe that so much had happened since he arrived back in Cornwall – he seemed to have lived half a lifetime in the space of two weeks – no, it was only twelve days since he set foot on English soil, only ten since he opened the kitchen door that morning and found hell opening up...

When he arrived at Seaspray the girls were

fighting. Red-cheeked and tearful, Dorcas was pulling Sophie's hair while her twin was backing off to give herself space to aim kicks. As soon as they saw him they ran to clasp his thighs, both shouting at once. 'She's being horrid, Uncle Dave!'

'She took my blue crayon and I want it to draw Daddy's box!'

'Hey, hey!' He took hold of them both and shot a look at Frances. Her face was still without colour, apart from the purple shadows under her eyes. 'Did you sleep?' he asked, reaching for her hand.

'No. Did you?'

He shrugged. 'Need you ask? I think we all need time to adjust, don't you? Let's have a quiet day on our own.'

'We can have a day on our own, but I'm not sure about the "quiet",' she answered, and smiled.

It was only a little smile, a weak, sad travesty of a thing, but when he saw it his heart turned over. He felt something for this woman who had been a second mother to him, something deep. Without giving his mind time to restrain him he let his heart speak. 'Frances,' he said out loud. 'I love you.'

He was still holding her hand and she lifted his and laid it against her cheek. This was David, saying he loved her. It should have been one of the happiest days of her life...

Then Delphi walked in with a sleepy baby Jonathan and sat with him whilst his sisters inspected him closely. 'He's going to sleep again,' announced Dorcas gloomily, 'and he still hasn't got any hair.'

'*Is* he going to grow?' demanded Sophie. 'Will he ever stand up? Will he ever be able to run?'

'Yes,' said Delphi. 'He'll do all those things, but they won't happen all at once.'

Dave watched them all. Jonny's son would grow, one day he would walk, and then he would run... He, Dave, had made a promise when he held him – a promise to Jonny that he would look after his children, look after his wife. Of course he'd been in the grip of emotion at the time, and everybody knew what that could do... Emotion had forced itself on him, battened on to him ever since he came back, but if he couldn't feel emotion over the death of his brother then life must be a sham. In fact, he was starting to think that emotion wasn't – well – that it wasn't completely bad.

The girls were squealing with laughter at something or other, but he paid no attention. Life was grim, life was hell, but he was beginning to see that there might still be something there for all of them. Beyond the present, with its misery and remorse and guilt, somewhere far ahead in the future, he thought he glimpsed a life of loving and hoping, and sometimes even laughing – a life of feeling things...

He'd just told Frances that he loved her and he knew it was true. He didn't, he couldn't feel love for Delphi, sitting there with the baby on her lap and her hair bundled up in its combs over her pale little face, but perhaps something was left between them, because he still *liked* her. That would have to be enough if he was to help her with her children – her children and Jonny's.

'Frances, Delphi,' he said. 'I'm going to stay in England, if you want me to. I'll help bring up the children. I'll watch them grow up.'

Frances looked at him. 'David – we can't expect you to give up your life like that.'

'You did it,' he said. 'Now it's my turn.'

Delphi didn't say anything at all, she just looked at him with her huge, shadowed eyes, then bent and kissed the baby's head.

'I forgot to say that Channon will be here soon,' said Frances. 'He rang to say he'd be here at eleven. Bozena's going to have the girls for an hour so we can chat to him. I think, I hope, he'll be able to explain things to us.'

Dave needed an explanation, he needed to be able to make sense of what had happened, and if anyone could talk sense it was the detective. He liked him, he respected him, he wanted to tell him he'd decided to stay with the family. He was pretty sure that Channon would be pleased.

The publishers hope that this book has given you enjoyable reading. Large Print Books are especially designed to be as easy to see and hold as possible. If you wish a complete list of our books please ask at your local library or write directly to:

Magna Large Print Books
Magna House, Long Preston,
Skipton, North Yorkshire.
BD23 4ND

This Large Print Book for the partially sighted, who cannot read normal print, is published under the auspices of

THE ULVERSCROFT FOUNDATION